IN TWO MINDS

Alis Hawkins

THE
DOME
PRESS

Published by The Dome Press, 2019
Copyright © 2018 Alis Hawkins
The moral right of Alis Hawkins to be recognised as the author
of this work has been asserted in accordance with the
Copyright, Designs and Patents Act 1988.

Map of Teifi Valley by Meredith Lloyd James

A CIP catalogue record for this book is available from the British Library

ISBN 9781912534180

The Dome Press
23 Cecil Court
London WC2N 4EZ

www.thedomepress.com

Printed and bound in Great Britain by Clays Ltd, Elcograf S.p.A.

Typeset in Garamond by Elaine Sharples

MIX
Paper from
responsible sources
FSC® C110794

For Edwina

Contents

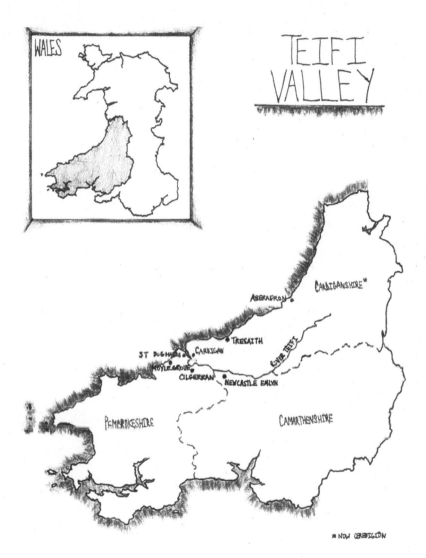

WALES

TEIFI VALLEY

ABERAERON

CARDIGANSHIRE*

TRESAITH

ST DOGMAELS   CARDIGAN

RIVER TEIFI

MOYLEGROVE

CILGERRAN

NEWCASTLE EMLYN

PEMBROKESHIRE

CAMARTHENSHIRE

* NOW CEREDIGION

Glossary of Welsh terms

'ngwas i: (colloquially) my lad

gwas bach: literally 'little servant'. A term reserved for the youngest or most junior servants.

Banc Yr Eithin: gorse bank

tŷ unnos: literally 'one-night house'

tai unnos: the plural form of *tŷ unnos*

crachach: gentry or upper classes

Duw: God

smwglin: a dockside drinking den where ale was brewed without a licence and smuggled spirits were sold.

betgwn: the outer garment of most Cardiganshire working women in the nineteenth century. It featured a tight, low-cut bodice and a long back, sometimes gathered up into a 'tail'. It would have been worn over a blouse and petticoats with an apron over the top.

Mamgu: grandmother

Arglwydd annwyl: Dear Lord

bara brith: a light fruitcake or tea loaf

'machgen i: my boy

trist: sad

hiraeth: a longing for times or places past

Glossary of Welsh terms

PART ONE

Harry

Is there any argument more futile than one with an aged parent? The mere fact that you persist in opposing them simply reinforces their poor opinion of you.

'This is preposterous, Henry,' my father announced. 'How can you even think of agreeing? I cannot conceive of Pomfrey's suggesting such a thing.'

'Not *just* Pomfrey. *All* the county magistrates.'

A brief, fraught silence. 'Not so,' my father said. 'There was one member of the bench who was not consulted.'

I clenched my jaw on the urge to roar with frustration. 'They couldn't very well make *you* a party to the discussions, could they? *I say Probert-Lloyd –*' I put on the exaggeratedly English tones of a Welsh squire – '*what d'you say to your son standing in for Bowen pro tem? Like a terrier with a rat in that business of the Jones girl's bones before Christmas – good coroner material, eh?*'

No. As my efforts to discover the truth behind Margaret Jones's death had demonstrated, the qualities that made a good death investigator were not entirely those of a gentleman.

'And,' I threw any remaining caution to the winds, 'however much *you* fail to conceive of it, the magistrates' *purpose* could not, in fact, be clearer. Leighton Bowen is dying and the county is in need of a coroner. Every member of the bench but you sees that I am eminently qualified to do the job.'

My father leaned towards me over his desk. 'Do they know you're almost blind?'

I resisted the temptation to lean forwards in my turn and meet him, nose to nose, across the desk. Apart from not wishing to give him the satisfaction of seeing that I was provoked, at such close range he would vanish completely into the whirlpool of my peculiar blindness. 'My sight is irrelevant. What they *know* is that I succeeded in disproving the inquest jury's ludicrous verdict when nobody else was even prepared to look at Margaret's death.'

He pulled back as if, in mentioning her name, I had committed a regrettable *faux pas*. Only he and I knew quite how embarrassing my investigations into Margaret Jones's death might have proved to our family.

I glared ineffectually into the blank whirl that hid his face from me. Was he attempting to stare me into submission as he had done when I was a boy? Failing sight did not confer many advantages, but at least it meant that I was immune to that particular form of intimidation.

'Harry, why must you insist on behaving as if your faculties were unimpaired?' His tone surprised me – sounding almost conciliatory. 'First there was all that nonsense about becoming a solicitor and now this.'

In other words: *why won't you stop being so stubborn, learn your duties as my heir and settle down as squire-in-waiting?*

'I'm not behaving as if I'm *unimpaired* as you so tactfully put it. I made it clear to Pomfrey that, my sight being as it is, I'd need an assistant. We've agreed that I will be allowed to appoint my own coroner's officer.'

'By which you mean Charles Schofield's clerk, I assume?'

'John Davies is an ideal assistant. He's observant, discreet and doesn't need to be told anything twice.'

4

'It's not his aptitude that concerns me. Do you not see how showing preference for somebody like Davies, valuing him above your peers, will affect your place in society?'

'I fail to see how having John as my assistant shows a *preference* for him. Or how the gentlemen of Cardiganshire can feel themselves slighted by his appointment.'

My father sighed. 'One day, Glanteifi will be yours. Don't make your becoming its master impossible.'

* * *

I rode to Charles Schofield's office through a clear January afternoon without wind or cloud, nothing overhead but a fading blue of frosty purity. The beauty of the day should have cheered me but, as I contended with a lingering fury with my father and a growing apprehension at the prospect of speaking to John's employer, my spirits remained anything but cheery.

In an attempt to master my mood, I turned my attention to the road ahead and tried to focus on what I could make out.

You'll find you become better at perceiving things you would not previously have noticed, my eye doctor had told me. *You'll learn how to make use of your remaining vision.* And he was right; despite the fact that one's peripheral vision is not designed to register detail, I was learning how to interpret the tantalising, sidelong view it offered. The problem was, I was not learning quickly enough. Much of my seeing now depended upon guesswork and familiarity; anything new was difficult to make out until I was very close to it.

I knew this road well but that did nothing to lift my mood. Everything around me – winter fields, hedges, ditches, leaf-bare trees, even the stretch of the cold brown Teifi away down the bank to my right – belonged to my father's estate, an inheritance and a responsibility I had never wanted, but which blindness seemed to have made inevitable.

Until today.

The magistrates' request that I become Acting Coroner for the Teifi Valley held out the possibility of a different future. Unpaid and *ad hoc* the office of coroner might be but, if I could secure it permanently, the job would offer independent occupation and a potential escape from the combined exigencies of filial duty and blindness. As coroner, I would no longer be a mere footman to the *status quo*, standing in wait behind my father, slipping – when the time came – into his warm space on the magistrates' bench, a prospect that was about as appealing as contemplating my own annihilation.

What cause does the jury find for the demise of this man?

He was stifled to death by gentility.

No. Whatever objections my father might raise, I was not prepared to play the docile squireling. Not while an alternative presented itself.

But, if I was to prove myself a credible coroner, securing John Davies as my coroner's officer was essential.

John

When Harry walked into Mr Schofield's office, I didn't know whether to be glad or furious. At last! Where had he *been*?

Christmas had come and gone. Then the New Year. Then most of January. What had happened to that new beginning he'd talked about when we'd been working together? That new start in Cardiganshire as a solicitor who needed *the right kind of clerk*?

I'd thought he was better than that. Dangling a job in front of a man and then disappearing for weeks on end.

Old Schofield stood up as Harry came in but, from the look on his face, I could tell he wished he hadn't. Force of habit though, isn't it, standing for the gentry? Mind you, Harry's gentility was questionable these days. In Newcastle Emlyn, anyway. All that grubbing about after a dead dairymaid. Not to mention speaking Welsh like a farm boy instead of honking English up his nose like the rest of the local *crachach*.

I stared at him. He was wearing one of those new Mackintosh coats that they advertised in the illustrated papers – do I have to say any more? About as smart as the seat of a navvy's trousers.

Mr Schofield cleared his throat in a way he probably thought was meaningful – though God alone knows what the meaning was – and he and Harry did the 'how's the family and can you believe it's eighteen fifty-one, where's the time going?' dance for a bit. Then – finally – Harry got round to what he'd come for.

'I'm afraid it's becoming an unfortunate habit of mine, Mr Schofield, to come and ask you to indulge me with the services of Mr Davies.'

Indulge him? That didn't sound as if he'd come to offer me a job.

'Shall we go into my office, Mr Probert-Lloyd? We can speak more privately there.'

I waited for Harry to insist on me coming as well. But he didn't. Just followed Old Schofield like a lamb.

Peter was watching me from the other clerk's desk. Waiting to see what I'd do.

'Privately be damned.' I slid off my stool, tiptoed over, and put my ear to the office door. Had to be careful not to touch it – it didn't fit very well and rattled on the catch if you put so much as a fingertip to it.

Harry was speaking loudly and distinctly. He knew a door with gaps round the frame when he heard it close behind him.

'What you grinning at?' Peter wanted to know. I shushed him and listened to what Harry was telling Mr Schofield.

So, Bowen the coroner was ill. That was no surprise. At the inquest before Christmas he'd looked as if he might drop dead in front of everybody. Grey, he'd been. Shrunk-looking.

Coroner's election in due course. Obviously.

Need for stand-in now. Body on Tresaith beach, dumped with a shipment of limestone. For obvious reasons, need for a suitable assistant.

A body on the beach. Drowned then?

Naked too, I heard through the door. As to drowning, Harry couldn't say.

So. A 'suitable assistant'. Harry wasn't here to offer me a job as his solicitor's clerk, then. I wasn't going to be making the bargain I'd been rehearsing for the better part of two months in my mind. *Yes, I'll be your clerk but you have to article me.*

Old Schofield was speaking again.

How long would you need Mr Davies for, do you think?

A week or so.

We weren't rushed off our feet. We'd get busier towards Lady Day with new contracts and agreements and so on but just now things were quiet. Mind, old Schofield didn't like giving something for nothing. And his silence must've told Harry that.

I will, of course, recompense you. I wouldn't expect you to pay John for the time he's spending with me.

Some mumbly muttering then. Probably my employer having his cake and eating it. Trying to make out he didn't need the money without actually turning it down. But what I hadn't heard him say was *yes*.

Harry upped the stakes. Said he'd be standing for election in due course. To be the coroner. Officially.

That'd make old Schofield sit up and take notice, for sure. Because once you'd been elected as one thing, other positions were easier to be elected to. As long as you didn't make a pig's ear of it, of course.

I could almost hear the cogs going round in Mr Schofield's head. Association with a member of parliament...

Perhaps, then, we should discuss this with the young man himself.

I was back on my stool, specs off to polish them so Mr Schofield didn't wonder why my pen was dry, by the time he called me through.

Harry's eyes were turned away slightly, when I went in, so that he could see me. Could see I was *there*, at any rate. Not much more. Which was why he needed me, of course.

When the question came, what I really wanted was to talk to Harry by himself. To ask him what his plans were. He owed me that. But Mr Schofield wasn't going to take himself off so I could speak to Harry like an equal.

'Well boy? What's your answer – will you help Mr Probert-Lloyd for a few days?'

I wanted to, God knows I did. After working with Harry, life in the office was even duller than before. Ruling lines a third of an inch apart. Copying wills and deeds and affidavits in a fair hand. Keeping the fire in and filling inkwells. Watching people walking up and down the hill outside the window. It was enough to make you want to gnaw your own arm off.

'Won't it leave you short-handed here, Mr Schofield?'

The old man gave me his 'you're a smarmy little shit but you're my smarmy little shit' smile. 'As Mr Probert-Lloyd values your assistance so highly, I'm sure we can spare you.'

I looked at Harry but his face was blank. I sometimes wondered whether not being able to see other people's expressions made him forget to pay attention to his own.

He had nobody else to turn to, I knew that. But if I was going to work for him again, there was going to have to be an understanding about my future. Because I did *not* intend to stay in Mr Schofield's office for the rest of my life.

'If you're sure, Mr Schofield,' I said. 'I'd be glad to.'

Harry

Given the need for a swift response to the suspicious death on the coast, Pomfrey, the magistrate, had arranged for a jury to be assembled from the local list and convened on Tresaith beach at ten the following morning, together with the man who had discovered the corpse. 'Get the corpse identified, instruct the jury as you see fit, and everybody'll be satisfied,' Pomfrey had said.

There was an inn on the beach where the proceedings could be held and I assumed that its keeper would have disseminated news of the proceedings so as to draw a good, beer-drinking crowd.

But as our horses picked their way down the hillside overlooking the little bay, John confirmed my impression that there was not a soul to be seen. 'Perhaps they're in the The Ship,' he said. 'Or the outhouse. You said that's where the body'd been put?'

Pomfrey had deplored the corpse's being lodged in a lean-to beer store, but, as the only buildings overlooking the sandy beach were a small cottage and The Ship Inn, there had been little choice.

'Actually,' I admitted, 'it'll suit me if we're here before the jury. We'll be able to take a preliminary view of the body in peace. Or rather,' I forced a grin, 'you can view it and tell me what you see.'

Somewhat disquietingly, however, on reaching the beach we found The Ship locked and deserted.

'Are you sure this is the time you agreed with Mr Pomfrey?' John asked.

'Quite sure. But, even if we were early, surely there'd be *somebody* here? Inquests usually mean good business.'

We tried the tiny cottage, which was set into the hillside behind two sea-facing limekilns. Though not locked, it, too, was unoccupied.

'If this is the lime burner's house,' I said, 'he's probably gone elsewhere for work till the season starts again.' Very little lime was burned along the coast in the winter months, the burners confining their activities to the times when building and agricultural lime was in demand.

'He's got plenty of limestone waiting for him,' John said. 'I don't know if you saw it but there's a huge pile of the stuff above the high tide line. Must be fifty tons or more.'

I nodded, though, as it happened, I had not seen it. 'Let's see if the outhouse is open,' I said. 'If not, we'll have to break in.'

John turned towards the inn. 'Who owns the place?'

'I can't remember his name, but he's a boat builder – or was, anyway. Hence The Ship. When I last came here, there was a smack being built on the beach.'

'No sign of any building now. The only boat here looks like it belongs to the lime burner.' He waved his hand vaguely towards the cottage beyond the limekilns, from which I inferred that the dark shape standing against the gable end was a rowing boat.

We walked to the outhouse. It stood at the back of the inn, tucked into the hillside, its only door facing north. With no fire inside, the lean-to would be constantly cold – suitable for the preservation of both beer and dead bodies.

'John.'

He turned. 'Yes?'

'It's not going to be very pleasant.' I had shared lodgings in London with Henry Gray, a student surgeon, who had insisted on dragging me to the mortuary in order to see a man dissected. It had been both fascinating and horrible.

'All right.' He moved towards the door, and I heard the thumb-latch click down. 'At least it's open.'

As we walked into the outhouse, I stumbled, suddenly deprived of vision. I was almost truly blind in dim light, and the small room had no windows. Standing aside so as to make the best use of the light coming through the door, I looked around as best I could. The object of our interest was immediately obvious – a pale-draped shape that lay on some kind of trestle table opposite the doorway.

'What have they covered him with?' I asked.

'Sailcloth. Probably trying to keep the rats off. Wouldn't've stopped them for long, mind. Got teeth like needles, rats have.'

He was speaking more quickly than usual. 'Would you rather wait for the constable and the jury?' I asked.

'No.' The word was sharp. 'I'll do it now.'

I nodded. If the state of the corpse was going to induce him to bring up his breakfast, better that he did it while only I was here as witness.

'Damn. The cloth's stiff with seawater. I can hardly fold it back.' His voice had the studied normality of somebody who was trying very hard not to be disturbed.

Folding proved impossible so, in the end, he grabbed the sheet and pulled it to the ground, where it stood in rigid folds. With a grunt of impatience, he kicked it to one side and bent over the naked corpse.

'God almighty!'

I thought he was referring to the smell which had filled the air with the sail's removal. 'He's been dead a while, evidently.'

'No. His face, it's–'

I heard voices outside. 'What's happened to his face?' I asked, quickly.

John stumbled past me, gasping air into his lungs. I hoped, for his sake, that deep breaths would bring his heaving stomach under control. If he threw up its contents now, the number of voices outside suggested that he would do so in front of the entire inquest jury.

I followed him, setting aside questions of what might have happened to the dead man's face and nerving myself to tell a group of men I had never met before that I was blind.

A blind coroner?

The words would go through every man's mind. Of course they would.

A flame of anger licked up inside me. What was a blind man *supposed* to do with his life? Beg on the street? Keep decently to his house so as not to embarrass others?

'Good morning, gentlemen.' I hoped that my speaking Welsh would take them aback just enough to allow me to assert myself. 'For those of you who don't know me, I'm Harry Probert-Lloyd of Glanteifi. I've been asked to stand in as coroner for the time being.'

A figure stepped forward, uniform blue coat and white trousers identifying him as a police officer. 'Good morning, sir. Constable Thomas Jones, Cardiganshire Constabulary.'

'Have you seen the body yet, constable?'

'No, sir.'

'Then can I suggest that you do so while I swear in the jury?'

He marched off in the direction of the outhouse, his footsteps muted on the sandy turf and I turned back to the jury, imagining looks exchanged amongst them. How far afield had gossip gone about my investigations before Christmas?

Sweet on Margaret Jones, he was. That's why he wanted to know who killed her.

'If you don't know me, you won't know that my sight is poor.' Let them wonder exactly what I could see. 'My colleague, John Davies, will oversee the view of the body with me. But first, we need to record your names. If you'd be so good as to introduce yourselves, I'd be grateful.'

A few awkward seconds followed while the jury silently decided who should speak first, then came the usual list of anglicised patronyms – Davies, Thomas, Williams, Jones, Evans, James. And one Vaughan – an ancient English spelling of *Fychan*, Small. It would be their responsibility to decide, on their viewing of the body and any other evidence that presented itself, who the deceased was and how he had met his end.

'Have you elected a foreman?' I asked.

They had and he spoke up: Vaughan.

'Thank you, Mr Vaughan. All that's left is to swear each of you in.'

I said it as if I had done it a hundred times before but, had it not been for John's help, I would have had no idea that the jury had to give their oath before viewing the body. Pomfrey had left a volume of advice for coroners with me at Glanteifi, murmuring, 'Perhaps your father...' But it had been John to whom I had given the book, and the task of instructing me in my duties.

Oaths duly taken, I suggested that, in order to allow each juror to scrutinise the body appropriately, they should conduct the view two at a time.

The first pair were stepping forward when Constable Jones emerged.

'Gone a nasty green colour, Jones has,' John observed, voice low so that the officer would not hear him.

Our corpse was evidently not a pretty sight and I wondered, again, what had happened to his face.

Inside, I turned to the first jurors. Were they feeling a queasy anticipation after witnessing Jones's reaction?

'May I have your names, please? I need to be sure that every man has viewed the body.' Of course, John would make sure of that, but I wanted to commit names and voices to memory as best I could.

'Twm Wern Fach,' the first man said, giving the name of his farm by which his neighbours would know him. 'Thomas Thomas on the jury list.'

'Obadaiah Vaughan,' said the taller figure. 'But only to my mother.' I heard the smile in his voice. 'Everybody else calls me Dai'r Bardd.'

Dai the Poet? I hoped flights of fancy would not affect his performance as foreman.

'Step forward, gentlemen –' I moved aside so that they could get to the body – 'and state what you see.'

They moved towards the corpse. I waited for one of them to speak but, after a single hissed intake of breath as they bent over the body, the kind a man makes when he cuts himself with a careless slice of his pocket knife, there was no sound.

'Do you know the deceased?' I asked.

They did not. Neither man turned from the body as he answered and I recognised the same horrible fascination that had fixed my own eyes to my first cadaver.

'Can we begin with whether the corpse is that of a man or a woman?' I prompted. I knew the answer, but it seemed an uncontroversial place to start.

One of the men cleared his throat. 'It's a man.' Dai'r Bardd. His voice had a youthful tone but there was something about it that made me think he might be one of those men who simply seem perpetually young, whose waistline does not thicken and whose hair does not recede as the years advance. 'A youngish man by the look of his hair,' he continued. 'No grey in it.'

'Colour?'

'Brown. Much as I can see in this light. Not dark but not fair either.'

'And his face?' I asked. 'Is that fair or dark?'

'That's difficult to say,' Vaughan's voice was steady, 'because his face has no skin on it.'

After what must have been half an hour of prompting, questioning and one swift exit to vomit loudly on the grass outside, I had a clear idea of what the dead man looked like. A little above average height and, variously, 'well nourished', 'muscular', 'strong-looking', or 'fit to fight you'. His arms were reported to be pale and hairy, as was his torso. Jurors also noted scars here and there but none so fresh as to have contributed to his death.

The corpse's hands were in a state similar to his face – the skin quite gone. But they did provide us with some information about the dead man. 'They're not a working man's hands,' John said. 'Not big enough. And, anyway, you'd expect his arms to be brown if he'd laboured for a living.'

'Are you sure there's nothing about him that you recognise?' I asked again and again. 'His hair? The shape of his face?'

Whatever had stripped the skin from the dead man's face had also taken his eyes, so I asked whether his teeth were unusual in any way – overlapping, missing some at the front, anything which would enable one of my jurors to recognise him.

But no. His teeth, like the rest of him, it seemed, were unremarkable.

When the last pair of jurors came in, I did not wait for them to shuffle uneasily around the body. 'Gentlemen, can you please confirm that this is a dead male, and that there are no recent injuries to the front of his body?'

I waited while they bent over the exposed corpse, examining the legs for thoroughness' sake before straightening up and confirming what I had said.

'And describe what you see on the back, if you'd be so good.'

John was already rolling the body over.

After a muttered oath from one of them, they agreed, as all the others had done, that his back was a mass of bruised flesh from shoulders to buttocks and on down his legs.

'Except there are some places which aren't bruised,' one of them said 'where the skin looks ordinary – here,' he apparently motioned to John to come and look, as if he imagined that nobody else had done so, 'across his shoulders, look. And here, on his buttocks.'

'What about his legs?' I asked. It was a leading question; I knew the answer, and not only because I had heard it from the other jurors.

'Same on the backs of his legs. Little patches where the skin isn't bruised.' He turned to me. 'What causes bruises like that?'

I had asked the twelve men not to confer about what they had seen until the last pair had emerged from the viewing and, evidently, they had followed my request to the letter.

'It's not bruising,' I told him, recalling my friend Gray's explanation of the apparent injury to one of his precious corpses. 'It's what the doctors call *livor mortis*. When the heart stops pumping, the blood settles in the lowest part of the body. This man was laid on his back after he died.'

'What about the pale patches?'

It was exactly the question I had asked in St George's hospital mortuary. In all probability, everybody asked it when confronted with the phenomenon for the first time.

'The blood settles around any unevenness in the surface that the body's lying on.'

'He must've been lying on something rough, then?'

I nodded. 'He was found lying amongst a load of lime on the beach.'

'Fell off the boat that brought the lime in then, is it?'

I ignored his question; that was for the public hearing of evidence. 'Can you look at his head, please?'

Their reluctance as they shuffled towards the man's skinless face was obvious. From the terse, tight-throated comments of the men who had already viewed the body, my mind's eye saw flesh that was both desiccated and wet, pitted tissue that looked somewhat less than human.

I shivered. 'There's nothing in his face that tells you who he might be?'

Subdued mumbles told me that there was not.

'Very well, if you could just have a look at the side of his head.'

Like the others, they quickly found the wound.

'Nasty.'

'Would you describe it for Mr Davies, please?'

'There's a lump, and broken skin,' one man offered.

'No blood,' the other said, 'but you can see where it's open, there.'

'Can you estimate its size for the record, please?'

'About two inches long. Lump's bigger – swollen around it.'

I knew that the swelling could have taken place even if death had occurred within a minute of the blow being inflicted. As a boy, I had once tripped in a hell-for-leather run and crashed my cheekbone into a rock. In the time it had taken to look around for witnesses to my humiliation, my eye had begun to close with the swelling.

'And its position?'

I saw a movement towards the body, imagined fingers pincered between ear and wound. 'About half an inch above his left ear.'

I was about to dismiss the men when one said, 'Nasty bump, granted, but he drowned, didn't he? If he was found on the load of lime in the sea?'

As I had asked him to do when previous jurors had suggested drowning as a cause of death, John returned the corpse to its original position. 'Watch,' he said, before pressing down on the dead chest.

The Thames gave up unidentified people with dispiriting regularity and drowned corpses had been a commonplace on Gray's dissection table. 'If he'd drowned,' I said, 'you'd see a fine froth coming out of his mouth. He might have come out of the water but he didn't drown.'

John

The man who'd found the body still hadn't turned up by the time we finished the view and neither had anybody else. I had a nasty feeling I knew what was going on. This magistrate – Pomfrey – had been hoping Harry'd just ask the jurors for a verdict and decide the inquest was done. But he didn't know Harry.

'An inquest is a public hearing,' he told the jury. 'Justice must be seen to be done or it's not justice. I'm sorry, gentlemen, I have no choice but to adjourn the hearing until public notification of it can be given.'

I watched the jurors exchanging the sort of looks that told me they'd been taking bets on this happening. But nobody said a word. Well, they wouldn't, would they? Not to the acting coroner. So, without the sniff of a suspicion that they'd second-guessed him, Harry thanked them all and off they went.

'What happened to the man who found the body?' I said as I watched the men drib and drab up the path to the headland in twos and threes. 'D'you think Mr Pomfrey forgot to tell him to be here?'

'No.' Harry's jaw was tight under his beard. 'I think Mr Pomfrey forgot to arrange a proper inquest hearing.'

So. It wasn't just me who thought the magistrates'd tried to use Harry to get this done quietly, on the sly.

'Right.' Harry'd made a decision. 'We're going to go and have a little chat with Theophilus Harris and find out why he didn't come and tell us how he happened to stumble across the body.'

Constable Jones gave us the man's details, then, when Harry

dismissed him, he saluted like a soldier and marched off up the hill, back to whatever duties he'd come from.

I fetched the mares, we tightened their girths, heaved ourselves into the saddle and followed the path Jones had taken.

Halfway up the bracken-covered hillside, I looked back down at the beach with its two peaceful looking buildings. You'd never credit that there was a faceless corpse lying down there, covered in a sailcloth. But then, if Harry became coroner, that'd be his life, wouldn't it? Seeing death everywhere.

I tried not to think about the corpse and stared out over the sea. All those colours of blue and grey and green. The immenseness of it. Stretching all the way down to Cardigan, up to Aberystwyth and, out there, out beyond the horizon, Ireland. Then America.

The vastness of it made you feel small. Like an ant in a field. It was so huge you couldn't see the size of it.

Once we were up on the headland, I turned to Harry. 'Was it Justice Pomfrey that this man, Harris, reported the death to?' I was wondering whether this fiasco of an inquest was all Pomfrey's idea or whether the other magistrates'd just volunteered him to talk to Harry.

'He didn't go to a magistrate to report the death,' he said. 'Seems he chose to favour the local registrar with the news.'

'Why? He couldn't have thought it was a *natural* death, surely? Not with a face like that?'

'Goodness knows what he thought,' Harry said. 'Fortunately, the registrar knew his job.'

'Knew he'd be in a whole lot of trouble if he just registered the death, you mean. You can't just give up a body for burial without a name. Especially if it looks like that.'

'I'll have to take your word for how it looks.' Harry smiled – sort of – which seemed like a good sign. Perhaps he was making peace with his blindness. Then again, I wasn't sure whether that was good or bad for my prospects. Perhaps he was making peace with being squire of Glanteifi as well.

Constable Jones'd told us that Harris's house was just off the turnpike road from Cardigan to Aberaeron. 'It's a *tŷ unnos*,' he'd said.

Harry's eyebrows'd shot up. 'I didn't think anybody still did that.'

Jones'd been too respectful to say so, but that just showed how much Harry didn't know. Building *tai unnos* might've been an old custom but it was still useful. If you could raise a house on common land between sunset and sunrise of a single night, and have smoke coming from the chimney as the sun came over the horizon, you were allowed to enclose the ground around it.

Mind, only desperate people built *tai unnos*. Enclosing common land takes grazing away from neighbours' animals, and this Harris'd be lucky if he hadn't made an enemy of everybody who lived within a walking mile of his house.

As we got to the turnpike road, Harry kicked his mare into a trot. 'What's the rush?'

'No rush, just want to get there and get on.'

Of course he did. He wanted this done. Finished. The reasons for this man's death presented to the world in an orderly fashion. He wanted to show he'd be a good coroner.

Damn. For the last month I'd been trying to tell myself that he was just taking his time thinking about the best way to go about setting himself up as a solicitor. But I think, in my guts, I'd always known he wasn't going to do it. If he'd been serious, he'd've done it straight away, as soon as we'd finished our investigations about Margaret Jones.

I'd just been fooling myself. Harry wasn't going to take me on as an articled clerk. Trouble was, I'd set my heart on articles now – on being a solicitor myself in due course.

Looked like I was going to have to find another way to do it.

Harry

Theophilus Harris's home was easy to identify from the name Constable Jones had given it – Banc yr Eithin – as the back wall was dug into the gorse-covered mound that rose behind it.

'Door's open,' John said 'but I can't see anybody about.'

I patted the neck of my little mare, Sara, and slid from her back. 'I don't suppose he's far away. There's not much labouring to be had at this time of year.'

John dismounted. 'Shall I knock?'

Before I could answer, we heard a voice behind us.

'Good day. Who's this paying a visit to me and my family?'

Though the greeting was civil enough, I detected a hint of displeasure in the voice. I turned, my pulse quickening.

'Good day to you. I'm Henry Probert-Lloyd, Acting Coroner, and this is John Davies, my assistant. Am I speaking to Mr Theopilus Harris?'

'Teff. Teff Harris. That's me.'

His tone was not welcoming. Perhaps he was surprised at my addressing him in his own language. He certainly did not want to speak to me in Welsh; despite my use of the vernacular, he had answered in English.

I saw his head turn to follow John who was leading the horses to one side. 'Don't tie them to that hurdle, *ngwas i,*' he called. 'One good tug and they'll have it over.'

'Where shall I tie them, then?' John sounded belligerent. He'd been 'Mr Davies' to the jury and clearly did not appreciate being addressed as 'my lad' by Teff Harris.

25

'You don't need to,' Harris said. 'I'll get my son to come and see to them. He can let them graze.'

We waited as he called the child from the house.

'You're here to ask me about the body on the beach, then?'

'Yes.' Given my suspicions about Pomfrey, I decided not to take Harris to task about his failure to attend the viewing of the body. 'I wondered why you didn't go to the magistrate to report it? It was obviously a suspicious death.'

Harris sucked in a breath. 'I'm not on terms with any of the magistrates,' he said.' But I know Jaci Rees, the registrar. Thought he'd know what the standing orders were.'

'You thought he'd tell the magistrate himself?'

'What they pay him for, isn' it?'

John spoke from behind me. 'Surely you knew that the first finder has to alert the magistrates? Or the police, in Cardigan. Procedures or not, everybody knows that.' His belligerence told me he was still smarting from that *ngwas i*.

Harris did not respond immediately. Was he considering John's use of that technical term 'first finder' and wondering who exactly this lad was?

'Cardigan's a long walk,' his voice was carefully neutral. 'I'd've lost a whole day going there and back.'

'Is there a *reason* you didn't want to go to the police or the magistrates?' John demanded. 'Do they *know* you?'

Harris was no fool. He knew what was being implied. 'Now look, boy – there was nothing forcing me to tell *anybody*. I could've dragged him into the sea and let him float away. Gone about my work as if I'd never seen him.'

I took over. 'But, Mr Harris, I'm sure you would never have done such a thing.'

Always flatter your witnesses, an old barrister once told me. Let them believe you think they're more law-abiding, more trustworthy than they really are. They'll be so keen to prove you right that they'll trip themselves up. Go after them and they'll give you nothing but monosyllables.

It was clearly advice I needed to pass on to John.

During the last few minutes, the sky had become noticeably darker and now rain started to fall.

'Come inside,' Harris said. 'You don't want to stand about in this.'

We left the boy outside with the horses. I hoped he would think to put something over the saddles or we were going to be unpleasantly damp on our onward ride.

'Your wife not home?' John asked. Unless she was hiding in the box-bed that stood against one wall, she was clearly not indoors. The cottage was small and bare to the point of austerity though somebody who knew what they were doing had made up the floor which was hard and clean.

'No.' I did not expect Harris to elaborate but he surprised me. 'Gone to her sister's. She's poorly.'

He did not clarify whether it was his wife or his sister-in-law who was unwell, and I felt we had no reason to ask.

'I can make you some tea if you'd like?'

'Yes, thank you.' I was cold and hungry; even weak tea made with leaves that had already been used once would be very welcome.

As Harris filled the kettle from a big jug on the side, John started interrogating him once more. 'So. What were you doing on the beach, Mr Harris?'

Did Teff Harris dart a meaningful glance at me? *Why don't you teach your boy some manners?* I could not tell, but he certainly took his time in answering.

'I was checking that the limestone had come in. Didn't want men arriving ready to bring it up the beach if it wasn't there.'

'You've been carting the stone up the beach?' I asked.

Because I was watching for it, I caught his nod. 'Last six weeks. Gets unloaded into the sea at high tide, we collect it off the beach at low tide and bring it up. It's there ready for the kilns, then.'

'We?' I could see John fidgetting uncomfortably on the stool he had perched on. It was probably meant for Harris's young son and was far too small for John's longer legs.

'Gang of men I bring in.'

'So, you're in charge?' John had mastered his irritation, and was now sounding more as I would wish.

Harris did not answer straight away. As we waited, I tried to get an impression of him. A small face under light-coloured hair; a feeling of sharpness, both of intellect and of temper. Not a big man, but one you would not wish to cross.

'Yes,' he said. 'Come to an arrangement with Mrs Parry. She pays me to get the stone up the beach, I do it as I see fit.'

'*Mrs* Parry?' I asked. 'The wife of The Ship's owner?'

Teff Harris spooned tea into the pot. 'Widow.'

'I see. So, she's taken over his business?'

I heard the sound of the lid going back on to the tin tea-caddy. 'Always was her business,' Harris said, 'husband or not.'

Interesting. But the widow Parry's business acumen was not something to be pursued just now. 'Describe to me how exactly you found the body, if you'd be so good.'

Harris stood and stretched his back. 'Went over to Tresaith as soon as it was properly light. Like I said, didn't want men arriving if there was no work to be done. But the stone was there. Could see it from the top.'

'From the headland?'

'Yes. So then, I went to get the horses.'

I had the impression that he was looking at me out of the corner of his eye, wondering. 'You use a cart to bring the stone up the beach, then?'

'Yes. Quicker than barrowing it. Don't need so many men, either.'

'Did you fetch the men as well?' John asked. 'Once you'd made sure the stone was there?'

'Didn't have to. They knew to come Tuesday morning.'

The kettle started to sing and Harris crouched at the hearth to pour water into the pot to warm it. I heard a knee popping and wondered how old he was; for all I knew, that fair hair of his could be greying, and his face lined.

'Whose horses do you use?' I phrased the question so that it was just possible to infer that I believed he might have horses of his own. It seemed unlikely, given the poverty of the cottage, but Teff Harris's accent and demeanour were not those of a labourer and I did not want to underestimate him.

'Got an arrangement to use a ploughing pair,' he said. 'Owner's glad to get them out of the stable and fit for the field.'

'And once you had the horses?' I asked. 'Did you get down onto the beach before any of the other men arrived?'

A pause, then I heard John's voice behind me. 'Mr Harris, can you answer, please? Mr Probert-Lloyd's sight is poor. He can't see well enough to notice you nodding.'

Though I had admitted as much to the jury, it rankled to hear John tell Harris. It was my admission to make, not his.

'Yes.' Harris bit the word off as if he would like to spit it at John. 'I got there before anybody else.'

I kept my face impassive, as if both my inability to see properly and John's drawing attention to it were things hardly worth mentioning. 'And, once you were on the beach, you saw the body. Is that right?'

'Yes.'

'Did you wait for the other men or did you go and look at it straight away?' John asked.

'I went straight over. Didn't know whether he was alive or dead. All I could see was somebody lying amongst the stones.'

'*Amongst* the stones, or on top of them?' I asked. If the body had been dumped along with the limestone then it might well have been half-buried.

'On top – right in the middle of the pile.'

As if somebody had placed him there. 'And then?' I prompted.

'Close up, I knew he was dead. That face didn't belong on a living man.'

I waited.

'So I put 'im in the cart and brought 'im up to the beer store.'

'Was he naked when you found him or did you take the clothes off his back?' From the harshness of his tone, I knew John had been rattled by the reference to the dead man's face.

Harris took his time before answering and I wondered whether he was trying to make John feel uncomfortable. 'And why would I do that?'

John did not answer but he did not have to. Clothes, especially the kind that a man with a gentleman's hands might wear, were valuable.

'Please, Mr Harris' – I allowed just a hint of pleading to enter my tone – 'just answer the question.' I would have to have words with John; personal antipathies could not be allowed to influence our investigation.

'As you saw him, so I found him.'

'Thank you. May I ask why you didn't leave him on the stones until the other men came?'

Harris stirred the tea, the spoon clinking against the rim of the pot.

'Two reasons. First, we had to get the load shifted before the tide caught us out, so I didn't have time to waste. Second, if that lot'd clapped eyes on him, half of them would've thrown their guts up on the beach and been useless for the rest of the morning. And the other half would've spent all their time gossiping about who he was and how he'd come to be there. I wanted to get on.'

'*You* didn't throw your guts up then?' John asked.

'I was in the Afghan War. Saw things a lot worse than his face.'

A soldier. That explained his English; not to mention his air of self-reliance.

'So, you just took him up to the shed then went about your business with the limestone as if nothing had happened?' John asked.

Harris got up and fetched some cups from a shelf on the back wall. 'Took the other men in when we'd finished. See if any of 'em knew 'im.' He crouched down again at the hearth. 'They didn't.' He began pouring the tea. 'I'm sorry, I've got no milk. The cow's dry and my wife usually fetches milk but with her being away…'

I assured him that I had drunk milkless tea before without ill-effect, and accepted a cup.

'How long have The Ship and the cottage stood empty?' I asked.

'You make it sound as if the one's empty because the other is,' Harris said.

'Isn't it? Wouldn't The Ship be open and welcoming people if the limekilns were burning?'

'Possibly,' he conceded. 'But Mrs Parry isn't generally one to be ruled by other people's comings and goings.'

'Where is she?' John asked.

'Seeing to business somewhere.'

I did not press him on that; I would speak to the lady myself as soon as she returned. 'And the lime burner?'

'Out with the herring-boats. Can't take to idleness. Needs the company.'

'How long has he been gone?'

Harris supped his tea. 'Wasn't here last time we got lime in or the time before. More'n two weeks that'd be.'

The lime burner was, therefore, unlikely to have had anything to do with our corpse's death. Nonetheless, it would be prudent to speak to him. 'Do you know when he'll be back?'

'Heard the herring boats were back in Cardigan yesterday. So, soon, I 'spect. Unless he's planning on drinking all his earnings.'

As we rode away – on saddles that were, thankfully, no more than slightly damp – I tried to decide how best to address the subject of John's tetchiness towards Harris. I could not afford to have him alienating witnesses. But, the more I struggled to find the right words, the harder it became. I did not want to reprimand him; if I did so, I reduced him to the rank of servant, a mere amanuensis, and I both wished and needed him to be far more than that. But I had to say something.

'He didn't mean anything by calling you *ngwas i*,' I began.

Nobody in Newcastle Emlyn knew that John had once been a *gwas bach*, a boy servant on a farm. But he could not forget the fact, and he did not like to be reminded that he had run away from that life in terror.

'He's an old soldier,' I said. 'He might just as well have called you "son". You're just a boy to him, that's all.'

'No. A *servant.* That's what I am to him. Specifically, *your* servant.'

'Assistant.'

'That's not what Teff Harris saw. He saw a servant, leading the horses.'

'What does it matter what Teff Harris thinks you are?'

'Easy for you to say.'

'What? Me the *blind man?*'

He made a sound that uneasily straddled dismay and dismissal. 'Still Harry Probert-Lloyd though, aren't you? Blind or not, you're still the heir to the Glanteifi estate.' He was working hard to keep his tone even, to point things out in a reasonable manner. But, underneath his attempt to be measured, I could feel something waiting to erupt. 'And I'm just *your assistant.*'

'Just?'

He did not reply but the set of his shoulders suggested an apple on his head and an arrow on the nock.

'*Just* the person without whom I wouldn't have considered taking on this job?' I insisted.

The lenses of his spectacles caught the sun as he turned his head and I felt his eyes on me. 'Why *have* you taken it on, Harry? What happened to being a solicitor?'

What happened to being a solicitor? My rebuke to myself.

'I told you. Pomfrey just turned up at Glanteifi and presented me with – effectively – a *fait accompli.*'

'You could have said no.'

'What? "No, Mr Pomfrey, don't be ridiculous, I'm blind?"'

'No.' John's tone was a study in reasonableness. 'Not "I'm blind". "I'm *busy.*" Busy becoming a solicitor.'

I turned my head away. The grey-blue of the sea, away to our right, curved around the central whirl of my blindness. I longed to be able to gaze at it directly, to see the patches of darker blue as cloud-shadows flitted across the surface of the water, the white horses racing in as the wind picked up the edges of waves and drove them into spume. But such things were invisible to me now.

Abruptly, I pulled my mount up, forcing John to do the same.

'Pomfrey asked me, as a favour to the magistrates, if I'd take on this one case.'

'One case *in the first instance*. But you're already talking about elections–' As I had anticipated, John had listened at Schofield's office door. 'So it's *not* just this case, is it? You want to *be* the coroner.'

'Is that such a bad thing?'

'It is if you think you're just going to keep dropping in to Schofield's office and *borrowing* me whenever you feel like it!'

I did not know what to say. I was mortified that John should feel so poorly used but, at the same time, I could not deny that his feelings were justified.

Finally, the chilly wind nudging at us like an impatient elbow, John spoke once more, his voice quieter now, more earnest. 'I don't want to be a solicitor's clerk all my life, Harry. I'm capable of more. I *want* more.'

'Of course, that's why I'm–'

'I'm going to ask Mr Schofield if he'll article me. I wouldn't need the full five years, I know a lot already.'

From the resignation in his tone, it was clear that, following our investigations before Christmas, John had expected to hear from me. To be offered employment as my legal *sine qua non*.

Of course I could be a solicitor, I had told him, our success in finding Margaret Jones's killer filling me with bravado. *I just need the right solicitor's clerk.*

John's new ambition was entirely of my own making.

'I'm only telling you this because, if you want to stand for coroner, you need to think about an assistant.' John's tone was that of somebody discharging a disagreeable but necessary duty. 'That's all I'm saying. I can't be at your beck and call, Harry.'

I swallowed disappointment and self-reproach. 'Of course. I should have realised. I appreciate your making things clear, John.' I paused but he deserved honesty from me. 'I suppose I'd assumed… well, that *you* wouldn't mind if Mr Schofield didn't. I thought it might make your life more interesting.'

I heard my own words and wondered that I had the nerve to articulate them.

'I'm sure it would.' He was not being kind, simply giving an honest response. 'But it wouldn't give me any *standing*.' I saw him shake his head, just slightly. 'I want something better than the life of a lawyer's clerk.'

I nodded. 'And you deserve it.' Of course he did; the abilities that I had seen in him were precisely those that were now compelling him to wish for more. I had discovered my ideal assistant and, simultaneously, alerted him to the fact that he could aspire to greater things.

I clucked Sara into motion once more.

'Harry? Where are we going?'

I did not know. Motion simply seemed better than stasis.

'We should go and see the inspector in Cardigan,' John said. 'He'll have something to say about all this.'

John

God, I wished I had gloves on that ride down to Cardigan! The wind kept thudding into us, like being hit with a goosedown pillow. And it wasn't just strong, it was cold – as if it'd picked up the chill of the Atlantic all the way from America. Why the lime burner would want to leave his little cottage and go out on the sea to be at the mercy of that wind was a mystery to me.

My fingers were frozen. I don't think I could've let go of the reins if you'd paid me.

And my insides were the same. Frozen. I'd gambled and lost. I'd been *so sure* Harry'd give me a job. He didn't have to offer me articles, just something better than what I had at the moment. But he'd just taken what I'd said. Taken it and said nothing. Perhaps he thought he didn't have any right to interfere. That would've been typical Harry.

Why in the name of sanity had I said I was going to ask Mr Schofield to article me? I hadn't meant to. I'd just opened my mouth and out it came.

Knowing Harry, now he knew I had a plan he'd just back away and let me get on with it. All respectful. But I didn't want his respect, I wanted him to give me a job.

Landed myself right in the shit, hadn't I? I could just see old Schofield's face if I asked him to give me articles for nothing. *I don't think that would be appropriate, do you, Mr Davies?*

I turned to Harry. Didn't want him to think I was sulking. 'Have you met the police inspector?' I asked.

'No. I know nothing about him. When the force was established

36

my father and I were barely on speaking terms. He wouldn't have felt the need to tell me magistrates' business.'

No, I didn't suppose he would. When the Cardiganshire police came into being, Probert-Lloyd of the bench was still getting over the scandal of his son being involved with a dairymaid.

'As it happens,' I said, 'he's got something in common with our friend Harris. He's an old soldier.'

'Aren't most policemen?'

'I wouldn't know, but Mr Bellis is. That's his name, William Bellis.'

Harry snorted as if I'd made a weak joke. 'I bet that's not what people call him.'

In spite of everything, I grinned. 'No, they call him Billy Go-About.'

He waited for me to explain. I glanced across at him, sitting there with his stupid soft-brimmed hat and his stiff Mackintosh overcoat. What was Mr Bellis going to make of him?

'The main reason the magistrates wanted a police force,' I said 'was to stop anything like the riots happening again. So, the inspector's always been keen to put an end to any kind of gathering that looks as if it might have an opinion about somebody or something. Gets his men together and appears on the streets. "Go about your business!" he shouts. "Anybody continuing to gather in unlawful numbers will be arrested immediately."'

'It's only unlawful after dark, surely?'

'Yes. Well. Billy Go-About takes a broad view of darkness. Late afternoon. Dusk. If he thinks too many people are loitering, out he'll come. Then it's *Go about your business!*'

'Not a popular man, then?'

'Popular with the magistrates.'

'But not generally?'

'He doesn't like civilians.'

Harry snorted again, but this time he didn't find anything funny in what I'd said. 'He's obviously failed to remember that the police may be uniformed, but they're not military. He's as much a civilian as you and I.'

No. Billy Go-About was definitely not going to take a shine to Harry.

If I'd been the chief constable, I'd've chosen somewhere else for Cardigan lock-up. Right next to where the old town stocks used to be wasn't the best place if he wanted to give the idea that he was in charge of a new, modern police force. To everybody in town, it looked like the same old story – the magistrates are the law. Only now they had men in uniforms to enforce it at the ratepayers' expense.

Mind you, inside the police station, the ratepayers didn't have much to complain about. No money whatsoever had gone on making the place look impressive. The walls were whitewashed – clean enough to show they'd been done recently – and the woodwork was polished, but that was all you could say. It wasn't a place that encouraged you to visit. *You don't come to us*, it said, *we come to you.*

There was a constable sitting behind a desk. His eyes followed us in, but he didn't bother stirring his fat arse from his chair. Looked Harry up and down, he did, as if he'd never seen a man in a Mackintosh coat before. To be fair, he probably hadn't.

'Help you?' he grunted, in Welsh. Not insolent exactly, but definitely not what your mother would've approved of.

Harry stared directly at him. As if he could see every blackhead in the man's face, every greasy brown hair on his head. As if he was disgusted by the crust of snot hanging from one hairy nostril.

'I am Henry Probert-Lloyd,' he said, in his most English voice. 'Acting coroner for the Teifi Valley. I would like to see Mr Bellis, please.'

That stood Mr Fat Arse up in a hurry.

'I'm very sorry, sir, but Inspector Bellis isn't here at the moment. Got a meeting with the magistrates, he has.'

'Do you know when he'll be back?'

He didn't.

'Very well, I'll leave him a letter if I may.'

The constable nodded, as if that was the best idea he'd heard all year. 'Yes, sir. Of course, sir.' But he didn't get the hint. Did he think I had a writing desk with ink and pens in my back pocket?

'We'll need a pen and some paper' I said. 'If you don't mind.'

As we went around to the back of the station to fetch the mares, I caught Harry grinning. It was a relief. 'What's tickled you, then?'

'That constable must've thought I was too grand to write my own letters – the way I stood there dictating to you.'

I glanced at the barred window of the lock-up room as we went past. Made me shiver. 'I know you had to leave that letter for form's sake,' I said, 'but the news'll be all round town before Billy Go-About gets back from his meeting. That constable'll be telling anybody in earshot that the inquest's been adjourned. You'll be lucky if Billy Bellis doesn't hear it in the street. And then he'll have a fit about it.'

Harry handed over a ha'penny to the boy who was holding our horses and waited for him to scamper off over the cracked cobbles. 'Why would Bellis have a fit?'

I let him take Sara's reins and kept hold of the little grey, Seren. 'Money,' I said. 'Take it from me, if the magistrates wanted you to get the whole thing done and dusted on the quiet this morning, Old Go-About'll be of the same opinion. Person unknown, not from round here, drowned. Very sad but not one of us. Stick him in the ground as cheaply as possible and that's the end of him.'

'Except he didn't drown.'

I'd never seen Inspector Bellis in the flesh but I had a pretty shrewd idea what an old army officer'd sound like if he thought his judgement was being questioned. 'Doctor now, are you, sir?' I barked at Harry. 'Qualified to say how a man died, are you? Man who comes out of the sea dead is drowned, sir, take my word for it. Drowned.'

Harry laughed. 'We'll see.'

He might not know Billy Go-About and his ways yet, but he would, soon enough. And if I'd had money to bet with, I'd've staked a good sum on him and Bellis not getting on. At all.

Harry

By the time John arrived the following morning, I had ruminated on his warning about the inspector's likely attitude, and determined that we must make another attempt to liaise with Bellis. However, there was something else that I wished to put in train first and I raised the subject with John as we walked around the house to the stableyard.

'As well as seeing Bellis today, I need to find a doctor,' I told him.

'Why? Who's ill?'

'Nobody. I want to arrange for an autopsy examination on the corpse.'

He pulled up abruptly. 'Is that really needed? Seemed pretty clear what'd killed him.'

'You mean the blow to the head?' I spoke quietly, aware that the grooms in the stableyard would be casting curious glances in our direction.

'Of course.'

'In my experience, what seems obvious isn't always what's true. And then there's the matter of his face.' The jury's various descriptions of the corpse's skinless face had stuck in my mind, marking this death as something out of the normal run of things.

'Having his face skinned didn't kill him.' John's voice was tight but it was not clear to me whether his reaction was due to recollection of the grisly sight or because he felt rebuked by my response.

'Possibly not,' I said, mildly, 'but it might have a bearing on how or why he died and I'd like to have a medical opinion on how he came to be in that condition.'

'Fair enough. But, I'm warning you, the magistrates'll complain. It's two guineas to have a corpse cut open.'

I knew he was probably right – after all, until I could acquaint myself with all the ramifications of my temporary position, he had the advantage over me when it came to both legal practices and local politics in Cardiganshire – but I was not going to allow financial considerations to sway me. 'Somewhere,' I said, voice still low, 'there's a family waiting for news of him. Where he is. Why he hasn't come home.' I paused to allow this putative family to take form in John's mind. 'And I'd rather not just take the easy option and tell them that he died from a blow on the head – accidental or otherwise. He may have died of some other cause. An apoplexy or seizure. After which, somebody found him, stripped him of his clothes for what they were worth and threw his body into the sea.'

'Is that what you think happened?' John clearly did not.

'It's what *could* have happened.' I hesitated. 'You and I both know that it'll be far easier to persuade somebody to come forward and identify him if an autopsy examination finds he died of natural causes.' Our investigation into the death of Margaret Jones had taught us that people were apt to be wary of getting involved in a murder, however innocent their knowledge of the victim might be.

John sighed. 'You'll never get elected as coroner if you start going into things in this detail. You'd cost the ratepayers twice what Mr Bowen did.'

His words sent a cold shiver over me but I could not simply sign my name to 'unlawful killing by persons unknown' and forget about the unclaimed Tresaith corpse. Whoever he was, he deserved better than that. Just as Margaret had.

'An autopsy examination will give us more information,' I said.

'Information we need.' I waited, but he made no response. 'So… do you know a doctor who might be persuaded to do the job?'

'People around here aren't too keen on dissectors coming to examine them,' John said, making for the stables once more as if he wanted to put a distance between himself and the topic of conversation. 'I know things are probably different in London but, here, people don't think it's decent.'

I kept pace with him. 'Are you telling me you don't know a doctor who'll do it?'

He stopped and sighed. 'No. There is *one*. But he's not what you'd call entirely respectable.'

'What's his name?'

'Reckitt. Benton Reckitt.'

The mares were well rested and skittish as John and I made our way up the hill to Treforgan. With a blue, cloud-skimmed sky above us and the warmth of the winter sun on my back, I felt cheered. Despite John's misgivings, I knew I was right to insist on an autopsy. We had to be sure.

'So,' I asked, 'who is this Dr Reckitt?'

'He's medical attendant to the Cardigan workhouse.'

That knocked my optimism a little. The Poor Law Unions paid their medical attendants a pittance and, as a consequence, workhouse doctors tended to be men who could not inspire confidence in patients who were able to pay for their services.

'I don't want an incompetent,' I said.

'Reckitt's not incompetent. He's a drunk.'

I was taken aback. 'Observation or hearsay?'

'Hearsay,' John admitted. 'But I've heard a lot of people say it.'

I felt Sara peck as she missed her footing. The road was better used than it was maintained.

'If he's unreliable, he's no use to us. We need somebody who knows what he's looking for when he cuts a man open. We can't have some drunk destroying evidence by butchering the corpse.'

'I've never heard anybody complain about his work, just his manner. He used to be a surgeon, from what I've heard. And they need to be quick, not chatty.'

A surgeon might perform better autopsies than a physician. But if he was a drunk, would this Reckitt retain the dexterity to anatomise our corpse and tell us how he had died?

'Where does he live?' I asked.

'Cilgerran.'

In half a mile or so, therefore, we would reach the point in the road where I would have to make a decision. A consultation with Reckitt would take us inland, delaying any meeting with Inspector Bellis.

'I wonder,' I said, 'if we should visit Dr Reckitt before going on to Cardigan? The days are short and it would be advisable to give him as much daylight as possible to get the examination done. If he agrees to do it, that is.'

'Don't you think it'd be more *diplomatic*,' – John emphasised the word as if he thought it might be foreign to me – 'to go and see Billy Go-About first?'

There was no doubt about it. Seeing Bellis first would be the politically expedient thing to do. But John's own warnings on the subject of an autopsy had put me on my guard and I suspected that it might be wiser to present the inspector with a *fait accompli*. I knew myself to be a mediocre liar and I wanted to be able to sound, if not contrite, then honest at least.

The autopsy is happening as we speak, Inspector. I couldn't stop it now if I wanted to.

There was also Reckitt's alleged intemperance to consider. 'Diplomacy is one thing,' I said, 'but, sometimes, pragmatism is required. Quite apart from the short supply of daylight, the longer we leave it before our visit, the more likely a habitual drunk is to be inebriated. I would far rather speak to Dr Reckitt sober, if I can.'

John made no response, and my inability to guess what he might be thinking aggravated me. 'If you have an opinion,' I said, 'feel free to air it. If we're not going to be working together in future, you have nothing to lose.'

A sudden jerk of his head in my direction told me I had shocked him.

'No. If you want to go and see Benton Reckitt,' he said, stiffly, 'that's what we should do.' And, before I could reply, he kicked Seren into a trot ahead of me.

Urging Sara after her stablemate, I thought with some sourness that my father would be gratified to know how closely John's opinion resembled his own. Only the previous evening, he had taken me to task, over dinner, in the matter of my relations with the Cardigan police.

'Henry, I gather you have not yet paid your respects to Inspector Bellis.'

I had tried to swallow my irritation with a mouthful of claret. 'That's not entirely true. I have not yet *spoken* to Mr Bellis but it's hardly for want of trying.'

'How so?'

'I went to the police station in Cardigan after the viewing of the body, as it happens. Expressly in order to confer with him.'

'But not, I gather, *immediately* after?'

I ground my teeth and wished I had excused myself from the table as soon as the remnants of our meal had been cleared away. Though I found the presence of a footman during dinner inhibiting, it did at least mean that my father confined himself to uncontroversial topics of conversation until we were alone.

'Given that the man who found the body lives less than two miles away from Tresaith beach, it seemed a more rational use of my time to speak to him first.' Rationality: one of my father's most prized virtues. 'I fully intended to speak to Bellis later but, when I enquired at the police station, he had already left.'

I saw my father extend a hand towards his glass but, instead of picking it up, he seemed to do no more than move it an inch or two on the starched surface of the tablecloth.

'I'd understood,' he said, 'that Pomfrey was having the finder summoned to the inquest.'

'As had I. Nevertheless, he did not appear. In common with the publican of The Ship Inn and every single member of the public. Hence the adjournment.'

My father ignored my implied criticism of the way the supposed inquest had been organised and concentrated on the missing witness. 'You should have sent the constable to fetch him.'

I took a long breath in through my nose. 'Be that as it may, I made my way to Cardigan after seeing him with the express intention of visiting Inspector Bellis. But he had already left for a meeting with the magistrates. Which is, I assume, where he complained of me to you.'

'Whining does not become you, Henry. It would have been politic if, instead of haring off to recruit young Davies, you had gone to see the inspector in the first instance.'

'Why?'

'*Why?* Because you and he are both officers of the law at the behest of the magistracy, and you would be well advised to work with him instead of alienating him.'

The need to contain my temper made me officious. 'Actually, Father, I'm sure I don't need to remind you that coroners do not make their investigations at the magistrates' behest. The coroner is an officer of the crown.'

My father did not hurry to reply. Giving me time to repent of my tone, no doubt. 'You seem unusually conversant with the office,' he said, eventually, 'for so new an incumbent.'

'As it happens, William Payne – the founder of the Society of Coroners – has a brother-in-law in my chambers. *Erstwhile* chambers,' I corrected before he could. 'The Society was quite the talking point in legal circles.'

A repressive silence was his only response but I was determined to make my point.

'Payne was concerned at the number of deaths that magistrates were allowing to go uninvestigated. *Unexplained* deaths that coroners were finding it necessary to investigate at their own expense. He established the Society so that the financial burden should not fall too heavily on individuals.'

My father steepled his fingers. 'In other words, he set up a society of men who would take the law into their own hands, in defiance of magistrates who have the public good in mind?'

I put my own elbows on the table and leaned forward. 'In defiance of magistrates more concerned with keeping the rates down and their own authority inviolate than seeing justice done.'

I expected a scathing riposte, but instead, he fell silent for a few moments. When he spoke again, his tone was strained.

'Is that what you think I am about when I sit on the bench?'

I could not answer him. Until three months ago I had always thought my father an honest man, a scrupulous one, but his role in attempting to deny Margaret Jones an inquest had shown me a different facet to his character. The truth, I had come to understand, was that my father had worked hard for almost fifty years to be accepted by the Cardiganshire gentry, to prove himself a useful and deserving addition to their ranks, and he was wary of anything that might threaten his position.

Which now, it seemed, included me.

John

You wouldn't've known there was a castle in Cilgerran if you lived on the high street – you had to go down a small, cobbled street towards the river before you could see it properly. But there the ruins were, overshadowing a little row of houses on the left, and, in one of them, lived Benton Reckitt. Not exactly a gentleman's house but then I wasn't sure Reckitt was exactly a gentleman.

I'd been to the house once before with Mr Schofield, to see about drafting a will. I would've told Harry, warned him what to expect, but that comment of his about me having nothing to lose if we weren't going to work together in future had stung.

Was that how things were going to be? Now I'd told him he wasn't going to be able to click his fingers and bring me trotting to heel whenever he wanted me?

As usual, I was the one to knock at the door. It swung open far more quickly than I was expecting and there was the doctor – feet in slippers, shirtsleeves rolled up to his elbows and no neck tie. Had we caught him dressing? It was getting on for midday.

'Yes?' Benton Reckitt looked from me to Harry and back again. Didn't recognise me, but then he wouldn't, would he? I'd just been Mr Schofield's note taker, a person of no importance.

I introduced us.

'Yes?' Reckitt said again, as if he hadn't heard me. 'Yes? Yes? *Yes?*' As if he was shaking us with it.

'I'd be grateful for a few minutes of your time,' Harry said. 'If we can just step inside? Is there anybody who can take the horses–'

'Livery stable down the high street,' Reckitt said, and slammed the door in our faces.

A quarter of an hour later we were back. This time, I noticed the cobwebs in the corners of the door frame and under the lintel. Lazy servants. Or a careless employer. I knocked and, again, Reckitt yanked the door open himself. He still wasn't properly dressed.

'You're back then.'

'As you see,' Harry said. 'May we come in?'

'What for?'

Harry blinked. 'I beg your pardon?'

'What do you want to come in for? Can't you say whatever you want to say out here?'

'If it's all the same to you, I would prefer not to conduct confidential business in the street.'

Benton Reckitt opened his mouth as if he was about to say that it wasn't all the same to him but then he closed it again and peered at Harry.

'Are you blind?'

Harry's eyes jerked up, as if surprise had made him forget he couldn't see. 'Yes, I am.'

'What is it?'

Harry hesitated. 'What's what?'

'What type of blindness are you suffering from?'

'Oh. Loss of central vision. Detail and so on.'

'But your peripheral vision remains intact, unchanged?'

'Yes.'

Reckitt nodded as if he'd scored a point, and stood aside. 'Come in then, if that's what you prefer.'

'You want me to perform an autopsy examination?' Reckitt said once Harry'd given him the bare bones of the situation. 'Why?'

'Because I don't want to make any lazy assumptions.' Harry was dealing with the doctor's directness by giving as good as he got.

Reckitt stared at him without speaking. Neither of them seemed bothered by the silence. Reckitt was studying Harry as if he'd have to draw him later in some examination and Harry just sat at his ease in an old, wing-backed chair, the newspapers he'd had to take off the seat in a pile on the floor beside him.

It looked as if Dr Reckitt was one of those people who never finish one thing before starting something else. The table was a mess. Piles of books, pages of notes in messy drifts, newspapers and periodicals on top of one another, half a dozen small bottles and a few pill-boxes scattered about.

'Are you paid?' Reckitt asked suddenly.

Harry didn't blink. 'No. But as long as the magistrates feel I've conducted the inquest appropriately, my expenses will be refunded.'

'And if they don't?'

'Then I'll cover my own expenses. In either case, I'll hold an inquest once I have sufficient evidence. Which includes reliable information as to whether the dead man succumbed to natural causes or was killed by a blow he'd taken to the head.'

Reckitt's nose went up like a pointer's. 'Is that the police's opinion? The blow to the head?'

Harry half-smiled. 'I don't know, yet. I chose to come and see you first.'

The doctor nodded. Just once, as if he was settling something in his own mind. 'Blow to the head – somebody biffed him. So, somebody'll need to be arrested. That's how the Bobbies think.'

I watched Reckitt while his eyes were busy with Harry. Rumours or not, he didn't look like a drinker. No broken veins or cherry-ish complexion. His face was the colour, and not far off the texture, of risen dough. His eyes were wide and blue, not yellowish or bloodshot like the sots I knew. Difficult to say whether drink might've aged him because he could've been anything between thirty and fifty. He wasn't bald, there was no grey in his brown hair and his face was as smooth and as chubby as the rest of him.

Harry was gazing calmly at him. Well, in the direction of the chaise-longue where he was sitting, at any rate. 'I'm not interested in what the police think. I want to get to the truth of the matter.'

'Why ask me though? I'm not in with the magistrates. Far from it.'

It was easy to see how Reckitt'd got his reputation for being difficult – he had the accent of a gentleman and the manners of a simpleton.

'I believe you're a surgeon.' Harry said.

'By training, yes. I was an anatomy demonstrator at Guy's Hospital. I'm more than skilled enough to do what you ask.' He wasn't boasting, just saying.

'Then will you?'

'Am I required to under the terms of my contract with the Union?'

'No. Tresaith belongs to a different workhouse union anyway. But this is a different contract. A doctor is paid two guineas for a full autopsy.'

Reckitt looked astonished. 'Two guineas?' I wondered how much his retainer for the Cardigan Union was. Not much, if the thought of two guineas had that effect on him. 'Where would you want the examination carried out?'

'That question's been exercising me somewhat,' Harry confessed. 'I think, for the purposes of allowing people to see him so that we can get him identified, I'm going to have the body moved to Cardigan workhouse – it's not exactly in town but it's more accessible than Tresaith beach. Would you prefer to examine him before or after he's been moved?'

'If it's all the same to you,' Reckitt said, standing, 'I shall open him up on the beach. Such fluids as are in him can be flushed away by the tide, and I'll have him neat and tidy for the mortuary.'

Harry

The sun was luring hedgerow birds into voice so John and I cantered along the road from Cilgerran to Cardigan to the accompaniment of fleeting snatches of song from blackbirds and robins. I pictured them, beaks agape, plumage coming into its lustrous prime.

'Spring's on its way' I said.

John grunted. 'Going to be another couple of months before the leaves are anywhere near out. That's when I think of spring coming in.'

It was a trivial disagreement. Ordinarily it would barely have registered as such but it put me on edge. I had let John down and it was clear that I could no longer expect his unequivocal support.

I shivered and spring slipped away.

At the police station, we were greeted by the constable we had seen the previous day. This time, however, his tone was entirely different.

'Good day, Mr Probert-Lloyd, sir.'

'Good day, Constable…?'

When he did not reply, John snapped, 'Mr Probert-Lloyd's asking your name, man!'

'Oh! Morgan, sir. Constable Morgan.'

I nodded, embarrassed on Morgan's behalf, and asked him to let the inspector know that we were here. Bellis was probably already aware of our arrival. The constable simply opened a door at the back of the room and spoke through it. 'Mr Probert-Lloyd to see you, sir.'

'Show him in, please.'

Inspector Bellis did not look up from his work as John and I entered his office. 'Do excuse me while I finish this sentence, gentlemen, or what I wish to say will have slipped my mind entirely.'

His tone was civil but the implication was clear. *In this office, you are not as important as the most trivial task I am required to do.*

Finally, he put down his pen and rose to his feet. He was unusually tall. 'My apologies. Good afternoon, Mr Probert-Lloyd, Mr Davies. Or should I address you as Acting Coroner?'

'Good afternoon, Inspector. You may address me as you see fit.' In response to his English accent I made sure that my own would not have been out of place amongst the Queen's Council; any hint that Welsh was my native language would simply give him leave to despise me.

'Acting Coroner, then,' Bellis said. 'It helps us all to know where we stand, does it not?'

Because I was watching for it, I saw him extend a hand, indicating the chairs on our side of his desk. I sat, carefully; it was not always easy to gauge the nature or height of a seat.

'I must confess,' the inspector said, 'I had rather expected to see you before this.'

I forced a smile. 'I *did* actually make my way here after the viewing of the body, as I hope Constable Morgan informed you. But I was told that you were otherwise engaged. Be that as it may, let me not waste your time now, Inspector. I'm here to give you formal notice that I have adjourned the inquest on the body found at Tresaith beach to allow further investigations into the circumstances surrounding his death.'

Bellis's chair creaked slightly as he shifted his weight in the silence with which he greeted my words. 'I wouldn't have thought an adjournment was necessary, Acting Coroner,' he said, finally. 'Surely a body washed up on a beach has drowned unless there are witnesses to say otherwise?'

So, John had been right. Bellis wished to dismiss this death as no concern of his. Or mine. 'This man did not drown. I am quite sure of that.'

'I see.'

'Moreover, there were other injuries, to his face and head which—'

'Then, surely, there is your verdict? Murderous blows to the head dealt by persons unknown. After all, as I'm sure you'll be aware, it is not the coroner's job to decide who dealt the blow, merely that it represents the cause of death.'

Hoofs clopped past the office window and there was an audible exchange of greetings. I allowed the voices to fade before responding. 'I wish to be satisfied that the blow was exactly that and that his injuries were not caused by something less culpable – an accident or a fall, for instance.'

'You think he fell and hit his own head?'

I did my best to ignore Bellis's tone. 'Since it seems unlikely that he died where he was found, it's impossible to say how he came by the injury to his head. I don't want to go looking for homicides where nothing more malign than an accident has taken place.'

'But if he fell,' Bellis said, 'then hit his head and ended up in the water, surely he would have drowned? And yet you say, categorically, that he did not.'

'There are physical indications that drowning was not the cause of death. But the autopsy will provide us with more absolute proof. Also, I wish to be satisfied as to the cause of the grievous injuries to his face.' Was the inspector even aware of the flayed state of the dead man's face? He had not referred to it though it was hard to imagine such a detail being omitted from reports made to him.

Bellis leaned back in his chair and rested one ankle casually on the other knee as if it was important to him that I should understand how completely at ease he was in his command of the situation. 'I admire your thoroughness, Acting Coroner, but surely an autopsy is an unnecessary expense for an unknown man who – however he died – has merely been washed up in our jurisdiction?'

I did not miss the significance of the plural pronoun.

'Unknown, as you say. If we can find out how and where he died, we may be able to find out who he is and attempt to inform his family.'

'You think he is missed?'

'He was well-nourished and in the prime of his life. He was no vagrant. Somebody, somewhere is waiting for news of him.'

'And you think the ratepayers should bear the expense of an investigation to provide it?'

'Is investigation not what the ratepayers *expect* of the police, Inspector?'

'It may be what they expect of the police force in *London*, Acting Coroner, but here, our function is to keep the peace. And, as the death of this unknown person is in no danger whatever of disturbing that peace, it seems wholly unnecessary that it should be the subject of such excessive diligence.'

'I must confess, Inspector, I have never been taken to task for diligence before.'

Bellis uncrossed his legs and leaned on his desk. Some primitive, watchful part of me reacted as if he had picked up a weapon. My muscles tensed.

'I gather,' he said, 'that you intend to stand for election as coroner.'

I already regretted telling Charles Schofield that. It was beginning to hang about my neck like the albatross of Coleridge's mariner.

'If that *is* your intention, you would be well advised to reconvene your inquest as soon as possible. Nobody wants a coroner who is going to search officiously for crime.'

His presumption in advising me raised my hackles. 'Would they prefer one who overlooked murder for the sake of a quiet – or should I say *inexpensive* – life?'

'Murder, Acting Coroner? I thought you favoured a theory of accidental death? The fall. The bumped head.'

Touché.

'My aim – indeed my duty – is to keep an open mind, Inspector. At the moment, it is entirely possible that this death was the result of an accident. However, by the same token, an autopsy may find that the deceased was killed by a deliberate blow to the head.'

I stood, and John followed suit. 'I shall see that you are informed of the results of the autopsy as soon as I have them myself.'

Bellis rose slowly to his feet. 'Please do, Acting Coroner. I shall be watching the progress of your investigation with great interest. As, I am sure, will the county magistrates.'

John

On Tresaith beach, Dr Reckitt had drawn spectators. As we rode down the hill, I saw two men standing on the dry sand a little way off, watching him work.

'Are they jury members?' Harry asked, when I told him.

'No, I don't recognise either of them.'

Reckitt had set up the trestle table from the beer store. Just below the high tide mark, he was far enough away from the sea to give him time to finish his work, but not so far that it wouldn't scour the sand clean when he'd finished.

The top of the beach was all pebbles thrown up by winter storms, so we dismounted and I found the same stunted sapling that I'd used last time to fasten the mares' reins to.

I staggered a bit walking over the stones. Still wasn't used to walking in the riding boots Harry'd given me. They had a built-up heel, and I had to think about how to walk in them instead of just doing it. Made me feel awkward.

Harry called out a good afternoon to the two strangers and they turned and gaped at him. Couldn't work out what he was in his odd, stiff coat and outlandish hat, could they? The look on their faces when I introduced him was priceless.

The shorter of the two whipped his hat off and said he was Tommy Moelfre. 'Dr Reckitt asked me to come. With my cart. To take the body down to Cardigan, after.'

I looked in the direction of his pointing finger and there, sure enough, was a cart, horse still between the shafts, standing to one side of the little cottage.

Harry told him to put his hat on again and not get cold which was a relief to mankind in general. Tommy Moelfre's hair looked as if it'd been cut with sheep-shears by someone with a grudge against him, great patches of scabby scalp on view.

The other man just touched the frayed edge of his knitted cap. 'Gwyn Puw, Pantmawr. I live over there.' He nodded at the little thatched cottage which looked as if it had just slumped down against the hillside facing the sea. Pantmawr. It was a name that belonged to a farm, not a cottage on a beach. It must've come with him.

'You're the lime burner?' Harry asked in Welsh.

Gwyn Puw's eyes flicked nervously to me as if he wanted an explanation but I wasn't responsible for Harry's ideas about what language he should use.

'Yes,' he said when I didn't help him out, 'I'm the lime burner.'

'I'd like a word with you, later on,' Harry said. 'After I've spoken to Dr Reckitt.'

Tommy Moelfre looked from Harry to me and back again. 'Beg pardon,' he said, 'but it might save you time if you have your word with Gwyn first, Mr Probert-Lloyd. Just a few minutes ago, the doctor said it might be another half an hour before he'd finished.'

The set of Reckitt's back said Tommy was right – as far as the doctor was concerned, we might as well not be there. So we followed Gwyn Puw into his cottage.

The first thing I noticed, going in from the clean, salty air outside was the smell – Puw was burning cheap coal in his grate. If I got too close to it, breathed in any smoke that blew back into the room, I'd be sneezing inside a minute, having trouble catching my breath. I was fine with anthracite and with culm, which was just anthracite dust mixed with clay, but cheap coal always made my chest tight.

If Gwyn Puw bought his own coal, instead of taking some of the anthracite he used for firing the kiln as a perk of the job, he was a better man than most of us.

Mind you, there are different ways of being good. If cleanliness is next to godliness, Puw wasn't even a near neighbour. There was no need to ask whether he was married – no woman would've tolerated the place. The strip mat looked as if it hadn't been shaken out since the coronation and just looking at the frame bed in the corner made me itch.

Puw pulled his rocking chair forwards for Harry. The cushion on the seat might've been blue and white once – now it was all sorts of dirty shades of grey from decades of backsides in work trousers.

Harry couldn't see the filth-shine, so he just sat down and waited for me to do the same. I found a stool and Puw rested his arse on the edge of the table under the little sea-facing window.

'You've been out on one of the herring boats?' Harry asked.

Puw nodded. If he'd noticed Harry not looking him in the eye, he was obviously putting it down to him being a gentleman. And eccentric. 'Back yesterday, late. Out nearly a fortnight, I was. Wanted company, see, with Mrs Parry away doing business for the American scheme.'

Harry waited to see if Gwyn Puw would explain. He didn't. 'Can you tell us what this American scheme is, Mr Puw?'

Stripped of Gwyn Puw's wandering about the subject, it turned out to be quite simple. In legal terms, Mrs Parry had contracted with an American business partner in a scheme to convey emigrants to a new foundry town that he was a party to establishing in America. Mrs Parry's part of the bargain was to build and equip a ship which would take the emigrants to New York. The American's job was to find the right people for his settlement and introduce them to their new home. Emigrants bought bonds which guaranteed a roof over their head and a contract of employment for a period of three years in whatever trade they had. Five if they were being apprenticed. The beauty of the scheme was that the emigrants wouldn't be strangers in a foreign land. Cardiganshire families'd been emigrating to America for more than thirty years and – according to Puw, anyway – Jackson and Gallia counties, in the state of Ohio, were home to so many of them that the place was known as Little Cardiganshire.

'And this is Mrs Parry's scheme?' Harry asked.

'Well, hers and Jenkyn Hughes. That's the American gentleman.'

'It would be very useful if I could speak to Mrs Parry. D'you know when she's expected back?'

Puw didn't, so Harry changed the subject. 'Have you had a look at the corpse, Mr Puw?'

'Well, not what you'd call a *good* look. Only from a distance, type of thing. Dr Reckitt...' he tailed off. Didn't do to criticise one gentleman to another.

'Dr Reckitt hasn't been keen for you to get too close, is that it?'

'Well, you know...'

Just then the door opened and Tommy Moelfre came in.

'The doctor says he can tell you what you want to know now.'

Harry

John and I pulled the mares up at the bottom of Glanteifi's drive.

'Put Seren in the livery stables again,' I told him, 'and perhaps you should drop in at Mr Schofield's – offer to do an hour or two's work?' I knew he must be as tired and saddle-sore as I was but it seemed only prudent that he should stay in his employer's good graces if he was intent on asking him for articles without the payment of a fee. 'We'll meet for breakfast tomorrow morning.'

'Here or in town?'

I imagined my father's displeasure should he come down to discover John at his dining table.

'At the Salutation?' I suggested. 'Say nine o'clock?'

'Say ten past and I can do an hour for Mr Schofield tomorrow morning as well.'

I kept him in my edge-sight as he rode away and found myself recalling the impression he had made when he first clambered up on to Seren's back all those weeks ago: a tense, jerking figure, all hands and elbows and ankles, bouncing up and down at the trot like a badly-strapped load.

Not now. As he disappeared down the road, I could detect the even bob of his head as he rose to the trot like a gentleman.

Turning Sara's head up the dusk-dim drive, his parting words came back to me. *Say ten past and I can do an hour for Mr Schofield tomorrow morning as well.* I had taken the comment at face value and simply agreed; in retrospect, the words had an obvious edge of sarcasm. Did John think I was punishing him for refusing to be *ad hoc* coroner's officer in perpetuity? I hoped he would not think so meanly of me. Perhaps I should have offered to pay for his articles with Mr Schofield – that, surely, would make it clear that I respected his right to choose his own path.

But unselfish though I knew such an offer would be, I had begun to hope that John might come to work for me in another capacity. It was increasingly clear to me that, if I was to have any effective kind of role in the world, I would need a private secretary. I could not read, and my writing – even with the aid of a bespoke apparatus – was inconsistent at best and illegible at worst. Managing the bureaucracy that accrues to any occupation was going to necessitate employing somebody.

Now that I knew of John's ambitions, could I ask him to lower them in order to come and work for me? Riding towards the glowing windows of my father's house, the day's colours muted by the fading light, I feared that I could not.

After a solitary dinner, I went to sit in the library. The fire had been made up for me, and the room was tolerably warm, particularly in the winged chair by the hearth.

Leaning my head against the high back of the chair I allowed my mind to flit amongst fragments of the day, like a bee alighting briefly on each flower in a patch. And, just as a bee will sometimes go back again and again to a particularly fruitful bloom, my mind kept returning to Dr Benton Reckitt.

Of course, he was nothing but an indistinct figure in my mind's eye – a large, pale man. His voice, however, was anything but indistinct. Slightly higher than his height and bulk would have suggested, its tone was didactic at best, hectoring at worst, and, like most men who are lecturers by predisposition rather than training, the cadences of his speech quickly fell into a favoured pattern. It had begun to grate as he had recounted his findings to me on the beach.

'You asked me to look specifically at this man's heart and brain,' he had said, 'but I took it upon myself to examine his other organs as well. Though rarer, a sudden crisis in one of them can cause collapse, particularly if there is an associated, generalised infection.'

He motioned me towards the table and, understanding that my presence at the corpse's side was for his benefit rather than my own, I moved forward to form the necessary audience.

'Here,' he said, bending over the rib-splayed chest of the dead man, 'you can see that I've opened the atria and the ventricles.'

'Actually, Dr Reckitt,' John spoke from behind me, 'Mr Probert-Lloyd can't see that. If you remember, he's lost his central vision?'

I smiled inwardly. It was typical of John to have remembered the actual term I had used when describing my condition to Reckitt.

'Oh. Yes. Apologies. *You'd* better come and see, then, hadn't you?' John moved forward a pace.

'Come on, don't be shy! This is what we all look like inside, you know!'

From a different man, the words would have been hearty. From Reckitt they sounded slightly perplexed, as if he was at a loss to understand John's reluctance to look at a butchered corpse.

'As I say, observe the atria and ventricles. No indication of any over- or under-growth which would suggest pathology and no signs of clots having formed and travelled to the heart. This is the right coronary artery – as you can see, I've dissected it out.'

If the doctor was going to deliver an anatomy lecture, we would be there all day. 'Dr Reckitt, I'm very aware that time is getting on. I'd like us all to be able to get home before dark and, as I'd appreciate your making the corpse decent for viewing, I expect you'll need some time to…' I floundered. 'To do whatever's necessary. May we have a summary of your findings, please?'

'Very well. If that's what you'd prefer.' He turned back to John. 'His liver, as you can see, here, is undiseased. He seems to have been a man of temperate habits because there is no evidence of the damage one sometimes sees in those who drink to excess.

'Then his kidneys, here. They too, are unimpaired. Indeed, I'd go so far as to say they are excellent specimens.'

If this was Reckitt's idea of summarising, God help us. The sea would be lapping at our boots soon.

'Doctor, I beg your pardon but have you managed to ascertain what killed him?'

Reckitt's head turned towards me. 'Oh yes. That's quite clear. If you look here, I'll show you.'

He moved around to the man's head which, I now realised, was missing half of its skull. I swallowed and shuffled forward, displacing John who moved away smartly.

'When I removed the brain, it was clear that a significant degree of bleeding had occurred following the head wound. This would have caused a substantial rise in intracranial pressure and a consequent compression of brain tissue leading to the failure of vital functions and subsequent death.'

'What kind of vital functions?' I asked.

'Heartbeat and respiration, crucially.'

'I see. And how quickly would that have happened? How long after the blow to the head would he have died – can you say?'

'A small number of minutes. The exact time would depend on the rate of bleeding. The condition of the vessel that was ruptured by the blow would suggest that it happened relatively swiftly, but I can't be absolutely sure.'

'What does that tell us about the force of the blow?' I asked.

'You're asking how hard he was hit?'

I nodded.

'There is no scale of blow force. All I can say is that it was a heavy blow.'

'And it *was* a blow, was it? He couldn't simply have fallen and hit his head?'

'Not unless he fell from a considerable height. And there are no other injuries to suggest that.'

'A premeditated attack then? With intent to kill?'

'That's beyond my scope.'

I nodded. 'Thank you.'

'There's one more thing I should make you aware of. On removing the brain, I saw immediately that its shape was markedly asymmetrical. Here, on this side – can you see?' He was clearly speaking to John, who moved towards the exposed brain. 'The frontal cortex bulges out.'

'Is that significant?' John asked.

'It would have been of great significance to the man while he was alive. The bulge was caused by a large tumour.'

I could tell, from his tone, that Reckitt expected us to be impressed by this.

'Would that have contributed to the pressure inside his cranium?' I asked. 'Might it have hastened his death?'

'An interesting question.' Reckitt sounded intrigued. 'It's possible that it made a very minor contribution to the speed of his demise. But that is not why the tumour is significant.'

A gust of wind flung squall-heralding drops of rain in my face and almost flipped my hat from my head. Clouds were darkening the western horizon, bringing night ever closer. 'Doctor, if I could ask you to make the body presentable so that it can be transported to Cardigan, I'd be very grateful.'

I knew he was keen to talk about the lump he had found but I wanted to be home before dark or deluge overtook us. 'If you're not too busy tomorrow,' I said, 'perhaps you wouldn't mind meeting me in Cardigan to give me your full report. We can discuss the significance of the tumour then.'

Now, opening my eyes to the library fire, I wondered what importance a growth in the dead man's brain could possibly have and whether I should, after all, have allowed Reckitt to tell me on the beach.

John

Who did Harry Probert-Lloyd think he was, telling me to drop in and do some work for Mr Schofield while he sloped off home to a nice warm fire? I should've told him where he could go. And, if I'd believed all the stuff he'd said to me when we were working together before Christmas – all that stuff about how we were equals, how he didn't want to have power over me – I would have, I'd have told him to go to hell.

But how could I believe him? Before, he'd as good as offered me a job as his clerk when he became a solicitor. Now, that was all forgotten and he was full of being coroner. In other words, he was just like every other under-occupied squire's son, full of whims and fancies. Because he could do what he liked, couldn't he? He didn't know how it felt to have to be as good as your word every day of your life, to work and work at convincing people you were somebody they could depend on, so they'd carry on employing you and you could carry on having a roof over your head.

So, now I knew. What I had to go by was what Harry Probert-Lloyd *did*, not what he *said*.

Been a fool to get my hopes up, hadn't I? Whatever he said, he was Harry Probert-Lloyd, heir to the Glanteifi estate and I was John Davies, solicitor's clerk, about a fortnight away, at any given moment, from the workhouse.

The way Mr Schofield spoke to me when I went in to the office didn't help, either.

'Oh, Mr Davies, good afternoon to you! Are we to infer that the inestimable Mr Probert-Lloyd has concluded his investigations?'

Hypocritical old fart. He was always nice as pie to Harry's face.

'No. Just finished for the day.' Because a gentleman could decide that his working day finished at four o'clock if he felt like it.

I took my coat off and hung it on the coat stand by the door. Harry'd given that coat to me. *I know they look ugly compared to cut-away coats,* he'd said, *but they're a lot warmer and more practical. London's full of them.* Mr Schofield'd raised his eyebrows at me the first morning I'd come in wearing it. All I'd had before was my ordinary jacket. Like every other working man in the world, if it was cold outside, I'd just got cold. Matter of fact, I'd been better off as a *gwas bach* – at least on a farm nobody cared if you wrapped yourself in sacks to keep warm because they were doing the same. But solicitors' clerks couldn't do that. Solicitors' clerks had a position to maintain. And it often left us cold.

When I turned around, Schofield was staring at me. 'And how, may a humble solicitor ask, are the coroner's investigations proceeding?'

The Cardigan inspector of police has been antagonised, a doctor everybody thinks is a half-mad drunk has been employed and Harry Probert-Lloyd's still got absolutely no idea who the corpse is.

The words ran into my head like floodwater over a threshold. And I might've said them, too, if it hadn't been for that 'humble solicitor'. As if I'd chosen Harry over him because I despised him. I'd've liked to know what choice he thought I'd had.

'I think the investigation's going well, thank you, Mr Schofield.'

The line between being polite and sucking up is so fine, sometimes, that you couldn't rest a hair on it. And, at that moment, it felt as if I lived my whole life balancing as I walked along that damned line. But I was going to have to put that aside.

I took a breath to ask him for what I wanted. To say *I don't want*

to work with Mr Probert-Lloyd any more. I want to be your articled clerk.
To have a future here as a solicitor. But then, in my head, I heard what
he'd say. *And who would pay for your articles, Mr Davies? What rich*
relative have you been hiding?

I had nobody to sponsor me. No rich kin. And, whatever I'd told
Harry, I knew Mr Schofield would as soon give me the contents of
his strong box as take me on without payment. So, I shut my mouth
and let the air out through my nose.

Mr Schofield looked at me with that 'Yes?' look of his. He knew
I'd been going to say something.

'I expect there's plenty for me to be getting on with?' I said.

To my right I could see Peter, mouth open, ignoring the work in
front of him and watching Old Schofield giving me the beady eye. I
knew Peter like I knew the surface of my desk. Better than I wanted
to. And he was waiting for something. What? Had the old man been
complaining about me – about how willingly I'd gone off with Harry?

My palms itched. Was I going to get the sack?

'Just come into the inner office for a moment, would you?'

Our desks in the front office were tall ones, designed for standing
at or using a high stool but Mr Schofield's desk in his private office
was a low one. About an acre of inlaid leather top, it had, with
expensive-looking things positioned carefully here and there for
clients to see and be impressed by. Brass blotter. Fancy brass inkwell
stand. One of those new steel-nibbed pens.

A delicately-made writing slope stood at one end of the desk, ready
for him to use. But no papers, obviously. That might suggest he didn't
employ enough clerks.

I thought he'd leave me standing but he waved me to the client's
chair. That made me even more nervous.

Mr Schofield picked up the blotter and frowned at it. From what I could see, the paper was barely marked but he started sliding it out to put fresh in.

I waited.

'Now. Tell me how the investigation is *really* progressing, John.'

I swallowed when I heard my Christian name. *Mr Davies* meant that everything was ticking along nicely, no nasty surprises in store. *John* … you never knew what was coming after that.

'I hope you feel that I'm entitled to know,' he said when I didn't reply straight away. 'Because, as you'll no doubt be acutely aware, anything you do in the company of Mr Probert-Lloyd reflects on this office. On *me*. Therefore, whilst I understand that you have a duty of confidentiality, I hope you understand that you have an equal duty to me. Your employer.'

I was in trouble. He was going to make me say things I shouldn't be telling him. He wouldn't say my job depended on it but he didn't need to. He was my employer and he was asking.

He took his specs off and pulled his polishing-handkerchief out of the desk's top drawer. 'So. How far have matters progressed?'

I looked at him, quickly, then away. He wasn't keen on being eyeballed, Mr Schofield. *Eyes on your work!* But I could see he wasn't going to be fobbed off.

'Well, Mr Probert-Lloyd had assumed that, as he was meeting the jury on the beach, a proper inquest had been arranged. At The Ship Inn, at Tresaith. But the inn was locked up and nobody turned up except the jury. And the dead man hasn't been identified, yet, so Mr Probert-Lloyd adjourned proceedings pending further investigations.'

Pending. A good lawyerly word. Mr Schofield would like *pending*.

'I assume that the constabulary is involved? Mr Probert-Lloyd isn't going to give us a repeat performance of his antics before Christmas, I hope?'

Mr Schofield had taken the magistrates' line when Harry started looking into Margaret Jones's death: that concerning himself with the fate of a dairymaid was unbecoming in a gentleman. And not in the public interest.

'We went to see the inspector today,' I said. It wasn't a real answer to his question but it sounded like one.

Old Schofield looked at me. 'Mr Probert-Lloyd *is* going to work with the constabulary, isn't he? Not *against* them?'

Like he worked against the magistrates last year.

What could I say? I wasn't supposed to be telling him any of this. 'John?'

'Mr Probert-Lloyd wants to leave no stone unturned.' Surely he'd see that as a good thing in a coroner?

'The whole county noticed his tendency to lift stones that should have been left *in situ*. As I recall, his actions brought the Rebeccas back into our midst.'

I wanted to tell him that, just because some men who'd ridden with Rebecca seven years ago had threatened Harry, it didn't mean they'd been *in our midst*, but I knew better than to dare. That would be *contradicting*. One of the things Mr Schofield didn't tolerate.

'Mr Probert-Lloyd would be well advised to allow the police force to do what the ratepayers pay it to do and not interfere,' he said.

But that was the trouble, wasn't it? Harry wasn't well advised. He wasn't good at being advised at all.

'One of the investigations he's set in train,' I said, carefully, 'is nothing to do with the police. It's something only the coroner can decide on.'

'And that is?'

'He's asked for an autopsy examination to be carried out.'

Mr Schofield gave a dry little sniff. 'Well, that, at least, seems prudent. It's as well to leave the jury with no doubts. Otherwise anomalous verdicts are apt to be delivered.'

Like the verdict the jury'd delivered in the Margaret Jones inquest. The verdict that'd set Harry – and me – off on his investigations. No wonder Harry didn't want to get this one wrong, he didn't want somebody coming along and unpicking the decision *his* inquest came to.

'Who has he asked to perform the autopsy?'

I knew I couldn't hesitate. Mr Schofield would think I disapproved and he'd want to know why. And, anyway, I didn't want to say anything against Reckitt. He might come across as odd, but I could see he knew exactly what he was talking about when it came to dead bodies.

'Dr Benton Reckitt, from Cilgerran.'

'Reckitt?'

'Yes.'

'Is he a fit person?'

A *fit person*. Not going to accuse Reckitt of being a drunk, was he? Not Mr Schofield. Too clever, too cautious.

'It's not my business to say, Mr Schofield. All I can say is that he seemed very competent.'

'Am I to understand that the post-mortem examination has already taken place?'

'Yes. Mr Probert-Lloyd was keen to have it done as quickly as possible. Before the body's moved to Cardigan workhouse.'

'Why is he having it moved there?'

'Mr Probert-Lloyd thinks more people'll come and see the body, in Cardigan. See if they know the dead man.'

And they would come, no doubt about it. As soon as word went around, people'd come in droves just to see his face. To see how horrific it really was.

Mr Schofield didn't so much purse his lips as purse his whole face. I knew what that look meant. *He's at it again, taking matters into his own wayward hands.*

'Does Mr Probert-Lloyd not feel that employing a man like Benton Reckitt might bring the coronership into disrepute? I've heard it said that he is not always sober.'

He stared at me, trying to force me to agree. Perhaps I should have. Just to keep him sweet. But the truth was, Reckitt hadn't been drunk. 'I can only speak from the evidence of my own eyes, Mr Schofield. He seemed very competent.' I sat there and let Old Schofield stare at me, eyes down so at least I'd avoid being accused of insolence.

'If Mr Probert-Lloyd is in earnest about standing for election to the post of coroner,' Mr Schofield was speaking in his listen-to-me-carefully-because-this-is-for-your-own-good tone, 'I cannot help but feel that he is going about it in an entirely misguided way.'

I flicked my eyes up. He was still staring at me. Suddenly I hated him. I hated him and I hated Harry bloody Probert-Lloyd. Neither of them was going to give me what I wanted. They both droned on about having my best interests at heart, but neither of them was prepared to give me what I deserved.

'People notice things you see, John. They will notice his choice of medical advisor and will draw their own conclusions about those in whom he puts his confidence. They will notice his tendency to keep the constabulary at arm's length and they will conclude that he is a law unto himself.'

'But, as I understand it, Mr Schofield, the coroner *is* a law unto himself.'

Why in God's name had I said that? Why had I suddenly jumped down on Harry's side of the fence and stood there with both feet planted, mouth open, singing like a stupid bird? Just for the moment's thrill of crossing Old Schofield?

'Explain.' The word could've frozen water.

'Well, obviously,' I stammered, 'nobody's *literally* a law unto himself. What I mean is, coroners don't have to be guided by the police. They're entitled to make their own investigations. In fact, they're *required* to do that. Aren't they?'

'Required to. That's what Mr Probert-Lloyd thinks, is it?'

I took a deep breath. Now that I found myself on this side of the fence, it was probably as well not to look weak by trying to climb back up. 'Yes, Mr Schofield. I believe it is.'

The way he looked at me, then, I felt like one of those dead butterflies stretched out and pinned under glass. 'I must counsel you to be very careful, John Davies. Mr Henry Probert-Lloyd is far from assured of being elected to the post of coroner. Very far. His recent conduct won him few friends amongst those who will vote in that election.' He paused, rocking his newly-filled blotter between us, to let his words sink into my unwise mind. 'You may find that it is not entirely beneficial to your future to fall in behind his standard. There is such a thing as taint by association.'

Why hadn't I kept my mouth shut? I'd never've said any of that before I met Harry. He'd given me what my father would have called *ideas above my station.*

And, now, those ideas had landed me in the shit. Right up to my armpits.

Harry

The embers had burned to ash in the grate and I was contemplating going up early to bed to see if sleep would come. Nights were not so bad in summer when I could be out and about in the long evenings but now, in the January dark, I was denied distraction and confined with my own thoughts.

Since my enforced return to Cardiganshire, it had occurred to me, more than once, that I should move into town, so that there would be readily-available society of an evening. But, without an independent income, such a move was impossible.

My friend Gus, whom I had last seen in December, when John and I had begged a night's accommodation at his family's London home, had suggested – only partly in jest – that I should look for a wife.

Who'd marry a blind man, Gus?

An ugly woman in search of a rich husband, obviously!

Sadly, there was more than a grain of truth in his quip. My position as heir to Glanteifi made me attractive to the ambitious parents of girls without fortune. Some of them – the buck-toothed or hirsute – might be grateful for a blind man, even if he did aspire to spending his time investigating unexplained deaths. But I did not want to be married for my position. Nor, if I was honest, did I wish to be pitied for my wife.

I stood up, determined to shake off such thoughts but the surrounding darkness pressed in on me from every corner. The candles reflected in the mirror over the mantelpiece seemed as feeble in the gloom as I felt. Feeble and ineffectual.

I wished that it were possible to have gas lamps installed at Glanteifi. The lights John and I had seen at Gus's London home had given night almost the appearance of day, and the thought of spending my evenings surrounded by such brilliance, even if I could not read by it, had been astonishing. But, in order to install gas lighting, it would be necessary to live in a town with a gasworks. Marooned here at Glanteifi by my financial circumstances, I seemed destined to spend my evenings sunk in gloom.

Perhaps I *should* become a solicitor, after all.

I was just beginning to give serious consideration to the thought when a knock at the library door made me jump.

'Beg pardon, Mr Harry, but Mrs Griffiths says did you know a letter arrived for you today and would you like her to come and read it?'

I left my dreary mood in the library and went to find Isabel Griffiths, Glanteifi's housekeeper, in her little sitting room at the back of the house.

'Thank you, Lizzie-Ann,' I said, as the maid who had lit my way retired quietly back to the kitchen where the rest of the servants would be sitting in the warm. All apart from Moyes, our butler. He left his staff to pass their evenings in Welsh while he sat in the pantry reading what my father liked to call 'improving literature'.

All the way from the library, I schooled myself to expect a letter from Gus, or – just possibly – some kind of communication relating to the adjourned inquest. I did not want to allow myself to think that it might, already, be from Lydia.

Lydia Howell and I had become acquainted when I travelled to Ipswich during the course of my investigations into Margaret Jones's death. Prior to that, we had met only briefly, in circumstances both of us refrained from referring to in our letters. Since the beginning of January, we had corresponded more and more often, and I had made increasingly frequent visits to Mrs Griffiths's sitting room.

'Describe your writing apparatus for me,' Lydia had asked in one of her early letters. *'I imagine, from the even spacing of the lines, that a ruler is involved?'*

'It's a frame,' I had written back, *'whose interior dimensions are the exact size of a standard letter-sheet. I insert the paper, wind up a central ruler which operates on a ratchet system so that each turn of the knobs on either end moves the ruler down one line, and begin writing. The frame shows me where to start and stop and the ruler keeps my writing even.'*

In truth, I was afraid that it gave my hand no more than the semblance of regularity. Though I worked hard on my letter-formation, sometimes the words I wrote were crushed, one against another, whilst at other times they were so spaced out that they appeared to want nothing to do with each other. I knew that to be the case because that was exactly what Lydia had written.

'I am not asking you to remedy it,' she had written. *'I'm merely telling you because you asked and because I find it rather endearing.'*

Endearing.

Very quickly our correspondence had begun to include such sentimental terms, though we were careful to limit ourselves somewhat. Miss Howell might be able to read my words in private but I did not enjoy the same luxury.

'Another letter from the young lady in Ipswich,' Mrs Griffiths said. I could hear her trying to keep a straight face and failing. 'You must be a fascinating correspondent, Harry.'

On my return from my first term at school, our housekeeper had tried to call me Mr Henry, and to speak English to me as she did to my father. But my thirteen-year-old self, appalled to think that I was no longer the boy who had been in and out of the servants' part of the house all my life, eating leftovers, getting under feet and being told off, had refused to respond. Eventually, Mrs Griffiths had relented, reverting to Welsh and calling me Harry, and I had insisted that she do so ever since. But Isabel Griffiths knew her place and she thought she knew mine, too, which was one more reason to dread the day I became squire of Glanteifi; I did not want to be 'Mr Probert-Lloyd' to her.

I lowered myself into the visitor's chair beside the room's little fireplace. Without asking, Mrs Griffiths poured tea and handed me a cup and saucer. I believe she felt that it would be easier for me to have my hands occupied while she read. In Isabel Griffiths's world, men did not passively receive, not unless they were in their dotage. Even if all I did was drink a cup of tea, something of the natural order was maintained.

I watched her unfolding the letter. I had already calculated that it could not have come in response to the news of my appointment as coroner *pro tem*; the mail took two or sometimes three days to reach Lydia and the same time for a return letter.

'Writing's even smaller than usual,' Mrs Griffiths said, hooking the spectacles she wore for reading around her ears in a way I remembered from childhood. 'Right then. *Dear Harry...*'

I smiled. In my last letter, I had asked Miss Howell if I might address her by her Christian name and invited her to do the same. But Mrs Griffiths, knowing nothing of what my letters contained, was clearly surprised at this sudden familiarity. 'Addressing you like a brother, now, I see.'

I found myself unexpectedly taken aback. Was that how Lydia Howell saw me – as a replacement for the brother she had lost?

'Dear Harry,' she began again, *'I have had a most rewarding few days since, as you suggested, I began trying to engage Reverend Mudge and his wife in conversation. Evidently you were right. Inviting me to sit with them in the evenings was more than a kindness to a servant, the Reverend Mudge seems very glad of a third person to speak to.'*

Isabel Griffiths paused and took another sip of her tea. I was being invited to explain the advice I had given.

'As you know from previous letters,' I said, 'Miss Howell felt that, because her employers barely spoke to each other in the evenings, she wasn't free speak to them either. But I suspected that the Reverend and Mrs Mudge simply had no common interests and I suggested that it might be a relief to them if somebody else spoke.'

It was advice born of endless evenings spent with my father, the silence between us anything but companionable.

'Yesterday,' Mrs Griffiths began reading again, *'the Reverend spoke of his youth at the Newington Green Chapel. I knew he was older than his wife by some years but I had not thought him well past fifty, as he must be, speaking as he did of the influence on his young mind of Richard Price.*

'Not being a Unitarian, you will not know the significance of the Newington Green Chapel but, without Richard Price, I doubt there

would be a Unitarian Church worth the name in our country today.
Newington Green has been influential in the intellectual life of the
capital, playing host, at one time or another, to every notable republican
of the last century.'

I felt a sudden shiver of misgiving. Our correspondence had allowed
Lydia to give free rein to her thoughts, something that had, previously,
been lacking in her employers' house. But, now that she had
discovered this rich seam of intellectualism in Mudge's parlour, would
she still wish to communicate with me, a reluctant squire-in-waiting
in Cardiganshire?

'In his conversation, I find the Reverend cast down by our society's increasing
tendency to believe that theology and scientific thought are now reaching
the point where no further investigation is necessary, where all questions are
answered and men of sense must submit. I fear that Mrs Mudge encourages
this view and I detect in her husband a tendency to wish that he had been
born half a century earlier than he was, into the ferment of thought and
debate and action that took place in the last century.'

A wish I might easily have shared, myself. The politics of our own
century seemed tame in comparison with its predecessor, the small
outbreak of insurrection with which Lydia and I had been involved a
mere puff of wind when ranged against the hurricanes of
Republicanism that had torn through France and America.

Mrs Griffiths stopped and fortified herself with several long sips of
tea. The quality of her silence left me with the distinct impression
that it was not the quantity of words she had read that had left her in
need of sustenance but their content.

She made no comment, however, and continued reading.

'But, whilst I rejoice that the world of ideas is opened to me once more, I fear that our conversations are not to Mrs Mudge's taste and I wondered whether Mrs Griffiths might be able to advise me on this?'

The housekeeper broke off her reading abruptly. She had something to say but would not volunteer it without being invited to do so.

'*Do* you have any advice for Miss Howell on this matter, Mrs Griffiths?'

She replaced her teacup, with a very deliberate 'chink', on the saucer. 'How long has Miss Howell been governess to the reverend's children?'

'More than seven years. But it's only recently that she's begun to be invited to sit with them in the evenings. Previously, she was needed to be on hand in the nursery.'

'How long is "recently"?'

'During the last few months, I believe.'

'And for most of that time, she sat quietly and waited to be spoken to?'

I nodded. 'Yes.'

'And she was well advised to do so,' Isabel Griffiths's voice was sharper than usual, as if she had nerved herself to deliver an unwelcome truth. 'I know a governess doesn't like to think of herself as a servant but that's what she is, in the end. She's a paid member of the household, same as I am. A servant.'

My mind rebelled against the idea. Maids and footmen were servants. They came and went from households at their whim, as did cooks. But butlers and housekeepers were different. I could not see

Mrs Griffiths as a servant. Without her, the household would fail completely. There would *be* no household.

'Because of the way you are,' Isabel Griffiths continued, as if my radical sympathies were some kind of congenital deformity, 'you think everybody of good sense thinks the same as you. And that they like to share their thoughts with all and sundry. But did you stop to wonder how happy Mrs Mudge would be to have a lively-minded young woman bandying views with her husband?'

She paused. Unsure what to say, I kept quiet.

'Is Miss Howell pretty?'

I had asked John the same question. His answer had been dismissive. *Not pretty but not a fright to look at. Wouldn't turn heads, either way.*

'No,' I said. 'I have it on good authority that she is nothing much to look at.'

But her voice would turn heads; a low contralto that I would know again anywhere.

'She should be thankful for that,' Mrs Griffiths said. 'If she was pretty, she'd probably be out of her place already.'

'But Mrs Mudge couldn't mistrust her husband, surely? He's a man of the cloth.'

'He might not *give in*. But no woman likes to see her husband tempted in front of her own eyes, Harry. If you want to be a friend to Miss Howell, you'll pass on my warning to her. If she values her position, she should go back to waiting to be spoken to. And she should take pains to be dull when she speaks.'

John

Harry'd told Reckitt that he'd be at the Black Lion Hotel the following afternoon. So, after our breakfast, off we went to Cardigan.

With the pace he set, it was difficult to talk but, to be honest, that was a relief. I was feeling awkward after what I'd said in parting the previous day and, if I wasn't careful, I'd be telling tales about Old Schofield and his views just to make things right between us again. But it wouldn't do Harry any good to know what people were thinking. Especially about his chances of getting elected as coroner.

I watched him as we cantered along. It was one of those changeable days, threatening rain one minute, the sun lighting everything up like a smile the next, but Harry didn't seem to notice. Something on his mind? I found out, soon enough.

'I've been giving some thought to how we should organise ourselves,' he said. 'I think we should let it be known that anybody with any information about the dead man can leave a message for us at the Black Lion. That might encourage people who'd be wary of going to the police station to come forward.'

He was right about that. Six or seven years on from finding that we suddenly had a police force, a lot of people still didn't trust the Cardiganshire Constabulary. Older people didn't like the fact that outsiders were there to keep order. Interfering, they called it. The old parish constables had been their own boys, known from birth. But the new officers might be from as far away as Aberystwyth or Llanelli. And their uniforms didn't help. Frock coats and tall hats. People weren't sure whether to think of them as soldiers or gentlemen.

'Are you planning to use the Black Lion for the whole of the investigation?' I asked. We'd be back and forth to Cardigan like the mail coach if he was.

'Yes. I'm going to see if they can accommodate us for a few days. As long as you're agreeable?'

No chance of being sent off to Old Schofield for an hour here and there if we were in Cardigan.

I was definitely agreeable.

When Harry put his proposal to Mrs Weston, owner of the Black Lion, I could almost see her working up the profit and loss of accommodating the coroner.

On the credit side: a gentleman and his assistant paying bed and board for a number of days. Not to mention the possible rise in reputation from being associated with the law.

On the debit side: seeing as the gentleman in question was the coroner, dead bodies'd be involved. There might well be talk of murder. And who knew what kind of people'd be coming in and out? Possible *loss* of reputation.

But Mrs Weston didn't want Harry to go to any of the other hotels or inns in town. And she knew that ninety-nine out of every hundred people who found themselves in her coachyard didn't care who else was there. Coach passengers wanted to stretch their legs, visit the privy and have something to eat, before getting back into the rattle-box and going on with their journey. They wouldn't give a second glance at comings and goings through the tradesmen's entrance.

So, terms agreed, Harry told Mrs Weston that we'd be back at one o'clock for Reckitt and anybody else who wanted to speak to us. Then we set off down Bridge Street towards the river.

The docks were bewildering. Crowded, busy, full of cranes swinging things on and off ships, men barely able to see where they were pushing their overladen barrows, carts trying to force their way through and constantly in danger of knocking somebody over. You wanted all your wits about you and I made sure I stuck close to Harry. Being half blind'd get him killed if one of us wasn't careful.

I'd never been down here before so it was news to me that each wharf handled different kinds of goods. The point where all the Pembrokeshire limestone for burning came in wasn't really a wharf at all – it was a breakwater built out from one of the wharves. Mercantile Breakwater they called it, owned by a company that brought in culm, lime, timber and other building supplies.

We made our way along, looking for somebody to ask about lime boats to Tresaith. Near the breakwater a huddle of pipe-smoking men were standing around one of those huge cast-iron lumps they use to moor ships to. Not a friendly pack of men. Looked as if nails'd bounce off them.

Harry told them what we wanted but all they did was shake their heads, eyes on the sea or the ground as if we weren't there.

'Any of you ever work on the limestone boats?' I asked. Harry couldn't be guaranteed to have seen the head-shaking.

They turned their eyes on me but not one of them spoke. The wind rattled the rigging of a ship moored a couple of dozen yards away and men called out to each other as they went about their work.

Harry tried again. 'We just need to know when the boats go in and out, that's all.' He was doing his best to look them in the eye but he wasn't making much of a job of it.

Without looking at his mates, one of the sailors suddenly took his pipe out of his mouth. 'Burning-stone that comes in here goes to Penyrodyn.' He jerked his head upriver.

I did my best to stare back at him but, try as I might to look him up and down as if his clothes compared badly with my own, I felt like a child with his arse out of his britches. The way he stood there, feet planted, head up, he made canvas trousers and a salt-stained smock look like the only clothes a man should wear.

Mind, that dead-eyed stare of his couldn't unnerve Harry. 'Can you tell us where we should be looking for Tresaith boats, then?' he asked, pleasantly.

Harry was nobody's fool. He'd heard the way the sailor'd pronounced Penyrodyn, and switched languages. That way, the man could answer in Welsh if he wanted to keep something from his English-speaking mates.

The sailor shook tobacco-piss out of his pipe and stuck the stem behind his ear. With the bowl nestling at his cheekbone, it looked like a growth.

'Kilns further up get their stone straight from Carew or Williamston,' he said, sticking to English. 'You could go there. Or you could go and wait for another load to come in.'

That's what he'd've done. You could tell. He'd've just gone and sat on Tresaith beach with his pipe and waited. Like a rock.

Harry thanked him, we turned and walked back along the breakwater, and I let my breath out for what felt like the first time in minutes. They hadn't raised so much as a finger against us but I'd still come away with the feeling that they'd've thrown us in the sea and let us drown as soon as look at us.

Didn't take much imagination to see one of them bashing a man's head in. All they'd've needed was a reason. Not a particularly good one, either.

'What now?' I asked.

'Back up the coast. Unless Mrs Parry's home, I think we need to speak to Teff Banc yr Eithin again. He'll know when the next boat load is due, and we can be there to meet it.'

When we went back to the Black Lion for the horses, a passing servant with a travelling box under each arm told us that there were two men waiting for us.

'Who are they?' Harry asked but the man just shrugged. Didn't know and didn't care.

We made our way through the dingy corridors of the inn, the smell of roasting meat making my mouth water. Breakfast had been a long time ago.

I opened the door into the bare little back room to let Harry in and, looking past him, I saw Gwyn Puw the lime burner and Obadaiah Vaughan getting to their feet. Puw dragged his ratty knitted cap off his head, leaving the hair under it sweaty and flattened.

'Good morning, Mr Puw, Mr Vaughan,' I said, for Harry's benefit.

They chorused their greetings back to us and Puw flicked a glance at me as Harry sat in the chair next to the fire. Like all fires in daylight, it looked weak and cold and it wasn't doing much to get rid of the smell of damp.

'Gentlemen,' Harry said. 'Before we start, can you just tell me, is Mrs Parry back at The Ship, yet?'

Puw shook his head. 'Haven't seen her.' He shifted his weight uncomfortably in his chair, all nerves. His eyes went from me to Harry and back to Dai'r Bardd. The so-called poet sat there, watching us, quite at ease. Still, at least he'd bothered to change out of his work clothes into Sunday best.

'You've got some information for us, I expect, gentlemen?' I said.

Dai'r Bardd stared at Puw. 'Gwyn has. Haven't you, Gwyn?'

The lime burner dug around in a pocket. When his hand came out, he thrust it at us and opened his fist.

'Coins,' I said and put my hand out for them. Unfamiliar-looking. I held one up to the light of the window and saw words around the edge. 'They're from America,' I told Harry.

Puw's eyes started flicking back and forth again. Me, Harry, me, Dai'r Bardd.

'Where did you find them?' I asked.

Puw looked at his friend. Dai'r Bardd nodded. Looked like permission more than encouragement.

'I found them in the draw-hole of my big kiln.'

Getting the details out of Puw was like getting seed out of a haystack but it turned out to be a long story easily cut short. After Harry and I had left the beach the day before, Puw had helped Tommy Moelfre get the sewn-up corpse on to the cart ready for Cardigan workhouse. Then he'd made his way back to his cottage past the bigger of his two limekilns.

'And I saw the waste had been disturbed,' he said.

'The waste?' Harry asked.

Gwyn Puw gave puppy-dog eyes to Dai'r Bardd, who sighed and started to tell us how the two wide arches in each kiln were there to suck air in, to keep the kiln burning, and to allow the burnt stone to be raked out. After a kiln had been emptied, he said, there was always a pile of ash and limestone dust left behind – the waste.

'The waste heap, see, there's always a certain shape on him,' Puw said when Harry asked him to explain what he'd seen. 'Grows up under the riddle, he does, with each load of stone we rake out. The wind and the rain do blow him a bit, after a time, but you get to know the look of that, with the wind always coming in off the water, see.'

'And the waste heap wasn't as you'd expect, is that what you're telling us?' Harry asked.

'That's it. A mess, he was. All over the place.'

We waited. Dai'r Bardd spoke up again. 'Gwyn showed me. There were footprints and evidence of shoveling in the waste.'

'Aye – somebody'd had my shovel out from where I left her. I gen'rally leave her laid down at the back of the draw-hole. Don't come to no harm there, she don't. But somebody'd used her.'

'What for?'

This was his big moment, but Puw was no storyteller. He looked pleadingly at his friend.

'Gwyn thinks – and I think he must be right – that they put the dead man in there and covered him up with the waste.'

'They?' I asked.

'Whoever killed him.'

As if he hadn't heard us, Harry suddenly asked, 'Mr Puw, how big is the draw-hole? It's a long time since I came up to fetch limestone on the carts as a boy.'

A picture came into my mind. Harry going up from Glanteifi to fetch limestone with the home-farm servants. I'd have laid good money that they'd never had to do what my father'd been forced to do – wait at the tollgate at midnight so that he could go down to the coast and back in the same day and only pay one toll on his cart and load of lime. Glanteifi's men would've had plenty of money for tolls. They'd've taken it leisurely. I could see it in my mind's eye – Harry and the servants sitting around the warmth of the kiln long into the night, the windows of The Ship bright in the dark, sounds of laughter and gossip as farmers and labourers caught up with friends and relatives they hadn't seen in months.

'How big?' Puw repeated. 'I don't know in feet and inches, Mr Probert-Lloyd. I can stand up in there with plenty of room to swing my shovel, I know that much.'

'About six and a half feet high and as many deep, I'd estimate,' Vaughan said.

Easily enough space for a body.

'And what makes you think the dead man was in there?' Harry wanted to know.

'The coins.' Puw nodded towards the cents in my hand. 'And his face and hands.'

All right, I'll admit it, I knew next to nothing about lime burning. But, according to Puw, we had to understand that if we wanted to know what had happened to our corpse's face.

'You explain it, Dai,' the lime burner said. 'You'll say it better than me.'

I watched Dai'r Bardd settle himself and find a place to begin. The man loved being the centre of attention.

'If you put raw limestone on the fields,' he said, 'nothing would happen except you'd have very stony fields. I don't know who found out that burning limestone changes it, or how they came to do such a thing, but when you put limestone in the kiln and burn it, what comes out looks the same but it's not. It's changed into quicklime. Now then, you can't just put quicklime on the fields, either, or it burns the grass. It needs to be slaked – watered.'

He looked at me, wanting to know that I'd followed so far. I nodded.

'You have to be careful with quicklime – it's dangerous stuff. As soon as it comes into contact with water, it blows – heats up quickly, fizzes, cracks and the lumps fall apart. If you put a big piece in a bucket with some water, it blows itself apart until, in the end, all you've got is lime slurry – and it'll be hot enough to burn your hand if you put it in. I've known carts catch on fire from quicklime blowing when a load's not covered and it gets rained on.'

'So, if a man was lying under a layer of quicklime waste and the wind blew the rain in and slaked the lime, the skin under it would burn because of the heat?'

Dai'r Bardd nodded, a sly smile on his face and one eyebrow up. *Not dull are you, boy?* 'Yes, he said. 'And not just because of the heat. Quicklime *itself* burns if your skin's wet from sweat or rain.'

'Funny thing,' Puw was happier to put his tuppenceworth in now the technical matters had been dealt with. 'You don't always feel it when it's just on your skin like that. I got blisters all down my arm, once, before somebody told me it was burning.'

'Would rain blowing in really be enough to do it?' Harry asked.

Puw nodded. '*Duw*, yes. Plenty, rain would be. Sweat'll do it, like Dai said.'

Harry frowned, chewed his lip. 'He'd have needed to be lying with his head to the entrance of the draw-hole then?'

We all sat there for a moment, thinking about it. Obviously, if Harry was right, the dead man had been dragged into the draw-hole feet first.

'When we saw him, he was naked,' Harry said, 'but only his face and hands were burned.'

'Must've still been dressed when he was covered with the waste,' Vaughan said.

'Wouldn't the quicklime burn through the clothes?'

'No.' Puw shook his head. 'Not like it does with skin. Never known it to go through my clothes.'

'But you said it could set fire to a cart,' I pointed out.

'Only a load still in lumps. Not enough heat in dust.'

'So where are his clothes?' Harry asked. 'What happened to them?'

'Haven't seen them, I haven't,' Puw was defensive. As if Harry'd accused him of robbing the corpse.

'And, if he'd been buried under the waste in your kiln,' Harry went on, thinking out loud, 'how did he come to be lying on that boatload of limestone when Teff Harris found him? Did somebody come and undress him and drag him down the beach?'

I felt Dai'r Bardd's eyes on me and looked over at him. He inclined his head towards the coins on the table.

'I don't know who killed him,' he said. 'But if those fell out of his pocket into the waste, then I think I know who he was.'

American coins.

'Jenkyn Hughes,' I said. 'The American that Mrs Parry's in business with.'

Harry

Benton Reckitt still not having presented himself by the time we had finished our midday meal, I decided to go and see Inspector Bellis in order to make him aware of what Puw had told us. I relished the thought of presenting him with evidence that, far from washing up on Tresaith beach, the body had been taken into the water from Puw's limekiln.

We walked into the relative warmth of the police station to be greeted by an eager Constable Morgan.

'Good afternoon, Mr Probert-Lloyd. You've heard then?'

I disliked the implied complicity of his tone. 'Heard what, Constable?'

A door opened. 'That will do, Morgan.' Inspector Bellis had heard us come in. Had he been expecting us? 'Please, gentlemen, come in to my office.'

I strode towards him, trying to dispel the feeling of being at a disadvantage, while Bellis held the door open.

Billy Go-About, I said to myself. *Don't think of him as Inspector Bellis, cut him down to size as Billy Go-About.*

'I trust your autopsy was illuminating, Acting Coroner?'

Your autopsy. *The one you so whimsically insisted on.*

I pulled out a chair and waited for Bellis to take his own seat behind his desk. When he did not, I remained standing. 'Very much so, thank you. As was the information I received prior to coming here. I now believe I have a far better understanding of how this man came by his injuries and how he ended up in the sea.'

'Oh, I think we shall know nothing less than the truth of the matter very soon, as it happens.'

His tone warned me that something had changed since our last meeting and I managed to stretch a smile over gritted teeth. 'How so?'

'We've made an arrest.'

Made an arrest? 'I see. May I ask who?'

'The discoverer of the corpse, Acting Coroner. Theophilus Harris. I'm expecting my officers back with him at any moment.'

Bellis's self-satisfaction was extremely aggravating. 'May I ask on what evidence you have arrested Harris?'

He leaned over his desk and picked something up. 'This was waiting for me when I arrived at the station this morning.'

He was proffering what I assumed to be a sheet of folded paper. John intercepted it. 'If you don't mind, Inspector?'

'Of course. I'm sorry, I'd forgotten.'

I was quite certain he had done no such thing. If it had been a *faux pas* he would have been highly embarrassed. No, Billy Go-About was making a point. *A blind man can't do this job.*

'*Ask Teff Harris what he did with the dead man's clothes,*' John read, '*after he took him out of the sea and stripped him.*'

I waited for him to go on but there seemed to be no more. 'Is that all?'

'It's quite enough!' Bellis barked. 'Tampering with a body, falsifying evidence, impeding identification, lying about the course of events… What reason could he have for doing any of those things unless he was guilty?'

'*If* he did them. We have only the word of an anonymous letter writer, Inspector. Which I consider to be very far from proper evidence.' I turned back to John. 'What kind of paper is it written on?'

There was a brief, considering silence. 'Half a sheet of ordinary letter-paper. Cut in half, not torn. Scissors, I'd say, rather than a knife along a fold, the edge is very clean.'

'You say it was waiting for you when you arrived this morning, Inspector. I assume, therefore, that it did not arrive in the mail?'

Bellis hesitated slightly. 'It was wedged beneath the outer door. Whoever wrote it thought they could slip it under, but our station is better constructed than that.'

I turned back to John. 'What's the handwriting like?'

'Legible and on a line,' he said after a moment or two. 'No misspellings. But I wouldn't've said it's the hand of somebody who uses a pen for his living. Looks as if time's been taken over it.'

The image of a slowly moving hand appeared in my mind, a tongue protruding slightly between lips set in concentration. But whose lips?

'I think you'll find that, when he realises he was observed, Mr Harris will soon tell us the truth.'

I looked up sharply and the inspector disappeared into the whirlpool of my central vision. Well aware of the methods used to arrive at 'the truth' in London police stations, I did not wish to be a party to such tactics, here.

'Inspector, if Theophilus Harris wishes to confess of his own free will that's well and good. But I would like your word as a gentleman that he will be offered no violence to induce him to do so.'

If I had asked for Bellis's word that he would stop consorting with prostitutes in dark alleys, the silence which greeted my request could not have been more outraged.

'Mr Probert-Lloyd, it is only your inexperience as coroner that prevents me from taking the gravest offence at that request.'

But feigned indignation was too common a barrister's trick for me to be discomfited. 'I may be inexperienced as coroner, Inspector, but please do not assume that I have no experience of what takes place in police stations.'

I could feel the look he fastened onto my face. Was he rethinking his opinion of me or allowing his impatience to swell into dislike? It was one thing to stand my ground with this man, I realised, but I could not afford to make an enemy of him.

'Very well,' I said, as if he had conceded the point. 'We will take it as a matter of record that Mr Harris will go unmolested. Perhaps,' I said, offering him a sop, 'I should have been more suspicious when he failed to turn up to the viewing of the body.'

To my relief, he took the bait. 'Indeed. His absence suggests that he was afraid he would give something away.'

Evidently, the inspector had not met Teff Harris. The former soldier had struck me as a man who would give away nothing he did not intend to part with.

Just then, a door slammed open in the outer room, followed by a burst of shouting. I heard Harris's unmistakable tones.

'Where is the inspector?' I heard him shout in Welsh, then again, louder, in his oddly accented English.

I turned to leave the office, but was preceded to the door by Bellis. 'Allow me to deal with this, if you'd be so good.'

He closed the door behind him. I opened it again and followed him out. Harris was speaking, controlled but furious. 'I demand to know on what evidence I have been arrested. There is a law in this country. You can't just take a man because you don't like the look of him.'

'Be quiet, Harris!'

If Bellis had hoped that the voice of command would instantly bring a subaltern to attention, he was disappointed.

'I will not! I am entitled to know on what evidence I have been arrested.' Harris faced the inspector, his figure, in my peripheral vision, so upright with fury that it seemed he might actually leave the ground. Then he turned in my direction.

'Are you responsible for this? You wanted to know why I didn't come to the police with news of the corpse. *This* is why! All I did was find him.'

Bellis spoke before I could catch my breath. 'We have ample evidence to arrest you, Harris. You were seen.'

'That's a lie! All I did was find him and put him in the shed.'

'We have reason to believe that is not true.'

'What reason?'

'A letter stating that you stripped the corpse before leaving it in the shed. Why would you do such a thing if you had nothing to hide?'

I waited for Harris to accuse Bellis of naivety if he could think of no other reason for a corpse to be stripped. In London, the assumption John had made – that the dead man's clothes had been removed in order to sell them – would have been universal. But then, unidentified corpses were hardly as commonplace in Cardiganshire as they were in the capital.

But Teff Harris surprised me by going to the nub of the matter. 'Where did this letter come from? Who wrote it?'

'That needn't concern you.'

'It *does* concern me! Any number of people have grudges against me! I can give you a list of half a dozen people who might have written a letter like that.'

'Quiet!' I jumped, startled at Bellis's unexpected vehemence. 'Take him into the lock-up, Williams.'

'Mr Probert-Lloyd.' Harris's voice took me by surprise.

'A moment,' I said, holding up my hand to Constable Williams who was attempting to drag Harris away.

'They've left my son on his own,' Harris said. 'He's only eight years old.'

'Didn't you tell him to go to a neighbour's house?'

'None of our neighbours would take him in.'

I can give you a list of half a dozen people who might've written a letter like that. Were all his neighbours on the list?

'Can you take him to the workhouse in Newcastle Emlyn until they let me out? Or until my wife gets back. If you leave a note for her in the house – she can read – she can go and fetch him.'

Had his wife really gone to care for a sister? A man who can kill one person might not stop at killing another to protect himself. It might be a good idea to do as he asked in order to have an opportunity to speak to his son.

I nodded. 'Very well.'

Williams, presumably following some gesture from his superior, jerked Harris towards the door.

'What about the cow?' John surprised me by asking.

'Tell Gwyn Puw I'll pay him to go up and see to her,' Harris called as he was bundled out. 'He'll do it for money.'

'What now?' John asked as we made our way back to the Black Lion.

I did not reply immediately; the concentration required in order to see where I was going and to avoid walking into things or people made coherent speech difficult.

'We continue with our investigation,' I said, when my way cleared slightly. 'Mr Bellis may choose to see an anonymous letter as sufficient reason to look no further but I don't.'

'You don't think Harris is guilty?'

'I don't think I should stop investigating just because it pleases Billy Bellis to arrest somebody on flimsy evidence.'

John dropped behind me to let a woman with a bundle go by, and I waited for him to resume his place at my side.

'If we assume, for now,' I said, 'that the dead man is this American, Jenkyn Hughes, we need to find out what he was doing at Tresaith and whether he was killed there. Also, it would be useful to find out whether he knew Teff Harris.' I hesitated. 'I'd like you to go and take Harris's son to Newcastle Emlyn while I wait for Benton Reckitt.'

John digested my request. 'You want me to go and fetch this child, and take him to the workhouse?'

'I'd do it myself, but I need to be here to talk to Reckitt. I want to ask him about this lime-burn theory of Puw's. But, realistically, the child will be more likely to speak to you than to me.'

'What, because you're a gentleman and I'm not?'

'Because I'm blind.' I had little experience of children but I knew that I would have found a blind man fearful as a child. 'If his father's attitude is anything to go by,' I said, 'the boy might be reluctant to speak. But if you put him on the saddle in front of you and take him down to the workhouse, it might just give him enough time to trust you and to tell you something.'

As I walked through the front door of the Black Lion, a servant approached and told me that a gentleman was waiting in the back room.

'Dr Reckitt, is it?'

'No, sir. A Mr Pomfrey.'

Pomfrey, the magistrate? What did he want?

He stood, courteously, as I entered the room. 'My dear Probert-Lloyd, how enterprising of you to station yourself here!'

I inclined my head in acknowledgement and asked what brought him to my door. I could not help suspecting that he had come at my father's request, whipper-in to a wayward hound.

'Oh, well, we rather threw you into the rushing flow, as it were, at Bowen's instigation, so I thought I'd just come and make sure that you were managing to swim without too much difficulty.' Pomfrey reached for the bottle on the table at his side. 'May I offer you a glass of Madeira?'

Though I did not particularly want the wine, I accepted and sat down. 'It's kind of you to be concerned,' I said, 'but I believe I am managing tolerably well.'

He moved in my direction and I put my hand out to meet the glass.

'Not lost your assistant already, I trust?'

'I've sent him to deal with a potential source of information.'

'Oh.' Pomfrey was trying to sound mildly taken aback but he was no actor. 'I understood that an arrest had been made. Perhaps it was foolish of me to believe that the investigation was, therefore, at an end.'

I sipped the Madeira which, as it happened, was more than tolerable. 'The situation,' I said, 'is that a man has been taken into custody on the basis of an allegation contained in an anonymous note. However, I'm far from ready to re-convene the inquest.'

'I see. And what is Inspector Bellis's view?'

'The inspector's opinion on the matter is, if I may say so, immaterial. He does not arrest suspects at my behest, nor do I hold my inquest at his.'

Pomfrey raised his glass to his lips. 'I see,' he murmured, once more.

'As I said, it's kind of you to be concerned as to my progress in this matter but I really mustn't trespass on your time any further. I'm actually here to meet with my medical witness and hear the results of the autopsy which took place yesterday.'

'Ah. Yes. The autopsy.' Pomfrey sounded uncomfortable, and I wondered whether I had, inadvertently, introduced the real reason for his visit. 'Was it *actually* carried out on the beach?'

'Yes. It seemed the most sensible arrangement. The shed in which the corpse had been housed was too dark and carrying out the procedure at the workhouse would have meant delaying it another day.'

'You didn't find it somewhat … eccentric? Irregular?'

'I found it practical. Expedient.'

'Yes. I see.' Pomfrey gave a species of nervous laugh. 'Actually, Probert-Lloyd, a question arose as to your choice of physician.' He paused but I was not inclined to help him out. 'Why, may I ask, did you choose Reckitt for the job?'

I sipped at the Madeira, taking my time. 'As a former anatomy demonstrator at Guy's Hospital, he seemed more than adequately qualified for the job.' I could feel my blood beginning to rise to the challenge Pomfrey represented.

'It's just that Prendergast is generally our man,' the magistrate said. 'Sound fellow, well regarded. Doesn't usually feel the need to cut a body open.'

I sipped on.

'His word carries weight at an inquest, you see.'

'I don't doubt it. However, I was given to understand that

Prendergast was generally very busy and that he was most unlikely to be able to perform the autopsy with the urgency I felt the matter required.'

'Urgency?'

'The deceased had been dead for an unspecified number of days already. I'm sure you're aware that dead bodies are apt to decompose and present more of a challenge to those who examine them in search of evidence. Reckitt was able to attend to the matter immediately.'

'Of course he was. He has no patients to speak of because he's–' Pomfrey pulled himself up.

'A drunk?' I suggested.

'The word I had in mind was *boor*.' I could feel Pomfrey's eyes on me. 'Of course, there are rumours as to his sobriety, but, speaking for myself, I've never seen the fellow in drink – or, at any rate, no more than anybody else. However…' He stopped. 'Probert-Lloyd, may I speak as one gentleman to another?'

Ho, ho! 'Please, Pomfrey, speak freely.'

'Thank you.' He put down his glass, as if he needed both hands in order to say what he wished. 'It's just that Reckitt is a damned queer fish. Odd manner. Behaves as if common courtesy is something only other fellows worry about. Orders other men's servants about as if they were his own. Once–' memories prejudicial to the doctor seemed to be pressing in on Pomfrey, now – 'sitting down to dinner at Llwyngwair, I saw him staring at one of the footmen. Observed some variety of growth on the man's face and nothing would satisfy him but that the unfortunate fellow should sit down and have the disfigurement explained to him. And to us, seated at the table. Poor man didn't know what to do with himself. Mortified. As, needless to say, was his master.'

'Does that make Reckitt a bad doctor?'

'It makes him a laughing stock!'

'But does it suggest that he would perform a less than adequate autopsy? As far as I can see, a man who's so seized by the need to explain medical facts that he makes a footman sit down at dinner is exactly the kind of person who should be asked.'

I heard Pomfrey sigh at my refusal to take his point. 'Inquest juries are asked to put a great deal of faith in post-mortem examinations, Probert-Lloyd. If they're sniggering behind their hands at the doctor's antics – I mean to say, not calculated to help them take his opinions seriously, is it? Not to mention the odd figure he'd cut as a witness.'

I knew I should be attempting to mollify Pomfrey; the magistracy had been sufficiently antagonised by my investigations into Margaret Jones's death to disapprove of me without further cause. But this stultifying need to preserve decorum set my teeth on edge.

'You mean we can't have the jury sniggering at the medical witness if they're already laughing at a coroner who's not only blind but has a well-known tendency to rush about the countryside investigating the death of dairymaids?'

Pomfrey's answering silence was worthy of my father. Finally, he rose to his feet. 'I'm sorry you can't see your way to being reasonable about this, Probert-Lloyd. I think we'd all hoped that responsibility would steady you.'

I was relieved of the need to produce an appropriate response by a peremptory rap on the door. Before I could answer, it was swung open, and Benton Reckitt's voice said, 'I'm told you're in conference with somebody, Probert-Lloyd, but I just wished to let you know that I have arrived. With my full report, as requested.'

John

Clear of town, I cantered Seren over Cardigan common and headed north. The sky was bright enough but it was getting colder and there were only a couple of hours of daylight left.

The reins in my hands were stiff and the saddle still wasn't properly warm under me. Damp, probably. A livery stable wasn't going to look after tack like the stables at Glanteifi. Still, at least I had my coat.

Seren slowed to a trot up the hill towards Tremain and I didn't push her. Let her keep her strength for when there were two of us in the saddle on the way to Newcastle Emlyn. I shivered. It'd be even colder by then.

Night would bring down a frost – I could smell it in the air – so it'd be freezing on the way back to the Black Lion in the morning. And, when I got there, there was a good chance I'd find Harry waving a note from Billy Go-About to say that Teff Harris had confessed. I knew he'd hate that. He didn't want Bellis to be right.

I didn't feel the same at all. I'd been quite happy to see Teff Harris dragged in to the police station. The man just made my hackles go up.

But that letter…

Ask Teff Harris what he did with the dead man's clothes after he took him out of the sea and stripped him.

Had Teff Harris stripped the body, or was somebody just trying to get him into trouble? From what he'd said about nobody being willing to take his son in, it sounded as if Harris had few enough friends amongst his neighbours. But if somebody wanted to cause trouble, why hadn't they said they'd seen him killing the man instead of accusing Harris of stripping the body? If it was a lie, it was an odd one to tell.

At Banc yr Eithin, I stuck my head around the cottage door but the boy wasn't there. I called for him. No answer. Damn. I'd have to tie Seren up and go looking for him.

I was threading the mare's reins through the loop-handle of the byre door when I heard his voice.

'Go away!'

I pulled the reins out and pushed the thumb-latch down. The door swung in, and the first thing I saw was the boy putting his free arm up over his eyes to stop the daylight stinging them. The other arm was around the neck of a white cow.

'You sent the police to take my father away.'

'No, I didn't. I was here yesterday to *talk* to your father but I didn't send the police.'

He stared at me. Defiant. Disbelieving.

'It was your father who asked me to come. He was worried about you all by yourself.'

'I'm all right. I'm looking after Gwenno.' He tightened his hold on the cow. She wasn't impressed with the arm and shook her head. Mind, she was gentle with him, she'd've shaken her head harder to get flies off.

'What's your name?' I asked.

No reply.

'My name's John. John Davies.'

'Pleased to meet you.' The words came straight out as if he'd had nothing to do with them. Dinned-in politeness.

'So? What *is* your name?'

'Clarkson.'

Clarkson? Why hadn't Harris painted a target on his son's chest and given the other boys a sack of stones to throw while he was at it? They'd already have picked up their own fathers' dislike of Teff, and a name like Clarkson would give them the perfect excuse.

'Pleased to meet you, Clarkson.' But there'd been a beat of silent surprise and he'd heard it. His teeth were clamped together.

'Your father's worried about you,' I said. 'He doesn't know how long he's going to be in' – *don't say gaol* – 'in Cardigan and he wants to know you're safe.'

'I'm not going!'

'I haven't told you where I'm taking you yet!'

'I'm not going anywhere. I can't leave Gwenno. She's in calf. She's our future.'

She's our future? That was straight from his father's mouth or I was an Irishman.

'It's all right. Gwyn Puw's going to come and feed her, make sure she's safe.'

'No. He can't! They'll take her!'

'Who'll take her?'

'The ones who tried to take her last time he was away.'

I got it all out of him, then.

Teff Harris took work where he could find it and, while he'd been away from Banc yr Eithin, a few months earlier, some men had tried to take Gwenno from the pasture at the side of the house. Mrs Harris had been fetching milk or gone to market with butter or some such, and men with cloths covering their faces had tried to drive the cow off.

'I jumped on her back – she always lets me ride her – and made her run away,' the boy said. 'The men tried to catch us but Gwenno can run fast.'

'That was brave,' I said.

'I couldn't let them steal her.'

I wondered how much of that was fondness for the cow and how much was the fear of a thrashing off his father.

'Why did they want to steal her?'

He shrugged.

'Did you know them?'

He shook his head.

'But if that happened last year, your father will've sorted it out by now.'

The boy just shook his head again. 'I'm not going.'

Light dawned, then. 'You didn't tell your father about the men, did you?'

I looked into his face. He was afraid. Of his father? Or of me making him leave the cow?

'Can you get out of that window?' I asked. The byre window was small but then, so was he.

'I think so.'

'Have you got any rope or thick twine about the place?'

He nodded and I sent him off to find it while I looked around. The job would've been a lot easier if this'd been a proper longhouse with a central passage and doors to the byre on one side, the house on the other. Then we could've just secured the passage door. But the byre'd been built on at the side of the one-roomed house and had its own separate entrance. We'd have to see to both doors.

I showed Clarkson how to tie the thumb-latch down, then left the byre and let him get on with it. A minute or so later he called out. 'Try it.'

I tried to push the latch up from the outside but it was solid.

'Good boy! Come out through the window, now.'

When he was out, and on his feet again, I nodded at the thick twine he'd found. 'You'll have to do the same to the house door. I'm going to see Gwyn Puw now – you know Mr Puw, the lime burner?'

He nodded.

'Does your father get on with him?' I wanted to make sure the boy was going to be safe.

He nodded again, sure.

'Right. I'll ask him to come up every day, if he can, until your father's back.' Then a thought struck me. 'How long's your mam been gone?'

His eyes moved about as he calculated. 'About a week, I think.'

'Do you know when she'll be back?'

'She said it'd all be over, one way or another, inside a fortnight.'

What was wrong with the sister, I wondered. Sounded like a fever if living or dying was going to be decided that quickly.

The boy'd decided he could trust me now, so I chanced a question for Harry.

'D'you ever go down to Tresaith to help your father with the lime loads?'

'When Mam's here, I do.'

'Have you ever seen an American man down there? A stranger who speaks differently?'

'D'you mean Mrs Parry's friend, Mr Hughes? The one with the white trousers and chequered waistcoat?'

'Yes' I said. 'That'll be him. Seen him recently?'

'No. Not since Mam went away.'

Harry

Benton Reckitt did not ask what Pomfrey had come to see me about; in fact, he made no comment on the magistrate's being there at all.

'I've put down my observations in writing, naturally,' he said, laying what I took to be his report on the table. 'But, as you're without your amanuensis, I shall summarise it for you.'

After his performance on the beach I very much doubted that he was capable of a summary, so I cut in before he could begin his organ-by-organ litany of the corpse's redundantly healthy body.

'I believe you said that the tumour in his brain was of interest.'

The alacrity with which he answered indicated that Reckitt was in no way put out by my redirection. 'Yes. Of great interest.'

I took my life in my hands. 'Can you elaborate?'

'The tumour was impinging on the tissue around it, disrupting function.'

'What do you mean? He couldn't think properly?'

I heard a deep sigh as Reckitt faced the task of bridging the gulf of ignorance that separated us.

'May I tell you a story, Mr Probert-Lloyd?'

'If you feel it's relevant.'

'Thank you. I believe it will serve an explanatory function.' He drew in a lungful of air through his nose. 'While I was working at Guy's, I became very interested in phrenology. I assume you know what that is?'

I had not expected to be quizzed. 'Umm ... bumps on the head?' I stumbled before righting myself and making a more creditable attempt. 'How the shape of the head tells us something about the character of the person?'

'A serviceable-enough definition for a layman,' Reckitt allowed. 'Phrenology posited *organs* of the brain to which were assigned particular *faculties*. It was believed to be an anatomically precise science. One which would change our understanding of human nature.'

I arranged my features to show interest, fearing that any verbal response would only prolong the story he was already failing to tell.

'The system has been discredited – at least in part– by anatomists but I, in common with many of my profession, was immensely interested in it for a time. So much so that I went to America in order to meet with like-minded professional men.

'While I was there, I met a medical student by the name of Harlow who was also a student of both phrenology and brain anatomy. After I had returned to London, we continued our association via correspondence. Two years or so ago, Harlow had the immense good fortune to be consulted on the case of a man who had suffered an extraordinary injury to his brain. A steel rod – a tamping iron I believe it was called – used in the insertion of explosives into rock, had been shot, by accidental ignition of the explosive, through the man's skull, causing extensive damage to the left front part of his brain. The rod had been fired at great velocity up through his cheekbone, behind his eye and out through the top of his skull.'

'Not a pleasant way to die, but a swift one, I image.'

'Oh, no, Mr Probert-Lloyd, Phineas Gage did not die. He was fortunate in having Dr Harlow as his physician. When Gage developed a cerebral infection, Harlow was able to drain it and to treat him appropriately. In a month or two, he was completely well again. But – and this is the point of my narrative, Mr Probert-Lloyd – Phineas Gage was a changed man.'

'I imagine he was. Such a close brush with death must change a person.'

'No! It was not through gratitude to be alive that Gage was changed. Nor did he repent of previous sins and resolve to live a better life. It was entirely the other way about!'

'How so?'

The doctor had not needed prompting; he was already answering before the question had fully left my mouth. 'Prior to having an iron bar tear through his brain, Phineas Gage had been known as a capable and intelligent man. He was efficient, energetic and shrewd and was regarded with great respect by both his employers and the men who worked under him.'

Reckitt paused, but I was beginning to realise that these narrative gaps were not designed to invite a contribution from his listener; they simply allowed him to order his next set of thoughts.

'Following his physical recovery, however, those who knew the man described him as "no longer Gage". He became impulsive, unreliable, surly. He took risks he would never previously have countenanced and appeared unperturbed by their consequences.'

'And you put this down to the accident he had suffered?'

'More specifically, I attribute it to the *damage inflicted on his brain*, Mr Probert-Lloyd. Though much of phrenological theory is now disregarded, I have no doubt whatsoever that its principal tenet – that particular functions are localised within specific areas of brain tissue – is correct. And, from the damage done to Phineas Gage, Harlow deduced – and I concur – that the moral character of a man is located in the front part of the brain, here.'

He raised a hand to tap his forehead.

'Dr Harlow is now devoted to looking for further evidence of our theory, particularly in those who have died after becoming, like Gage, *not themselves*. But his research is being hampered by the reluctance of relatives to allow autopsies to be carried out.'

Though I did not say so for fear of provoking him, my sympathies lay with the relatives rather than the inquisitive doctor. 'So,' I said, 'to bring us back to your autopsy, you believe – if I understand you correctly – that the tumour growing in the brain of the dead man would have affected his character?'

'I believe it is highly probable.'

'And how quickly might this have happened?'

'If I had a hundred tumours and their attendant case histories I would know the answer to your question, Mr Probert-Lloyd! But I haven't!' Reckitt was impassioned rather than impatient and a sudden suspicion bloomed in my mind.

'Do you perform autopsies on the paupers in the workhouse?'

He did not hesitate. 'If necessary.'

'And by necessary, you mean...?'

'I mean, as I imagine you would, in order to understand their death.'

'Whether or not there is an inquest?'

'As you will know, an inquest is always *supposed* to be conducted when a death occurs in a public institution,' Reckitt said. 'But if the death follows a period of obvious disease or decline, often the magistrates see no need to involve the coroner.'

I knew he was right. The investigation of workhouse deaths was, effectively, an extension of the obligatory inquiries into deaths in prison or police custody where, as I had indicated to Bellis, the use of force might well be suspected. But, whilst deaths in poor law union premises were hardly a rare occurrence, they were usually due to old age and infirmity rather than anything more reprehensible.

'So, in the absence of calls for an inquest, if you suspect that the deceased had been suffering from a growth on the brain, you ask for the body to be released to you in order to perform a dissection?'

'If I've been attending the patient, I believe I have a moral right to do so.' Reckitt paused and made a gesture which I was not quick enough to interpret. He might have been running a hand over his face.

'When the requirement was introduced for deaths to be certified before they could be officially registered,' he said, 'I believe most medical men saw it as a way of earning another fee for attendance. As a matter of fact, some doctors of my acquaintance are notorious for decamping from a bedside where they suspect that death is imminent so that they will be obliged to come out again to certify the death.' He paused for a second as if he was passing judgement upon such behaviour. 'But some of us see certification in another light entirely. It represents – or *could* represent – an unparalleled opportunity to look at illness and death not just on an individual basis but on the basis of whole populations. If certification demanded universal post-mortem examination, we could look at what illnesses claim most lives, compare the age at which individuals succumb to those illnesses, see the districts or counties where diseases of particular kinds are most prevalent! We could, in short, begin to look at *cause and effect*. At the conditions prevalent in particular locations or professions that lead to declining health and premature death.'

He stopped but I did not know what to ask him. I could not see the point he was trying to make in relation to the corpse on Tresaith beach.

'I conceived the idea that if I could identify those workhouse inmates whose circumstances had deteriorated prior to their being admitted, I might be looking at a sub-population of individuals whose illness had *precipitated* such circumstantial decline. And, of those illnesses, some would reside in the brain.'

'And you became the workhouse doctor in order to further your research?'

This time the silence which preceded his answer seemed of a different quality.

'Not for that reason alone, no. The truth is, I have never caught the trick of wooing patients. I am not a Prendergast. But I believe I have made more than a virtue out of necessity. I have made a vocation.'

I nodded. His was the zeal of a man following a calling, not pursuing a lucrative career. 'And the tumour in the brain of the Tresaith corpse?' I asked.

'Is significant, I believe. Allow me to explain.'

I listened to him carefully and, when I was fully apprised of the facts, I realised that Reckitt was correct. The presence of a tumour in our corpse's head could, indeed, be of great significance.

John

With Clarkson safe in his house, I didn't need to go to Newcastle Emlyn so I decided to nip down to Tresaith and see if Mrs Parry was back yet.

Why? My devil's advocate wanted to know. *Why are you still trying to impress Harry? He's not going to give you a job, is he?*

I'd dreamed of that job. I'd seen the brass plaque with our names on it so many times in my head. *Probert-Lloyd and Davies, Attorneys at Law.* Because I *knew* Harry'd give me articles if I was his solicitor's clerk. Of course he would.

But now, he'd decided he wasn't going to *be* a solicitor. He was going to be coroner for the Teifi Valley. *If* he could persuade the electorate. And with people like Mr Schofield and Billy Go-About not fancying his chances, that wasn't a small if.

What if there *was* a chance, though? If I had to be a solicitor's clerk, wouldn't it be better to have the odd outing as coroner's assistant?

Or Assistant Coroner.

Tell him you made a mistake. Tell him you're sorry.

No. It was a climb-down too far.

Mrs Parry was back, but only just. The pony that was tied up outside The Ship, tail to the wind, still had luggage strapped to its back.

I looked in through the open door and called out a greeting.

'Good God alive,' a voice said. 'Back two minutes and they're here already!' A woman followed the voice towards the door. Middle aged, stout, man's hat, man's cloak. She stopped when she saw me. 'Well.

You're not one of mine, are you? You'll be here about the body, I suppose?'

I nodded. I wasn't surprised she knew about the corpse. News like that travels with the wind.

'Not here anymore. Know where it's gone, do you?'

Her information wasn't quite up to the minute, then. 'Cardigan workhouse.'

'Why?'

'See if anybody'll come and tell us who he is.'

She snorted and folded her arms. 'Hoping one of the girls from down the docks'll recognise him by something other than his face, are you?' I tried to keep my face blank but I can't've made a very good job of it. 'Oh, don't look so shocked, boy. Didn't think you'd find a lady running a shipwrights' tavern, did you?'

There was no answer to that question that was going to help me so I ignored it. 'I'm John Davies, acting coroner's officer.'

She nodded. Didn't bother introducing herself. We both knew who she was.

'The acting coroner, Mr Probert-Lloyd—'

'What?' she interrupted. 'Not *George* Probert-Lloyd, the magistrate?'

'No. His son. Henry.'

'Ah, yes. Heard he was back from London.' She shut her mouth then as if she might've said more but realised, just in time, that it'd get back to Harry if she did.

'Mr Probert-Lloyd would like to speak to you. Can you come down to Cardigan tomorrow? He's staying at the Black Lion.'

'No. Not tomorrow. I've got things to do here. Might be able to come down and see him the next day.'

Another day to wait. Harry wouldn't be pleased. But, on the other hand, he owed Mrs Parry a certain amount of leeway. A dead body'd been housed on her premises in his name.

'Mrs Parry, do you own the limekilns as well as The Ship?'

She frowned. 'I do, as it happens.'

'Did you check them before you went away?'

'Check them? For what?'

'Just to make sure everything was as it should be.'

'Telling me it wasn't, are you?'

'Did you?'

We had no idea how long our corpse had been dead. If Mrs Parry could testify that he hadn't been lying beneath a pile of kiln-waste when she left, that would help.

But she was shaking her head. 'I leave the kilns to Gwyn Puw. You'd have to ask him.'

'We spoke to Mr Puw today.'

'There we are then.' She looked around as a girl came in from the back. 'Bets, hurry up and get the fire lit in here, will you? It's colder inside than out.'

I threw a sympathetic glance at the girl who'd staggered in carrying a bucket full of coal.

'Mam, I'm going as fast as I can, all right?'

So Mrs Parry had her daughter skivvying for her. Still, as Mr Schofield would've said, you don't get rich by squandering your assets.

'I told you we should've come back earlier,' Bets complained. 'We'll never get the pony up to Hendre before it's dark.'

'Don't fret about the pony. He can stay with us another night.' Mrs Parry unfolded her arms and stood, hands on hips, looking at her daughter. 'Why've you brought the cheap coal in, girl? That's Gwyn's stuff.'

'Well, that's all there was. There's no anthracite out there.' She glared back at her mother, giving as good as she got. 'Go and look if you don't believe me.'

Mrs Parry sniffed. 'Somebody's been a naughty boy.'

'Not Puw,' I said. 'We were in his cottage the other day and he was burning the same stuff as you've got in that bucket.'

I got a sharp look for that. It wasn't my business to defend Puw and Mrs Parry was wondering why I was doing it. Well, the truth was that Gwyn Puw had helped us. The lime-waste's disturbance and the American pennies he'd found in it were the only clues we had so far.

'Puw told us you're in business with an American called Jenkyn Hughes,' I said. 'Is that right?'

She folded her arms again over the old-fashioned cloak. I wondered if it had belonged to her husband.

'What's it got to do with the coroner who I'm in business with?'

I wasn't going to let her fob me off. 'When did you last see Mr Hughes, Mrs Parry?'

My change of tone got nothing from her but a lifting of one eyebrow. She might just as well have said, *Ooo, listen to him! Getting above himself just because he's somebody's assistant.*

I looked her in the eye. 'We think he might be the dead man who was found on the beach.' All right, I wanted to shock her. She obviously wasn't going to tell me anything otherwise. But she barely blinked.

'You think it's Jenkyn Hughes? Why didn't you just ask Gwyn, then? He's seen Hughes about the place enough to know what he looks like.' When I didn't answer straight away. she peered at me. 'Or was his face that much of a mess?'

'Puw thinks it might be a quicklime burn.'

Mrs Parry turned away, then, but only to fetch two stools. She put

one of them in front of me. 'You obviously know all about it, John Davies,' she said, planting her backside on the other stool. 'So tell me.'

It didn't take long but, by the time I'd finished, Mrs Parry's mood had changed. An unknown corpse in her beer shed had turned into what might be a dead business partner. I could see that she was already working out how his death might come back on her.

'It'll be a simple matter to find out whether he's still alive,' she said. 'He's lodging at Captain Coleman's, the other side of Cardigan Bridge. On the St Dogmaels road.'

Captain Coleman, St Dogmaels road, I repeated in my head. I didn't want to stop and take my notebook out while Mrs Parry was feeling helpful.

'It was Teff Harris, Banc yr Eithin, who found the body,' I said. 'He says he's working for you. Carting the lime.'

She nodded. 'He brings in a gang to fetch it up the beach.'

I opened my mouth to speak, then stopped. I'd been going to say 'Apparently, he found the body, naked on the lime,' but that would've told her I was suspicious of him. Better if I got her opinion of Teff Harris, first. So I just said, 'The body was lying on the lime that was waiting to be carted up the beach.'

Her face didn't change. She just waited for me to go on.

'Mr Probert-Lloyd got the impression that Teff Harris wasn't very popular with his neighbours,' I said. 'Do you know why that might be?'

She tilted her head slightly to one side and looked at me. 'Asking me to gossip, is it, Mr Davies?'

'Not at all. I'm asking you for an opinion as to why people might've taken against Mr Harris.'

I looked away to give her time to consider what she wanted to tell me. Bets was kneeling on the hearth making a meal of getting the fire going. I could tell she was listening to us and pretending not to. I'd done the same often enough myself.

'Well,' Mrs Parry said, 'he keeps himself to himself. He's ambitious. Hard working.'

I waited for her to go on. What she'd said might not make him popular but there had to be more to it than that for Harris to've asked Harry to make sure his son would be safe.

'Let's say he's not what you expect from a man who lives in a *tŷ unnos.*'

I nodded, slowly. We knew that much already.

'Then there's the house itself. How it got built.'

I felt a flicker of excitement.

'You're most likely too young ever to have seen a *tŷ unnos* going up.' She didn't wait to find out whether or not it was true. 'Not that there were dozens a year even in the old days – people go on as if every young couple without two ha'pennies to rub together would be building one. But if that was true, we'd have no common land left, would we?'

It was a rhetorical question.

'I saw it done once. Hell of a thing – like a wedding night! Lamps and lanterns everywhere, people swarming about like a pack of Irishmen digging and building and trimming and throwing. It's not a small undertaking to build a house in a few hours. Even if you've got everything you need with you, you need all the people you can call on to help you with it.'

She stopped, looked at me. Waiting.

'But that wasn't how Teff Harris did it – is that what you're saying?'

'The building of Teff Harris's house was a military operation. The first thing anybody knew was a gang of men marching up to the bank in two rows, like soliders. Spades and axes and saws and hammers they had, instead of guns, but that was the only difference.'

'You saw this?'

'I did. Somebody came down to fetch my husband in case there was going to be trouble. Parry was good in a scrap. Knew what to do.' She nodded, satisfied, as if that was the most any wife could want of a husband. 'Anyway, they marched up to Banc yr Eithin – late in the day, this was, getting on for sunset – and then they just sat down on the ground to wait.'

'For the sun to set?'

'And for people to start making trouble. Because they were ready for trouble, you could see that.'

'And did it come?'

'Parry went and asked them what they were doing. They said they were going to build a house. Of course, somebody wanted to know by what right they thought they were going to build a house in our parish and that's when Teff Harris stepped forward and said he'd bought the land.'

'Did they believe him?'

'Didn't matter if they believed him or not. His friends were there to make sure the house got built. And to say that if anybody tried to pull the house down, they'd be back.'

'They threatened people?'

'Not exactly. They just said what they said. If anybody tries to damage the house we build tonight, we'll be back.'

I thought of the tidiness of the little holding, how it had been cleared and the soil improved. 'How long's he been there?'

'Years. The boy was born there.'

'And *did* anybody try to damage the house?'

She looked me squarely in the eye. 'Teff Harris keeps a gun. Nobody lifted a finger.'

I thought of what the boy, Clarkson, had told me about the cow but I left that alone for now.

'Not the way to make friends,' I said.

'Teff Harris isn't interested in friends. He's interested in making enough money to go to America.'

Just then we both heard an exasperated sound from the hearth. 'This wood is so damp it won't catch,' Bets Parry complained.

I stood up. 'I can try something if you like?'

'Miracle worker with fires, are you? Or have you got some dry kindling in your pocket?'

She was as sharp tongued as her mother, but she moved aside all the same. I knelt down on the hearth and took out my pocket knife.

Nearly all the little bits of catch-wool and leaves and dry grass that she'd been using to try and get the fire going had burned up. I scraped everything that was left into a little pile then took one of the sticks of kindling and split it down the middle. Like I'd hoped, it was drier inside than out. I stood the blade on edge to the cut surface and scraped the wood into feathers along its length. I did the same with the other half, then took two more twigs and feathered them as well. I put them all on the pile of dry stuff and motioned to Bets to get going with the steel and flint.

In less than a minute, the sticks had caught and Bets was cautiously feeding the fire with thicker twigs.

She looked over her shoulder to see if her mother was there. When she saw Mrs Parry 'd got up off the stool and was busy, she leaned closer to me. 'If it is Jenkyn Hughes,' she muttered, 'then, pound to a penny, it'll turn out somebody killed him over a woman.'

I found myself copying her, looking over my own shoulder. I shouldn't have. Mrs Parry saw me checking and came over.

'Good. You've got it going. Right, go and get the warming-stones out of the bedrooms then come and help me see to the pony and the packs. I'll see Mr Davies off the premises.'

Harry

Alone in my room at the Black Lion later that afternoon, at a loss for occupation, I felt my lack of companionship more acutely than at any time since I had been forced to leave London.

Having been largely absent from Cardiganshire for the best part of eight years, I had not a single friend in the county, a fact that I determined must be remedied as soon as possible. Looking to my father for an introduction to society was unthinkable – acquainting myself with his circle would simply tighten the net of social expectation around me. No, I must look elsewhere; and the obvious place to begin was with my mother's family.

Jemima Lloyd, who had died giving birth to me, had been a solicitor's daughter from Cardigan, respectable but not landowning. Lacking her presence to bridge the social gap between them, my father had maintained little contact with her family after her death and I had no memory of any of my Lloyd relations. However, occasional reference had been made to a cousin – a Mrs Philips who lived in St Dogmaels, just upstream from Cardigan, on the Pembrokeshire side of the river. If I left now, while it was not yet dark, it would not be too late to call. Especially as I was family.

When I went to retrieve Sara from the stables, the head ostler suggested that I take one of the stable boys with me to look after the little mare when I got to St Dogmaels. He also provided a lantern for the return journey.

'It'll be dark later on,' he said. 'You don't want to go stumbling about, Mr Probert-Lloyd. Some people do what they're supposed to and hang lanterns out but most don't bother. Too tight, they are. Sooner we get proper lighting in town the better.'

Used to the gaslights and link-boys of London, I heartily agreed with him.

The stable boy, whose name was Evan, could barely stammer a response when I told him to jump up on the mounting block and sit on the saddle in front of me. 'Me? Ride?' Evidently, the suggestion trumped even my speaking to him in Welsh.

'No point you trotting along behind,' I told him. 'I can't see very well so I need you to keep a sharp eye on what's in front of us.'

He did not need telling twice and, with him up, we rode through the yard and on to the High Street.

I told him to keep his toes in against Sara's shoulders so that she was not confused by the bouncing of his heels against her, but the necessary effort seemed to make him tense and the little mare, sensing his unease, threw her head up and sidestepped as if she was being spurred.

I transferred both reins to my right hand and put my left arm around his chest. Immediately, I felt him sag with relief.

As we ambled down towards the bridge over the Teifi, the pressure of my arm holding Evan secure against me reminded me very forcefully of the physicality of boyhood. Boys are forever nudging, kicking, wrestling, flinging an arm around a companion's shoulders, clutching at each other while fording a stream; such contact is as natural to them as it is to puppies. For myself, as I became older, such casual bodily commerce had been replaced by more gentlemanly contact – football, boxing. Then, as an undergraduate, the carousing which inevitably takes place when young men spend their allowance on alcohol had seen us leaning on each other for support.

Now, the casual intimacy of such contact was lost; my blindness seemed to have immured me in an invisible cell into which others dared not venture. Only Gus, whom I had followed from Oxford to the Inns of Court, still cuffed at me and wrung my hand on coming to see me. Far away in London, at that moment, he might as well have been the Man in the Moon.

'There's a man on the bridge looking at us.' Evan's voice yanked me out of my doleful reverie.

'What kind of man?' I asked, quietly. Whoever he was, I did not want him to hear us speaking about him.

'A sailor, I think,' he whispered back.

'How do you know he's looking at us?' I could see the figure now, but dimly, the dusk muffling what remained of my sight.

'His body's leaning towards the river but his head's turned towards us.'

The man's apparent interest made me very aware of our approach to the bridge. Each footfall on the damp ground, each yard closer, wound a growing tension in me.

'He's turning around. His body's facing us now, too.'

It probably meant nothing, but not being able to see this man and form my own judgement made me feel ill-prepared for whatever might happen.

I urged the mare on to the bridge and heard the change in tone as her feet left the muddy road and slithered slightly on the bridge's cobbles. I wondered if Evan could feel the beating of my heart against his back. I did not like feeling so exposed and devoutly wished John were with me.

Eyes askance, I could make the fellow out now. His arms were folded across his chest as if he was waiting for something. My wariness communicated itself to Sara and her steps faltered. I urged her on, keen to get past the waiting man.

'Well, look! It's Mr Coroner.'

He knew me. Had I met him before or had gossip about me simply scurried through the docks like the ubiquitous rats? His voice seemed somewhat familiar but I could not place it.

'Good evening,' I said, pleasantly.

'Where's your other boy tonight then?'

Other boy? I realised that he must mean John. He did not wait for an answer. Perhaps he realised he would not get one.

'This one doesn't look as if he'd be much use to you.'

I half-expected Evan to protest and the fact that he did not told me he was afraid.

'You think he'll be able to look after your mare if somebody decides to take her?' As far as I could tell, the man did not move but I felt Evan shrink against me. 'You'd do better with me. I'd make sure nobody came near her.'

Was that a threat? Was he implying that harm would come to the mare if I did not employ him? The last thing I wanted was to put Evan in any danger.

'I've promised the boy tuppence, now,' I said, forcing myself to smile. 'Another time, friend.' I nudged Sara into a walk once more.

'Another time?' The man took a step towards me and Sara pulled up, uncertain. 'How will you know me *another time*, Mr Coroner?'

And then it came to me.

'I'll know you by your voice. You were the man I asked about the limestone-hauling boats. *I* might not recognise you by sight but Mr Davies would.' Two could play the implied threat game.

He withdrew slightly. 'Find your stone boat, did you?'

'Not yet, no.'

'Want to arrest the crew, is it? Think they dropped the body on the beach – ten tons of lime, one man with no face?'

My heart and stomach seemed to contract simultaneously and I felt the pulse surging along my veins at his question. What did he know about the dead man? But then reason prevailed – news of the body would be up and down the docks and shipyards on both sides of the river by now. He could easily have seen the dead man. The workhouse was less than half an hour's walk from where we were standing.

'I'd just like to speak to the men who took the limestone up to Tresaith,' I said, 'and ask them if they saw anything.'

Did I hear a grunt, or just expect one? In my agitated state, I could not be sure.

'If you happen to be speaking to any of the men who work the limestone boats,' I said, 'I'd be grateful if you could mention that I'd like to see them. I can be found at the Black Lion.'

'Nobody likes talking to the magistrates.'

'The coroner isn't a magistrate,' I snapped. 'Now, if you don't mind, I need to get on.'

'I'll come along. Your boy'll need help with the mare.'

But I had had enough. 'No,' I said. 'You will not.' Even as I spoke, I hated him for forcing me into behaviour I had always detested. 'No help is needed. Now, let me past or there will be trouble. I may not be able to see, but I know who you are.' I squeezed Sara's sides again, pushing her forward. 'Good evening to you.'

I could scarcely draw breath as we passed him and my skin crawled in anticipation of being laid hold of. But nothing happened. Sara walked steadily on, over the bridge and, as we left him behind, I murmured, 'Don't look back yet, but when we turn after the bridge, look and see if he's following us.'

I waited, and, as we left the bridge, the boy did as I'd asked.

'He's going up into town.'

I sighed with relief.

A great advantage of having the boy with me was that he could ask passers-by if they knew where Mr and Mrs Athur Philips lived. To my relief, their house was quickly identified and we arrived before a generously-sized, double-fronted house.

'Just stay here and don't get in the way of anybody,' I told Evan. 'If anybody asks, tell them the mare belongs to Mr Henry Probert-Lloyd and that I'm visiting Mr and Mrs Philips.' I didn't think he would be questioned but it was as well to give him something to say.

Approaching the front door, without conscious thought my hand slipped into my pocket for my card case. Then I hesitated. Would Mr and Mrs Philips be accustomed to visitors presenting cards? I could not decide which would be more awkward, not to offer one and cause offence, or to present one and find the household in a flurry of uncertainty as to what to do with it.

As I stood in the gathering dusk, contemplating my dilemma, misgivings crowded in. How would the Philipses greet me? I had had no communication with them for twenty years. Might they not ask themselves why, if I had not found them worthy of my notice before, they should suddenly be worthy of it now?

'Can I help you?' The question spun me around. Whoever was there had spoken in English, his accent sufficient to tell me that he was a local man, though, from the absence of a 'sir' on the end of the question, I deduced that I was not being looked up and down by a servant. I smiled and looked firmly into the whirlpool.

'Good evening,' I replied. 'I understand that this is the home of Mr Arthur Philips.'

'It is. I'm Arthur Philips – how can I be of assistance?' His accent had shifted to meet mine. Speaking English, I knew I sounded very much the gentleman and his opinion of me – influenced at first, no doubt, by my Mackintosh and hat – had been altered.

'Mr Philips, I'm sorry to intrude unannounced. I am Henry Probert-Lloyd of Glanteifi.'

'Henry! Jemima's boy! Heavens above! Come in, come in!'

I turned vaguely to indicate the mare and Evan. 'Shall I leave my horse here? The boy'll be all right with her, will he?'

'Hold on, now. You haven't ridden over from Glanteifi at this time of the day?'

I explained that I was staying in town.

'Let the boy take your mare back then. The landlord at the inn down the road rents his dog-cart out as long as it's not too late. I can drive you back.'

I thought of the man on the bridge and did not want to risk Evan's safety. 'It's kind of you but I've promised the boy a ride back with me. He'll be fine if he can sit somewhere. The mare won't try and wander if he has her reins.'

Philips sent Evan around the end of the street and told him how to find the back of the house. 'Knock at the back door. The servants will tell you what to do with the horse. Then you can sit by the kitchen fire.'

Knowing servants, I very much doubted that Evan would get anywhere near the fire but it was reassuring to know that he would be indoors.

Philips threw open his front door, speaking all the while. 'We keep early hours these days and we'll be sitting down to dinner in an hour or so. Will you join us?' He opened a door and called out to a Mrs Knowles that, if it wasn't too much trouble, there would be a guest for dinner. 'She'll grumble at the short notice,' he said, turning back to me and hanging his overcoat on the hallstand, 'but she'll put a dinner in front of you that you won't forget in a hurry.'

I caught a moment's hesitation and knew what it was. He was looking at me and trying to work out what was wrong.

'Mr Philips – before we go in, I must just tell you, my sight is not what it should be. I'm not exactly blind but I can't see you. That is, I can see that you're there but that's all.'

For weeks I had been trying to settle on a simple and elegant form of words to explain my predicament. As yet, however, elegance eluded me.

Just tell them you've gone blind, Gus had advised. *Then you'll have them at a disadvantage when you catch them trying to sneak out without you noticing. They'll think you've developed preternatural hearing.*

'I tend not to bump into the furniture, so people don't necessarily notice immediately.' I smiled. 'They just think I'm being shifty.'

'Yes, I see,' Philips said. Then, as so many people found themselves doing, he corrected himself. 'I mean, I understand.'

'Please,' I smiled again, trying to put him at ease with a situation I had yet to feel easy about myself, 'don't give it a second thought. I'm always saying "I see". It's just a metaphor, isn't it?'

Dear God, what fatuity this blindness was driving me into! Not two minutes in the man's company and I was offering grammatical analysis. Fortunately, I was saved from any more drivelling by his opening a door and announcing, 'My dear, you will be astonished to hear who I have found on our doorstep.'

Arthur Philips had not been over-praising his cook. The meal was the best I had enjoyed since leaving London.

'Mrs Knowles is constantly refusing offers to go and work for better-off families around and about,' Mrs Philips confided when I complimented the meal. 'She prefers to stay with us, as she has a widowed daughter and three grandchildren living with her. We're less than five minutes' walk from her own house here, so she can come and go as she needs to without the constraints of living in.'

I felt a rush of affection for my mother's cousin. Most servants were not treated with such kindness and, as I smiled in Mrs Philips's direction, I wondered how her little cousin – my mother – had viewed her own role as mistress of a whole houseful of servants at Glanteifi. I judged it to be far too early in our reacquaintance, however, to begin asking that kind of question. Not that the subject of my mother was avoided; far from it. Mrs Philips, who had been the oldest grandchild in the family while my mother had been very much the youngest, had fond memories of 'little Jemima'.

'Of course, I was so much older than her – nearly grown-up when she was born – we were never playmates, but I remember her so well. She was a sweet child and she had that kind of harmless mischief about her that late-coming children often have. She could be demure when she wanted to be but I'm sure it was her mischievous streak that bewitched your father. From the first time they met, he couldn't take his eyes off her.'

My father bewitched? I found that not only hard to imagine but vaguely indecent. From my earliest memories, my father had seemed old – he had been past fifty at my birth – and, as far as I recalled, he had never shown much enthusiasm for anything. He had always managed to convey the impression that his continued existence proceeded solely from a sense of duty. I could no more imagine his head being turned by a mischievous girl than I could picture him cavorting naked in the rain.

'Was she so very pretty?' I asked, trying not to sound as hungry as I felt for details of my mother.

'Yes, she was. But I believe it was her vivaciousness which caught men's eye.'

A vivaciousness which had been snuffed out by my birth.

Arthur Philips coughed slightly in the sudden silence. 'We hear that you've been asked to stand in as coroner, Henry.'

Ah, the social advantages that attached themselves to the entertainment of a blind man; his wife had evidently caught his eye and mouthed 'change the subject'.

'Indeed,' I acknowledged. 'Mr Bowen obviously saw talents in me which I had not seen in myself.'

'I trust it wouldn't be indelicate to ask whether you've identified the poor man?'

His sympathy for the victim caused another upwelling of affection in me. Was it that that made me more confiding than I might otherwise have been? Whatever the impulse, I was soon to be glad of it.

'We believe he might be a man called Jenkyn Hughes,' I said.

A gasp came from Mrs Philips.

'Jenkyn Hughes the American?' her husband asked.

'Yes.' I nodded, acutely aware that information was being exchanged between husband and wife. 'Do you know him?'

'Rather more than that,' Mr Philips said, clearly agitated. 'Our family is in business with him. How did he die?'

'That's what I'm trying to find out. But it seems clear that it wasn't an accident.'

'Somebody killed him deliberately?'

'It seems so.'

I caught a movement from Mrs Philips's direction. 'Oh, the poor man. Why on earth would anybody want to do him harm?'

'That's another question I must find the answer to,' I said, keeping my tone rueful so as to avoid sounding officious. Her husband raised his glass to his lips but did not comment. Was he less surprised than his wife that somebody should wish to see the American dead? I forced a smile. 'But this is no topic for the dinner table. Perhaps I could come and speak to you tomorrow, Mr Philips, at your place of work? I will have my assistant with me then. He makes notes for me.'

'Of course. We're entirely at your disposal – myself and everyone I employ.' He hesitated before adding, 'However, you might find it more useful to speak to my son, James. He is slowly but surely taking over the business from me and he has – *had* – more to do with Jenkyn Hughes on a day-to-day basis than I did myself.'

'Thank you.'

Unsurprisingly, conversation became somewhat strained after that as Mr and Mrs Philips struggled with the knowledge that somebody they knew personally, somebody who had, more likely than not, sat at this very table, had died a violent death. So, after an exchange of mutual assurances of future visits and an enquiry as to where I might find the Philips' business premises, Evan was alerted and Sara brought to the front door.

Despite apprehensions which neither the boy nor I needed to articulate, we did not encounter the sailor on the bridge again.

John

I slept badly. Always do if I've got to get up earlier than usual. Afraid to go to sleep for fear of not waking up in time. Still, at least I managed to leave the house without seeing my landlady. Sour as sloes she'd been, when I told her I'd be staying in Cardigan for a few days.

'I hope you're not looking for a reduction in rent, John Davies. It's not as if I can offer your room to anybody else while you're away, is it?'

It'd been on the tip of my tongue to remind her that she wasn't going to have to feed me morning and evening either, but I managed to keep my mouth shut. She could easily turn nasty, and I didn't want to have to look for new lodgings. I wasn't exactly sitting pretty but at least it was a decent roof over my head at a rent I could afford.

I was out of bed before it was properly light and off to the livery stables. Harry was a man of routine and I knew he liked his breakfast at nine o'clock. If I could be at the Black Lion just before that, I'd get breakfast too.

The ostler's boy gave me a surly look when I walked into the stableyard, but I'd warned his father I'd be there before sunrise so he couldn't complain. I still half-expected him to tell me to tack the mare up myself but, as usual, Seren was ready – saddled and bridled. She knew me now and she made that friendly half-breath, half-whinny that horses use to their friends. It made me smile. I'd got attached to her, too.

I settled myself in the saddle. It was a quarter past seven by the watch Harry'd given me and I was confident of being in Cardigan well before nine. There was still most of an hour left before sunrise but that cold, grey light that creeps over the countryside before the sun appears was plenty to see by and I followed the road out of town towards Cenarth.

I was happy enough on horseback now to let my mind wander as Seren trotted steadily along the road. Whatever Harry thought, it seemed to me that today might be our last day investigating. All we needed to do for the inquest was to go over the river, knock on Captain Coleman's door, confirm that this American was missing and we'd have all we needed. Identity of corpse: Jenkyn Hughes. Cause of death: murder.

Teff Harris seemed to be everybody's favourite for the crime and it was easy to see why. Firstly, he was always coming and going at Tresaith beach with the limestone hauling he'd got himself contracted to do. With Mrs Parry and Gwyn Puw away, the place had been deserted, so he could've easily arranged to meet Hughes there. No witnesses.

Secondly, he was a soldier. Bashing somebody over the head wouldn't be as difficult for him as it would be for the rest of us.

Thirdly, there was no love lost between him and his neighbours. That might not seem like much but it told me a lot. Our house'd been not much better than Teff Harris's and my parents had depended on their neighbours to see them through hard times. Likewise, their neighbours had depended on them, turn and turn about. That's how things were. Life was too hard, too chancy, to think of falling out with the people around you, and you had to be suspicious of anybody who did.

Then there was that anonymous letter. *Ask Teff Harris what he did with the dead man's clothes after he took him out of the sea and stripped him.*

I knew it might be nothing more than somebody trying to make trouble for Harris. But, then again, it might just as easily be from somebody who'd seen exactly what they said but was afraid of Teff Harris's gun if they came forward in person.

Coming up to Llechryd bridge, I stared over the sodden meadow at the river. Flat as beaten metal. Until it went over the weir and got tossed into tumbling froth, you wouldn't even know it was water. Things didn't always look like what they were.

Teff Harris had said he didn't know the corpse. Well, if he'd stripped it, he was lying – even the boy, Clarkson, described Hughes by his clothes. But, if the body really had been naked when he found it, I knew that, more than likely, Teff wouldn't've recognised it. I'd seen my father blacked with soot and I knew I'd've walked past him as a stranger if he hadn't been in our own kitchen. With the corpse's face as it was, unless he had reason to suspect that it was Hughes, Teff Harris might well not've known him.

I kicked my heels lightly into Seren's sides until she rocked into a canter. Two heads were better than one and I hoped Harry's had more in it than mine.

But, when I got to the Black Lion, Harry didn't want to talk about Teff Harris. He was full of Benton Reckitt. Or, at least, what Reckitt'd found inside the corpse's head.

Made no sense to me. I couldn't see what having a lump growing in his brain had to do with Jenkyn Hughes getting hit over the head.

Mind, when Harry told me what else Reckitt had said, it was suddenly crystal clear why people gossiped about *him*. Cutting up dead paupers to see what'd killed them was downright strange.

'Did you ask him about the burns on Hughes' face?'

'We don't know it *is* Jenkyn Hughes yet,' Harry said. 'But I did ask and Reckitt didn't have much to offer. He said he's only seen minor burns from quicklime and only ever in the living. He couldn't rule it out as the cause of the damage but he couldn't say with any certainty that it *was* the cause, either. But he did tell me one thing I didn't know. Quicklime acts as a drying agent. That's why they used to throw it into plague pits – to absorb the liquids from putrefying bodies.'

'I thought it was to break the bodies down. Dissolve them, kind of thing?' Now I'd said it, it seemed stupid. As if quicklime could dissolve bone like salt melts a slug.

'No. It was to stop the bodies stinking. To prevent disease.'

'If it was a drying agent,' I almost interrupted him, 'that would fit. I said the skin looked leathery, didn't I?'

Harry nodded. 'Which means he probably *was* buried in the kiln waste.'

'With his clothes on. Clothes that were stripped off him later. Just like the anonymous letter said.'

Harry ignored that so I told him everything I'd got from Clarkson, including the American's flashy white trousers and chequered waistcoat. 'Very recognisable clothes,' I finished. 'Nobody in Cardigan goes around looking like that, do they?'

Harry thought for a bit. 'Do you think whoever buried him in the kiln waste knew what would happen to any exposed flesh?' he asked. 'Or was it just an accident?'

I said nothing. It was himself he was asking, not me.

'On the other hand,' he said, 'why bother hiding the body at all? Why not just take him out to sea, tie him to something heavy and drop him overboard? Nobody'd have been any the wiser.'

'Perhaps they wanted him to be found.'

'Why?'

I didn't know. I'd just heard the idea coming out of my mouth.

'And why take him *out* of the kiln?' Harry wanted to know. 'What was the point of leaving the body there, on the load of limestone?'

'We've only got Teff Banc yr Eithin's word that it was on the limestone. Well, his, and whoever wrote that anonymous letter.'

'But let's say, for the sake of argument, that it was there,' Harry insisted. 'Why? Why leave it there?'

'For it to be washed out to sea and come ashore somewhere else?'

'But that would go against your theory that whoever put it there wanted the body to be found. Once it'd got washed out to sea, goodness knows where it would have ended up.'

'We could ask Gwyn Puw. He'd know what would've happened to it. He lives on the beach. Bound to know about tides and currents and so on.'

Harry nodded but I don't think he really heard me. From the stillness of him, he was thinking hard.

'It'd be a good idea to go back to Tresaith, anyway,' I said. 'To talk to Mrs Parry's daughter.' I told him about my visit to The Ship the day before. And about Bets Parry's suggestion that Jenkyn Hughes was a womaniser.

'I also think it might be a good idea to try and find out where *Mrs* Teff Harris is,' Harry said. 'It could be that we're barking up the wrong tree. Maybe she and Jenkyn Hughes ran off together and our corpse is somebody else entirely. A few coins have seduced us into thinking we know who he is.'

'The boy, Clarkson, seemed pretty sure that his mother'd gone to her sister's.'

'I don't suppose she'd tell him she was running off with her lover.'

True.

'Right. Let's get on.'

He got to his feet but I stayed where I was. 'Have you told Inspector Bellis about those coins yet? Does he know the dead man might be Jenkyn Hughes?'

Harry sighed. 'No.'

'We should do that first, then, shouldn't we?'

Harry pulled in another breath and held it while he chewed his lip. 'Let's go and see Captain Coleman first,' he said. 'No point troubling Bellis if Jenkyn Hughes is alive and well and eating breakfast in his lodgings.'

We didn't have to ask which house belonged to Captain Coleman. He'd hung a ship's wheel next to the front door.

'What on earth for?' Harry asked when I told him.

'Advertising his trade, I suppose.'

Turned out I was wrong. Captain Coleman himself was long gone and it was his widow who let rooms in her house to lodgers. 'Captain Coleman's is what it's always been called,' she told us as she saw us in to her front room. 'No call to go changing it now, just because my husband's gone.'

There were sailors' trinkets everywhere in the tiny parlour. Little ships in bottles. One of those things they use to tell where they are at sea. Carvings made out of ivory like you see old sailors selling on the streets sometimes. And a flag, hanging in the corner. Either the widow was fond of all the paraphernalia, or she'd been very fond of her husband.

'I'm sorry you've had a wasted journey, Mr Probert-Lloyd. I don't know when Mr Hughes will be back, you see. Not for some time, going by what his cousin said.'

'His cousin?' I asked. Hughes was an American, what was a cousin of his doing here?

'Yes. Came to fetch Mr Hughes's things. I didn't know him but he had Mr Hughes's signet ring to vouch for him. I knew it was his ring, I'd seen it a dozen times.'

'When did he come, this cousin?'

She looked at me, twisting her face with the effort of remembering. 'A few days ago. I can't tell you exactly, I'm sorry. The days all seem to go into one at my age.'

'That's all right, Mrs Coleman,' Harry said, giving her a little smile. 'Did Mr Hughes's cousin say *why* he was collecting his things?'

'Mr Hughes was delayed in Aberaeron, he said, so he'd asked him to fetch the boxes to his house. Mr Hughes didn't want me to be out of pocket when I could be letting the room, you see. He'd only paid up to the end of the week and the cousin said Mr Hughes didn't know when he'd be back.'

'I see,' Harry said. 'This cousin, do you happen to remember his name, Mrs Coleman?'

'Shoni Jones. From out Moylegrove way, he said. I don't know the family but he said his father's got a farm out there.'

'He didn't mention the name of the farm, by any chance?' I asked.

'He did, *bach*, but I don't remember. Didn't think it was important, you see. Not when he showed me the ring and said Mr Hughes wanted me to be paid what I was owed.'

'Did he say when exactly he'd spoken to Mr Hughes?'

'No, *bach*. Just that he'd seen him in Aberaeron, that's all. He was his cousin, you see. It wasn't my place to start asking questions like that.'

Harry, who must've been wondering what the cluttered little room was full of, turned back to her. 'Mrs Coleman, this is going to sound like a strange question but what colour hair does Mr Hughes have?'

The old woman turned to him. 'Brown, it is. No grey in it at all even though he's nearly forty years of age.' She smiled as if she was Jenkyn Hughes's mother. 'Very proud of his hair, Mr Hughes is. A full head of hair into old age runs in his family, he says. His father and his grandfather both had all their hair till the day they died.'

I wondered if Harry was thinking what I was. That the dead man would've been able to say the same thing.

The tide had come up, even in the short time we'd been in Captain Coleman's, and the estuary mudflats were almost covered as we rode back towards Cardigan. The wading birds were closer to us now, dipping their beaks in the narrow strip of sandy mud between the reeds and the water. I didn't know anything about water fowl and it was no use asking Harry what the little black-and-white birds were. Red legs, they had. We were so close I could see the colour of them.

'What do we think of this cousin?' Harry asked.

I turned away from the river. 'Do you mean is he really a cousin? Did Jenkyn Hughes really ask him to move his things? Or was he involved in killing him?'

Harry blew out an impatient breath. 'All of those. Dammit, it shouldn't be this difficult to find out whether somebody's dead or not!'

He was frustrated – you could see it coming off him like steam off a cow's back in the rain. When he'd agreed to do the inquest, I don't suppose he'd thought it would take half this long to find out who the dead man was. He'd've been hoping to present a nice clean account at the inquest and impress the voters.

'We could go and see whether Teff Harris has confessed,' I suggested. 'If he has, we'll know who the dead man is.'

Harry chewed his lip. 'Alternatively, we could go and see Mrs Parry. If she was in business with Hughes she might know who this cousin is. Or what Hughes was doing in Aberaeron.'

'*Or* we could go to the police station,' I pressed him, 'and find that they've got all the information we need to re-convene the inquest. There might be no *need* to go riding about the county.'

Harry narrowed his eyes. Why, I don't know – he couldn't focus that *peripheral vision* of his. Habit, I suppose.

'You know I'm right,' I said. 'I don't know why you're trying so hard to avoid Bellis.'

'Because he thinks I'm a know-nothing foreigner.' I'd never heard Harry's voice so clipped, so tight.

A seagull screamed and I turned. A dozen or more were following a fishing boat in on the tide. I shook my head. 'He can think what he likes, can't he? You just have to hold your ground.'

'*What* ground?' His voice was bitter. 'My barrister's training? My position as heir to Glanteifi? What *is* my ground, John?'

We'd been through this before. Harry'd grown up here and thought of himself as a Welshman but, the truth was, he'd gone to make his fortune in England and everybody assumed that he saw things through London-tinted specs.

'Well?' he tilted his chin up.

I was uncomfortable. Didn't want to tell him unwelcome news. But then, as he'd said himself, we weren't going to be working together in future so what did it matter?

'Like it or not,' I said, 'people see you differently from the way you see yourself. Not just Bellis – everybody. If you're going to be coroner'

– God knows whether that was a reasonable ambition but I wasn't going to be the one to tell him not to try – 'you're going to have to work with the police. With Bellis. And the magistrates. To work in the way they're expecting. Or, at any rate,' I said when I saw him draw breath to object, 'more in the way they're expecting than you do now.'

That's what you think, is it?' His voice was flat but I could tell he was surprised. I should've stopped there. But that 'well?' of his had been a challenge.

'Yes, it is what I think. And another thing, stop speaking Welsh to people who can speak English perfectly well. It just confuses them.'

'Welsh is my mother tongue!'

'Maybe so, but you're the squire's son. It makes people uncomfortable when you speak the language of their own hearth to them.'

'What am I supposed to do – pretend I can't speak Welsh and use you as an interpreter?' He was getting angry now and I felt a little rush of fear. I stamped it down.

'Just try and sound a bit more formal. Help people out. How are they supposed to take you seriously as coroner if you sound like them? It'd be like the minister reading the Bible out in everyday speech.'

He'd turned his head away, now, as if he could see the birds and their little red legs.

'I know you don't want to be Harry Glanteifi, heir to the estate,' I said, 'but that's who you *are*. You'd be better off making use of that and not trying to pretend that you're some *gwas bach* made good.' Like me.

Without looking round, he gave a sudden bark of a laugh. 'No, please, don't hold back, John, tell me what you really think!' Sarcasm. He only ever turned that on me when he was feeling hurt. Seren tossed her head suddenly and I had to grab the reins to stop them being pulled through my fingers. She didn't like the way the wind was blowing up her tail.

I sighed. 'I'm sorry. But you need to behave properly if you're going to get yourself elected.'

He still didn't look round, but I didn't need to see his face. The mixture of surprise and acceptance was in his voice. 'You wouldn't give me so much as an opinion when we first met and now you're telling me how to behave.'

I tried to smile for him. 'You've taught me well.'

He dropped his chin to his chest in defeat and I sucked in a deep breath. The air smelled of salt, stinking mud, and traces of old fish and tar.

'Come on then,' he said, his head coming up again. 'Let's go and see if Billy Go-About is at home. And I'll see what I can do about being emollient and squire-ish at the same time.'

Harry

After the sharp, frosty air outside, Inspector Bellis's private office was stuffy and, by the time I had shared with him the evidence we had gleaned from Benton Reckitt and Gwyn Puw, I was sweating beneath the coat I had not been invited to remove.

'And Mr Puw brought this information to you rather than to the police?'

I felt a stab of childish pleasure at the question but was careful not to show it. 'He'd already met me. As had Mr Vaughan. In fact, Mr Vaughan is a member of the inquest jury.'

'But he himself had no actual evidence to present?'

'No. I believe he came simply to help Mr Puw articulate his evidence more clearly.'

But, as I spoke, I wondered whether that was true. Though we knew that Puw had gone to Obadaiah Vaughan for advice once he suspected that the limekiln waste had been tampered with, we had not asked who had found the coins. Bearing in mind John's suggestion that somebody wanted the body to be discovered, could the coins have been 'found' so as to identify him? If so, the articulate Vaughan seemed a likelier suspect than the lime burner.

Bellis was speaking. 'Of course, this Jenkyn Hughes had already come to my attention. Plenty of people emigrate but the sort of scheme Hughes had devised was unusual enough to be of note.'

'How so?' I asked, grinding my teeth; if I had followed my instincts and gone to speak to Mrs Parry before coming here, I would not have been forced to display my ignorance.

'Emigrants generally just get on a boat and hope for the best at the other end,' Bellis said. 'Or they join family who've gone before and can help them get established. But Hughes was offering guaranteed employment and somewhere to live. No need for family support or letters of introduction. More expensive, of course. Jenkyn Hughes wasn't just selling a ticket for passage, he was selling a bond for a whole new life.'

Possible motives for Hughes's murder sprang to mind as Bellis spoke: rivalries, exclusions, arguments over cost. 'How long had Hughes been in Cardigan?' I asked.

'He seems to have been coming and going for a number of months. He has two partners, I believe. Mrs Parry, who runs an inn and builds ships at Tresaith—'

'And Mr Philips of Philips and Lloyd.'

'I see you're well informed.'

I said nothing. I was not going to admit that I had come by the information fortuitously at a family reunion. Let him think I had means of obtaining intelligence which did not rely on his officers.

'Perhaps Mrs Parry or Mr Philips could provide more information.' He paused. Was he expecting me to respond or thinking before he spoke again? I waited. 'Are you intending to ask Mr Philips if he would view the body in order to attempt an identification?'

It had not occurred to me but, now that Bellis suggested it, I saw that it was the obvious course. 'I am, yes.'

'Good.' Bellis's tone was decisive, as if we had just shaken hands on a bargain. 'Assuming he is able to make the identification to your satisfaction, when can we expect the inquest to be re-convened?'

The question took me aback. 'I believe we are some way off from that, yet.'

'You surprise me, Acting Coroner. I understood your autopsy to have confirmed that a deliberate blow to the head killed him.'

'Deliberate, yes. But we have no evidence as to whether it was murder or manslaughter. Or indeed the remotest idea why he should have been killed.'

'I do not believe that is the coroner's business.'

'Then we shall have to agree to differ, Inspector. I mean to continue my investigations in order to satisfy myself that the witnesses I call will provide the public, and Mr Hughes's family, with an adequate explanation of how he died.'

'Then it is fortunate for the ratepayer that investigations by you and your assistant will not be necessary, Acting Coroner. My officers are already speaking to Theophilus Harris's neighbours. I believe they will be able to supply adequate evidence to reach a verdict.'

How I wished I could stare defiance into Bellis's eye! His insistence on pursuing Teff Harris seemed, at best, lazy and, at worst, vindictive. From everything we knew about Harris's relations with his neighbours, evidence was likely to be in shorter supply than dislike and hearsay. But, given the way that reputation quickly solidifies into accepted character, such testimony might well be sufficient to prejudice a jury's verdict.

'I would like to speak to Harris, myself, if I may.'

'You think he will give you different answers from those he has given my officers?'

'I suspect that I will ask him different questions, Inspector.'

Of course, Bellis had no good reason to deny me, and within five minutes John and I were in the lock-up at the side of the police station. If I had been uncomfortably warm in Bellis's office, I had the opposite affliction now, and shrugged my way further into my coat as we waited for the stools we had been promised. Harris sat in the corner on what I assumed was a mattress of some kind.

'How are you, Mr Harris?' I asked.

'Never mind me. How is my boy? Did you take him to the workhouse as I asked?'

I tried not to bridle at his assumption that he could hold me to account. 'I will let John tell you about your son. He went to Banc yr Eithin while I was busy with other matters.'

Just then a constable appeared with two stools and set them down before standing himself in the corner of the cell.

'Thank you, Constable,' I said. 'We won't need you for anything else.'

'I need to be here to lock up again, sir.'

'Then one of us will come and find you when we need to leave.'

The constable out of the way, I turned to Teff Harris. 'Have you been well-treated?'

'Well enough. They haven't beaten me. I'm fed, after a fashion. But they can't just hold me here!'

'No. The inspector has his officers out trying to get evidence against you at the moment. Unless there is eye-witness testimony or a strong suspicion that you had a compelling motive, I will ask for you to be released.'

'When will that be?'

'Tomorrow at the latest.'

'Meanwhile, my son is in the workhouse!'

'No,' John said, 'he's not.'

While he explained his encounter with the boy, I tried to get an impression of the cell. Despite persistent rumours of medieval treatment, there was no stinking straw on the floor and, if there was any water trickling down the walls, then I could neither hear nor smell any evidence of it. The air was cold but not damp and the flags underfoot felt dry. Since my sight had failed, I had begun to take a great deal more notice of the ground under my feet and I had learned to notice the difference in texture between dry and wet paving. There was a surprising grittiness to damp that was not there in a dry surface.

'Why do you think Clarkson didn't tell you about the men trying to steal your cow?' I heard John ask.

'Didn't want trouble, did he? But my wife told me what had happened.'

'About your wife,' I began. 'When do you think she'll be back?'

Did he guess at my suspicions? There was no suggestion of it in his voice. 'Her sister was sick with a fever. They're generally over pretty quick, one way or the other. She'll be back soon, I dare say.'

One way or the other. If I wasn't mistaken, that was the phrase John had reported Clarkson using to estimate when his mother would be back. Perhaps Mrs Harris really had gone to look after her sister.

'Where does her sister live?' I asked.

'Llandysul.'

'It might be necessary to talk to her before she comes back. Where exactly would we find her?'

'Her husband's a shoemaker – Dai Davies. If you ask for him in the town anybody'll know where his shop is.'

An artisan. It was a decided social rung above *tŷ unnos* builder. Either Mrs Harris had come down in the world or her sister had gone up. If it was the former, I could not help wondering whether Harris's wife had had enough of privation and begun to look elsewhere.

I hesitated before asking my next question. I wanted John to take careful note of Teff Harris's reaction and I needed to think how to make sure he did. 'Mr Harris. I would like you to think very carefully, now, and tell me whether you are acquainted with a man called Jenkyn Hughes.'

Clarkson had told John that his father knew Hughes. If Teff denied it, now, Bellis might be right in his suspicions.

'Hughes? Yes, I know him.'

'How did you become acquainted?'

'He's in business with Mrs Parry. He's often at The Ship and so am I.'

'And away from The Ship?'

'What d'you mean?'

I was trying to find out whether he had other dealings with Hughes. Interestingly, Teff Harris suddenly sounded wary, as if he suspected me of setting a trap for him. 'Do you only see Mr Hughes at The Ship or do you see him elsewhere?' I followed Harris's lead and referred to Hughes in the present tense.

'Why do you ask?'

I stared into the whirlpool that hid Harris from me, willing John to follow my gaze. 'We have reason to believe that the body you found was that of Jenkyn Hughes.'

He said nothing which was a point in his favour. Guilty men are apt to be too obviously surprised when told things they already know.

'You saw the body,' I went on. 'Do you think it could be that of Jenkyn Hughes?'

'If you were able to see his face, Mr Probert-Lloyd, you wouldn't ask me that.'

I nodded, allowing him to understand that others had expressed the same opinion. 'But the body's general features – height, build and so forth?'

'Mr Harris?' John prompted. He had his notebook on his lap and was, presumably, waiting to record the answer verbatim.

'I'm trying to remember what the body looked like.' Harris said. He drew an audible breath. 'Jenkyn Hughes is average height and well-built. As I recall, the body was pretty well-fleshed, so that fits. The hair was wet and tangled so I couldn't say about that.' He paused, as if he was weighing up the evidence. 'It could've been him. But I can't say definitely that it was.'

'Can I just ask you, again, to describe how you came to find the body and put it in the shed?'

I had half expected him to complain at the request, but he did not, simply repeating the same story we had heard from him at Banc yr Eithin. He had seen the body lying on the limestone, he had gone to investigate, seen that the man was dead and, not wanting the limestone-carting to be delayed, had taken it upon himself to remove the body to Mrs Parry's beer shed.

'What state was the tide in when you arrived at the beach?' I asked, remembering, as I did so, that we needed to ask Gwyn Puw about currents and so forth.

'About an hour off bottom tide.'

'So, was the limestone load still covered?' John asked.

'Not when the waves drew back. That's how I saw him.'

There was nothing to be gained from questioning Harris any further, so, assuring him that we would petition for his release as soon as practicable, we took our leave.

John had found a boy to take the mares back to the Black Lion before we went in to the police station and we were walking through the inn's carriage arch towards the stables when I suddenly realised that the unidentified body had now been on display at the workhouse for more than twenty-four hours. Given that the workhouse master had been instructed to send anybody who recognised the corpse to the Black Lion, we might be awaited inside.

I put a hand on John's arm, halting him. 'Let's just ask whether anybody's here to see us. I don't want people hanging around indefinitely and making me unpopular.'

We were scarcely inside the door before I heard my name.

'Mr Probert-Lloyd!'

I turned. 'Twm?' Twm James, one of the grooms from Glanteifi, was standing there. I knew him by his weak 'r'.

'I've been sent to bring you home, sir.'

I was about to protest, then the tone of his voice registered. 'Why, what's happened?'

'It's your father, sir. He's been struck down by an apoplexy.'

PART TWO

John

Harry's reaction to Twm James's news took me by surprise. I'd seen Harry with his father. Only briefly, but I'd seen how they treated each other. Civil, distant. When we'd worked together before Christmas, I'd heard a dozen stories about how, when Harry was a boy, he'd been closer to the servants at Glanteifi than to his own flesh and blood. So, if you'd asked me to tell you how he'd react to news that his father was gravely ill, I would've been a long way from guessing that it'd drive every sane thought from his head and make him rush around issuing orders, asking questions and achieving nothing but distress for him and confusion for the rest of us.

Maybe it's harder if you can't look around you and see the people you need to speak to, right there. Maybe only being able to see the edges of things made Harry feel like a man in the dark, not knowing which way he was going, stumbling against things he'd seen in their places every day of his life. Whatever the reason, it was hard to watch.

In the end, I took him by the shoulders. 'Harry. Just go. Sara's saddled and ready. I'll pack your things and send them back with Twm.'

He nodded, but his face looked as if he was hearing my words from a long way off and only just catching them.

'I'll get Mrs Weston to make up an invoice for the magistrates, shall I?'

That seemed to bring him back to himself. 'No! You'll need the rooms to go on with the investigation till I can get back.'

Till he could get back? Unlikely. He'd either be tending a very sick father or organising a funeral. He wasn't going to have time for inquests.

Harry grabbed my arm as if he might drown without something to hold on to. 'Keep on with the investigation for me. Please, John. You know as much about it all as I do. Just use your judgement.'

He gave me no time to argue. Just did as I'd told him and went.

After I'd spoken to Mrs Weston and arranged to move into the room Harry'd had, I went up to see about packing his things.

The room was small and barely furnished. At first, I thought it was Harry penny-pinching for the magistrates but then I remembered that the Black Lion was a coaching inn – not much required beyond a bed for the night.

Still, somebody'd put a little table in the room and Harry's writing things were on it.

On top of his writing box was the wooden frame he used, still folded in half. He hadn't had any need for it yet. I put it to one side and opened the writing box. I don't know why but the sight of the half-used ink stick and the empty inkwell made me sad for Harry. Could he still make his ink up himself, or did he get somebody to do it for him? There'd be plenty of servants to do it at Glanteifi but perhaps he'd have had to see to it himself, here. Or asked me.

I looked at the steel-nibbed pens in their little compartment. Who had Harry thought he'd be writing to while we were in Cardigan? If he hadn't brought the frame as well, I might've thought he'd brought the writing things for me. And I might need them, yet. All I had in the way of writing equipment was a pencil and a notebook.

I closed the box. I'd keep it and send the frame back to Glanteifi with the rest of his things.

I gave Harry's portmanteau to Twm and told him I needed word from Harry as soon as possible about how I should proceed. *Just use your judgement* might show his confidence in me but it could let me in for a whole lot of trouble from Billy Go-About if my judgement wasn't to his liking.

I watched Twm riding out of the yard. I knew I'd get no word from Glanteifi until the following morning at the earliest. Which left the rest of that day for me to do whatever I judged best.

Whatever Harry thought, my gut told me that Teff Harris was the obvious suspect for Jenkyn Hughes's murder. Always assuming the corpse *was* Hughes. Granted, we didn't know why Harris might've wanted to kill the American but it wasn't my job to find that out.

I knew Billy Go-About had sent his officers to get what they could out of Harris's neighbours but I'd've been willing to bet good money that they wouldn't go near The Ship. Which was exactly where I was intending to go because two things were clear to me. One, Bets Parry knew something. Two, judging by the way she'd hustled me out the day before, her mother didn't want Bets talking to me. But I was pretty sure that if I threw Harry's name and 'Acting Coroner' about enough, I'd be able to speak to Bets alone.

I looked into the stalls. Seren was getting a rubbing-down from one of the grooms. Not that she really needed it – we hadn't been far. Still, it was better than seeing her neglected.

'Have you fed her since she's been back?' I asked.

The groom shook his head.

'All right then, tack her up again for me, will you? I'm going out.'

Seren hadn't even put her nose beyond the coachyard arch when I saw a horse and trap bowling along at a determined clip past the Black

Lion and down towards the quayside. The driver, still wrapped in that thick, man's cloak of hers, was Mrs Parry.

My first thought was to ride straight up to Tresaith and talk to Bets while her mother was out of the way. But then I remembered something that made me think again. When I'd spoken to her, Mrs Parry'd been very definite that she couldn't come down to Cardigan that day to talk to Harry. Far too busy. But that'd been before I'd told her that we thought the dead man might be Jenkyn Hughes. Was that why she was in town now? To speak to Captain Coleman's widow, ask after the widow's lodger?

I turned Seren's head and followed the trap down Bridge Street. But, instead of driving on to the bridge, Mrs Parry turned the pony's head and drove along the quayside. I followed, slowly, hanging back in case she looked over her shoulder and saw me.

On the wharves, between the lines of moored ships and the huge, slab-fronted warehouse buildings, there was all sorts of to-ing and fro-ing going on. I crooked my finger to one of the boys who'd come rushing up to me, offering to look after Seren for tuppence, and agreed that he could have a ha'penny if he stood on Bridge Street with her and waited for me. Without Seren I was just another clerk. Invisible.

Mrs Parry'd tucked the trap in under the lowest windows of one of the warehouses and was giving instructions to a handy-looking boy who took the horse's reins from her.

I looked up at the warehouse. Big, painted capitals on the middle storey spelled out its purpose. PHILIPS AND LLOYD, TIMBER AND GENERAL MERCHANTS. Harry'd mentioned Arthur Philips and his wife over breakfast. Philips was Harry's cousin by marriage. He was also Jenkyn Hughes's partner. Was that going to be awkward for Harry?

From a distance, I watched Mrs Parry going down a passage between the Philips and Lloyd building and the one next to it.

I squared my shoulders, tried to look as if I had the right to walk wherever I liked, and followed her.

At the end, the cut-through turned into a narrow street running behind the backs of the warehouses. Most of the buildings looked like offices and one had the Philips and Lloyd name in big letters above the first-floor windows.

I couldn't see Mrs Parry. She must have gone inside. Damn. I couldn't follow her in. Had no business in there, did I?

Except ... Harry'd said he needed to go and talk to his cousin about the company's business arrangement with Hughes.

You know as much about it all as I do. Just use your judgement.

Right then, I would.

I quickly ran through what I should say.

My name is John Davies, I'm the acting coroner's assistant. No, better say *coroner's officer* – people were used to coroners' officers looking for inquest witnesses.

I'm the acting coroner's officer. I need to speak to Mr Philips.

With a bit of luck, I'd be able to wait outside his office – there was always a chance I'd overhear what Mrs Parry'd come for.

Before I could change my mind, I marched up to the door and pulled it open.

I don't know what I was expecting but it wasn't scuffed deal floors, plain board walls and low ceilings. Whatever money was to be made in shipping, Lloyd and Philips weren't spending it on impressive offices. But then, I was used to a solicitor's office. Most likely the kind of people who did shipping business didn't care about smart premises. They'd be more fussed about the state of the company's ships.

I looked about. No sign of Mrs Parry. She must've gone into a room behind one of the unpainted deal doors. I stopped a passing clerk of about my own age and asked where I'd find Mr Philips.

'Older or younger?'

'Younger.' I remembered the name Harry'd mentioned. 'Mr James Philips.'

The clerk jerked his thumb back over his shoulder, then thought better of it. 'I'll show you.'

I followed him to the back of the building. The door he stopped in front of looked like all the rest.

'This is Mr Philips's office,' he said, keeping his voice low so it didn't carry through the door. 'But you'd better wait. I saw one of his business partners going in a minute or two ago. They won't take kindly to being disturbed.'

I nodded. 'Thanks.'

'What d'you want him for, anyway?'

'I'm the coroner's officer. I need to speak to him on official business.'

His eyes widened. 'Coroner?' His voice was even lower, now. 'Who's dead? Anybody I know?'

I nearly said *How should I know who you know?* but I stopped myself just in time. Clerks know more of their employers' business than those employers ever suspect.

'We think he's a man called Jenkyn Hughes.'

The clerk suddenly had the look of a man who's put two and two together and made twenty-two. Because he'd realised what Mrs Parry was doing here or for some other reason?

'You saw Mrs Parry coming in,' I said, leaving the subject open.

'Yes. Crisis meeting, that's what they'll be having in there, sure as eggs.'

'Crisis?'

He chin-pointed along the corridor and we moved quietly away from the boss's door.

'If Jenkyn Hughes is dead, then yes. Him and Mr Philips are partners in this emigration scheme, you know that?'

I nodded. 'But why should there be a crisis?'

'Because not one of them can step into the others' shoes,' he said.

I waited. With any luck he'd want to show off what he knew. Turned out to be my lucky day.

'They've each got a third share in the venture, see,' he said, eyes flicking up and down the corridor in case anybody heard him. 'Mrs Parry's the one responsible for getting the ship built and provisioned up.' He glanced at the door of Mr Philips's office as if he thought Mrs Parry might have her ear pressed to the other side of it. 'Mr Hughes's job is – or *was* – to find people who wanted to emigrate, and act as their agent. Mr Philips's side of the business is supplying the new town with whatever he can sell over there at a profit – slate, mostly. Then he'll bring timber back the other way. From Canada. For his timber-supply business, see. All this railway building – you wouldn't believe how much timber's needed.'

I nodded again, trying to look as if I would believe it.

The clerk glanced nervously up and down again. 'If he's dead, the other two might be in trouble.'

'Because they'll have to find somebody else who can take over as agent, you mean?'

His voice said 'yes' but his tone said there was more to tell.

I waited but he didn't say anything else. Maybe he needed the coroner's officer to ask officially. It wouldn't be him tattling, then, would it? 'That's not the only reason, is it?'

'Well, it's just rumour, remember.'

'What is?'

'Will I have to say this at the inquest?'

'Depends. If we can find it out some other way – like Mrs Parry or Mr Philips saying they already know if I suggest it to them – then no.'

The need to tell me and the fear of getting into trouble were wrestling in him, I could see. 'This is important information,' I pushed. 'Billy Go-About's got somebody in custody and if he shouldn't be there...'

That decided him. He knew as well as I did how keen the police were to let a man go once they'd got hold of him.

'Hughes is a card player,' he said. 'Well, more than that. He gambles. Big money.' He dropped his voice till I could barely hear him. 'What I heard is, he's been borrowing money from the scheme, to pay his debts with.'

'Borrowing?'

He made a face. *You know what I mean.*

I stared at him. 'So the emigration scheme's missing some money, is it?'

He shoved his hands in his pockets, shrugged. 'I don't know – maybe he's paid back what he owes.'

'And maybe not?'

He just looked at me.

'If he's died without paying the scheme back, Mrs Parry and Mr Philips are in the shit, that's what you're telling me, isn't it?'

A sly look came over his face. 'Well ... maybe not quite as deep in it as you'd think.'

'Go on.'

He looked up the passageway to his boss's door, then back at me. 'Took out life insurance, didn't they?'

'On Jenkyn Hughes?'

He nodded. Know-it-all man of the world. 'Standard practice, of course, with risky ventures. But ... they took out a lot more insurance than usual. More than his share of the business was worth.' He stared at me. 'A lot more.'

'How do you know?'

A door opened, and both of us turned. A fat man came out into the passageway, crammed his hat on his head, and pulled the door to behind him. He turned to leave the building without even looking in our direction.

My heart was going like locomotive. Just from a door opening when I wasn't expecting it.

'Well?' I pushed 'Do you know about this insurance for a fact, or it is just clerks' gossip?'

'Know it for a fact. See papers, don't I?'

'When did you see them?' I don't know why I asked that but, later, I was glad I had.

'When?'

'Yes. If it's standard practice to insure partners' lives, there'll be a standard time to do it as well, I suppose?'

His eyes turned shifty. 'D'you know something about this already?'

I gave him a knowing look. Let him think I'd catch him out if he tried lying to me.

He licked his lips. Good, I'd made him nervous. 'Well. Funny thing. Mostly, people take out insurance at the beginning. You know, when they sign up as partners?'

I nodded but he didn't go on. Needed another push. 'But these three didn't?'

'No, they did.' His gaze twitched over my shoulder. 'But then Mr Philips and Mrs Parry took out another policy, together. On Jenkyn Hughes.'

When?'

'About six weeks ago.'

I had no idea how long it took to build a ship and start an emigration business but I had a fair idea that six weeks ago would've been pretty late in the day. 'And the partnership was formed when, exactly?'

'More than a year ago.'

I thought for a second. Money from life insurance was a motive for murder. My informant would see that as well as I did.

'How much did they insure Mr Hughes for?' I waited. 'I'm not being nosey, here. You understand that, don't you? I'm working for the coroner. If I need to know something, I can go to the life insurance offices and check. But I'd just as soon not waste the time.'

He stared at me. As if he was trying to pass the number from his head into mine through the air. 'It was a sum that'd make your eyes water. That's all I'm saying.' He saw me open my mouth and held his hands up. 'No. That's it. I'm not saying any more.'

Fair enough. He had his job to think about. I glanced at the door to Mr Philips's office. Still closed. 'This gambling. D'you know where Jenkyn Hughes did it?'

He stuffed his hands back in his pockets, shoulders hunched as if he'd just felt a chill on his back. 'Not for definite. It's just what I've heard, right? I'm not standing up in any inquest or court and saying anything about it.'

I spat on my palm and held my hand out to him. 'Just between us.'

We shook, and he sucked in a lungful of air as if he was determined to tell me all in one breath. 'There's a *smwglin* down on the docks where they play for potloads of money. Gentlemen go there as well.'

Gentlemen? In an illegal drinking den? Didn't sound very likely, but I wasn't going to get up his nose by telling him that.

'That's what I've heard, anyway. But I haven't seen it with my own eyes so I can't stand up in court and say it, can I?' I'd already got the message. He wasn't going to be a witness. Didn't he trust my handshake?

'All right then.' I gave him a little break then asked the question I should've asked at the beginning. 'When was the last time Jenkyn Hughes came here?'

He looked away, thinking. 'Three weeks ago? Can't remember exactly. He doesn't come here a lot – I think he mostly deals with Mrs Parry, up at Tresaith.'

Still using the present tense. Whatever I said, he wasn't ready to believe Hughes was dead, yet.

'That makes no sense,' I said. 'He was lodging over at Captain Coleman's. Why would he go all the way up to Tresaith when he could do business here?'

The sly look was back. 'Very charming to the ladies, Mr Hughes is. P'rhaps it's easier for him to get what he wants from Mrs Parry than from the boss here.'

I seriously doubted that he'd ever had any dealings with Mrs Parry, if that's what he thought. She didn't give away anything she didn't want to and I was pretty sure no amount of charm would change that.

'So, when he came here, that was the last time you saw him? You didn't see him in town or anywhere else?'

He shook his head, clear on this. 'No. Just here.'

'Thanks. What's your name, by the way?'

'Whoah! I told you, I'm not standing up at an inquest!'

'I'm not asking you to. But my boss might want to speak to you and I need to know who to ask for.' He still looked unhappy. 'I can always ask Mr Philips what your name is – I don't suppose he's got many clerks with hair the colour of yours.' It was bright ginger, even in the dim light of the passageway.

The glare he gave me then told me he'd happily punch me in the face. Fair play, nobody likes Hobson's choice.

'David Daniels,' he said, jaw stiff. 'But I'm telling you, I'll say nothing that'll get me in trouble with Mr Philips.'

While I waited, I made a plan. Mind you, Mrs Parry and Mr Philips weren't in any hurry and, by the time the door to the office opened, I'd talked myself out of my plan and back in to it at least twice. I jumped like a startled kitten when the latch clicked up, then straightened up away from the wall.

'Morning, Mrs Parry.'

She looked into my face. 'John Davies. What's your business here?'

I swallowed. I couldn't get used to the way she always behaved like a man. Left me feeling flat-footed for the right response.

'I'd appreciate a word with you and Mr Philips. Together, if you'd be so good.'

'Mr Probert-Lloyd too busy with more important people, is he?'

'Not at all. I know he wanted to speak to you himself. But he's been called home by an urgent family matter.'

Her eyes met mine. There should have been a clang. 'What kind of urgent family matter?'

Would Harry want his father's condition spread about? Probably not. But I knew it was important not to let these two feel slighted. 'His father's been struck with an apoplexy.'

She gazed at me steadily, as if she was weighing up my honesty. 'I'm sorry to hear that. Please pass on my sympathy to Mr Probert-Lloyd.' Then she turned and pushed the door open again. 'James? Seems we need to give an account of ourselves.'

Harry

I took the road through Llangoedmor. Though more up-hill and down-dale, it was a couple of miles shorter than the valley road through Llechryd. Sara was fresh and responded eagerly to my encouragement, breaking into a fast canter.

I was both desperate to get to Glanteifi and dreading my arrival. What condition would I find my father in? Would he even still be alive?

To my shame, I found myself transfixed by the thought that, if my father were to die, it was inconceivable that I should continue as acting coroner.

But what if he survived in a state of incapacity? Would I be expected to be at his side night and day?

The road was quiet. I kept what sight I possessed on the middle distance lest I needed to avoid cart or carriage and gave Sara her head. She knew she was going home and needed little guidance.

Home.

Glanteifi.

Seat of the Proberts, a family whose name I bore but whose blood I did not. On marrying into the estate, my father had been obliged to relinquish his own family name so that Glanteifi would continue to be owned by Proberts. He had added Lloyd, my mother's maiden name, on his marriage to her, an act which had always struck me as violently out of character.

That daily reminder that Welsh blood ran through my veins might have been enough, on its own, to awaken egalitarian sympathies within me; but fate had conspired to make me a thoroughgoing Radical. Following my mother's death, a concatenation of circumstances had ensured that I was brought up by a nurserymaid who, for reasons of her own, had taught me to consider myself no better than Glanteifi's servants. Consequently, as I grew from boy to man, I had come to feel that the ownership of such acreages as my father and his kind possessed was immoral; that natural justice was in no way served by an economic system in which a tiny few owned so much whilst the many owned so little.

Now, however, given that such possession was about to become my lot, I was faced with a stark question: did I have the courage to overthrow the accepted order?

The tenantry would not thank me for it; I knew perfectly well that they were likely to be as scandalised as the local squires by any suggestion that leaseholders might buy the freehold of the acres they farmed.

This – this damned decision was why I had fled to London, trained as a barrister, lived as if I had nothing further to do with Cardiganshire. And, had blindness not forced my hand, I might have continued to do so. Ormiston, my father's steward, could have been left in charge while I made my living at the bar, taking not a penny from the estate's revenues.

But that path was no longer open to me; I was now dependent, one way or another, on Glanteifi for my living.

I arrived in an unusually muted stableyard, and an unexpected feeling of dread filled me. Had my father died as I made my way home?

'Is there news?' I asked as I swung myself down from Sara's back. 'Is Dr Prendergast still here?'

'Yes, Mr Harry.' Michael, the head groom. 'We're all very sorry about what's come upon your father.'

Mr Harry. He was still alive, then; I knew the servants would insist on calling me Mr Probert-Lloyd the moment my father died.

As I walked towards the house, I heard my name called. Mrs Griffiths's small, upright figure, dark in her usual sober clothes, was easily visible against the pale stucco of the walls.

'You're here quicker than I thought,' she said. 'I was worried Twm might have to wait all day for you.'

'If I hadn't remembered an errand at the Black Lion, he would have. I was about to ride up to Tresaith.'

'Well, thank God he caught you in time.'

A chill hand wrapped its fingers around my heart. 'Is it that bad?'

'Dr Prendergast says that today and tonight will be critical.'

'Is he able to speak – conscious, even?'

'Barely. He seems aware that people are there, some of the time. But he can't speak – only make sounds.' Her voice wavered to a stop.

I hesitated. 'Shall I go up and see him?' Though I had ridden home post-haste to do exactly that, now I was here, I was afraid of what I would find. And afraid of my own reaction.

Perhaps Mrs Griffiths could see my wavering, for she was mercifully direct. 'Yes. Go up now, don't bother about your muddy things. Dr Prendergast wants to speak to you.'

Despite her injunction, I took the time to scrape my boots carefully before entering the house. Making my way through the subdued servants' quarters and out into the front hall, I stopped on the black-and-white tiles and drew in a long breath.

Then, more gingerly even than I had become used to doing, I set my feet to the shallow, curving staircase. With each step, I heard the heaviness of my own footfall and was reminded of the way I had bounded up the stairs as a boy, taking three at a time, my toes hardly touching the treads. Now, the staircase had never seemed so long. With every step, I dreaded what I would find in the bedroom at the end of the landing.

At the top of the stairs, I stopped to gather my thoughts and master them. Then, face set to greet whatever news Dr Prendergast had for me, I walked along the landing and opened the door.

For some reason, I had been expecting a darkened room but the curtains stood open to the low winter sun.

'Henry.' The doctor strode quietly across the room and clasped my hand. It was an unexpectedly intimate gesture and I had to prevent myself from pulling back.

'How is he?' I asked.

'The initial attack would have killed a lesser man.' He turned to look at my father's bed. 'However, at the moment he is unable to swallow, and if he does not regain the ability to drink and take nourishment...'

He did not need to complete the sentence.

'Do patients normally recover the ability to swallow?'

Prendergast turned back to me and I made out what I could of his face. He wore long side-whiskers, iron-grey like his hair.

Unbidden, Reckitt came to mind. His hair was brown, still that of a young man. Did Prendergast see him as a rival, or was Reckitt's oddness enough to ensure that nobody of any consequence would prefer him?

What strange thoughts spring to mind in dire circumstances.

'With a stroke as severe as this, I'm afraid there is always the possibility that no recovery will occur.' The doctor's voice was soft, regretful. Was it from professional courtesy or genuine feeling? I knew that he and my father had been acquainted for many years but whether they were friends I could not say.

'I'm sure it's a comfort to him to be attended by somebody whom he has known for so many years,' I said.

'Any service I can render allows me to repay a longstanding debt,' the doctor replied. 'When I first came into the district, your father was a good friend to me. He introduced me to the people who could make my career here a success. He understood what it is to have to make one's way in a place where one is unknown.'

I nodded, uncomfortable. It had not occurred to me to think of my father's early, friendless years in Cardiganshire in that way. In truth, I had seldom, if ever, thought about his youth at all.

Warily, I moved towards the bed. 'Will he hear me if I speak to him?'

'He seems aware of people's presence but that's all I can say.'

I stood where I hoped my father would be able to see me and leaned towards him.

'Father? It's me, Harry.' I felt foolish, as if I was speaking into a void. I could see him lying there but I could not see his face in any detail, could not tell whether it was twisted. Then, suddenly, I thought his eyes opened.

'Father? I'm here.' I did not know what else to say.

I saw his mouth open wide, like a baby bird searching for a beakful of food, and my sudden unease bloomed into full-blown fear when he produced a harsh, effortful sound that seemed to have been forced out of him rather than being uttered in the normal way.

Without thinking, I put out a hand, as you would to a wounded animal. 'It's all right, Father, I'm here.'

His hand clutched at mine, gripping with unexpected force. Again, that sound, more urgent this time, as he tried to raise himself from the bed.

'I think perhaps he's trying to say your name,' Prendergast said.

As if in confirmation, the sound came again and again as my father struggled and gripped my hand.

'I'm here,' I repeated, stupidly, wishing to God that I knew words that would calm him, stop him making that terrible noise.

Suddenly, the pressure on my hand loosened and my father sank back on the bed with a gasp. Now a different sound came from him. A thin, panting sound, broken up as if to form unintelligible words. Then it stopped. His hand gripped at mine again and I saw Prendergast moving quickly around to the other side of the bed. He bent over my father.

'What?' I asked. 'What's happening?'

'I fear he may be having another attack.'

I backed away from the bed. Was this my doing? Had my presence agitated my father unduly?

The last time we had spoken, I had as good as accused him of being more concerned with maintaining his own position than with seeing justice done. I had meant to go and see him the next day, to apologise and smooth things over between us but he had left the house before I had finished dressing. Had he been dwelling, ever since, on my opinion of him? And if he had, if my solipsism had contributed in some way to the apoplexy that had struck him, was it now too late to hope that I could put things right between us?

John

James Philips's office was exactly what you'd've expected from the state of the rest of the building. It had one small window, bare floorboards and exactly three pieces of furniture. A desk, which looked as if it had been manhandled from cart to destination more times than was good for it. A carver chair with a cushion on the seat for the user of the desk. And another chair, without arms or cushion, in front of the desk. No paintings on the walls, just shelves stacked with ledgers and small boxes.

No desks for clerks, either. David Daniels and those like him worked their fingers to the bone elsewhere.

Mrs Parry moved the armless chair to the other side of the desk and sat down. Mr Philips shot her a look and sank back into his carver.

Taking the chairs was meant to show me my place, but standing or sitting made no difference to me. I wasn't just a clerk, here, I was the coroner's assistant. And that gave me the coroner's authority.

I started putting my plan into action straight away. No niceties. Be civil but take them off their guard.

'The body of a man we believe to be Mr Jenkyn Hughes has been found, stripped naked and facially disfigured, on the beach at Tresaith,' I began. I was pleased with 'facially disfigured'. Mr Schofield would approve. No sensational penny-blood talk about a 'man with no face'.

'I understand that you were both in business with him as part of what people call the American Scheme.'

Eyes on me, they waited. I'd picked up the spade and they were going to wait and see what sort of hole I'd dig myself into.

'Is that information correct?'

'It's properly called the Cardigan-Ohio Emigration Company,' Philips said.

No wonder people called it the American Scheme. Who'd want to come out with that mouthful every time?

'Thank you.' I wrote it down in my notebook. Taking my time over making notes was part of the plan. I hoped it'd put them on edge.

'What makes you think it's Jenkyn Hughes?' Philips asked.

I'd had a long time to think about this while I was waiting outside his office and I didn't want to get scoffed at for identifying a body by a handful of coins. So, instead of answering the question, I asked one of my own. 'When did you last see Mr Hughes?'

It didn't work. Philips just tapped the desk with a hard finger. 'I asked you a question. What makes the coroner think that the dead man is Jenkyn Hughes?'

My knees began to shake, but I put as much confidence into my voice as I could. Thank God I'd practised all this in my head.

'I'm afraid I'm not at liberty to say, Mr Philips. When the inquest is re-convened, all the evidence will be laid out. Meanwhile, I've been asked to speak to people who might be called as witnesses in order to discover as much as possible about the circumstances of Mr Hughes's death.'

Neither of them said anything. I flipped a couple of pages back and pretended to read. I had to work to keep my voice steady, my fingers were jerking with every heartbeat. 'Mrs Parry, you last saw Mr Hughes a couple of days before you left Tresaith on business a fortnight or so ago, is that right?'

Mrs Parry stared at me, face blank, eyes shrewd. I was pretty sure she knew I hadn't just read those words. 'Yes,' she said. 'That's right.'

I sucked in a breath as I turned to Philips. 'And you, sir?'

I hadn't called anybody *sir* since I left Mr Davies's school in Adpar. Mr Schofield had been clear on the matter. *I am your employer, not your master, and you will both address me and refer to me when speaking to clients, as Mr Schofield.* I was banking on James Philips being the kind of man who liked to be called sir.

His face was as expressionless as Mrs Parry's but his eyes weren't half as shrewd. He struck me as the sort of man who's generally pretty pleased with himself. His hair and beard were snipped close and neat, as if they were barbered every week, and his coat looked new and expensive. Its seams lay very flat and it was fitted snug to his body, as if it'd been made for him very recently.

'I can't exactly remember,' he said. 'I didn't have as much to do with him as Mrs Parry did.'

'But you were equal partners in the Cardigan-Ohio Emigration Company?'

He blinked. Did he think I was too stupid to remember the American scheme's proper name? Arrogant pizzle.

'Yes,' he said. 'But each of us had different areas of responsibility.'

I waited. It was a trick I'd got from Harry – give most people a silence and they can't help filling it up. Mind, I knew I wouldn't get away with that trick with Mrs Parry.

'I'd put in my share up front, to start getting the ship built. My part of the scheme involves import and export. I had no reason to see Hughes.'

Hughes. Not Jenkyn or Jenkyn Hughes or even Mr Hughes. Just Hughes. It was cold. No love lost there. I made a note of what he'd said. Slowly. The information tied in with what David Daniels had said about not seeing the American here much.

I finished writing and looked up at James Philips. 'So you only knew Mr Hughes as a business partner, sir? You didn't associate with him for any other reason?'

'Such as?' He was wary.

'Socially?'

'No.'

I was pretty sure he was lying. The answer had been too quick, too definite.

'Can you tell me a bit more about Mr Hughes' part in the scheme?' I wanted to give him every opportunity to let something slip.

But he wasn't having any of it. 'I think Mrs Parry'd be better placed to tell you about that.'

So I turned my attention back to her. The difference between the two of them was striking. Him in his expensive coat, a silk necktie around his shirt collar and a watchchain draped just so from his waistcoat pocket. Her in her man's cloak over a working woman's *betgwn* and apron, a squat hat on her head that had nothing to do with looks and everything to do with keeping her warm on the drive down from Tresaith.

'Our friend Jenkyn liked to see himself as a sharp businessman.' Matter-of-fact, just a suggestion of an indulgent smile. No coldness towards Hughes from her. But then, maybe she was canny enough to know that a bit of warmth would look less suspicious. 'The money for his third of the business comes from the fees the emigrants pay him,' she said. 'But he had something else on the go, as well. To make a bit of seed-corn money for his next venture.'

'Did he have another business venture in mind?' I asked.

'Not that he'd told us. But men like Jenkyn always have something up their sleeves.'

I nodded. 'So can you tell me what he was doing to make this additional money?'

'He was bringing coal up from Pembrokeshire. Some anthracite and some cheaper coal as well. Mostly for the limekilns at Tresaith. But also to sell up and down the coast.'

'To other lime burners?' There'd certainly be little or no market for anthracite amongst the farmers on the coast. If they were lucky, they burned culm. If not, they burned turf and brushwood faggots and any dead wood they could find. There might be the odd one here and there who was doing well enough to afford brown coal but even they'd be pretty few and far between.

'It was mostly for the kilns, yes. And I bought some of the anthracite off him. For The Ship.'

I could see why she'd want it. Anthracite burns brighter and hotter than any other fuel and, with The Ship standing empty whenever she was away, it'd be no quick job to warm it up again. Walls that thick hold the cold.

Then, something occurred to me. 'Would the boats that brought the lime up from Pembrokeshire bring Mr Hughes' coal at the same time?'

'Only the coal I was buying off him to fire the lime. No more than that.'

'Does Teff Harris unload coal as well as limestone?'

Jenkyn Hughes wouldn't have got far playing cards against Mrs Parry. She gave nothing away. 'Teff Harris'll do most things for money,' she said.

'Just for money?' I asked. 'I remember you saying he wanted to take his family to America. Might he have done a deal with Mr Hughes for labour in exchange for a reduction in the price of his ticket?'

Mrs Parry raised one eyebrow about a quarter of an inch. 'Possibly.'

I made them wait while I wrote another pointless note. 'Can either of you think of anybody who might have been glad to see Mr Hughes dead? Anybody with a grudge against him? Anybody he'd made an enemy of?'

For the first time, Mrs Parry and Mr Philips looked at each other.

Philips turned to me. 'He wasn't well liked. Not what we're used to here. He was loud. A bit too pleased with himself.'

Hah! I thought. Pot. Kettle.

'But he was a sound-enough businessman.' Mrs Parry put her tuppence worth in. 'When you're in business with someone, you don't have to like them. Just trust them.'

'And you trusted Mr Hughes?'

A flicker of something crossed her face. 'Yes, I did. I wouldn't have gone into business with him otherwise.'

Was she lying? At the very least, her choice of tense was interesting. Not *I wouldn't have been in business with him* but *I wouldn't have gone into business with him*. Had she trusted Jenkyn Hughes in the beginning but come to regret going into business with him later? Dr Reckitt'd be like a dog with two tails if he heard that Hughes's trustworthiness had slipped. He'd put it all down to the famous lump.

'We still haven't formally identified the body,' I told them. 'Do either of you know of any identifying marks Mr Hughes might've had – scars, birthmarks, anything?'

We'd seen nothing that you could've described as distinctive at the view so it was a surprise when Mrs Parry nodded.

'Yes. You'll find a scar – quite a recent one – here on his ribs.' She demonstrated on herself.

I must have looked scandalised because she gave me a twisted smile.

'He came in to The Ship with blood on his waistcoat. I insisted on looking at the wound and dressing it. He tried to explain it away. But I could see he'd been knifed.'

Harry

The sky in the window clouded and cleared by turns and, every half an hour or so, I rose to shake the stiffness from my limbs and keep the fire fed.

My father had been quiet since the easing of his second attack but it was the quiet of insensibility rather than of calm. Dr Prendergast had sat with me for an hour or so before excusing himself and promising to return in the morning unless he was summoned earlier.

As he left, in spite of his protestations of long friendship with my father, I could not help recalling Reckitt's claim that doctors were known to leave deathbeds so that they would be owed another fee when they returned to sign the death certificate.

Reckitt. What would he give to be able to see into my father's brain now, to see what had caused his abrupt descent into inarticulate sound-making, the paralysis of his right side that Prendergast had described to me, the potentially fatal inability to swallow?

Unwilling to contemplate the enthusiasm with which Reckitt would discuss the exact cause of my father's apoplexy, I distracted myself by recalling his examination of the corpse on Tresaith beach. At the time, his decision to carry out the autopsy on the wet sand had seemed entirely pragmatic. However, seen through the eyes of his detractors, I could not help but acknowledge a certain Canute-like quality to the whole thing; the surgeon cutting, dissecting, examining and probing as the tide drew ever closer to the table on which he was working.

In the event, Reckitt's thorough dissection of Hughes's body had added nothing to our understanding of how he had died. Admittedly, the autopsy examination had ruled out other causes, and had raised an odd little footnote in the form of the tumour in Hughes's brain, but the outcome had been as blunt as the dint to his head. The American's death had been the result of a sudden violence – a blow of an obvious, physical kind.

My father lay on the bed beside me, felled by an attack less visible, but scarcely more subtle. I gazed, sidelong, at his motionless, effigy-like form beneath the cover.

Would he revive once more, or would his breathing simply become shallower and shallower, each breath separated from the last by longer and longer intervals until he passed from life, almost imperceptibly, to death?

A verse of John Donne's slipped into my mind.

As virtuous men pass mildly away,
And whisper to their souls to go,
Whilst some of their sad friends do say
'The breath goes now', and some say, 'No'...

Was my father a virtuous man? I had always thought him conscientious and dutiful but virtue was a different matter. Duty bound him, in my opinion, too uncritically to the role of squire, magistrate, upholder of family status.

But could I do differently?

I pushed the question aside and turned to my father again. Studying him, as best I could, I felt a sudden flicker of panic; how would I know if he had died? Leaning over him, I cocked my head to his face, my ear a bare inch from his mouth. For what felt like a minute I could hear nothing but the obtrusive beating of my own heart, becoming louder and more insistent in proportion to my fear. Then, as if the faculty of hearing had been extruded from my ears and into the air between us, I caught the faintest trace of breath. He was still alive.

Without thinking, I put my hand out to him. At some stage, someone had removed his jacket and he was lying under the covers in his shirt and unbuttoned waistcoat, his arms left free.

His hand was cold but, as I clasped it, his fingers feebly gripped my own.

I was startled. I had been expecting no response to my touch and this answering pressure made me uncomfortable. But, though I flinched, I managed not to let go.

'It's me, Father. Harry.'

I knew that, in his right mind, he would laugh at my words, call them fatuous. *Who else would address me as Father?* But who knew what delirium the apoplexy might have caused? I could not be confident that he knew me, that he did not mistake me for his firstborn, George, dead these thirty years.

I remembered, with the greatest possible clarity, the words he had used when I had finally brought myself to broach the subject of my half-brother during my investigations the previous year.

When you were born, it was my greatest wish that you would not grow up to be like George. Not in any way. I was ashamed to have fathered such a person.

His wish had been granted. I had grown up to be entirely unlike George. But had I brought my father greater pride? Now, with his hand in mine, his fingers curled with no more strength than those of a newborn around my own, the question seemed a stark and necessary one.

I had certainly never gone out of my way to give my father a good opinion of me. Indeed, many people, observing my childhood and young manhood, might have said the opposite. I had chosen the company of servants over his. I had spent my school holidays making hay with labourers and rabbiting with stableboys. As John had pointed out so painfully, I had persisted in speaking Welsh when, by custom, I should have begun using English as soon as I started learning Latin. I had been banished from the house when I had fallen in love with a dairymaid and, not two months ago, I had defied my father and investigated the death of that same dairymaid when her bones had been discovered in a nearby wood. I might have been a barrister and well-thought of in London legal circles prior to my sight failing me, but what had I done in Cardiganshire that would make other men envious of the son George Probert had fathered in his later years?

I gazed at him as best I could, a small part of me wishing that I could see his face, the greater part glad that my last clear memory of him would not include the drooping eye and drooling mouth that Prendergast had hinted at.

I could not bring myself to think of my father brought so low, did not know how to respond to a man so toppled from the place he had occupied for my entire life. Always, I had been the underdog, and fought him from that position; I had never exerted myself to imagine what it would be like to find myself the stronger of us. But circumstances may alter our views in unanticipated ways and recent words of Lydia Howell's came to mind.

'I know all too well,' she had written, *'that, whilst in one situation a particular opinion may be defended with perfect rationality, in another*

situation that same opinion may come to look unfeasibly utopian.
Consider, if you will, my current circumstances as compared with the life
I previously lived and tell me, if you can, that I may express the same
views now as I did then, and live them out with equal vigour.'

Of course, in reading this, Mrs Griffiths would assume that Lydia was
referring to her life before becoming a governess. I, however, knew
her to be speaking of a different life entirely.

'It may be easy to assume that everybody should share one's philosophy,
that if only the whole world would acquiesce to such a shining example
of reasonableness, mankind would be a happier race. But what <u>might be</u>
is coloured, as I have discovered to my cost, by what <u>is</u> and, when one is
constrained where previously one was free, it becomes more difficult to
assert that the way in which most people live could be altered for the better
if only they would take courage and fling off the shackles of custom. I have
been forced to realise that freedom of action encourages freedom of thought
whilst having one's actions constrained brings constraint to one's thoughts
and one's ideals. It diminishes one.'

Stiff from sitting, I relinquished my father's hand and stood.

'I'm not leaving,' I said, forcing myself to speak as though he could
understand perfectly 'I just need to stand up and walk about for a
minute.'

I moved over to the window and gazed, obliquely, at the world
outside. My father's room overlooked the river's course towards
Cenarth and I knew the lie of the meadows on either side, the woods
to the west. All those things my residual sight was able to confirm
but I could see nothing else, nothing that was particular to this

moment. No movement of bird or otter on the river. No men in the bare, dun-coloured winter meadows. The sky – a bright, promising blue when I had entered the house – was washed out now, darker on the eastern horizon than over the woods to the west. The afternoon was wearing away.

I had been here since a little after noon. It seemed a lifetime.

I thought of John, abandoned in Cardigan. What had he done in my absence? I hoped he had gone to Tresaith to speak to Mrs Parry. It was essential that we identify this cousin who had swooped into Hughes's lodgings and removed all his effects.

Also in Tresaith, of course, was Bets Parry. I was eager to learn the truth behind her suggestion that Jenkyn Hughes had been a womaniser.

The other possibility was that John might have gone to Llandysul to look for Teff Harris's wife. If she could not be found, things would look bleak for her husband.

I tried not to fret about how John would fare on his own. Though I was aware that most coroners' officers worked at the coroner's instruction rather than at his side, John's situation was different. He was not a policeman, nor even an old-fashioned parish constable, he was a coroner's assistant specifically because of the limitations imposed upon me by my sight.

I looked, sidelong, out of the window. Would I be able to function as coroner if I had only the kind of officers normally assigned to the role? Possibly, but not with anything like the efficiency I enjoyed with John. If I was going to stand for election, I desperately needed either to persuade him to continue to work with me or to find an alternative assistant.

Again, I wondered whether the way forward was to offer to pay for his articles at Schofield's office. But that presented problems of its own. Not only might John feel that his services were being bought against his better judgement; if he was to be articled, Mr Schofield could quite reasonably protest that he should not be absent from the office at my whim. Furthermore, if John were to become a solicitor in his own right, it was impossible to imagine him agreeing to ride about the countryside with me investigating deaths. He would have his living to make.

No. I had to think of an alternative solution.

John

I barely noticed anything on my way from the docks to the workhouse. My head was still full of my conversation with Mrs Parry and James Philips.

I could tell that Mrs Parry'd thought I'd be all 'many thanks and good day to you,' once she'd told me about Jenkyn Hughes's knife wound. Corpse identified, knife wielder supplied as candidate for murder, job done. But I'd still had the last part of my plan to put into action.

My heart was sprinting in my chest but I wasn't going to give up now, however cowardly my innards were. So, as smooth as I could, without so much as introducing the subject, I'd asked, 'Why did you take out such a large sum in life insurance on Mr Hughes?'

I couldn't watch both of them at once so I fixed my eyes on James Philips. I was pretty sure he'd give away more than Mrs Parry. And I was right. He frowned and his face flushed. 'That's a confidential business matter! How dare you?'

My heart was still trying to run away but I forced myself to keep my eyes on him. 'I'm sorry to have to ask but it's a business matter which concerns a man who has died in suspicious circumstances. The acting coroner needs to look into everything that might have a bearing on that.'

Self-protection, that was – using phrases Mr Schofield would've been pleased with. I was shaking, now. Well out of my depth. Whatever I said, I had no real idea whether the coroner was allowed to look at confidential business documents. I was just praying these two didn't know either.

'I hope you're not suggesting that Mrs Parry and I had anything to do with Hughes' death?' James Philips's voice had gone up an octave.

'No. Not at all. But I am interested in why you took out a second life insurance policy on Mr Hughes?'

I watched Mr Philips's Adam's apple go up and down. He wasn't happy about that question. 'That's a confidential matter,' he tried again but Mrs Parry cut him off.

'Stop looking so guilty, James! It's not a crime to guard against losses.'

'No but—'

'If you're worried about the scandal, give it up. That horse has bolted. Next time we see it will be at the inquest.'

She turned back to me. 'I don't know how you know about this, John Davies, but you're clearly a capable young man so you probably already know that Jenkyn Hughes was a gambler. And that he was in debt. I don't doubt that it was one of his gambling cronies who put a knife to his ribs. Mr Philips and I had to protect our business. As it's turned out, it's fortunate we did.'

'Fortunate for you?'

'And for the people who'd bought a place on the Cardigan-Ohio scheme. It was their future he was gambling with. Without the life insurance, the scheme would be bankrupt and nobody'd be going to America.'

'But their investment's safe now, is it?' I asked. 'All money paid to Jenkyn Hughes will be covered?'

'Bondholders' money will. We'll have to see about the rest.'

'Didn't everybody who'd paid get a bond?'

'Jenkyn was allowing people to pay in installments if they needed to.'

'But he must've been keeping a record of who'd paid what?'

Her eyes were steady on mine. They held not a trace of pity. 'So far, we've seen no records. Jenkyn Hughes was responsible for the emigrants and for their money. If he kept no records, we can't be held liable.'

Anger boiled up inside me. My family could so easily have been one of those paying in installments. 'You don't feel morally obliged to honour what people have already paid?'

The question didn't ruffle a single one of Mrs Parry's feathers. 'Not without records, Mr Davies. There are no moral obligations in business. Only contractual ones.'

With my hands shaking even more than before, I made a note. *No moral obligations in business.* Then I changed the subject.

'Did Jenkyn Hughes actually tell you that he was knifed by another gambler?'

Mrs Parry sucked her tongue. 'No.'

I waited but she didn't say anything more. James Philips was looking anywhere but at me, as if I might disappear if he ignored me long enough, but Mrs Parry's eyes never left me. And they were sharp, her eyes, sharp as ice. She was one of those people who could see without being seen, if you know what I mean.

'Did he tell you he had gambling debts?' I asked her.

James Philips snorted. Neither of us paid him any attention.

'No. He wouldn't've admitted anything like that to us.'

'To keep up appearances?'

'To stop us going down to the *smwglins* and pulling him out by his ear.'

By 'us' she obviously meant herself. I couldn't see Philips walking into a drinking den. Not in that coat.

'So how did you find out? About the gambling?'

Her face didn't change. She just blinked, once, quite slowly, as if her eyes were dry from staring at me. 'It pays to know what your business partners are up to, Mr Davies. Nasty surprises'll bankrupt you if you're not careful.'

And she was careful, I thought, as I urged Seren up the hill towards Cardigan workhouse and the corpse. That much was quite clear.

Harry

Deciding that I had had my fill of unprofitable introspection, I opened the door and called down into the hall. 'Wil-Sam?'

Feet scrambled in the hall below and pounded up the stairs.

'Yes, Mr Harry?' He always answered me in English, regardless of the language I'd addressed him in; Wil-Sam was keen to better himself.

'You came up those stairs at a rate,' I remarked. 'Did you go and see Mrs Griffiths about your boots, like I told you?'

'Yes, I did!' He laughed at his own audacity.

'And what did she say?'

'Same as you, Mr Harry – I mustn't go round in boots too small. There were some old ones in the bootroom cupboard and they're much better.'

William Samuel Jones had been our hall boy – carrier-out of all menial errands and taker of messages for the household – for a little over a year. In that time, not surprisingly, the hand-me-down boots that had come with him had started to pinch and I had found him hobbling about the house one day the previous week. Like all the servants, he knew better than to bother Isabel Griffiths with things of no account but I had assured him that our housekeeper would not want her hall boy crippled by his own footwear.

'Right, Wil-Sam, do you know if Twm has brought my things back from Cardigan yet?'

'No, Mr Harry, I don't.'

'Go and ask Mrs Griffiths for me, will you? If the answer is yes, tell her I'd like you to bring my bag up to me, all right?'

'Yes, Mr Harry!' And he was gone at a clatter, keen to pay me back for his new boots.

When the knock came a few minutes later, however, it was not Wil-Sam who entered at my invitation but Isabel Griffiths herself.

'How is he?' Her voice wavered uncertainly. It was only natural; she was not accustomed to being in my father's bedroom, and I do not suppose she had ever been in it while he was in his bed.

'Quiet,' I said. 'Resting, I hope.'

She came forward. 'I brought your bag. I thought I'd bring it up myself – I wanted to let you know there's a letter from your friend in Ipswich here as well.'

'I don't want to leave him,' I said, quietly. 'Would you mind reading it to me here?'

Mrs Griffiths did not reply immediately. I wondered whether she was looking over at my father's unconscious form.

'You think he'd object to your being here?' I suggested.

'I'm sure he wouldn't be so rude as to object once you'd invited me, Harry. But I'm sure he'd *mind*. Me seeing him like this, I mean.'

I knew that the kind thing would be to let her make up her own mind but I was tired of my own company and keen to hear from Lydia.

'I don't feel comfortable leaving him,' I said. 'And I have nothing to do but sit here and think. My own thoughts are not the best company.'

She sighed. 'Very well.'

I moved my chair to the fireside and we sat facing each other on either side of the small hearth.

Prior to my loss of vision, the tearing of a sealing wafer had been just one more barely-noticed sound in a world full of sights. Now, when letters brought news of life outside Cardiganshire, it was a sound that made my heart beat more quickly.

Lydia's letter began with congratulations on my temporary position and gratifying compliments as to my suitability for the task. She went on to reflect on the anguish attendant upon sudden death far from home.

'It saddens me,' Mrs Griffiths read, *'that a person should die alone, as this poor man on Tresaith beach did, uncomforted by friends or family. I am reminded, inevitably, of my poor brother's death. Though I take comfort from the fact that I was with him at the end, the pain of having to bury him where we were, far from all who knew him, was very great and I would not have considered doing so had I possessed the means to take his body home and bury him next to my father.'*

The recitation stopped. Isabel Griffiths required an explanation.

'Her brother, Nathaniel, died on the way to his new parish,' I said, carefully speaking the truth while knowing that I was misleading her. 'She was travelling with him, intending to be his housekeeper.'

'Poor dab!' Mrs Griffiths was moved. 'I hadn't heard that he'd died.'

I did not reply immediately. I was trying desperately to recall how Lydia had accounted for her failure to correspond with Nathaniel's congregation at Treforgan.

'Nobody, locally, had met Lydia,' I said eventually, 'so she wouldn't have known who to write to. By the time a new minister could reasonably be expected to be in the manse, I think she'd reached a point where she couldn't bear the thought of recounting the details of his illness and death again.'

'Yes. I'd feel the same.'

Her tone indicated a fellow-feeling born of shared experience and, to my utter chagrin, I realised that I knew nothing about her family. As a child you take the adults in your world for granted, their presence a given, requiring no explanation. But my failure to rectify this situation since I had returned home now seemed shameful.

'Do you have brothers, Mrs Griffiths? Or sisters?'

'Three brothers and a sister, as it happens. All younger than me and all living, thank God.' She paused for a second or two. 'But I well remember the death of my mother. Straight away afterwards, you're caught up in all the mourning and the way things have to be done. You write and tell anybody at a distance that you think needs to know – and that's all right. It's part of every death, like sitting for the wake and marking the month. But, later, when people came to the forge who didn't know she'd died – then it was hard to talk about it.'

I nodded. 'Your father was a blacksmith?'

'Yes. In Moylegrove.'

I nodded, but my thoughts were torn away from Isabel Griffiths's early life to my own current preoccupations. Moylegrove was where Jenkyn Hughes's alleged cousin was supposed to live.

Mrs Griffiths raised the letter and resumed her reading.

I am glad to know that John Davies is going to be working with you again. He seemed a competent and intelligent young man who might do a great deal better than solicitor's clerk. Working with you will expand his horizons, I am sure.'

I caught something in Isabel Griffiths's voice. 'Don't you approve of my expanding John's horizons, Mrs Griffiths?'

She sat very still and I could read nothing in her posture. 'It's not for me to say anything about who you employ or in what capacity,' she said.

'But if I were to ask your opinion?'

The letter came to rest in her lap once more, and she gave a soft sigh. 'Seeing new, exciting horizons is all very well. As long as they're within your reach. But showing somebody a life they might dearly wish for but can't have is cruel.'

'But who knows what's within John Davies's reach?' I protested. 'Your own life tells you that you may aim higher than you dreamed, surely? Did you think, as a blacksmith's daughter, that you would one day run a house like this?'

'No, Harry. I thought one day I would run a house of my own.'

Her voice was calm, kind; but I was so discomfited by her words that she might as well have slapped me.

'You say I run this house,' she went on, 'and that's true. I've been happy to run it. But I would have been happier with a husband and a home of my own. If I upset your father–' She faltered, worrying, perhaps, that he was listening. 'If I upset him, he could turn me out and I'd have nowhere to go and nothing to depend on but the charity of my family.' She paused and, in spite of the discomfort her words caused me, I willed her to go on, anxious to understand the uncertain truth of a life I had always taken for granted as settled and secure.

'To the maids and the footmen and to young Wil-Sam,' she said, 'I'm Mrs Griffiths, queen of the house. Perhaps I'm that to you, too.' I heard the small, sad smile in her voice. 'But I have no more claim on my place here than Elsie-Margaret, who arrived a month ago. I may be running the house because there's no mistress but I'm still a servant, Harry.'

I swallowed. 'This is why I don't want to be squire,' I told her. 'This business of gentlemen always living in houses that are ludicrously too big for them, so big that they require an army of servants to run – servants who must live in, not employees who can come and go to their own homes.'

'But those servants are better off in the big houses, Harry. Most of the girls and boys we employ can't live under their parents' roof because there are too many mouths to feed. You won't have been able to see but Elsie-Margaret's put on at least half a stone since she's been working here and eating three meals a day.'

'That's not the point though, is it? The big houses don't *exist* to provide employment!'

'Don't they?'

Her question pulled my gaze to her in surprise, and she disappeared into the whirlpool.

'What would you do, Harry? Sell this house and live in a Newcastle Emlyn bow-front with a cook and a girl coming in every day?'

'Why not? That's what my mother's cousin, Mr Philips in Cardigan, does.'

'And is he a justice of the peace? Does he make decisions that affect the whole of the county, the way your father and the other county magistrates do?'

'No, he's a merchant. He's responsible for a great deal of the wealth which the magistrates spend!'

'I never thought to see you turn your back on your family's traditions, Harry. I thought you'd come to your senses, with time.'

'But they're *not* my family's traditions, Mrs Griffiths! I'm not a Probert by blood. I have no right to Glanteifi. I'm a Lloyd – grandson of a Cardigan solicitor.'

'And of an English landowner. Just as much.'

'If I have to choose a family tradition,' I said, 'I choose the Lloyd one.'

'We aren't put here to choose, Harry,' she said, quietly. 'All we can do is accept the place God has put us in and make the best of it.'

I couldn't help myself. 'Is it? Ask Lydia Howell what Nathaniel preached. According to him there is no Greek or Jew, male or female, slave or freeman in the Kingdom of God. Everybody's equal!'

'And is that why you're corresponding with his sister so confidingly?' she asked, her voice still low, as if she did not want to disturb my father. 'Because you were so taken by her brother's ideas?'

Her words pulled me up short. *Was* I corresponding with Lydia because of Nathaniel? An image – clear and sharp as only memories were, now – came to mind; Nathaniel Howell in a huge straw wig, face blacked, eyes blazing in the light of lanterns and torches, shouting the challenges of Rebecca and being cheered to the echo by the band that followed him. Was that figure the reason why I looked forward to every new letter from Lydia? Was I looking to hear that same challenge, that same catch-me-if-you-can devilment?

'No, Mrs Griffiths,' I said. 'I'm corresponding with Lydia Howell because I may go mad if I do not hear views that are in agreement with my own every once in a while.'

Lydia's letter finished, Mrs Griffiths and I parted friends, as I devoutly hoped we always would, and she went back to ordering the household. But I was left to ponder her parting words.

'Of course, you'll have to find somebody to take over the inquest now, things being as they are.'

I knew she was right. That was exactly what I should do.

I was simply not ready to do it yet.

John

Cardigan workhouse. From the front entrance, you might have mistaken it for a mansion. High walls with gables in the roof, long windows and fine stonework. But, once you went through into the yards, there was a grim feeling to the place. It was in the air. The quietness of it. There were dozens of people in these buildings – men, women, children – but you'd never have known they were there. There was no singing, no cheerful shouting, no sound of playing. Just that ringing 'tonk' of hammers breaking road-stone. The female inmates did other work, but you wouldn't hear linen being washed or oakum picked.

The sun was a bare touch on the back of my neck as I walked through the damp, grey courtyards. The man who'd been called to take me to the dead house at the back of the site hadn't spoken when he was given his instruction, just started off walking. Hadn't even looked around to see if I was following him.

Word of 'the man with no face' would've gone around town quicker than a dirty joke, so I'd asked the workhouse master whether anybody'd been to see the corpse before me. There was a type of person who'd stand in a queue and pay a penny to see a face like that.

The master's response was terse. 'A few.'

I pictured the timewasters – mob-handed and giggling. But even timewasters may know a man.

'Nobody's come forward to the coroner with a name,' I told him. 'Has anybody said anything to you?'

They hadn't. But that didn't mean he hadn't been recognised. Any one of the gawpers might've done what I was here to do, and had a look at the dead man's ribs for a knife scar.

For the umpteenth time I tried to remember whether any of the jurors had mentioned a partly-healed wound on his ribs. There'd been talk of a scar here and there from the first couple of pairs to see him but then Harry'd started telling jurors he only wanted them to testify about wounds that might've happened around the time of the man's death. Fresh wounds. The gash Mrs Parry had described had been serious enough to bleed through Jenkyn Hughes's waistcoat but not to threaten his life.

'Just here,' she'd said, putting her fingers to her own ribs just below her left breast and looking me in the eye. 'That's where it was.'

My guide stopped, jerked his head at a low, whitewashed building, then turned and stomped away without a word. I watched him go. His jacket was frayed at collar and hem, and you could tell from the way his boots sounded that he had no stockings. If he hadn't been so surly I'd've felt sorry for him.

I opened the rattling plank door. I supposed there was no need to have a well-fitting one on a store for dead bodies – not going to feel the cold, were they?

If what Harry'd said about quicklime drying a body out so it wouldn't stink was true, it hadn't worked on our corpse – he'd begun to smell pretty badly. Then again, if he'd been clothed, the lime probably hadn't been able to do its job.

Somebody'd wrapped him in an old sheet. It'd been sides-to-middled at one time and, when I pulled it open, the hemmed edges felt as thin as muslin under my fingers. If I didn't have to look at that face, I wasn't going to, so I managed to leave his head covered and just get at the hairy torso of him. Had a bit of a nasty moment when

I saw the crude seam where Dr Reckitt'd stitched all his innards back in, but I swallowed hard and pulled myself together.

The dim light from the small windows was enough to see that his skin was rotting. Even when Reckitt had done the autopsy examination it hadn't looked right. Loose and soft as if a fingertip'd pull it off his flesh. Hoped I could touch it without heaving my guts up.

Gingerly, I felt about under the hair of his chest. Found the wound pretty quick, thank God. About an inch and a half long, it was, but if it'd been deep when it was done, I couldn't tell. The edges had closed together. Most likely, it'd been a slash rather than a stab. Or Hughes'd jumped back smartish when the knife came at him.

Had Hughes got into a fight at the *smwglins* or had he been attacked elsewhere? Because this *was* Jenkyn Hughes, no doubt about that any more. Mrs Parry'd doctored a wound in a very specific place on her business partner, and here it was on our corpse.

Gravely ill father or not, I knew Harry'd want to know.

Harry

In the wake of John's brief visit with news from the dead house, I felt more alone than I had done before. That morning, I had been acting coroner; now, my role was suspended and I had had to cede responsibility to John, who – despite a valiant attempt to present the things he had discovered in a calm and businesslike way – was very obviously reveling in his new autonomy.

Finding myself incapable of sitting, I paced my father's room, my mind flinging itself from one thing to another like a lunatic in a lucid phase.

Would my father die tonight?

How could I possibly take responsibility for Glanteifi?

Who had killed Jenkyn Hughes?

Why had his body been taken out of the limekiln?

Where and who was this supposed cousin?

If my father recovered sufficiently to take nourishment tomorrow, would I be able to resume my investigation?

The clamorous questions were like the recrudescing heads of the hydra: the more I tried to put them aside, the more insistent they became, until I was almost dementedly restless.

When Mrs Griffiths brought my supper on a tray, she must have seen my agitation. 'I think a glass of brandy would do you good, Harry. When you've finished your supper, I'll have a bottle sent up.'

The door closed behind her and I contemplated the tray of food. Would it be heartless to eat as my father lay there, insensible? But taking nourishment could hardly be less filial than willing him to recover simply so that I could get back to preparing for Hughes's inquest.

Though London had taught me to love hard, strong cheese, as I bit into our own dairy's soft curd, I found myself somewhat calmed by memories of standing at the dairy door, watching the cheese being made. Cream skimmed in wide, slate troughs, curds pressed in cloth, young cheese being salted. I made myself rehearse each stage of production before my mind's eye. I could not abide the thought of being a useless dilettante who was dependent on the labours of others and, in my somewhat less than rational state, I fastened onto the notion that, if I could make my own cheese, people would not be able to dismiss me.

I spread and cut and chewed and thought in this rather warped manner for a few minutes, my father's still form lying in the bed at my side. In the gloom of the lamplit room, he was scarcely visible in my peripheral vision and the fear that he might have died without my knowing seized me again.

I stretched out my hand, laid it on the blanket over his chest. Nothing. Then, after a second or two of skin-crawling apprehension, the smallest rise and fall.

Slumping back in the chair I waited for my heart's suddenly clamourous beating to subside . My appetite had disappeared and I put the tray of food aside.

The panic I had felt when I thought my father had stopped breathing shocked me, and I examined it like a chemist analysing a suspect powder, weighing its contents. What proportion of that panic came from the knowledge that, if he died, my life would no longer be my own, and what proportion from fondness? The answer did not improve my current opinion of myself.

I want to be coroner.

I want to find out who killed Jenkyn Hughes.

That the Tresaith corpse was Jenkyn Hughes now stood beyond doubt. Mrs Parry's testimony as to the wound and John's inspection of the body confirmed it.

What did we know about Hughes? He was an emigration agent. A gambler. A womaniser? That still needed to be looked into.

He was an American. Or was he? Everybody we had spoken to had referred to Hughes as an American but, if the man who had appeared at Captain Coleman's to take possession of Hughes's effects was indeed a cousin, then Hughes had roots in the Cardigan area. The first emigrants from Cardiganshire had sailed for America no more than thirty years before; therefore, as Captain Coleman's widow had described Hughes as a man of forty or thereabouts, it was likely that he had been born and spent at least part of his youth here.

Old enmities die hard in rural areas and, if Jenkyn Hughes had been behaving less than discreetly, those enmities might have been re-awakened.

We urgently needed to find the man claiming to be Hughes's cousin.

John

If my mother, God rest her, could've seen me riding away from Glanteifi, she'd've wagged her finger at me for being full of myself. And I was. I was full of what I could do now.

With Harry stuck at his father's house, I was in charge. To all intents and purposes, I was the coroner.

Harry and I had talked through what I might do next but he'd left it to me to decide. 'You're the one doing the work, John. It's up to you how you want to do it.'

So, I had to make a decision about where I should go now.

If we wanted to keep Billy Go-About sweet, I knew it'd be wise to let him be the first to hear that we'd identified our corpse. But it was too late for me to go back to Cardigan today. I wasn't going to disturb him and Mrs Go-About on their own hearth, thank you very much. Even if I knew where he lived, which I didn't.

And, to be honest, it wasn't just that. If I went and told the inspector who the body was, I had a pretty good idea what he'd say. *Very well, tell Mr Prober-Lloyd that, in his absence, I shall re-convene the inquest.* Because, as far as Billy Go-About was concerned, he had his man in the lock-up. All he needed the inquest to do was confirm identity, say it was murder, and he'd commit Teff Harris for trial at the assizes.

But Harry didn't want Teff Harris committed for trial. He'd promised Harris that he'd get him released if Bellis hadn't found any actual evidence against him by the following day. Trouble was, Harry was stuck at Glanteifi. And I couldn't go marching up to the police station and start demanding things, not without good evidence against somebody else.

Some time before he'd been bashed on the head, Hughes'd been stabbed, we knew that much. But had the stabbing happened at the *smwglins* or somewhere else? All we knew was that he'd turned up in Tresaith with blood on his waistcoat.

Same with the blow that killed him. We didn't know whether he'd got it on the beach, or whether somebody'd taken his corpse there later, to put it in the kiln. Far as I could see, the only reason to run the risk of carting the body to the beach was if the killer believed that the lime waste would get rid of it. Burn it away. But, seeing as most people probably believed that old wives' tale, that wasn't much help.

Besides, it seemed more likely that Hughes'd been killed on the beach and his killer'd panicked and hidden his body in the only place they could see.

So, if he'd been killed at Tresaith, we needed to know what he'd been doing there. And when.

I was going to have to go back to The Ship and speak to the Parry women.

And while I was there, I might be able to find out when the next lime boat was due in. We – *I* – still had to find out whether the lime boatmen had seen anything.

I took my watch out of my pocket and looked at it. Quarter to four. The sky was clear, nothing to cut the daylight short. Nearly an hour before sunset.

I turned Seren's head up the hill towards the road that would take me to the coast.

* * *

As I rode up to The Ship's front door, Mrs Parry came out and stood there, arms folded.

'Twice in one day, John Davies. People will talk.'

I grinned. Nerves. I wasn't sure how to deal with Mrs Parry, what tone to take with her. So I said nothing, just swung one leg over the pommel of the saddle and jumped down from Seren's back.

'Is it me you want, or Bets? I heard what she told you the other day, the little gossip.'

'Always a grain of truth in gossip though, isn't there?' I sounded like my mother.

'Grains are small, John Davies. *Very* small.' She stared at me for a bit, waiting for that to sink in, then cocked her head to one side to direct me. 'Put the mare round the back, out of the wind. There's a ring in the wall for you to tie her up. There's water there too.'

Inside, with the shutters open to the setting sun, the main room was lighter than it had been the day before and I could see that The Ship was a well-kept place. The table in the middle of the room was pale with proper scrubbing and the sand on the floor was fresh. Not as absorbent as sawdust but a lot more plentiful. And free.

Mrs Parry latched the door behind us. 'Bets is in the kitchen. I'll get her to make some tea.'

I'd been wondering how I was going to speak to Bets without her mother interfering so I jumped in with both feet. 'No, don't disturb her – I'll go and talk to her in there. She can make the tea at the same time.'

I turned and marched towards the kitchen door. If Mrs Parry followed me, I'd have to be more direct but I didn't want to get into an argument with her on her own premises.

Mercifully, she left me to it.

Being at the back of the building, the kitchen was gloomier than the taproom but it looked well-kept – as if it'd had money spent on it. The main evidence of that was the new cooking range that stood against the back wall. I didn't have much to do with kitchens but I knew these ranges were the big thing now. No more cooking over the fire, it was all putting things in the oven with a range. My landlady would have pulled out her eye teeth with her own fingers to have one. I knew that because she was always running them down, saying how they were difficult to keep alight and she didn't know why anybody bothered with them.

Bets caught the direction of my eye.

'If you're thinking it's a modern marvel,' she said, 'that's because you've never had to clean and polish one.' She stepped towards me and held up her hands, palms out. They were covered in little black lines, every fold and crease stained.

'Blacklead' she said. 'Can't get it off. That stove takes more work than everything else in the kitchen put together. And you know the worst thing?'

I shook my head.

'I have to make bread now. We never had a bread oven before. Too much bother to build one. But now we've got that,' she curled her lip at the stove 'I have to make bread. Every day!'

'You'll have to make sure that whoever you marry doesn't mistake you for a houseproud woman and buy you one then,' I grinned. All right, I know it was a bit forward but she was the sort of girl I always found myself flirting with.

'*Marry?* Who'd marry me? I'm Mrs Parry's daughter.'

'So?'

'She's Mrs Parry, The Ship. And I'm not just talking about this place. She has ships built for her, out there on the beach. She's in business with men. She gives men orders and they do what they're told.'

'I thought we were talking about you not her.'

'Haven't you ever heard of *Like mother like daughter?*'

Of course I had. It was on the tip of my tongue to say that some men admire a woman with spirit but, thank God, I heard the words in my head before I said them, and kept my mouth shut. Flirting's one thing but I didn't want Bets Parry to think I was after her.

'Look,' I said, 'I'm sorry but I've got to ask you some things. Can we get on?'

She looked at me as if I'd just proved her point for her. 'If you like.'

'Your mother was going to ask you to make some tea,' I said.

'For you or her?'

I shrugged. 'Both, I suppose.'

Bets reached for the kettle on the stove and topped it up from a tapped barrel in the corner. The kitchen wasn't quite modern enough to have water piped in yet, then.

'What did you mean yesterday?' I began. 'When you said that if the dead man *was* Jenkyn Hughes, it'd come out that he was killed over a woman?'

'Did I say that?'

'Yes, you did.' I watched her move over to the stove. 'Come on, Bets. I know your mother's probably given you a row for gossiping about him but I need to know what you meant. Was Jenkyn Hughes a womaniser?'

'Is it him, then?'

Her eyes were big as she asked the question. Like a small child at Michaelmas asking where his friend the pig's gone.

'Yes. Your mother told us about the knife wound. That identified him for us. Were you here when she dressed it for him?'

Bets looked away, as if she wasn't sure whether she should answer that.

'Were you?'

'I'm here all the time, aren't I? Got nowhere else to go.'

'You know what I mean, Bets! Did you see your mother doctoring Hughes?'

She kept her eyes on the kettle. 'I did, but she doesn't know I saw.'

There was something in her tone. 'Spying, were you?'

'I wanted to know what was going on.'

'Between your mother and Hughes?'

'Did she tell you how she knew he'd been stabbed?'

'Said she saw blood on his waistcoat.'

Bets turned to face me. 'Well, she lied, then.'

'Go on,' I pushed her when she said no more. 'How *did* she find out?'

'She rubbed herself up against him like a bitch on heat and he flinched.'

Her voice was as cold and sour as three-day old beer. In my mind's eye, I saw an image of Bets spying through a crack in the door and it told me everything I needed to know. She'd wanted Jenkyn Hughes for herself but her mother'd got there first. No wonder she was bitter about her chances of marriage, if Mrs Parry seduced any man who came within reach.

'Right,' I said, not sure how far to take this. 'So ... were they ... you know...' *Come on, John, you're here on official business. Spit it out.* 'Were they lovers?' I asked, hearing myself speaking too loud.

She looked me straight in the eye, as if she despised me for being awkward about her mother's behaviour when she had to live with it every day. 'I don't know. But it was what she wanted. I could tell.'

Well, well. I'd never've guessed Mrs Parry'd had feelings for Hughes. I tried to remember how I'd come to ask her and James Philips about identifying marks. Had she led me into asking? Had she wanted to know for herself whether it was him in the mortuary at Cardigan workhouse?

Mind, even if it wasn't personal, having him publicly identified would suit her. Once his death was announced, she and James Philips would be able to claim their life-insurance money. Was that why she'd given me the information?

'My mother's used to getting what she wants,' Bets said. It felt as if she'd read my thoughts but, actually, she was just carrying on from where she'd left off.

'And what does she want? In general?'

Her answer was bitter. 'To be in charge.'

'Well, I suppose she's had to be since your father died.'

'Oh, don't fool yourself. Dada wasn't the boss here. He was a strong man – physically strong, I mean – and she admired that. But it was always her who did the thinking. The planning. He let her make all the decisions.'

Parry was good in a scrap. Knew what to do.

Just as well he was dead or he'd just have become my main suspect for killing Jenkyn Hughes.

'If your mother was after Hughes, she can't've been very happy about his womanising – if that's what he was up to.'

She raised her eyes to me then. I hadn't noticed before – not enough light the previous time I'd been there – but she had bright blue eyes. Really bright blue.

'I don't know whether you'd call it womanising exactly but he *liked* women. And women liked him. At least, at the beginning they did.'

'At the beginning of what?'

She put her hands in the pockets of her apron and looked at the floor. Deep pockets they were – you could've put a bottle in each. Perhaps that's what they were for. 'When he first got here,' she said. 'That's what I meant.' She frowned as if she was remembering something unpleasant. 'Jenkyn Hughes changed. Or, better to say his *behaviour* changed. Maybe he was just behaving himself at the beginning but he couldn't keep it up.'

She went up in my estimation then. Not many people make the distinction between what you *are* and what you *do*. I gave her time to think about what she was going to say next.

'When he first came, he was nice. Charming. But in a nice way – not smarmy. But then he started getting more ... I don't know ... He started saying things to you, putting his hands where he shouldn't be putting them, that type of thing.'

I felt myself blush. Couldn't help it. 'Was this just with you?' I asked.

'No. Well – I mean, I was the only woman here, a lot of the time – me and Mam and she wouldn't've let him touch her in public. But when there were other women about, with them, too. It's just men here, most of the time, with the lime and the ships and everything. But sometimes women'll come and help with loading the lime or raking out – an extra pair of hands, you know.'

'And Jenkyn Hughes ... put his hands where he shouldn't with them, too?'

'The younger ones.'

'How did the women take it?'

''Spect most of them were flattered. And because it was in front of everybody it couldn't go anywhere, you know.'

'But there were some who weren't flattered?'

She pulled a face. 'Some he went after a bit more. You know, not just a bit of messing about.'

'Anybody in particular?'

Her eyes were troubled. 'Look, if I tell you this, it's just because you're asking and because I have to tell the truth, all right? It's not because I think anything came of it or because–' she stopped.

'Fair enough,' I said, cautious now. 'So who was it?'

She looked me in the eye. 'Ruth Harris, Banc yr Eithin. Teff's wife.'

I'd been half expecting it. 'And she's disappeared, hasn't she?'

'Disappeared?' From Bets's surprise, that was the first she'd heard of it.

'Hasn't been seen in nearly two weeks.'

'Well, somebody's seen her now. Dai'r Bardd – that's Obadaiah Vaughan.' She looked at me to check that I knew Vaughan's nickname. 'He came down to Gwyn Puw's earlier. Stuck his head in here to say she was back.'

'Why would he do that? What's Ruth Harris to you?'

Bets pulled the kettle off the range with a pot-holder and poured a spoutful into the teapot on the side. 'My mother's got a contract with Teff. For the lime-hauling. With him not here, she'll want to give Ruth the option of carrying it on.'

'D'you think Mrs Harris would want to?'

Bets raised a nicely-shaped eyebrow. 'Most likely. Need the money, don't they? And Ruth Harris won't have any trouble with the gang her husband recruited. She can get men to do things. Especially–'

She stopped but I knew it was only so that she could let me get it out of her. If she hadn't meant to tell me she'd've held her tongue. She'd've had plenty of practice at that around her mother.

'Especially who?' I asked.

'Well,' she gave me a sly little smile. 'Let's just say that I'm not surprised it was Dai'r Bardd who came to tell us she was back.'

When I went back out into The Ship's main room carrying two cups of tea, Mrs Parry was sitting in front of the inglenook, her back not three yards from the kitchen door, calmly smoking a pipe. The door wasn't exactly thick – how much had she heard? I had to assume she'd heard everything, including Bets's suspicions about her designs on Jenkyn Hughes. But, from the look of her, I was the embarrassed one.

'Bets helpful, was she?'

I kept my eyes on the cup as I passed it to her. 'Yes, thank you. Could I have a few minutes of your time now?'

She took the pipe out of her mouth and leaned forward to rest it against the coal bucket. 'Sit down then.'

I turned my back on the last rays of sunset and sat in the rocking chair by the fire. 'We're still trying to work out when Jenkyn Hughes was killed,' I started. 'You last saw him two days before you left The Ship – was that here or in Cardigan?'

If she'd last seen him here, in Tresaith, there was always the possibility that he'd never left, that he'd been killed soon after.

'Here. He was staying overnight before doing a trip to sign papers with some families. For the Ohio scheme.'

'So he stayed here and then went off the following morning?'

She lifted one eyebrow at me. 'The Ship's an inn, Mr Davies. We have plenty of rooms for people to sleep in.'

So, she had heard everything Bets said.

'Of course. Did you happen to see him ride off?'

'No. I saw him walk out of that door there,' she nodded at the front door, 'and go past that window at the front. He was walking up to Hendre. That's where he had his horse – in Hendre's stable.'

'Do you know whether he ever got there?' I asked.

She shook her head, eyes still on me. 'No. You'd have to ask Matthew Davies.'

'He's the tenant at Hendre?'

She nodded.

I needed to go and speak to him, see if Hughes had picked up his horse.

'You said, earlier on, that Hughes was a gambler. Do you know who he was gambling with?'

She returned my stare without heat. 'Sailors.'

'*Just* sailors?'

'That's who drinks in *smwglins* as a rule.'

I remembered David Daniels's reference to 'gentlemen' and James Philips's silence. 'Is Mr Philips a card player?'

Mrs Parry smiled as if she could read my mind and found it more interesting than she'd given me credit for. 'James is my business partner, Mr Davies, not my husband. If you want to know his vices, you'll have to ask him.'

There was something about that smile of hers. It warmed you. Made you feel more of a man.

'One more thing, if you don't mind. The lime boats. There were two loads delivered while you were away, is that right?'

She blew on her tea. 'It is, yes.'

'And Teff Harris was contracted to bring men in and cart the stone up the beach.'

She took a cautious sip. 'That's right.'

'Is it all there?'

She frowned and leaned forward slightly, resting her elbows on her thighs like a man. 'The lime? You've seen that great pile out there, John Davies. There are dozens of tons. Scores. I've got no way of knowing if it's all there.'

I considered this. 'What about the coal? The coal that Mr Hughes was bringing up from Pembrokeshire to fire the kilns. Where was that stored?'

Her eyes narrowed. She could see what I was getting at. 'On the landward side of the limestone. And, before you ask, that's *not* all there – I do know that.'

I already knew that. The previous day, Bets had said there was only cheap brown coal outside. 'You're missing the anthracite?' I asked.

Mrs Parry nodded.

'Maybe Mr Hughes got a better price elsewhere and was going to bring in more for you?'

'No. He knew better than that. I'd paid half in advance. He wouldn't've gone back on a deal with me.'

'Then where is it? All I've seen is brown coal.'

She nodded and leaned back in her chair, crossing one leg over the other, as if she was wearing trousers, not a *betgwn*. 'That's the question, isn't it?'

Harry

From some previously unsuspected store of such things, Mrs Griffiths produced a camp bed and suggested that I lie down and rest my eyes, even if I could not sleep. I was sincerely grateful for the gesture but, once I had closed the door behind her, I returned to the chair at my father's bedside. The brandy I had consumed earlier had cured me of my restlessness and, if I could not keep my mind steadfastly on my father, the least I could do was to remain awake at his side.

I stretched my legs out and let my thoughts return to John. Would he be able to find the man who claimed to be Jenkyn Hughes's cousin? If not, I had a plan to root him out: a meeting of all parties with an interest in the Cardigan-Ohio Emigration Company. Hughes's death and the resulting need to appoint a new agent could be explained to the would-be emigrants, the security of bondholders' investments made clear, and any payers-by-installments could be asked to provide proof of their deposits. I was confident that the self-proclaimed cousin would see such a meeting as the ideal opportunity to present himself and lay claim to any interest he had in the business.

My mind occupied with planning the meeting, I was brought up short when I caught myself making a mental note to ask my father whether the magistrates would allow it to be held at the Shire Hall. That habits of mind could be so engrained as to allow me to formulate such a thought whilst sitting beside his stricken form astonished me. It was as if I had two, quite distinct levels of awareness – one for the habitual, routine aspects of life, the other for more active thinking and planning – like an efficient private secretary and his lively-minded employer.

Did such a state of affairs truly exist? Was that what lay behind our ability to feel that we were 'in two minds' about something – the phrase representing a confusion which arose from a difference of opinion between the conscious, spontaneous mind and the hidden, private secretary-mind?

Reckitt would, no doubt, have an opinion and, indeed, the case of the patient whose unfortunate encounter with a steel rod he had described to me suggested such a dichotomy. Had the destruction of parts of engineer Phineas Gage's brain left him in only *one mind?* Reckitt had described a transformation from shrewd, affable and reliable to surly, taciturn and erratic. The injured man had *been no longer Gage.* Had the affable and surly elements of his personality always co-existed, the more acceptable imposing itself, in the whole brain, on the less?

Eyeing my father in my peripheral vision, I allowed myself to consider the possibility that, if he were to regain his senses, he might no longer be himself.

Unless he recovered from the paralysis described by Prendergast, he would look different, that much was certain. But, not having seen my father for the three years during which my sight had deteriorated to its current extent, I no longer knew exactly what he had looked like before the stroke. Had he begun to acquire the androgynous look of the very old? Had slackening muscles and sagging skin fallen away from the steady firmness of virility towards something softer, less insistently masculine, the second childhood of senescence rendering his countenance as genderless as a baby's?

More resolutely than before, I put my hand on his chest. This time, though I could not feel the rise and fall of breath, I felt the small pulse of his heartbeat beneath my palm. It seemed such an insignificant movement, like the beating of a tiny fist against the inside of his chest, rapping out the insistent iambic of existence – a-*live*, a-*live*, a-*live*.

Until Reckitt had tried to explain the consequences of the fatal blow to Jenkyn Hughes's head, I had not grasped that the brain regulated the workings of the internal organs. Without consciously thinking about it, I believe I had envisaged the heart, lungs and other viscera going about their business of their own accord. Of course, my friend Henry Gray, these days an anatomist of some note, had talked endlessly about the brain and spinal column and nerves, but I had come away with the idea that nerves were for executing movement and supplying us with sensation. That the heart required nervous instruction to beat had come as a revelation.

Did those unacknowledged instructions arise in that unobtrusive private secretary-mind which did not answer to logic and reason but which, nevertheless, had a wisdom that was all its own? The mind that, governed by habit, had not yet learned that it could not ask my father whether Shire Hall could be used by the coroner.

These thoughts caused me to wonder, somewhat despondently, whether mankind was quite the rational species we congratulated ourselves on being. Perhaps, even in the best of us, some of our actions were not governed by reason at all. The philosophers tell us that our passions can be controlled, tamed by reason but, in the reflective mood I had fallen into, I was obliged to acknowledge that my own experience had suggested otherwise.

Once, in the grip of romantic love, I had knocked a man to the ground, stood over him and defied him to call the virtue of my beloved into question a second time. Given that he had been a head taller than me and half again as heavy, that had not been a rational act. Indeed, rationality had not entered into it. I had heard the insult and, the next thing I consciously knew, I was standing over him, my fist still raised, heart pounding. Had I held a weapon in my hand, I cannot say with any certainty that I would not have hit him about the head.

Could that have been what happened to Jenkyn Hughes? Had somebody snatched up a weapon and hit him with it before their rational mind – their *right mind* – had a chance to understand what was happening?

I pictured Hughes's body, dragged up the beach by its heels and lying on the floor of the draw-hole, a figure shoveling lime waste over it until it was completely covered. Had that burial been the action of a man panicking at the result of a moment of utter irrationality? Or the calculated act of a murderer concealing the evidence of his crime?

John

I should've slept like the dead that night. I'd been up since before first light and riding over half of south Cardiganshire all day. But I never slept well away from home.

Back and forth I rolled, twitchy and uncomfortable. I swore as bedclothes twisted themselves around me. Got in a stew about sheets that were still clammy hours after I got into bed. Wished I had my nightshirt and wasn't lying in my underlinen. Changed the side I was lying on for the twentieth time. Hit the pillow to get the clotted feathers out of their lumps. Longed for sleep or morning and didn't care which.

I cursed myself for staying at The Ship instead of going back to Newcastle Emlyn. But it'd seemed like a good idea to take Seren up to Hendre and kill two birds with one stone – stable for the night and a short conversation about Jenkyn Hughes and his horse.

I should've gone home after Hendre. That would have been the sensible thing to do. Go home to my lodgings. Visit Harry on Sunday.

I banged the pillow again, lay down, and stared up into the dark. I felt stupid about being so excited earlier. Stupid to think I could carry on by myself. Harry was going to be at Glanteifi with his father for days – weeks even. He was the heir, he had no choice. He'd have to pass his duties on to another acting coroner. Rushing about the countryside wasn't going to do me any good. Nobody was going to be impressed. Mr Schofield would soon hear about Justice Probert-Lloyd having an apoplexy and he'd expect me back at work. None of this was my responsibility any more.

So what was I doing here?

I wasn't Harry. I was the monkey, not the organ grinder.

But still ... Matthew Davies up at Hendre'd answered my questions happily enough.

Yes, Jenkyn Hughes had come for his horse.

Yes, they'd had a bit of a chat. Mr Hughes was a friendly gentleman. Bit over-friendly if I wanted to know the truth.

Where he'd gone?

Cardigan.

Not up the coast, then? Not to Aberaeron?

No. He'd said he was going to Cardigan.

Maybe he'd changed his plans?

Perhaps. Wouldn't be the first time.

I squirmed around the mattress, trying to find the warm dent I'd been lying in a minute before. This was useless. I was fooling myself. Tomorrow, I'd go and see Harry. Tell him I was leaving all this and going back to work. To the law.

I knew how he'd be. *Of course, John, it's your decision ...* But I could see the look of disappointment on his face already.

Damn him, what was I supposed to do – put my whole future at risk? And why was I feeling guilty about letting him down when he'd let me down just as badly?

Probert-Lloyd and Davies, Attorneys at Law. A solid, bow-fronted property. Two grand offices, one on each side of the hallway. Clerks knocking on our doors. 'Mr so and so to see you, Mr Davies.' 'Mrs whatshername to see you, Mr Probert-Lloyd.'

I'd built and furnished that office so many times in my mind. The pedestal desk. Rugs on the floor. A comfortable leather button-chair for clients. Gaslights on the walls. Why not? In my imagination, Newcastle Emlyn could have a gasholder.

Probert-Lloyd and Davies. Huh! At this rate I'd be lucky if Mr Schofield kept me on as his clerk. I was pretty sure he wasn't going to put up with much more of this running about after Harry.

You may find that it is not entirely beneficial to your future to fall in behind his standard. There is such a thing as taint by association.

And yet ... Mr Leighton Bowen must think differently. He was the coroner for the Teifi Valley – even if he was too sick to do the job – and he'd passed the post on to Harry. Which implied two things. One, he trusted Harry to do the job competently. Two, he thought it was a fit occupation for a gentleman.

But, gentleman or not, as of the previous day, Harry wasn't doing the job. I was. And there was a big difference between *I hear your clerk's assisting young Probert-Lloyd as stand-in coroner* and *I hear your clerk's acting on his own initiative, let loose by young Probert-Lloyd.*

There was something else, as well.

I try not to believe in fate. It's just a sop for people without the sense to plan for the future. But there was something about this investigation that was making me shiver.

America. Death.

America'd been the reason I'd gone for a *gwas bach* on Price's farm when I was eleven. My parents'd put me in service so I'd get board and lodging, plus a suit of clothes and a pair of boots, and – just as important – sixpence a week put by. One pound and six shillings a year. That would have paid for my ticket.

But I'd never collected any earnings. After six months, I'd run back home in fear of my life. Except there'd been nobody there. My father, my mother and my little sister had all died of an infectious fever weeks before.

I lay still and stared up into the thick darkness above me, listening to the sound of the waves down on the beach. What would my life've been like if we'd gone to America?

My father would've wanted me on the land with him. No doubt there. But I'd never been cut out for farming. Even when I was small, I always preferred being indoors to out and, when I went to the Sunday school, I'd taken to reading and writing like a terrier takes to ratting.

What would my father tell me now? Who should I stick to – employer or squire's son?

With no shutters, the window was a pale square floating in the dark and I fixed my gritty eyes on it. Out there was the sea. All the way to America if you managed not to bump into Ireland first.

Until I met Harry, I'd never seen the sea. Only the estuaries at Cardigan and Carmarthen. Never waves and sea all the way to the horizon.

Tell Harry you've changed your mind. That you'll work for him. Be his assistant.

I turned away from the window and stared up without blinking until the blackness pulsed and flickered. If we didn't find out who'd killed Jenkyn Hughes, Harry could whistle as far as getting elected coroner was concerned. If I wanted even the possibility of being his officer again in the future, I couldn't afford to let him down.

But it wouldn't be easy. Matthew Davies, Hendre, might've been happy to talk to me, but not everybody would. I knew that from going to see Gwyn Puw the previous evening. When I'd knocked on his door, straight away he'd looked over my shoulder for Harry.

'What do you want?' he'd wanted to know, when he realised I was on my own.

'Only a quick word, that's all.' There was brown coal burning on his hearth again. With the wind in the wrong direction it was blowing back into the cottage and I could taste it on my tongue. 'About tides and that sort of thing,' I told him when he just stood there, blocking the doorway. 'Just some things I need to know.' He still didn't move. 'Come over to The Ship and I'll buy you a drink – easier to talk over a pint by the fire.'

Puw looked at me from beneath the ragged edge of that knitted cap of his. 'Where's your boss, then?'

'Family matters.'

He eyeballed me some more then nodded and turned to pull his door shut. 'Come on then. There's no beer in but the missis'll have some rum.'

In the taproom, I held my tongue while Mrs Parry got our rum for us. I didn't want to talk to Puw with her standing there. She wasn't above suspicion herself. Not with the life insurance she'd taken out on Hughes.

Luckily for me, she was no keener to stay and gab with us than I was to have her there. 'You'll be good enough, I'm sure, to call me if any other customers come in.'

Puw waited until she'd gone into the kitchen before speaking. 'Won't be any customers,' he said. 'Wintertime, nobody comes in unless there's a boat on the beach or a fire in the kiln. And, anyway, this time of year there's no money about, is there?'

The mention of money gave me a good way in.

'So nobody's going to come and try and make a bit of money on the cards or the dice?'

His eyebrows disappeared into the edge of his cap. 'Gambling? Not in The Ship, boy.'

'Doesn't allow it, does she?'

He took a gulp of his rum. 'No,' he said, licking his lips. 'Says it stirs up trouble. And you don't go against Mrs Parry.'

I took a chance. 'So where did Jenkyn Hughes go to do his gambling?'

Puw shook his head. 'Don't know. You'd have to ask somebody else about that.'

'He'd got himself in a lot of debt, gambling,' I told him. 'Did you know that?'

A shrug. He'd heard rumours. But he wasn't going to go as far as to look me in the eye.

'Did you happen to hear what he was doing to pay off his debts?'

I'd asked the question to see if I could find out whether any ticket holders for the Ohio scheme might've heard that Hughes was playing fast and loose with their money. But, judging by Puw's reaction, he thought I was getting at something else.

'I don't know *anything* about what was going on here,' he mumbled furiously, still not looking at me. 'I told you. I was on the herring boats.'

I took an eye-watering swallow of rum. My chest was beginning to feel tight with the brown coal smoking in the grate. I wished Gwyn hadn't chosen to sit right in the inglenook.

'You're talking about the coal that's been stolen?' I said, as if I knew all about it. 'The coal and the lime?'

Puw didn't look up. 'I told you. It's nothing to do with me.'

'You weren't paid to be somewhere else, then – while your kiln was fired and tons of Mrs Parry's lime was burned?' I thought he might let something slip if I went on the attack. But it was me that'd slipped.

'Don't be stupid, boy! Nobody's fired my kiln. Everybody for miles'd know.' Now I had his eye. 'Never seen a kiln burning, have you, boy? Can't've. Smokes like the fires of hell, it does. See it for miles.'

'If the lime's not gone into your kiln, where's it gone?'

'Know for a fact there's lime gone, do you?' Puw was angry now. Or at least, he was raising his voice and giving me the beady eye.

'What about the coal, then?' I said. 'No question that that's gone, is there?'

He stared at me, hard. 'Look, boy. I've told you. I wasn't here. I don't know anything about it. And it's none of my business, anyway, until it's time to fire the kilns.'

Something clicked in my head. 'When is it time? When d'you usually start burning?'

Puw glared at me and I thought he wasn't going to answer. Then he changed his mind. Maybe he'd worked out it wasn't a trick question. 'March or April. Depends on the weather. No point burning till people can get here. Don't want piles of quicklime standing about.'

April was when emigrant ships started embarking for America. Had Jenkyn Hughes been selling the shipped-in anthracite twice, hoping he'd manage to replace enough for Mrs Parry's use and then disappear to Ohio before Puw realised there wasn't enough to fire his kilns?

The lime burner took my silence as a sign that I'd finished with him. He drained his beaker and put his hands on his knees to push himself up. 'Before you go,' I said, quickly, 'could I just have a minute to ask about tides?'

Puw didn't reply but he settled back down and started digging in his pockets. I waited until he'd taken a pipe from one and a roll of oilcloth from the other. If I let him light up, he might stay long enough for me to find out what I needed to know.

Once he'd packed his stained pipe with tobacco, he reached into his pocket again and pulled out a dried gorse-top.

'Teff Harris says he brought the body up the beach off the limestone,' I started, as Puw lit the gorse spill from the fire and put it to his pipe. He sucked the spitting, smoking flame into the tobacco, eyes on the spill, not on me. 'Out of the sea, in other words,' I said. 'What do you think about that?'

The strands of tobacco crackled as they caught fire and Puw sucked at his pipe, eyes on the glowing clump. 'If that's what he says.'

'If the body was dumped in the sea, wouldn't the current've carried him away instead of leaving him on the beach?'

Puw blew smoke out. He still wasn't looking at me. 'Only if he was dropped in a depth of water. Not if the tide was nearly at the bottom.'

'But if somebody dragged him on to the limestone when the tide was almost out, Teff Harris would've seen whoever put the body there, wouldn't he? Either on the beach or coming away up the track?'

'Maybe he did see them.'

'He says not.'

Puw shrugged. He wanted the subject dropped. But I wasn't ready to satisfy him yet.

'Harris says he found the body naked.'

Puw shook his head but not in denial. *None of my business what another man says.*

I'd been thinking about Hughes's naked body. There'd been no gashes from the limestone. No signs that the waves'd pulled him this way and that over the unloaded rock. 'D'you think he *could've* been naked?' I asked. 'Wouldn't the waves've moved him about – even at low tide? Torn his skin?'

Puw pulled a face, shifted in his chair. 'Most likely, yes. Unless he was dumped when the water was completely off the stones.'

'But then,' I pointed out, 'if there was no water on the stones at all, he'd've still had limestone dust on him. In his hair. On his skin. And he didn't.'

Puw'd had nothing to say to that. Not that it'd really been a question, to be fair.

Now, lying sleepless in the dark, I thought about how it all came back to that anonymous letter.

Ask Teff Harris what he did with the dead man's clothes after he took him out of the sea and stripped him.

I decided to ride into Cardigan first thing and ask him that exact question.

Harry

I woke to a dry mouth and a hand on my arm. In the second or two that it took me to recall that I was in a chair at my father's bedside, I also realised that I had a painful crick in my neck.

My father was conscious. And leaning towards me.

'Father!' I felt a rush of emotion. Relief?

''A'ey.' My father's voice was not his own; he produced this attempt at my name with the force of a small explosion, as if he had gathered such sounds as he was master of, bound each carefully to the next and then propelled them out past some invisible impediment.

I put my hand over his, where it was still clamped to my forearm. 'Yesterday…' I began, then stopped, unsure of what I had been going to say. Would my father even be aware of what had happened to him yesterday?

'Ye'day…' After he had expelled the truncated word, I heard another sound that might have been the sucking of saliva into a mouth not wholly in charge of itself. 'Aw-hul.' Awful. He remembered enough, then.

His efforts at speech told me that my father was in his right mind but that all was far from well.

'Yes,' I said. 'I think we've both had better.'

His hand gripped my arm with renewed force and I felt the effort required as he spat a single word.

'Closet.'

All the principal bedrooms at Glanteifi had closets containing a close-stool and lime bucket. Indeed, until I was old enough to know

234

much about agricultural husbandry, I had thought the only use for quicklime was to sprinkle in the close-stool bucket. Experience later taught me – both at school and at the homes of friends – that most people did not trouble themselves to reduce noxious odours, but my father was a fastidious man and he had always insisted on it.

Hoping devoutly that he was asking for no more assistance than would be required to get him through the closet's door, I helped him from the bed and lent him my shoulder.

We made decent progress until his right leg, stiff and unbending, caused the rug to ruck up. I am sure we were a comical sight, my father refusing to let me go lest he fall over, me tugging at the rug beneath his feet, but it was not amusing to me. I had endured a long and uncomfortable night and felt tetchy and unreasonable.

Once we were inside the closet, the full reality of his paralysis made itself clear. Unwilling to let go of me, my father was using his only useful hand to clasp my arm and had no means of unbuttoning himself.

The mutual mortification of the next few minutes was exacerbated by my own struggles with buttons: I could only unfasten them by feel.

Leaving him safely ensconced behind the closet door, I made my way to my own chamber. A wash and fresh linen dispelled some of my ill temper.

However, on returning to my father's room, my hope that he might have got himself off the stool and out of the closet was crushed by a sound of entreaty from behind the door.

Something was going to have to be done about this situation, and swiftly. I would ten times rather have followed my father on to the bench of magistrates than into his closet. If his command of his limbs did not improve, Justice Probert-Lloyd was going to have to submit himself to the services of an intimate kind of valet.

The day loomed, long and uncertain, and I wondered what John was planning to do with it. Whatever it was, I should communicate with him.

I put my head around the door and called down for Wil-Sam.

John

Breakfast at The Ship wasn't up to the Black Lion's standards but it was better than nothing

'You can thank Bets for the porridge,' Mrs Parry told me. 'She went up to Hendre and got the milk straight from the cow an hour ago, else it would've been made with water like we usually do. She brought your mare down, too.'

I hoped Bets'd strained the milk before putting it in my porridge. I'd seen milk straight from the cow often enough – flakes of shit and particles of straw floating in the froth on top. Still, it didn't do to be too fussy. As my old *Mamgu* used to say *you've got to eat a peck of dirt before you die.*

'By the way,' I said, eyes on the scalding porridge, 'I know Mr Probert-Lloyd wanted to speak to the men on the lime boat. When's the next load coming in?'

Mrs Parry shook her head. 'There'll be no more deliveries until I can sort out what's happened to the coal.'

Ruth Harris would miss the money with her man still in the Cardigan lock-up.

'Do you think Teff Harris's got anything to do with the coal going missing?' I asked.

Her face didn't change. 'I doubt it very much.'

'You trust him, then?'

She folded her arms. 'Teff Harris is busy pulling himself up in the world. If he pisses on people, it'll only be on those beneath him who can do him neither good nor harm.'

A full stomach almost made me forget my gritty eyes, and I felt quite cheery as I rode up the hill away from the beach. The sun was up and I didn't think it was too early to go and have a word with Mrs Teff before heading down to the police station.

But when I got to the *tŷ unnos* I found the boy, Clarkson, by himself. He started to run towards the house, but then he recognised me.

'Where's your mother?'

'Gone to Cardigan. To take food to my father.'

I knew Billy Go-About's men had been feeding Harris, so I wondered if there was more to the visit than that.

'Everything all right with the cow?' I asked.

He beamed. 'Yes. She's grand.'

'Did anybody come and try and take her?'

He shook his head. 'Mam said they wouldn't have dared. But I was ready for them if they had, wasn't I?'

'You were.' But Mrs Harris must be confident in her own judgement. No mother willingly puts her child in danger. Perhaps she'd asked her beau, Dai'r Bardd, to keep an eye on him.

'You know that man we were talking about before?' I said. 'Mrs Parry's friend with the chequered waistcoat?'

Clarkson cocked his head, nodding at the same time.

'Did he ever come here, to the house?'

'No.'

'Sure?'

'People don't come here. Not much.'

I thought about that as I rode down to Cardigan. And about 'Mam said they wouldn't have dared'. What had happened after the last time Teff Harris's neighbours had tried to steal his cow? In Mrs Parry's terms, how exactly had Harris pissed on them?

Something else to ask husband and wife when I got to town.

It had rained in the night but the morning was bright and clear with little clouds racing each other like children in an innocent blue sky. Wet grass caught the low early-morning sun and seemed alight with it in the long shadows. I was so busy looking at it that I almost rode straight past Dai'r Bardd. Luckily, something about the man's lanky lope elbowed me into paying attention and I pulled the mare up.

'Good morning.' His greeting was civil enough but he didn't take his hat off. Mounted or not, I was no better than him.

'Off to chapel?' As if I didn't know perfectly well where he was going.

He smiled easily. 'I thought charity could come first today. I'm going to see if Mrs Harris, Banc yr Eithin, needs any help.'

'I thought you'd know.' I kept any expression off my face. 'She's not there this morning.'

'Why should I know that?'

'Didn't you visit her when she got back yesterday?'

He frowned. 'No.'

And yet he'd known she was back because he'd told Mrs Parry. Had he been spying on her? Watching the *tŷ unnos*? 'Well, I've just been there and she's gone down to Cardigan. To see to her husband's needs.'

'Oh. Of course. I should have realised.' He couldn't keep all the disappointment off his face, though he tried hard. 'Has the boy gone with her?'

Interesting question, I thought. Had Vaughan been one of the cow-stealing neighbours? Fancying Ruth Harris needn't've stopped him trying to impoverish her husband. Might've suited him to be in a position to come to her rescue, in fact.

'No, Clarkson's at home. I'm sure Mrs Harris would be grateful for you looking in on him. You could make sure there's water hauled in and everything for when she gets back.' I paused fractionally. 'I'm off down to the police station, now. I'll mention to her that you're going over, shall I?'

He kept his face bland, but I was sure he was seething inside. He'd been hoping for a quiet few minutes with another man's wife and here I was offering his services to the man's child instead. I knew Dai'r Bardd's type. He was the kind of man who was accustomed to being the cleverest in the room. Men like him didn't always do all the talking, but they did always want the last word. And he made sure he had it now.

'Yes. If you'd be so good, give her – give them both – my best wishes. Tell them I hope that this whole business is resolved as soon as may be.'

I smiled maliciously to myself as I bade him good day and rode on. He hadn't sent hopes that Teff would be released, only that things would be resolved. Well, if Teff was committed for trial and hanged for murder, that would certainly resolve things in a way that Dai'r Bardd would like, wouldn't it?

If he'd been watching Banc yr Eithin for Ruth Harris's return, had he spied on Teff, at other times, to know when it was safe for him to 'happen' to drop in? Had he stood on the headland watching Teff Harris on the beach, seen him stripping Jenkyn Hughes's corpse? Vaughan was literate – he'd made a point of reading through my record of the wounds we'd seen on the body and signing his name to it with a steady hand.

Was it him who'd written the anonymous note to Billy Bellis?

Harry

As the morning wore on, I brooded impotently about when John would get the letter I had sent to the Black Lion via Twm.

My father was dozing, having exhausted his meagre resources of energy in consuming a few spluttered spoonsful of the broth Isabel Griffiths had carried up for him.

'Shall I send for Dr Prendergast?' she had asked, clearly anxious at my attempting to manage without medical advice.

'No, thank you. I'd prefer that somebody went and asked Dr Reckitt to come from Cilgerran.'

'Dr Reckitt.'

I was glad I could not see the look she favoured me with; her tone was sufficient to tell me that she disapproved most strongly of this idea.

'Yes.' I did my best to sound warm rather than contrary. 'I've had professional dealings with him. I found him to be intelligent and far more modern in his thinking than Dr Prendergast. It doesn't do to live in the past where the only thing a doctor could think to do was to bleed his patient, Mrs Griffiths.'

Once she had gone, I sat waiting for time to pass and trying not to wish myself elsewhere. I had no idea when John would next come to me for instructions, or whether, without me, he would run into impediments to our investigation.

I thought about the public meeting of those with an interest in the American Scheme that my letter had suggested. Was there any chance that I might be able to attend? How much would my father's condition have to improve before others would consider it reasonable for me to be anywhere but at his side?

Trying not to allow the chair to creak, I got up. Inactivity was driving me to distraction. Since returning to Glanteifi, I had become used to taking Sara out every day for several hours; in the absence of mental stimulation, achieving physical exhaustion had become my only recourse. On horseback, I was required to do no more than keep to the road or work with the mare to ensure we kept a decent line across the fields, and being outside allowed me a freedom which being cooped up with books I could not read and people I could not see denied me. But it was unthinkable that I should go out riding today.

I sat down once more and tried to think rationally about what must be done for my father. A valet would see to his personal needs but the bureaucracy of managing the estate must now fall to me. Or, at any rate, to myself and the estate steward, Mr Ormiston.

I spent the next half an hour going around the estate in my head, naming farms and tenants and trying to see, in my mind's eye, the state of each farm's house and outbuildings.

How soon should I arrange a meeting with Ormiston?

I saw the steward in my mind's eye and imagined going through all the details of Glanteifi's finances with him. It would be an uphill task. I knew next to nothing about the estate's administration. My years of absence had made quite sure of that.

I shied away from the thought of having to submit to Ormiston's instruction and rose to pace the room once more. But I could bear neither my own company nor the contemplation of my fate. I located the handle that rang a bell in the servants' hall and pulled again and again. I had to know whether there was any reply from John yet.

Mrs Griffiths herself answered the bell, and the panting haste with which she flung the door open made me realise that my insistent ringing on the bell had made the poor woman fear that something awful had happened.

'What is it?'

I hung my head. 'I'm sorry. I didn't mean to worry anybody.'

'Is it your father?'

'No.'

'What then?'

'I didn't know you'd come.' It was true, I had not expected our housekeeper to respond personally to my fretful summons. But, if I had given it even a second's thought, I would have realised that Mrs Griffiths had answered every bell from my father's room since he had been taken ill. She wanted to be the first to know of any change, whether for good or ill.

'Harry. Why did you ring?'

'I just wondered – is Twm back from Cardigan yet?'

Mrs Griffiths drew in a slow and audible breath. I knew she meant it as a rebuke and I felt suitably chastened. 'He is. Now, this minute.'

'Did he bring any answer from John Davies?'

'He did not.'

I sighed. 'I expect he stayed in Newcastle Emlyn last night and then went over to Cardigan this morning. He probably hasn't even called in at the Black Lion yet.'

I sincerely hoped that he would think to do so before the day was out. Quite apart from my communication, there could be any number of informants waiting to speak to him.

'There is a letter, though,' Isabel Griffiths said. 'From Miss Howell.'

If being forced to ask others to read my correspondence aloud to me was not the most humiliating aspect of my blindness, it came extremely close.

Had I been able to, I would have read Lydia's letters three or four times, committing her thoughts to memory so that I could mull them over before giving a response. But I could not ask Isabel Griffiths to read her letters more than once. Once was a sufficient imposition on both of us.

How I wished for the impossible – a lector who could read English, but not understand what they were reading. Someone who would read without judgement, who would repeat any word or sentence as often as I asked, without imputing any significance to the request, mouth moving like an automaton, dead eyed and hinge-jawed.

One section of Lydia's present letter did, however, print itself more vividly on my memory than the rest because it chimed so exactly with my own current American preoccupations and I sat, pondering it, long after Mrs Griffiths had left me alone with my father once more.

'To re-visit something of our last discussion' – Lydia had written – *'my conversation with Mr Mudge yesterday evening touched on whether there is a greater freedom of thought abroad in the new states of America or whether, as we have seen at home, the radical strains of nonconformity that seemed, at first, to offer a greater degree of equality to all are becoming attenuated by time so that they come to look not so different to the old order of Anglicanism. Mr Mudge is pessimistic.*

For myself, I cannot help feeling that, perhaps, in the New World, there might be found – or founded – a more enlightened church. Where lives are being forged anew, should it not be possible to think new thoughts?'

With each letter from Lydia, I now detected an increasing dissatisfaction with her position and I wondered whether this reference to America meant that she might be contemplating a new and more independent life for herself there. Recent as our epistolary relationship was, it had become important to me and I was forced to admit that the thought of its coming to an end was disturbing.

John

As I trotted Seren past the hump of Banc y Warren and began the long slope down towards Cardigan common, I started fretting about what I'd say to Billy Go-About if I found him at the police station. I was hoping he wouldn't be there but, if he was, how much should I tell him? I was pretty sure that, if Harry was here, he'd tell Bellis as little as he thought he could get away with.

Then again, he was the inspector of police. I'd have to tell him something.

Or perhaps not. I might be in luck. It was Sunday so perhaps he'd be at church with Mrs Go-About.

But, as it turned out, luck wasn't on my side. I'd barely opened my mouth to say good morning to the constable on duty before Bellis was marching out of his office with a face fit to turn milk. Maybe he'd thought Sunday'd be quiet. Should've gone to church like a Christian, shouldn't he?

'It's one thing when you're with your master,' he said, looking me up and down, 'but I don't want you here asking questions by yourself.'

No point arguing about who was or wasn't my master. Standing on my dignity'd only make things worse

'I know it's not a usual situation,' I said, all apologetic, 'and I'm not saying I like it – puts me in a difficult position, to tell you the truth – but Mr Probert-Lloyd has asked me to carry on the investigation while he's at home dealing with a family matter.'

'What family matter? Can't it wait? Being coroner isn't something to be picked up and put down on a whim!'

I gritted my teeth. 'It's a delicate matter, Mr Bellis, but I know you're a man of discretion. Justice Probert-Lloyd has suffered a stroke of apoplexy. Harry rode out to Glanteifi yesterday morning to be with his father. He was still alive yesterday afternoon but I can't tell you any more than that.'

Was it the slip I'd made in referring to Harry by his given name or the news about Mr Probert-Lloyd that rocked Billy Go-About back on his heels? Either way, he lost his bluster. 'I'm very sorry to hear that,' he said.

I nodded. 'I'm waiting to hear from Mr Probert-Lloyd with further instructions and I'll be going up to the Black Lion after this to see if there are any messages. But I do know he wanted to speak to Mrs Harris. Is she still here?'

Bellis pulled himself back from whatever calculation was going on inside his head. 'No. She's been and gone.'

'Can I speak to Mr Harris? He may know where I can find her.'

The inspector looked me up and down. 'Do you understand the term *quid pro quo*, young man?'

Didn't he know what I did for a living? Of course he did. He was just putting me in my place.

'I'm a lawyer's clerk, Mr Bellis,' I said, keeping my voice flat. 'I should hope I know what a *quid pro quo* is.'

'Then you'll understand what I want.'

I nodded. I'd have to tell him at least some of what we knew. Apart from anything else I'd look hopeless otherwise – as if I'd been going about, asking questions, and nobody'd told me a damn thing.

So I informed him that I'd been able to positively identify Jenkyn Hughes. And I gave him Mrs Coleman's news about the as yet unidentified cousin who'd come and taken away all Hughes's belongings. Then, when he still didn't look very impressed, I passed on the information I'd got from David Daniels about Hughes's gambling habits, and the fact that his business partners had insured his life for an unusually large sum. Which was definitely not something he wanted to hear, believe me.

'Are you accusing Mr Philips of Philips and Lloyd of being involved with this death?'

I held my hands up. 'I'm not accusing anybody of anything, Mr Bellis. I'm just telling you what I've found out.'

But not everything. For some reason, I was getting as bad as Harry on the subject of Teff, Banc yr Eithin. I left out the fact that the dead man had shown too much interest in Mrs Harris. And the fact that, if Gwyn Puw was right about what would happen to a naked body on the limestone, then Jenkyn Hughes's corpse had been stripped naked *after* it came out of the water.

'It's not appropriate for somebody like you to go around asking impertinent questions of your betters,' Bellis told me. 'I don't want you to go bothering Mr Philips again.'

All my *gwas bach* instincts, all Mr Schofield's careful training in what was appropriate to my station opened my mouth to say, 'Just as you like, Mr Bellis.' But then I heard Harry's voice – as clear in my head as if he was standing next to me – and closed it again before I could say a word.

You know as much about it all as I do. Just use your judgement.

'Can I see Mr Harris, now, please?' I asked. 'In my position as coroner's officer.'

Old Schofield's beady eye was like a kitten's wide-eyed innocence compared to the look Bellis gave me, then. My stomach clenched. I half expected him to hit me.

'You can be smug if you like. But coroner's officer's going to be your only position after I've informed Mr Schofield of your insolence.'

I should've backed down. I should've apologised in the hope that he wouldn't complain about me.

'If I could see Mr Harris now, I'd be grateful.'

Icy politeness. I'd learned that from Harry, too.

A finger. Bellis's. Right in front of my face. 'Let me give you a piece of advice, *Mr Davies*. Do not make an enemy of me.'

I managed to squash an insane urge to wave a finger back at him, thank God, and just gave a brief nod. *I understand.*

Teff Harris surprised me by getting up when I went into his cell, and I took a step backwards before I realised that he was holding his hand out.

'Mr Davies – thank you again for what you did for my boy.'

I shook his hand. 'He was very determined to look after that cow of yours.'

Harris grinned and I realised how like him his son was. 'My wife said he was strutting like a turkey-cock when she got back and saw how he'd got the place defended.'

Time to make the most of his gratitude. 'I saw Clarkson earlier on today, as a matter of fact, and he said your wife told him that nobody would've dared come for the cow again.' I hesitated. 'What did you do to make sure they wouldn't?'

Teff Harris went back to his mattress and sat down. 'That's my business.' He crossed his legs in front of him and sat there, straight backed, as if he was holding court, not sitting in Billy Go-About's lock-up.

'I know how you threatened anybody who lifted a finger against your house,' I told him. 'Did you take your gun and threaten your neighbours with it again, Mr Harris?'

He stared at me, cheeks sucked in and I was afraid he was pulling back into himself. Then he surprised me for the second time in as many minutes.

'What sort of coward goes to a man's house, when they know he won't be there, and threatens his child?' I was familiar with questions I wasn't supposed to answer. 'Those men *deserved* to have the fear of God put into them. They'd turned up at my home, faces covered, and tried to take my property from my child. No man does that twice. Not to me.'

Arglwydd annwyl! Teff Harris and Billy Bellis were cut from exactly the same cloth. *I'm in charge. You do what I say or it'll be the worse for you.* No wonder Bellis wanted to find Teff guilty of something – he knew exactly what the man was capable of.

I decided that there was no point picking my way about like a cat in a yard full of shit.

'Mr Harris. We know you stripped Mr Hughes's body.'

I braced myself but he just stared up at me. 'You're taking that anonymous note as gospel?'

'No. The body wasn't damaged by the limestone. It should've been cut to ribbons but it wasn't. So it stands to reason that, when you found him, Mr Hughes was clothed.'

'Not damaged? Where he'd been lying on those rocks his body looked like meat.'

I shook my head. 'That wasn't from the rocks. It's called *livor mortis*. It's where blood settles after it's stopped running around the body.'

He looked at me as if he was going to call me a liar but then changed his mind. 'You'd think I'd know that. But we always buried them in their uniforms.'

Them. His comrades. Dead in the Afghan War. Briefly, I imagined mountains in a dry and dusty land, Teff Harris standing over the grave of a fallen comrade. He'd seen things I never would.

'So why did you strip him?'

He looked up at me but said nothing.

'Mr Harris, Inspector Bellis thinks you murdered Jenkyn Hughes. Mr Probert-Lloyd doesn't.'

'Funny way of showing his faith in me. Staying away.'

'His father's dying.' I was hoping to shock him. From the way he blinked, I was pretty sure I'd succeeded. 'He's had an apoplexy, and Harry's gone home. I'm acting for him at the moment.' I looked Harris in the eye, man to man. 'I can help you. But I need to know the truth.'

His expression didn't change but his stare was fit to suck the thoughts out of my head. I waited. Still, he said nothing.

'All right,' I said, 'I'll tell you what I already know. Inspector Bellis believes you're guilty because of the note. But I think there are a lot of other people who might've wanted to get rid of Jenkyn Hughes.'

'What? Like the poor sods whose emigration money he was stealing to gamble with? That does me no good. I was one of them.'

'Were you a bondholder or were you paying in installments?'

He looked at me sharply. 'I never do work without something to show for it. I told Hughes I'd have my family's bond up front and work off what I owed him unloading his coal.'

'So *you* owed *him* money?'

'No. I owed him *labour*.'

Just the hardness in his voice was enough to make my balls shrivel. If Teff Harris had decided that Jenkyn Hughes'd crossed him, I wouldn't've wanted to be in the emigration agent's shoes.

'That coal,' I started. 'Was he trying to be too clever with it – selling it twice – once to Mrs Parry, and then again to whoever'd come to the beach for it?' I got nothing, not so much as the flicker of a change of expression. I carried on. 'Because he could've been away to America before anybody realised that it wasn't all there, couldn't he? Gwyn Puw doesn't burn lime before April and that's when the emigrant ship was supposed to be leaving.'

Harris sucked his teeth and stared at me. 'He was enough of a gambler to do what you've just suggested for some of the coal but not for all of it. Not enough for me to notice at any rate. He knew I wouldn't stand for it.'

I nodded. 'Maybe somebody took the rest, knowing that Hughes wasn't going to come after them.'

'Because they'd killed him, you mean?'

I shrugged. 'Because they knew he was dead, at any rate.'

I could almost see Teff Harris weighing things up. He didn't want to trust me but he knew he didn't have much choice. 'The inspector thinks he's got all the evidence he needs,' he said. 'Been very pleased to tell me that all my neighbours are quite prepared to believe I killed Jenkyn Hughes.'

And then I knew. Beyond any shadow of doubt, whatever Harris said or didn't say. 'That's why you stripped him, isn't it? To hide his identity. Because when you saw who it was, you knew nobody'd believe that you'd just happened upon his body. Not him – the man who was trying to steal your wife. The man who was trying to swindle a woman you respect.'

I stared at him. He might've been waiting for a cart to give him a lift into town, not listening to evidence that could hang him. 'Did you threaten him?' I asked. 'Tell him he'd better not steal from Mrs Parry or he'd have you to answer to? Did somebody hear you?'

Harris tilted his head from one side to the other. The bones in his neck made a wet clicking noise. 'Anybody accused me of threatening him?'

'I don't know. All I know is that Bellis's officers've been talking to your neighbours.'

His face didn't change, but he knew the kind of things his neighbours were likely to say. 'We'll see then. But I'll tell you this. Jenkyn Hughes was a chancer and a fool. Made a fool of himself over Ruth. My wife. Didn't care who heard him talking nonsense to her.'

'Including you?'

'Including everybody.'

Harris's wife must be bewitching beyond belief for a man to be so careless of his own reputation. Not to mention his safety. 'Was she flattered?' I asked. 'Did it turn her head?'

Teff Harris's gaze rested on me with all the subtlety of an iron bar. 'My wife is the truest woman you'll ever meet. She'd beg with me in the streets before she'd betray me.'

If another man had said it, I might've thought he was trying to convince himself. But not Teff Harris. That was what he believed to the marrow of his bones. 'So you had no need to get rid of Mr Hughes.'

He gave a bark of a laugh. 'If I had to kill every man who made eyes at my wife – or wrote poems for her like that fool Obadaiah Vaughan – the parish'd be stinking to high heaven with the corpses.'

'But you did strip the body, didn't you? Because you knew what everybody else would think?' He still wasn't going to admit to it but even Teff Harris couldn't make silence look like anything other than guilt. And I knew that's how a jury would see it, too. 'But why did you try and cover it up – not go to the coroner with it?'

He shook his head. 'I wasn't covering it up. I told Mr Probert-Lloyd that first day – I didn't have time to go chasing around the county looking for the police or the coroner. I knew Jaci Rees would know what to do.'

God help me, I believed him.

Harry

Benton Reckitt arrived as I was writing a response to Lydia's letter. Shown in by the maid, he strode over to where I sat.

'What an extraordinary device,' he said, by way of greeting. 'Did you design it yourself?'

'Partly. I outlined my ideas to a cabinet maker and he was able to construct what I needed.'

'It's ingenious. And I see it works tolerably effectively.'

He was clearly reading my letter to Lydia but, even as I drew breath to object, it struck me that, as he was about to attend my father, I might do better to keep my censorious words to myself.

'As you will have gathered,' I began, 'my father has had an apoplectic stroke.'

'No. He has not.'

Reckitt sounded quite certain of it and, just for a moment, I felt a surge of hope. Was it possible that this had all been a terrible mistake and Prendergast had misdiagnosed my father's condition? 'What do you mean?' I asked, trying to see what Reckitt was doing at my father's side.

'Apoplectic strokes result in the obliteration of all mental functions,' Reckitt said, folding the blankets back from my father's sleeping form. 'Followed, not necessarily immediately but swiftly thereafter, by death. Your father is alive and, I believe, has been conscious and speaking.'

Somewhat thrown by this diagnostic summary, I mumbled, 'Yes. He has.'

Reckitt applied what I assumed was an ear trumpet to my father's chest. He said nothing for the space of half a minute or so. Then he straightened up abruptly. 'Tell me about his speech.'

Did that mean that his heart sounded satisfactory? I did not dare ask.

'He can't produce sentences. Only single words.'

'Impaired, then. There will be a lesion, for certain.'

A lesion? I racked my brains in vain for any memory of Gray having spoken in this way. 'What does that mean?' I asked, vexed at being forced to admit ignorance.

'It means that your father has suffered an interruption in the proper supply of blood to his brain. This may be occasioned by one of two things. An effusion into his brain from a ruptured vessel. Or a thrombotic blockage which has occasioned what the French call *ramolissement* in surrounding tissue.'

I mentally translated *ramolissement* but was none the wiser when I realised that it implied a softening of my father's brain tissue. 'Will he recover?'

'Recover his speech, d'you mean?'

I shook my head uncertainly. 'Recover completely, survive the stroke.'

'He has survived. Whether he will be alive tomorrow or next week or next month nobody can say. But the immediate danger from *this* stroke is past, if he has regained his senses and spoken to you.'

I was having trouble adapting to Reckitt's absolutism. It was so unlike the vague prognostications of Dr Prendergast that I did not know whether to be reassured or dubious.

Reckitt turned back to my father. 'Is he generally in good health?'

'I believe so. It's not something we discuss.'

'Does he suffer shortness of breath? Pains in his legs?'

Had he heard evidence that might suggest such things in the beating of my father's heart? 'Not as far as I'm aware.'

'And has he experienced anything like this before?'

I shook my head, as much in sorrow at my own failure to provide a definitive answer as in ignorance. 'Again, if he has, I'm not aware of it.' Was it possible that my father had suffered a milder version of this stroke, from which he had entirely recovered, while I had been in London? I thought it unlikely. Whilst he might have been unwilling to admit to bodily frailty himself, I did not imagine for a moment that Isabel Griffiths would have allowed me to remain in ignorance.

'It's highly likely that he will suffer a further stroke in the days or weeks to come,' Reckitt said, as if he were discussing something of no more significance than the likelihood of my father's eating lamb or beef at future dinners.

'I see.' Reckitt was still standing at my father's side. What was he observing? 'Is there anything that can be done?'

'I would recommend bleeding him.'

I was horribly disappointed. 'Isn't that somewhat old-fashioned?'

'That depends on one's rationale for the procedure. If one is stuck in the dark ages of humours and spirits and their release, then you are quite correct. Generally, blood-letting serves to do nothing but weaken the patient, to his or her detriment. However, if this stroke has been occasioned by an effusion as a result of pressure on vessel walls, then reducing blood volume will bring about a reduction in pressure and a lessening of the chance of a catastrophic event. D'you see?'

'And if the stroke arose from the other cause – the *ramolissement*?' I asked.

'Thrombosis is more likely with an excess of blood,' Reckitt stated. 'In either case, bleeding will only be of benefit.'

Dr Prendergast arrived as Reckitt was bleeding my father. He had not waited to be announced but had come up to the sick-room of his own accord. After a stiff greeting, he gave vent to his annoyance.

'Mr Probert-Lloyd, as your father's physician for many years, I must object to Dr Reckitt's presence here.'

'I beg your pardon, Dr Prendergast.' I would be courteous, even if I was the only one in the room who felt the need to bother. 'Reckitt has been consulting with me in the matter of the death at Tresaith and, as he is an expert in diseases of the brain, I thought he might have something valuable to contribute in this case.'

'An expert?' Prendergast clearly found this a laughable idea.

'Indeed,' Reckitt said, keeping his face turned to my father's arm and the basin he held beneath it. 'Though I don't expect you've read my monographs on tumours of the brain, they've gained me some degree of regard amongst my peers.'

'Then why the blazes aren't you in London pursuing your macabre interests with them instead of lurking here?'

Though tellingly ill-mannered in its phrasing, it was a question that had occurred to me, too.

'That is neither any of your business nor relevant to the present case,' Reckitt snapped. 'Mr Probert-Lloyd, would you be so good as to take this basin, so that I can bandage the arm?'

I moved over and, carefully, took the blood-filled basin from him. I put it on the nightstand and turned to Prendergast.

'No offence was intended, Doctor. Nor did I wish to exclude you. I merely felt that Reckitt might have something to contribute.'

There was a few moments' tense silence during which I had the impression that Prendergast was glaring at Reckitt. Then he turned to me. 'Henry, may I speak with you in private, please?'

I tried not to be offended by his familiarity but it was hard not to feel that he was putting me in my place. *I'm your elder, you must listen to me.*

'Very well, shall we step out onto the landing?'

Once we were out of my father's chamber, Prendergast used the pretext of standing where the light was better to draw me away from the door to the very end of the landing, where a round-topped window looked out over the river.

'Henry, I know you have been away a great deal until recently so you perhaps do not know—'

I did not let him finish. 'You think I haven't heard the gossip about Reckitt? Actually, Prendergast' – two could play at the familiarity game – 'I would have to have stuffed my ears pretty thoroughly to avoid hearing how the doctor is a drunk, a fool, a buffoon.'

'And yet you still employ him in your father's care?'

'Because I prefer to judge on my own observations. And I have found Reckitt to be intelligent, well informed and sober.' I might have added that he was odd, abrupt and lacking in courtesy to the point of rudeness but did not wish to oblige Prendergast by criticising Reckitt in any way.

'Am I to infer that you find me less than well informed?' I was given no leave to answer before he swept on. 'What you may not appreciate, Henry, is that in medicine, experience is as valuable as any *monograph*. Frequently more so. And I have been your father's physician for decades.'

I have always disliked being browbeaten. It is nothing more than a rarified form of bullying. 'And does experience tell you what the causes of apoplexy are?' I asked.

'Experience tells me the likely *course* of the illness, which is more to the point.'

'I disagree. If one understands the cause of a disease then a remedy may suggest itself. Following a brief consultation with Dr Reckitt, I am now able to give two causes for apoplexy and the reasons why, in this case, bleeding is more than a conventional response born of the need to be seen to be doing something.' I paused fractionally, as if I were challenging a witness and felt a frisson of ruthless excitement. Dear God but I was sick of being nice to people! And of enduring the suffocation of their niceness to me. At that moment, I missed the bar with the intensity of a knife under the ribs. 'Can you, Dr Prendergast, do the same?'

Prendergast said nothing for several seconds. 'Reckitt,' he spat, eventually, 'is a theorist—'

'On the contrary, he is an anatomist. A practical investigator. He does not theorise about what causes illness and death, he opens the bodies of the dead and investigates until he finds a cause.' I should have stopped short of that last sentence, for Prendergast pounced upon it.

'And will you let him open your father's body? Investigate the cause of his death? No.' I heard the sneer in the voice he had raised, presumably to carry as far as Reckitt at the other end of the landing. 'You may applaud Reckitt's dissection of paupers but you will not allow him to anatomise your own father.'

Hoist with my own petard. Serve me right. But those reactions came in retrospect. At the time I had only one wish. To thwart Prendergast and prove that, whatever he thought about me, he was mistaken.

'You're wrong,' I said. 'I will allow it.'

John

So, the anonymous letter had told the truth, as far as it went. Teff Harris *had* stripped the body after bringing it up out of the water. And, ironically, he'd done it so as not to be suspected of exactly the crime that Billy Go-About had put him in the lock-up for.

After leaving Harris in his cell, I walked smartly away, as if I was going somewhere. Just in case old Go-About tried to get me to tell him what Teff had said. Within two minutes, I found myself halfway to the docks, standing at the end of a lane opposite the Custom House.

What should I do next? Go down to the quayside and try and find the boat that had delivered the limestone to Tresaith?

No. Go back to Newcastle Emlyn. Go and see Harry and tell him that if he's not able to continue the case, neither are you.

That would be the sensible thing to do.

I took a breath and looked around. I don't know what I was looking for – an excuse not to go back to Newcastle Emlyn, probably – but something caught my eye. Or, rather, *someone*. A familiar-looking figure was standing fifty yards away, on the far side of the High Street, leaning against the wall at the entrance to Market Lane.

I started walking towards him, trying to look like anybody else going up and down to the docks. By the time I'd halved the distance between us, I knew I was right. I recognised him. He wasn't doing anything, just leaning against the wall, looking up the High Street in the direction of the Black Lion.

Watching. Waiting. For Harry?

I'll be honest, I wasn't keen to speak to him. Last time we'd met, down on the docks, he'd managed to give the impression that, for sixpence, he'd rip our arms off and beat us to death with them. But we were in a public place, where a man having a limb torn off would be noticed, so I scraped my courage together and marched up to him. 'Good morning! Are you watching for the coroner?'

I spoke to him in English. It was the language he'd chosen to use with Harry. His expression didn't change. He just moved his eyes from the street to me.

He looked exactly the same as last time we'd met. Same canvas trousers. Same stained smock, same knitted cap on his bald head. And that cold pipe stuck bizarrely behind one ear.

'If you remember, I'm the coroner's assistant,' I said when he just carried on looking at me. 'The coroner's not here. And he won't be. Not for a few days. Urgent family matters.'

He stood there, watching me gabble.

'If you have information, you can speak to me.'

'Not here.'

I jumped. Hadn't really expected him to say anything.

'Come to the Black Lion then. We've got a room set aside.'

'No.'

No. On second thoughts, he was right. If he walked into the Black Lion in those clothes, he'd look like a pig in a cake shop. 'Where, then?' I asked.

He turned and started walking down Market Lane towards Mwldan and the foundry. I followed.

At the end of the lane, where you could smell the stink that came off the culverted stream, he stopped and turned to me. 'The lime boats to Tresaith,' he said in Welsh. 'I was on them.'

I hesitated, trying to remember what Harry'd been going to ask the men on the boat. There'd been two loads of lime delivered while Mrs Parry was away, the second on the day before the body was found.

'Did Jenkyn Hughes go in the boat with you on the last trip?'

'No.'

'Did you see him at all?'

'Not the last time.'

That fitted with the theory that Hughes'd been dead and buried in the lime for days before Teff found him.

'What about the other times? The time before last – while Mrs Parry was away?'

The man's eyes had about as much life in them as marbles. 'He was on the beach. Waiting.'

'Did you speak to him?'

'No.'

'Who did?'

'Albion Thomas. He was in charge.'

'Who else was on the lime boat?' I asked.

'Me, Scrim Richards and Shoni Jones.'

My pulse jumped. 'Shoni Jones from Moylegrove? Jenkyn Hughes's cousin?'

Another man would've shrugged. Maybe he was too musclebound.

'Don't know. He didn't speak to Hughes. He just unloaded with me and Scrim.'

'So Albion Thomas went ashore to talk to Jenkyn Hughes and you three unloaded the lime?'

He didn't agree or disagree. Just looked at me.

I tried to picture the scene in my head. Three of them unloading the stone into the sea off the beach, Albion Thomas with Hughes on the sand. I wasn't exactly sure where the limestone would've been dumped but it must've been a fair way out, where the water was deep enough for the boat. 'How did you know it was Jenkyn Hughes on the beach?' I asked.

'Square patterned waistcoat. Light coloured trousers. Seen him before.'

Those very identifiable clothes. Like some kind of calling card. 'Where'd you seen him?'

'About.'

I stopped and gathered my thoughts. The stream's stink was making me breathe through my mouth, and I could almost taste the stench on my tongue. Disgusting.

'Look,' I said, as if I was letting him in on a secret 'Mr Probert-Lloyd – the coroner – he knows about Jenkyn Hughes gambling down on the docks.' I didn't say *smwglins*. Nobody who went there would call it that. It'd be like a criminal saying to his wife *see you later, I'm just off to do a bit of aiding and abetting.* 'He knows Hughes was in debt.' I was watching the big man for any sign that he knew what I was talking about but I'd've got as much information from watching the wall behind him.

'We don't want to get anybody into trouble,' I said. 'We're not the police. It's nothing to us who drinks where or who takes whose money off him at cards. None of our business. All we want is to find out who killed Jenkyn Hughes.'

His eyes hadn't moved from my face. It was a struggle not to look away from him, that stare of his was unnerving. 'D'you know any of the men Jenkyn Hughes played cards with?' I asked.

'Played with anybody who sat down at the table with him.'

I couldn't tell if he was genuinely stupid or trying to be unhelpful.

'Anybody particular he owed a lot of money to, then?'

'One or two.'

'D'you know who they were?'

He blinked, then. Hesitated. It was the most emotion I'd seen him show. Hughes's gambling wasn't what he'd come to tell me about and he didn't know how much to let on.

I was uncomfortable, standing there. The dirt and coal dust and kicked-out cinder had been trodden into a gritty mud that seeped in through my boots. And the air around us was foul – not just from the stream, either. Smelt as if the foundrymen and labourers who worked here used this patch between buildings as a privy. They'd've done better to sit on the edge of the stream and shit in there. It was a public sewer anyway by the look and smell of it.

His silence was making me nervous and I looked about. Being a Sunday it was quiet but that cut two ways. Fewer threats but also fewer witnesses.

Suddenly, he spoke. But not to answer my question. Not exactly.

'Some owed *him* money as well.'

So far, we'd only heard about Hughes's gambling losses. Could somebody have decided to get rid of him because they owed him more than they could pay?

'Who?' I asked.

'Nobody that would've killed him.'

'What, like a gentleman?' I was sure James Philips'd been lying when he said he hadn't seen Jenkyn Hughes anywhere but at the office.

He gave a single forward tilt of his head. As if he thought he'd be able to take it back if he needed to.

I pushed him. 'Mr James Philips – of Philips and Lloyd?'

No response. But I was pretty sure he'd've said no if it hadn't been Philips.

Well, well, well.

'So,' I said, keen to bring things to a close and get back to safety. 'The night of the last-but-one delivery, you sailed up to Tresaith, you unloaded the limestone while Albion Thomas talked to Jenkyn Hughes, and then you sailed away again. Is that right?'

He didn't answer, but something about his cliff of a face told me there was more. 'What else?' I asked. He stared at me but still didn't answer.

The missing coal. It had to be. 'You loaded some coal on board, didn't you? And took it up the coast?'

His mouth stayed shut, but I knew I was right, otherwise he'd've given me that deadweight 'No' of his.

'How did you get the coal on board from the beach?'

'Used the skiff. Sacks. Winch.'

'And did you take the coal up the coast or down?'

For several moments I thought I'd got all I was getting. But then he opened his mouth again. Briefly. 'Up.'

'To Penbryn?'

Another deniable nod. I thought hard. 'Shoni Jones,' I said. I'd been going to ask if he knew where Jones lived but there'd been a flicker of something when I mentioned the name. 'What did he do? He did something didn't he?'

The eyes on mine were flat, full of nothing. 'He watched the beach with his telescope. Tresaith.'

His *telescope?* I waited. Nothing. 'What did he see?'

The sailor put up a huge hand and rubbed one eye with his knuckles, like a child. 'Don't know' he said. 'But he was watching something. The telescope never came away from his eye.'

They were the longest sentences he'd uttered. Perhaps it was the relief of finally getting it out. 'Why didn't you tell Mr Probert-Lloyd this when we spoke to you on the docks?' I asked.

No shrug. No shifting of the feet. Nothing moved except his eyes. They moved away from my face. It was as much of an admission that he wasn't entirely happy with his own behaviour as I was going to get. 'Some things it pays a man not to see.'

He didn't want to get a reputation for a loose tongue.

'Why are you here now, then, talking to me?'

His eyes moved back to mine. 'Tried to speak to your master. But he had a boy with him.'

A boy? When had Harry had a boy with him?

'So you came to wait for him.' I said. 'Something was important enough to make you come.'

'A duty was owed.'

I waited, curious, but he'd said all he was going to say. And curiosity didn't make it my business to ask.

'Did you see the cousin – Shoni Jones – again after that?'

It wasn't a hesitation because none of his answers had come quickly but he seemed to think even longer about this one. I looked away from him, giving him time, putting my eyes on the shitty scum on the far edge of the Mwldan where it left a crust on the walls of the buildings above.

'Heard he'd been at Captain Coleman's.'

Harry

Prendergast left me on the landing and I listened to him making offended haste down the stairs before opening the front door and banging it shut. Moyle's sense of household decorum would be outraged that nobody had been summoned to show the doctor out but, as far as I was concerned, Prendergast had departed as he had presumed to come up: without so much as a by-your-leave.

I turned and went back to my father's room.

'Prendergast left, has he?' Reckitt asked.

Suddenly irritated beyond reason by the whole situation, I chose to hear a smug kind of triumph in Reckitt's question.

'Yes. And now, unless you have anything profitable to offer, I'd like you to leave too, please.' I regretted my rudeness as soon as I heard the words leave my mouth, particularly as it had been entirely calculated. I put a weary hand up. 'No. I'm sorry Reckitt. Forgive me. I'm afraid I had an almost sleepless night and it hasn't agreed with me.'

'Understandable. Think nothing of it. But I will leave if you'd prefer.'

'No, please, stay. I can't tell you how sick I am of my own company.'

Reckitt took the chair he had been sitting on and moved it away from the bed in the direction of the fire.

'What advice has Prendergast offered about your father's condition?' he asked.

Though the question was somewhat abrupt, I was glad of it. I needed advice and it was a relief to have the subject broached for me.

'When I arrived yesterday, he told me that the next twenty-four hours would be crucial.'

'Meaning that your father was highly likely to suffer another stroke and die of it.'

Reckitt's failure to leaven facts with empathy was shocking but, oddly, I found myself glad of its sinew-stiffening effect; I did not want my emotions roused in the presence of a near-stranger. 'Yes. And he did appear to suffer another. He became unconscious. But this morning he woke and spoke.'

'But not well.'

'No. As I said, earlier, single words. And those effortfully.'

Reckitt rested one ankle on the opposite knee, entirely at ease speaking about sudden illness. 'Cerebral seizures – especially when they result from *ramolissement* – are often associated with disease elsewhere in the body.' From his measured tone, Reckitt might have been speaking to the medical students at Guy's. 'Of course, one would, in any case, expect a man of your father's age to be showing signs of physical decline. I have to counsel you to expect no great future length of life for him.'

I pulled in an uncertain breath. It was no more than I had suspected myself but, still, it felt as if a sentence of death had just been pronounced.

'Just as well that your appointment as coroner was *ad hoc,*' Reckitt observed. 'Your time will soon be taken up learning the ropes of squiring. A far cry from being a barrister, eh?'

I sat down, heavily, in the chair opposite him, my attention removed from my father's future to my own. 'Was medicine your father's profession, Reckitt?' I asked. 'Have you followed the family trade?'

'No. My father is a clergyman.'

'You weren't tempted to follow him?'

'I am a man of science. I prefer that things are visible and tangible. I dislike being told that I must simply have faith and live by a set of precepts apparently laid down by a being I can neither debate with nor disagree with.'

'You're an atheist, then?' Even saying the word in my father's bedroom felt transgressive.

'I wouldn't presume to rule out the existence of a deity altogether. But, if such an entity exists, it is unlikely to be the anthropomorphic vision we are invited to believe in.'

'A scientific God, then?'

'One not at variance with science.'

A brief silence fell between us, the only sounds in the room rising from the stableyard behind the house.

'You don't seem shocked,' Reckitt said. 'The effect of London society, I suppose.'

'Possibly,' I conceded. Then, because it was more pleasant to speak about abstract notions than about the potentially imminent death of my father, I asked, 'You don't agree with Edmund Burke then, that man is, *constitutionally*, a religious animal?'

'No. I think he is religious by education and inculcation. As a means of social control, organised religion is without its equal. Voltaire implied as much when he said that, if God did not exist, it would be necessary to invent him. He felt that the excesses of the Revolution would have been far greater without the ameliorating effects of Christianity.'

I smiled somewhat ruefully. 'Should my father recover, may I advise against expressing that view in his presence? He thinks the Revolution was the most godless thing to have happened since the sack of Rome.'

No sooner had I heard myself laughing with Reckitt than I felt guilty. How could I be mocking my father when he lay, close to death, not two yards away? And yet, the sensation of being able to open my mind to another person without the fear of being judged scandalously radical was a luxury I had almost forgotten.

'Do I detect that you are not overjoyed at being expected to play the feudal lord?'

From his tone, I imagined a slightly quizzical look on Reckitt's face. How would a doughy face look quizzical? I realised that, in my mind's eye, Reckitt had the corpulent appearance of an oriental panjandrum in a *Punch* cartoon; except that they were always depicted as inscrutable and Reckitt seemed to me entirely the opposite.

'I always promised myself that I would never play the squire,' I said. 'I ran away to London and trained as a barrister to avoid it. I wanted to provide for myself, not be dependent on the labour of others.'

'And then you went blind and that choice was taken from you.'

His forthrightness was as liberating as it was shocking. 'Yes. And I was forced to come home.'

'And now?'

'I wanted to stand for Coroner,' I found myself admitting. 'I hoped it would keep me off the bench. Squiring I can bend to, I think, but not being a magistrate. However, if I'm now to be denied the chance to show that I can be an effective coroner, I'll come under ever-increasing pressure to sit on the bench.'

'Just say no.' Reckitt made it sound as simple as the uttering of a single word.

I sighed. 'If I refuse, I'll offend every member of the gentry in the county.'

'Why should you care? You aren't squire of Glanteifi by their permission. You can do what you like.'

'No man is an island,' I said, quoting Donne for the second time in two days. 'Nor should he be. We all need society.'

'Not me.' His tone was definitive. 'What I need is my work. Society is a distraction at best.'

'And at worst?' I asked, intrigued at the suggestion that he might regard local society with all the esteem it felt for him.

'A hindrance. The better people become acquainted with me, the more they feel free to tell me what I must and musn't do. I find it intolerable.'

Had I been able, I would have stared at him. I had never met a man who was so taken up with his calling that he truly did not require social engagement. Even Gray, obsessed as he was with his anatomical studies, was an entertaining companion. 'You genuinely don't have any regard for the judgements people make on you?'

I saw Reckitt moving his head to and fro in a vague kind of denial. 'If they pronounce me rude and rough in my manners, I dare say they're right. I've never mastered the arts of refinement. But if they criticise my work, or my giving my time to it, it simply shows that they have not understood the seriousness of my endeavour.'

'Which is?' I asked, noting how quickly my own conversational style had fallen in with his.

Uncrossing his legs, he leaned towards me and his tone took on a new passion. 'To grasp the workings of the brain in all its different manifestations. To understand its diseases and their causes. Perhaps, in the fullness of time, to use anaesthesia to probe the material of the brain itself in living subjects.'

'You would cut people's heads open while they're *still alive*?'

'Alive but insensible. Anaesthetised. Conscious of no pain whatever.'

'And then what?'

'Perhaps it might be possible to remove tumours. Restore people to health.'

'How?' I asked, incredulous.

'I can't tell you, yet. But that's why it's vital that we carry out post-mortem examinations. To find out what effects tumours have, we must follow the path of a person's illness, then dissect their brain and other organs. If our ambition is to cure patients, then first we must be able to investigate these tumours – discover how integrated they are with surrounding tissue and how much damage would be done to the patient by their removal.'

I was silenced by the thought of such dissection.

'Probert-Lloyd.' After a brief silence, Reckitt's tone was restrained once more. 'I couldn't help overhearing what you and Prendergast said to each other outside the door.'

Momentarily befuddled, I shook my head.

'You told him that you would allow me to perform an autopsy on your father. Were you trying to confound him or did you mean it?'

'For God's sake, Reckitt,' I hissed, instead of answering his question, 'have some kind of care for my father. God knows what he can hear in his state.' My alarm was partly fuelled by guilt because, truth be told, Reckitt had hit the nail on the head. Yes, I had been trying to *confound* Prendergast. But, now that I was put on the spot, I found that I did not know my own mind on the subject. The dissection of my father's corpse was not something I had ever thought to be confronted with.

'I'm sorry,' Reckitt said. 'I was taking it as read that he was unconscious and would hear nothing. I beg your pardon.'

I could not decide whether he was genuinely contrite or whether this was simply an attempt to mollify me. His next question did nothing to clarify the issue.

'What would be his opinion on the matter? Would he greet the proposal with distaste?'

I opened my mouth to reply, but discovered that I did not know the answer to this, either. In many respects my father was a traditionalist, a man of conservative opinions. But, in others, he looked resolutely to the future. It was he who had insisted on close-stool chambers being constructed in all the main bedrooms at Glanteifi and piping running water into the kitchens so that the servants did not have to bring water in from the well. But whether such progressive tendencies would be reflected in his attitude to his own mortal remains I had no idea.

I confessed as much to Reckitt.

'Would you permit me to ask him? Should he regain sufficient comprehension to understand the implications, obviously.'

Everything in me rebelled against it. Surely the question was insensitive, implying, as it must, that his imminent death was not only a foregone conclusion but one that was being eagerly anticipated by Reckitt, a man of whom my father was unlikely to approve.

And yet, what right had I to deny my father an opinion as to what should happen to his body after his death?

As I struggled inwardly, Reckitt, presumably inferring that he should not press the matter, rose to his feet and returned to the bedside. Reaching down, he took my father's wrist and held it. 'His pulse is encouragingly strong.'

It seemed enough, for now.

John

I was still wondering how to go about finding Jenkyn Hughes's cousin when I called in at the Black Lion to check for messages and Harry's letter provided the answer. His idea of a meeting for bondholders was a stroke of genius.

Go and see my cousin, Philips, he'd written. *I'm including a note to him with this. He might be able to refuse you but he's less likely to refuse me as acting coroner.*

I put Harry's letter down and had a quick look at the note for his cousin. It was short and to the point – just what you might expect from a blind man in a hurry. But haste hadn't stopped him referring to me as his *valued and trusted assistant.*

I wondered whether those words were for my eyes as much as for his cousin's. He must've known I'd read the note.

To be honest, I wasn't keen to ask a favour of James Philips. He'd barely spoken to me when I went to his office, apart from getting shirty when he thought I was accusing him of something over the life insurance. Without Mrs Parry there, I wasn't sure he'd even see me.

A knock startled me out of my thoughts, and I looked at the open doorway.

Straightaway, I knew this must be Teff Harris's wife. She was easily the most striking-looking woman I'd ever seen outside of a picture. Even in an old *betgwn*, with a man's jacket over it instead of a shawl, she was beautiful. Perhaps she looked more beautiful *because* of the jacket. It gave her an exotic look, a hint that she wasn't like other women.

'Mr Davies?'

I nodded.

'I'm Ruth Harris,' she said in Welsh. 'Teff's wife.'

Belatedly, I got to my feet and pulled a chair forward for her. 'Sit down, please. Can I get you something to eat? I'm sure they'll bring something if I ask.' Especially if I asked using the words 'coroner's account'.

She asked for a cup of tea and off I went to find somebody to make us one.

When I came back with a tray, she was sitting, looking around at the room and, for the first time, I felt how its bareness reflected on our work. There were no pictures like there were in the more public rooms, only a set of shelves for a few pots. The wainscot made it look a bit less like a labourer's kitchen but the paneling needed a new coat of paint. Still, it covered the damp that was creeping up the walls, even if it didn't stop the air smelling of it. No wonder Mrs Weston'd been happy to give us this room, she probably got very little use out of it otherwise.

I poured the tea and put the pot on the hearth to keep warm. I'd persuaded the kitchen maid to nip a portion of sugar off the loaf for both of us and my mouth was watering at the thought of it. I'd take my tea without and just let the sugar melt on my tongue.

'Have you seen my husband?' Ruth Harris asked.

'Yes,' I said, passing her the tea and sugar.

'Thank you. Oh, sugar! I'll save it for Clarkson.' She slipped the sugar into a jacket pocket. 'What did Teff tell you?'

I passed her my chunk of sugar. 'Give Clarkson this as well.' The smile she gave me in thanks was so sweet that I almost forgot what she'd asked and I had to sip my tea to give myself time to remember.

'Teff told me that it was him who stripped the body,' I said. Not strictly true, of course. He hadn't actually said those words. But we both knew that's what'd happened.

'Have you told the police?' she asked.

I shook my head, swallowing tea. 'No. And I won't. Not yet.' I needed to speak to Harry before I did anything like that. 'But why didn't your husband tell the inspector himself when he was arrested?'

Ruth Harris put her cup down. 'Inspector Bellis is enjoying having my husband in his lock-up, Mr Davies. He'd love to be able to hang Teff for this murder. If Teff'd even told him that he *knew* Hughes, Bellis would've sent him to gaol to wait for the assizes.'

'Why?'

She looked past me at the fire, as if she was trying to decide something. Then she turned to me. 'About a year ago, our neighbours tried to run us off our land. They tried to steal our cow and they dumped a barrowload of cow shit into our spring. Teff went to report it but Bellis did nothing. Said we were squatters so we deserved all we got. But we're not squatters. Teff *bought* that land. He has papers to prove it. So he went to the magistrates and complained.' She looked straight into my eyes. 'Bellis isn't going to forget a thing like that. He thinks he's the law. He didn't like it when the magistrates told him otherwise.'

Mrs Parry had told me that Teff claimed to own his land but the way she'd described his house being built, it hadn't seemed all that likely. Now here was Ruth Harris telling the same tale. 'So your house isn't a *tŷ unnos* then?'

'If you mean, did we built it in one night, yes we did. We had to build it quickly and cheaply because we'd spent all our money on the land and the cow. And we wanted to get it built without interference. But it's not a *tŷ unnos* in the old-fashioned meaning. We're freeholders, not squatters.'

'But your neighbours still objected?'

'Of course they did! The land we bought had grazing, gorse and a spring. Our neighbours'd been using them all for years without paying anybody. Of course they objected. But they couldn't complain to the crown, could they? Or the magistrates? We hadn't committed any crime. They just thought if they could get rid of us, they'd have those things back.'

'Is that why you're going to America?'

Ruth Harris made a face that said it was all a lot more complicated than that. 'The prospects in America are just better. For us and for Clarkson.'

I had to ask. 'Why did you call your son Clarkson?'

She looked away from me. 'He's named after a soldier who saved Teff's life. He promised he'd name his first-born after him. And Teff's a man of his word.'

'But didn't the man have a Christian name?'

Her eyes came back to me again. 'That *was* his Christian name. Clarkson de Vere Mounton. He was Teff's commanding officer.'

I wanted to ask what an officer was doing saving the life of a private soldier but she said no more, and it wasn't my business to ask. I got back to the point. 'So Bellis is just looking for evidence against Teff to get his own back?' I asked.

Ruth Harris looked steadily at me. 'To be fair, Bellis might believe Teff is guilty. People are apt to believe anything of an old soldier, aren't they?'

Especially one who hadn't been too squeamish about threatening people with a gun.

'Can you help him?' she asked.

'We're looking for Jenkyn Hughes's killer,' I said. 'Once we've found him, Teff'll be out.'

'But not before?'

I felt uncomfortable. 'If Mr Probert-Lloyd was here, I'm sure he'd put pressure on the inspector to let your husband go. But he's been called home and Bellis isn't going to listen to me. It was a miracle he even let me see Teff.'

Her eyes were showing signs of strain – little crows' feet at each corner. And she had other lines on her face that a beautiful woman shouldn't have. Looked as if life with Teff Harris wasn't easy. But she carried herself in a way that told you she knew her own worth. Her husband knew how to value her. Lucky bastard.

'I'll be seeing Harry – Mr Probert-Lloyd – later on today,' I told her. 'I'll see if he'll write a letter to Inspector Bellis asking for your husband's release.'

'Thank you, Mr Davies.'

We both knew it probably wouldn't work. But it was all I could do. 'Can I ask you something else?' I asked.

'Of course.'

'Is Teff a card player?'

If she was surprised by the question, she didn't show it. 'In the army he was. Everybody plays cards in the army when there's nothing else to do. But only for pennies.'

'And not since?'

'No.' She shook her head, certain. 'According to Teff, only fools gamble and nobody wins except those who cheat.'

Jenkyn Hughes'd been in debt so, according to Teff's definition, he couldn't've been a cheater. But what if he'd caught somebody else cheating and threatened to expose them? Or even tried to blackmail them?

That might've been very unwise.

Harry

Having his pulse taken seemed to have roused my father for he stirred sufficiently to convey that he would like to sit up. Reckitt and I took an arm each to help him.

'Thank you.' Unlike his earlier utterances, this was delivered with all the ease and fluency of his speech before the stroke.

'Are you feeling better, Father?'

In response, he produced a barely distinguishable word.

'You feel strange?' I guessed.

'Yes.' Again, this word was entirely clear.

'Only to be expected, Mr Probert-Lloyd.' Reckitt spoke from the other side of the bed. 'Your brain has suffered a significant injury. You are lucky to be alive.'

My father made an indeterminate sound which might as easily have been derision as agreement. Was he glad to be alive or would he prefer not to have survived in this diminished state?

'From what Harry tells me, you've made great progress since yesterday.' Reckitt spoke slowly but not as if to an imbecile, and I had the impression that he was watching my father very carefully. 'I consider it likely that you will continue to make progress.'

In response, my father managed to expel sounds which were identifiable as, 'another' and, 'stroke'.

'It's possible that you will suffer another stroke, of course.' Reckitt would not sweeten the pill. 'But, if you do not, I think we can expect continued improvement.'

Though I could not see my father's reaction to this news, the word 'good' was perfectly distinct.

In my peripheral vision, I saw him raise his left hand and wave it between myself and Reckitt. 'Talk,' he spat.

I crushed a reflex resentment; he could not help but sound harsh, though he was simply encouraging us to continue speaking freely as we had been.

How much, I wondered, had he heard of our previous conversation? I decided that, in any case, it was time for a change of subject.

I turned to Reckitt. 'Our dead American apparently had a tendency to pursue women in a rather unrestrained manner. Could that be a symptom of the tumour in his brain?'

'It could be, certainly. The mores of American society aren't particularly different from our own, so that kind of behaviour can't be accounted for by being in an alien culture.'

'And gambling? Could it have made him more inclined to take unwarranted risks?'

This time, Reckitt's answer was both less swift and less definite. 'Again, it's possible. But I would need to know his character before the tumour developed.'

'You mean perhaps he was always an inveterate gambler?'

'Precisely.'

Had that been his reputation, I considered it highly unlikely that Mrs Parry would have entered into business with him; she was too shrewd for that. It seemed far more probable that the lump in Hughes's brain had caused him, like Phineas Gage, to become *not himself*.

I was about to ask Reckitt whether Hughes would have become more and more unreliable or, indeed, whether his tumour might have produced other symptoms, when I heard the sounds of a carriage coming up the drive. The pace of hoofs slowed from a trot to a steady clop as the driver manoeuvred on to the area below the terrace, and the jingle of bits and martingales carried up to the first storey as the horses blew and tossed their heads.

'I'd better go down, Reckitt.' Wil-Sam would be scampering for somebody to come and open the door to whatever important visitor had arrived. 'Would you mind staying here? I don't like to leave my father alone.'

I got to the bottom of the stairs just as a gentleman was being admitted.

'If you could let Mr Henry Probert-Lloyd know that his cousin, Mr Arthur Philips, would be glad of a moment of his attention.'

'It's all right, Moyle,' I called. 'I'm here.'

'Very good, Mr Henry.' The butler turned and stalked away. This sudden visitation by a cousin would be a wonder in the kitchen.

'Cousin Arthur, welcome to Glanteifi,' I said, allowing him to hear my pleasure at his arrival.

'Thank you. James tells me that your father has suffered a stroke. How is he?' He allowed the footman who had appeared to take his coat and hat.

It was a brave question. He must have known that there was a good chance my father had succumbed to a second, fatal attack by now.

'His condition is improving, thank you. He is sitting up and, if not conversing, then at least able to speak single words. He seems to understand what's being said to him, which is a blessing.'

'Indeed! I'm very glad to hear it.'

'Come up. He'll be glad of the diversion.' As I led Arthur Philips up the stairs, I acknowledged, guiltily, to myself that it was I who was glad of the diversion. My father might well be mortified to receive visitors in his current condition.

'Do you think he'll know me?' Arthur asked, cautiously. 'After all this time, and after … the apoplexy?'

I heard what he was not asking. 'He seems to know who's who. And before the seizure he was as sharp as ever. His memory was unimpaired.'

Philips did not reply and I wondered at his being here. Cousin by marriage or not, it was an extravagant gesture after one evening's reunion with me.

'Father,' I said as I closed the door behind us, 'do you remember my mother's cousin, Letitia? This is her husband, Arthur Philips.' I ushered him forward.

'George, my dear fellow. What a pleasure to see you again after all these years. I'm only sorry that it's in such unfortunate circumstances.'

My father emitted some vowels which I took to be an enquiry after Philips's own health. Evidently, Philips made the same assumption for he replied that he and his family were well. At my invitation, he sat in the chair I had vacated and proceeded to speak about his wife and son, telling my father that the 'whippersnapper, young James' was now nearly forty and married with children of his own.

Reckitt had risen to his feet as we entered. 'I should be going,' he said.

'Will you come back this evening? We have room to put you up so you needn't worry about getting home.'

Reckitt agreed to return after attending to whatever duties generally occupied him, then made his goodbyes.

I put a hand on Arthur Philips's shoulder. 'If you are settled for a few minutes, I'll go and find some refreshments for us.'

It was such a relief to be out of my father's room and in the world where people scurried about and spoke loud and clear that, after arranging for tea to be sent up, I did not hurry back to my cousin.

When I eventually returned to the bedroom, I found Arthur Philips standing at the window and my father asleep once more.

'I fear my nervous prattling has put him to sleep.'

'No, no. Reckitt assures me that a great deal of sleep is quite usual.'

'I must confess,' he admitted 'I was surprised to see Reckitt here. I assumed that Prendergast would be your family's doctor.'

'He is. Or, rather, he's always been my father's doctor. But Reckitt is more up-to-date. More modern in his thinking.'

'Yes. I know of his methods.'

'Do you have a personal connection?' I asked. His tone suggested as much.

'I'm on the board of guardians of the Cardigan Union workhouse. Dr Reckitt sees to our paupers' needs. And he applies to us, from time to time, for permission to perform dissections. Or autopsy examinations as he calls them.'

'So I understand.'

'Strictly speaking, of course, he needn't ask permission. Not if the body's unclaimed.' Arthur cleared his throat. 'Do you mind?'

I was caught off guard. 'I beg your pardon?'

'My dear fellow, do excuse me. May I take this seat, here?' He had obviously indicated the chair by the fire, forgetting that I could not be relied upon to notice such casual gestures.

'Of course. Please.' I fetched the other chair and sat opposite him.

'I must confess, I am glad of a few moments to speak to you, Harry. My wife and I were most troubled by the news you gave us when you visited the evening before last. About Jenkyn Hughes.'

So this was why he had come. 'Yes. A bad business.'

'Our disquiet was added to when our son, James, came to tell us of your assistant's visit to the office,' Philips said, carefully. 'Not simply because he brought news of your father's stroke but also because…' He paused, and I could feel him looking at me. 'As I believe I mentioned when you were kind enough to visit,' he began again, 'James is taking over more and more responsibility for the company, as is only right. One day, he will be in charge, in partnership with his cousin, Lloyd.'

Again, I waited.

'I intimated to you the other evening that we were in business with Mr Hughes – part of the Cardigan-Ohio Emigration Company.' He hesitated. 'In fact, it was not Philips and Lloyd that entered into the partnership but James himself. This was something he embarked upon as an independent investor. With my blessing, naturally. But Philips and Lloyd has no liability in the Cardigan-Ohio Company.'

'I see,' I said, though, in fact, I did not. Though Arthur clearly felt that Hughes's murder had come too close to his business for comfort, I could not yet see what this had to do with me.

'James brought to my attention something that I had not previously been aware of,' he continued. 'Apparently, rumours had begun to circulate that Hughes was a gambler. And not a successful one. Mrs Parry and my son began to have reservations about the security of their investments in the emigration company and Mrs Parry suggested that they would be wise to take out an insurance policy on Mr Hughes's life.'

'They were afraid that his gambling threatened his life?' I did not mention the gambling den that John had told me about. I was intrigued to see whether Arthur knew anything about it.

'The places Hughes had apparently chosen for his gaming activities were quite unsavoury,' Arthur said, confirming that he did. 'So, yes, I believe my son feared for his safety.'

'But isn't it quite usual, anyway, for the partners in a risky endeavour like this to take out insurance on each other's lives?' I asked, hoping John's information was correct. I did not want to seem an ignoramus in the ways of business; not when the subject of my inquest was a businessman.

'It is, yes,' Arthur Philips said, slowly. I imagined his eyes on my face, watching my reactions. 'But, in this case, both my son and Mrs Parry seem to have decided to take out insurance for what might be called a precautionary sum. To cover not only the losses which would be inevitable in the event of a partner's death but also any additional sums which might have been incurred as debts.'

John had, of course, passed on to me Mrs Parry's ruthless comment on the company's terms of business and each party's liability for the other's debts. But perhaps James had not been as explicit with his father, leaving Arthur to assume that all parties in the Cardigan-Ohio Emigration Company would be equally liable for the embezzlement of bondholders' money.

'I'm aware,' he went on, his tone still careful, 'that insuring a life for large sums like that might raise suspicions. Particularly in the light of Mr Hughes's death.'

There was no point denying it. My cousin cannot have been ignorant of the regular newspaper reports of murders motivated by the sums available from life-insurance policies.

'Harry, I am going to presume on your discretion and tell you something which I trust you will not disclose to anybody else.'

I shook my head. 'I beg your pardon, Arthur. I can't promise such a thing without knowing what you're going to tell me.'

'On my honour – and that of my son – it has nothing to do with Jenkyn Hughes's death.'

I believed him. That is, I believed he was speaking the truth as he knew it.

'I can only promise that, if it truly proves to have nothing to do with Hughes's murder, you have my word that it will not be revealed to a soul.'

The subsequent silence told me that Arthur was not entirely happy with this formulation but knew I could offer nothing more.

'Very well. The fact is that James owed money to Jenkyn Hughes.'

'Gambling debts?' I asked, my eyes lowered so as to keep what I could see of my cousin above the whirlpool. He did not stir.

'Yes.'

'Large enough to cause the firm embarrassment?'

'Large enough to cause James *personal* embarrassment. He could not take money out of the firm without my being aware of it and I would never have sanctioned such a thing.' He stopped, abruptly, as if he feared that he had been too much the businessman and too little the loving father. When he spoke again, his voice was hard. 'James complained that Hughes was no gentleman, that he would not give him the chance to win his money back. But only a fool blames bad luck for his losses and banks on his skills at the table to make them good.'

My mouth was suddenly dry. 'May I ask how you are able to say so definitively that this has no bearing on the death of Jenkyn Hughes?'

'Because my son has given me his word.' Then, clearly realising that the word of a man prepared to gamble in an illegal dockside drinking-house might be worth less than he would like, Arthur added,

'If you knew exactly when Mr Hughes was killed it would be easier to prove that James had nothing to do with his death.'

I agreed with him. The whole investigation would be easier if we knew when Hughes had met his end. Or even where. As it was, we knew nothing of Hughes's movements between his taking his leave of Mrs Parry and the discovery of his body. And that lack of certainty was, presumably, why Inspector Bellis felt able to keep Teff Harris in custody.

But here was a clear motive. Gambling debt.

I felt a surge of excitement. Did this explain the removal of Hughes's papers from Captain Coleman's? Had James – or another of Hughes's gambling cronies – charged Shoni Jones with finding the IOUs which confirmed sums owed? After all, debts did not die with the creditor but would now be payable to Hughes's heir.

'Who inherits Hughes's portion of the business?' I asked. 'Do you know?'

'Interesting that you should ask. James had assumed that we would have to wait until after the inquest had formally identified Hughes and probate could be applied for. But then an heir presented himself. Some sort of cousin.'

'Shoni Jones of Moylegrove.'

'Yes.' Arthur was audibly surprised. 'How did you know?'

Why had neither Mrs Parry nor James Philips told John about the cousin's claim? Were they hoping that he could be paid off? Or had he tried to threaten them in some way?

'We think Mr Jones may have evidence to bring before the inquest,' I said.

'Do you think he might have been involved in Hughes's death?'

I prevaricated. 'We simply need to speak to him.'

Genial as Arthur Philips was, he had obviously come to Glanteifi as much to ask me to keep James's gambling debts out of the inquest as he had to see my father. And, family or not, I could not ignore the possibility that he had also hoped to find out how much I knew.

In fact, he had learned very little from me. I, on the other hand, had learned a great deal. As soon as he was gone, I would write to John. It was imperative that Shoni Jones be found as soon as possible.

John

As it turned out, I didn't have to speak to James Philips. He was busy playing the respectable businessman at church.

When I went to the office, it was Mrs Parry I found sitting at Philips's desk, and she didn't need any persuading that a meeting of Cardigan-Ohio bondholders was a good idea.

'It's something we'd have had to do ourselves, anyway,' she said. 'As soon as word gets out that Jenkyn Hughes is dead, people will be bound to be worried.'

She asked me whether I had a particular day in mind for the meeting and we agreed on Friday.

I nearly asked her whether she knew where I could find Shoni Jones but I caught myself in time. I still wasn't altogether sure we could trust Mrs Parry, so the less she knew about our interest in the Moylegrove cousin the better.

I was about to leave when she surprised me by asking after Teff Harris. 'Billy Go-About still got him in the lock-up, has he?'

'Yes. His wife came down to see him this morning.'

Mrs Parry nodded, eyes on me as if she was waiting for the next piece of information. I kept my lips shut.

'Ruth Harris is fortunate in her husband,' she said, as if she was just making conversation.

I tried to resist. And failed. 'Oh, yes?'

'He knows it's not her fault men fall for her. A lesser man might think she was leading them on.'

I looked her in the eye. It was the only way with Mrs Parry. 'You're telling me Teff Harris didn't kill Jenkyn Hughes because Hughes was after his wife, are you?'

'Ha!' She laughed and slapped her palm down on the table. 'You're a sharp one, aren't you, John Davies?'

So I'd been told. Sharp enough to cut myself, I was.

By the time I left Mrs Parry, it was well after noon. The sun was hidden somewhere behind a sky of dirty white and it was already beginning to weaken. I decided that enough was enough and set off back to the Black Lion to fetch Seren. If I left Cardigan now, I could get to Harry, give him an account of what I'd been up to and still be back before it was properly dark.

I walked up the hill into town past shuttered shop-windows and locked doors and tried to imagine this meeting of the American Scheme. All the would-be emigrants in one place, desperate to know whether the bonds they held were still good, whether any money they'd already paid in installments would be honoured. People who'd been saving for years, convinced that life would be better in America.

A better future. Could that be the answer for me? Emigration?

Jenkyn Hughes had left the Cardigan-Ohio Emigration Company in what Mr Schofield would call a state of disorder, so there were probably still bonds to be had. I could use my savings and sail to a new life. In this iron town Jenkyn Hughes'd been recruiting people for, they'd be in need of articled clerks and lawyers. Why shouldn't I be one of them? American law couldn't be so different from ours and it certainly wasn't beyond me to learn the ways it differed.

A new life in Ohio. No more Mr Schofield. No more grumbling landlady. No more worrying about the future – it would all be decided. I'd be a lawyer in the new town.

I could almost hear my father's voice. *Arglwydd annwyl, boy, go! There's nothing here for you now. America's a new country. Anything's possible. You could be rich!*

But I'd be leaving behind everything and everybody I knew. My future would be completely separated from my past. There'd be nobody I'd shared anything with for the first twenty years of my life. It'd be like being born again on the other side of the Atlantic Ocean. Was that what I wanted?

I didn't know. I just didn't want to have to keep deciding between Mr Schofield and Harry.

Before going to the stables for Seren, I made a detour inside the Black Lion to check that there was nobody there waiting to see me.

There was. Sitting in what the Black Lion's maids and bootboys were already calling 'the Coroner's Room' was a little rat-faced man with tobacco-stained teeth and a shirt whose colour made you suspect he didn't have a wife. I introduced myself and explained that Harry wasn't here.

'I'm Benjamin Matthias,' he said, standing and taking his hat off to me. 'Ben the tailor. I'm the registrar of births and deaths.'

'Registrar' was what he said, because nobody calls themselves a sub-anything. But I knew that the Cardigan registration district covered dozens of parishes. Ben Matthias would actually be sub-registrar of a smaller district.

I looked him over quickly as we sat down by the almost-dead fire. I hoped he was a better registrar than he was a tailor, because he was no great advertisement for his trade. His coat was old and his trousers were baggy at the knees. But, like they say, the shoemaker's children always go barefoot.

'If you've come about Jenkyn Hughes,' I said 'you'll have to wait till the inquest for cause of death. You can register him then.'

'No, no. I know that.' Matthias spoke quickly, as if he was used to not being allowed to finish anything he said. 'It's another death I'm here about.'

I left space for him to go on but he obviously needed permission. 'Whose death is that, Mr Mathias?'

'Well. Now, then. Illegal burial it is, see, really. Burial without the death being registered.'

'Registered or certified?' Strictly speaking, the system wanted a doctor to see every dead person and say not just that they were dead but also how they'd died, but allowances were made for circumstances where no doctor was available or affordable. The registrar was allowed to record the death as 'uncertified' if he was satisfied that a doctor's opinion wasn't needed.

'No. Unregistered, it was. No doctor came but I'm not worried about that. What happened was, the burial was done and *then* the minister came to me to register the death.'

'The minister who'd performed the burial?'

'Yes. Reverend Williams from Blaenywaun, St Dogmaels.'

The Reverend John Philipps Williams. Everybody within a dozen miles in any given direction had heard of him. Taken a moderately successful chapel, JP Williams had, and made it into what the papers called a *phenomenon*. Sometimes he preached to congregations so big they couldn't all fit into the building.

'He said he had no doubt whatsoever that the death was natural,' Matthias went on when I didn't reply.

He was waiting for me to tell him how to make this all right, but I couldn't. I didn't know whether this was any of my business. Was it my job to take these details? This death was nothing to do with the inquest Harry'd been asked to conduct.

But then, if he was acting coroner, I supposed every unexplained death was his business.

Matthias started scratching at a splash of mud on his trousers, trying to get it out of the weave with his nail. He looked nervous.

'So why did Reverend Williams perform the burial before coming to you to register the death?' I asked. 'Did something happen to keep him away?'

Matthias shook his head. 'No, no, nothing like that. Just – as soon as the grave was dug, see, the body was in it and buried.' He made his point by doing a half clap, half brush of one hand with another. *That's how it was done – quick-smart.*

I took out my notebook. Time to stop asking random questions and bring some order to proceedings. 'Right, Mr Matthias, who is it that's died?'

Matthias shifted in his chair. 'A little girl. Elizabeth Abel. Been ill for some time, she had.'

'Yes?' I said, waiting for the rest. Nothing came. 'A child dies after an illness. A very respectable minister buries her – according to the parents' wishes, I suppose – and then comes to you to register the death.' I kept my eyes on Matthias's face. He wasn't looking at me. 'All right,' I allowed 'it's *technically* an illegal burial but–'

'That's not why I've come. I wouldn't've bothered for that. I know I said illegal burial at the start...'

He stopped speaking so I helped him out. 'Why *have* you come then, Mr Matthias?'

'Because of the father. Elizabeth Abel's father. People are talking, you see.'

I waited. I wasn't going to do *all* his work for him.

'They're saying that it's lucky for him the little girl died.'

The hairs stood up on the back of my neck. 'Lucky? Why's that?'

Matthias put one hand in the other and cracked his knuckles. I don't think he knew he was doing it. His eyes were on me the whole time.

'I don't know the parents, myself, but I heard there was a disagreement between them. About going to America. The father'd bought one of those emigration bonds – for the ship that's going over in April. But the mother didn't want to go. Because the little girl was poorly. Said the journey'd kill her.'

'And you're worried that the father hurried her on her way so they could go.'

'Well,' Matthias looked shocked at my directness but I didn't have time for tip-toeing. I needed to find out whether there was anything suspicious here to pass on to Harry. 'The reverend says it's nothing to be concerned about. Says it'd been obvious that the child was dying for weeks. The doctor was giving her laudanum. But the mother couldn't accept it, see. Kept going to the reverend after services and asking him to pray with her. Looking for a miracle, she was.'

Which was just the kind of thing I'd've expected a man with Reverend Williams's reputation to encourage. 'Has the mother made any accusations against her husband?' I asked.

'Don't know. Haven't spoken to her.'

'But the Reverend Williams is happy that it was a natural death?'

'*He* is, yes. But not everybody is. I don't want the rumours to cause trouble.'

'What kind of trouble?'

He shrugged but we both knew what he meant. The death of a child provokes people.

'All right. I'll speak to the coroner. To Mr Probert-Lloyd. Just one thing. Who was the doctor who was giving her laudanum?'

Matthias cracked his knuckles again. 'Dr Reckitt from Cilgerran.'

Harry

By mid-afternoon, Arthur had been gone a little while and Reckitt had not yet returned, leaving me to navigate my father's short periods of wakefulness as best I could alone. Our conversation was, necessarily, largely one-sided but it did allow me to comprehend both that my father was feeling somewhat restored and that he did not wish me to remain perpetually at his bedside.

'Out,' he had insisted, at one point, with an accompanying movement of his good arm towards the door. 'Work.'

I had demurred, saying that it was Sunday and that, anyway, I wished to see him a good deal better before I left him. But another visit to the close-stool closet had taught me that, at the very least, I would have to leave him in order to make arrangements for his intimate care.

Arthur Philips had offered to return the following day, and I was fairly confident that he could be persuaded to sit for an hour or two and read to my father.

Meanwhile, I paced.

How did women endure this, day in, day out? How did they manage the demands of others and subjugate their own needs to those of their family – husband, children, elderly parents? Before knowing Lydia, I had not given it a thought, but our correspondence had opened my eyes somewhat.

'I think you will agree,' she had written in one letter, *'that I, more than most, am capable of giving an opinion as to the relative position of women*

and men, and I know that women are not constitutionally inferior to men. I believe that society has merely discovered it to be expedient to incarcerate the gentlewoman in her home, to enfeeble her body by her dress and to deprive her of an education for her mind.'

Mrs Griffiths had, predictably, bridled against such notions, but when I had pointed out to her that – with the keys to the house and an almost unlimited license to spend my father's money on behalf of the household – she had considerably more power and freedom than Lydia enjoyed as a governess, she admitted that perhaps Miss Howell was speaking from a position of greater knowledge.

'Even a small farmer's wife or a farm servant has more freedom than a so-called gentlewoman,' Lydia had suggested. *'The farmer does not say that his wife is too weak to go out and work in the fields with him; he requires it because he needs her labour. The employer does not keep the girls on his farm from hard physical labour out of deference to their sex but works them as hard as he may for their board and lodging. But society's conception of the gentlewoman is of a being somehow both superior to her working sisters and, simultaneously, inferior by reason of her frail body and easily-overwrought mind which cannot be allowed to consider abstract thought but is good only for gossip and for social pleasantries at the dinner table.'*

Though, when we had met in Ipswich, Lydia had given me to understand that she had entered into employment as a governess with some relief, I wondered whether, with the passage of time, she regretted giving up the freedoms she had enjoyed in her previous life.

I was beginning to long for a real conversation with Lydia, a conversation that did not have to be censored in accordance with Mrs Griffiths's sensibilities and that was not forced to proceed in three-day jerks, obliging me to recall my own words a week after they had been written.

However, given the circumstances in which she had left Cardiganshire, the chances of Lydia Howell returning here seemed remote.

As the trees outside the window turned black against the sky, John arrived and, judging my father to be sufficiently recovered to withstand my absence for an hour, we sat in the library.

I was astonished at how much he had discovered. For me, time appeared to have slowed to a snail's pace and my accomplishments that day consisted of antagonising Prendergast, one of my father's oldest friends, and making an ally – if not a friend – of Reckitt, a man generally regarded as a pariah.

John, meanwhile, had so much to tell me that darkness had fallen by the time he had imparted all his news. Not even my conversation with Arthur Philips enabled me to surprise him with new information; he already knew that my cousin James had been in debt to Teff Harris.

'James Philips could have been working with Hughes in double-selling the coal,' he suggested, 'as a way of paying off his debt. If so, perhaps Hughes tried to blackmail him. It'd be the end of Philips as a businessman if people found out he was involved in fraud.'

I did not want to disagree too much in case John thought I was closing family ranks so I gave his suggestion due consideration; even so, it did not strike me as particularly likely. 'Seeing James Philips as a suspect involves two or even three assumptions,' I pointed out.

'Firstly, that he was involved with the coal scam. Secondly, that Hughes was blackmailing him. And, thirdly, that he decided that murder was a good way out of both problems.'

'All right, but Teff Harris has less motive. We know he doesn't gamble, so, if he did kill Hughes, that wasn't the reason.'

'That's if we believe Mrs Harris,' I said.

'If you'd met Mrs Harris,' he said, simply, 'you'd believe her. She's … remarkable.'

I hid a smile. 'I suppose that's why Hughes was making a nuisance of himself over her.'

'And Obadaiah Vaughan.' John perked up again as he remembered something else he had to tell me. 'He's been spying on her since she's been back. I think that's what he does. Spies on Banc yr Eithin to watch for her. I think it was Vaughan who wrote that anonymous letter. Remember – I said it was the hand of somebody who was used to writing but who probably didn't use a pen every day, for his living. That's Dai'r Bardd to a 't'.'

'So,' I said, 'Vaughan spies on both husband and wife. Then he writes the note implicating Teff Harris, hoping that he's guilty and the police will remove him, leaving the way to Ruth open.'

'Or he points the finger at Teff after killing Hughes himself.'

'You think he'd see an innocent man hang?'

'If he murdered Hughes, he's not going to care about that, is he?'

'There are too many motives for Hughes's murder,' I complained. 'Women, embezzlement, gambling.' I got up to ring the bell at the side of the fireplace. 'Let's have something to eat.'

'At least we've got a better guess about when Hughes died, now,' John said after Clara, one of the maids, had been and gone again in search of tea and cake. 'The same time as that last-but-one lime load was dumped on the beach.'

'You think whatever Shoni Jones saw through his telescope included Hughes's murder?'

'Well, he turned up at Captain Coleman's to claim Hughes's papers before the body went to the workhouse, so he must've seen something. How else would he've known Hughes wasn't coming for his stuff himself? Unless he killed him, of course.'

I nodded. 'What was your informant's reaction to Hughes not being on the beach to meet them the second time?'

'He didn't give a reaction. We didn't really talk about that last load of lime. Just the one that Hughes met.'

My mind was slotting things into place. 'Somebody took Hughes's body out of the kiln and put it on the last delivery of lime for Teff to find. Who was going to benefit from his death being discovered?'

John pulled in a considering breath. 'The partners in the emigration company – because of the life insurance – and the cousin, as his heir.'

'And we know that the cousin watched something happen on the beach. And that he had Jenkyn Hughes's signet ring. I think you need to find this sailor again and ask him whether Shoni Jones was on the boat the second time and whether he stayed on the beach after the lime was unloaded.'

John sighed. 'I'll try. But he's not an easy man to talk to. There's something else I need to tell you about, as well,' he said. 'Nothing to do with Hughes but it's still a coroner's matter. Do you have responsibility for other deaths, too?'

At that moment, there was a knock at the door followed by Clara carrying a large tray. Once she'd set it down and been assured that

John could pour tea quite adequately, she took a poker to the fire to stir it up, shook some more culm on and left.

In between eating *bara brith* and drinking tea, John told me about the illegal burial of the child and Reckitt's involvement in the case.

'Matthias raised the possibility that the father hastened the child's death so that he could persuade his wife to emigrate,' he concluded. 'Says people are a bit worked up about it.'

'Reckitt'll be here soon. He can give us his opinion on whether the child really was at death's door or whether the death was sudden,' I said. 'I'd trust his judgment on medical matters.'

John

Not long after Harry'd been upstairs to see his father, Reckitt turned up.

'How is the patient?' he asked after we'd done all the good evenings.

'He managed a sentence,' Harry told him. 'Or perhaps I should say a phrase – *When's dinner?*'

'Considering that, yesterday, he had an absent swallow reflex, he's making a remarkable recovery,' Reckitt said. 'Nevertheless, I'd recommend giving him nothing too challenging – no meat. Perhaps a broth with some soft potato.'

I stared at him. He was still flushed from the cold ride over but otherwise he looked like he always did, as if he couldn't care less. I couldn't work him out. Giving advice about broth and soft potatoes seemed out of character.

Mind you, everything about Reckitt's behaviour seemed out of character that evening. There was none of the odd jumpiness we'd seen in Cilgerran. He looked at ease, more comfortable in Harry's home than he'd been in his own. Maybe it was more what he was used to. Glanteifi mansion might be a bit shabby but you could've fitted the whole of Reckitt's little house into the library where we were sitting.

After a bit more discussion about his father, Harry cocked his head in the way he did when he was trying to watch somebody's reaction. 'Reckitt, John has been approached with another potential inquest case. It's one I believe you're familiar with.'

Reckitt leaned back from the fire to look at him. 'What case is that?'

Harry didn't reply and I realised he wanted me to do the talking.

'A child,' I said. 'By the name of Elizabeth Abel.'

Suddenly, Reckitt was bolt upright. 'Abel's child has died?'

I was flustered by the look on his face. 'Yes,' I managed.

'When?'

I looked over at Harry. Maybe he saw my head move or maybe he just took his lead from the sound of me desperately saying nothing. 'Tell us what you know of the family, Reckitt.'

Ten minutes later, things were a lot clearer. Ben Matthias had told me that David Abel and his wife'd been arguing about the emigration bond he'd bought, but it looked as if that wasn't all they'd been arguing about.

According to Reckitt, they'd brought their seven-year-old daughter, Elizabeth, to see him when she began falling down in fits and complaining of headaches and 'things in front of her eyes'. Reckitt had suspected some disease of the brain – an infection or one of his famous lumps. He'd given the parents laudanum for the child's pain and told them that he'd come and see them in a week.

The week passed. Elizabeth'd had no more seizures but the headaches seemed to be worsening. Reckitt prescribed more laudanum.

'Before six weeks had gone by, I was convinced that the child had a tumour on her brain. There'd been no head injury and, in the absence of any infection, a tumour was the obvious explanation.'

Elizabeth's condition had grown steadily worse. She became more unsteady on her feet and lost the power of sight. Now, as well as the headaches, she had fits of vomiting.

'By the New Year the child was consuming laudanum several times daily. It was clear to me that she would not recover.' Reckitt might've been giving a report on livestock prices. No compassion for the Abels at all.

I remembered my mother being almost beside herself when my little sister Sali-Ann had the whooping cough. I couldn't imagine what she'd've been like if Sali-Ann had died.

'It's been suggested,' Harry said slowly, 'that there was disagreement between Abel and his wife about a proposed emigration to America. That Able might even have hastened the child's death so that her illness would not prevent them going.'

Reckitt wrinkled his nose as if he'd smelled dogshit on his boot. 'Absolute nonsense. Abel had no need to resort to such a thing. The emigrant ship isn't sailing until April and I'd been quite honest with Abel and his wife – there was virtually no possibility that the child would live past February.'

I looked over at Harry. He was sitting opposite Reckitt and the fire cast a pink glow over his face. It made him look young, in spite of his beard.

'With the child suffering from a tumour on the brain,' he said, eyes on the fire so he could see Reckitt in his peripheral vision, 'you must have been interested in her condition. In performing an autopsy.'

I tensed, waiting for Reckitt to be offended, but he just nodded as if what Harry'd said was the most normal thing in the world. As if dead children were cut up every day to satisfy doctors' curiosity. 'I was. I remain so. In fact, David Abel and I have an agreement on that front.'

That explained why Reckitt'd sounded so shocked to hear that Elizabeth Able was dead. He'd've been expecting to hear from her father. I swallowed. The thought of a child ending up like Hughes on that table at Tresaith beach made me feel sick.

'Any agreement's been broken, I'm afraid,' Harry said. 'The child has been buried.'

He didn't mention how desperately hasty the burial had been. Sparing Reckitt's feelings, or just not wanting him to know?

Reckitt was on his feet, now. If there'd been a dog to hand, he'd've kicked it. 'Damn and blast the man!' He took a step towards the door then he stopped and looked around at Harry and at me. You could almost see him getting a grip on himself. Whatever he'd agreed with Abel, there was no law that could compel a man to allow his child be dissected.

The doctor stood there, hands in fists at his side. Perhaps he wasn't so different from before.

Suddenly, all I could see was my sister. Eight years old she'd been when I went off to be a *gwas bach* – almost the same age as Elizabeth Abel – and annoying like all little sisters are. I remembered her fine dark hair that would never stay back in a ribbon. And her big brown eyes. And her little pinching fingers.

'Don't you think It's a terrible thing?' I heard my own voice as if somebody else was speaking, somebody who was only just holding his temper. 'To propose cutting up a child while her parents have barely begun mourning her?' *A thousand times worse*, I wanted to shout in Reckitt's stupid, fat face, *than dissecting the poor friendless sods who die in the workhouse.*

Reckitt frowned. 'No, Mr Davies, I do not. You, in common with the vast majority of people, evidently find the dissection of cadavers abhorrent. But I believe that abhorrence to be misplaced. We are living in a scientific age and parliament recognised that more than a decade ago when they made provision for anatomists.'

'Yes. I know.' My hands were shaking. 'The Anatomy Act. I don't suppose anybody asks the paupers, either, do they?'

My words didn't touch him. He just looked at me, steadily. 'I believe you are allowing emotion to obscure reason. The dissection of cadavers is of enormous importance to the study of pathology. How can we hope to treat diseases until we know their symptoms and their course?'

'That's not relevant here, though, is it?' I wanted to be calm and rational like him but it was difficult when I also wanted to punch his stupid face. 'You can't treat a lump in the head. It's impossible!'

'Not at all!' Reckitt sat down again, leaned towards me. 'So much is possible now that couldn't be contemplated even five years ago. In ten years time, you will be astonished at what may be accomplished. Have you heard of ether? Chloroform?'

'Of course I have!' Did he think I never opened a newspaper?

'In ten years time, painless surgery will be performed everywhere! Patients choosing to die rather than go under the knife will be a thing of the past!'

I'd heard religious zealots before but never a scientific one. 'If that's the case, why do you need to cut up dead people? You can just open up people who're sick and see what needs to be done.'

I was expecting him to put me in my place but he seemed to take no offence at all, just shook his head like a dog shaking off water. 'I can see how a lay person might make that mistake. But all procedures that open the body have their dangers. Many patients die of infection following surgery and it's impossible to predict whether anaesthesia will have any effect on that. No, Mr Davies, if we are to perform surgery as effectively as possible it's essential that we are allowed to perform autopsy examinations in order to see *exactly* what each specific disease process entails.'

'But to cut up children—'

'Children or adults, it makes no difference! The more we know about disease, about how diseases begin and proceed and how they kill their victims, the more we can help the living!'

I shuddered. I didn't want to talk about this anymore. 'All that notwithstanding,' I said, the legal word stiff but right on my tongue, 'there's only one question I need answered about the death of Elizabeth Abel.' I turned my head towards Harry. 'Is it something I need to look into on your behalf, or not?'

Harry hesitated, head cocked towards Reckitt in case the doctor wanted to say anything. He didn't.

'As we seem unable to do much more on the death of Hughes until the meeting on Friday, it might be as well for us to pay the Reverend Williams a visit. See if he can do anything to quash the rumours and save us from having to insist on an inquest. We've enough to do at the moment, what with one thing and another.'

PART THREE

Harry

Riding to St Dogmaels with John the following day, I felt my liberty most acutely. Though it was a mere two days since we had been in Cardigan together, weeks might have elapsed as far as I was concerned. Each hour I had spent in my father's sickroom seemed to have taken days to pass and I felt both aged and sobered by my vigil.

Fortunately for my sanity, Arthur Philips had returned and, with Isabel Griffiths suggesting that he and my father be given time alone to mend neglected familial fences, I was able to leave the house with a passably quiet conscience.

'It doesn't matter that your father mayn't be able to say much,' she maintained. 'He can listen. He has years and years' worth of listening to do and he'll do it willingly, Harry.'

I knew what she meant: he would do it in order to restore relations with my mother's family and provide me with friends and allies. And I would need them. Hours of enforced contemplation had led me to a decision about my future. Come what might, I would stand for election to the post of coroner. Glanteifi had a steward so, whether my father was alive and capable or not, the estate would not founder while I prepared my campaign.

However, though Ormiston could be relied upon to run the estate, I knew I would need somebody to help me manage my campaign, a secretary or an agent who would be able to attend to all the bureaucratic requirements of standing for election. John was obviously the ideal candidate but his mind was set on becoming a solicitor and I could not stand in his way.

From its position, out in the countryside a mile or so beyond the village of St Dogmaels, I concluded that Blaenywaun chapel must have been built by the Teifi Valley's early Baptists who had chosen to site their meeting houses well away from the censure of churchgoing people.

Though we had called in at the manse in the village only to be told that Reverend Williams had gone out on pastoral duties, it was clear that they had not brought him here.

'We should've taken up his wife's offer and waited for him at his house,' John said. 'It's freezing out here.'

But I had had enough of sitting indoors, these last few days. Even the icy wind could not dent my pleasure at being outside and purposeful. 'Ah well,' I said. 'At least we've seen the famous Blaenywaun chapel.'

John made a dismissive sound. 'It's just a building.'

A big building. And necessarily so; I was given to understand that Williams's congregation was constantly on the increase.

As we rode away from the chapel, I registered the raw earth of a new grave, its mound – as far as I could tell – unsunk. Lizzie Abel must, surely, lie beneath. Had her precipitate burial had anything to do with the agreement Reckitt had spoken of? Faced with his little daughter's lifeless body, had her father realised that, whatever agreement they had reached, he could not allow Reckitt to cut her open? If so, then I hoped Lizzie's parents were able to take some comfort from the fact that her body was safe beneath the soil.

Though the legal provision of cadavers to medical schools had, by and large, put a stop to graverobbing, tales of the Resurrectionists' trade had still been rife amongst medical students when Gray and I had first met and he had relished them as only somebody untouched by their horrible reality could.

I recalled the grim pictures he had conjured up. The bereaved, guarding the graves of their loved ones, night after night, until sufficient decomposition was judged to have taken place to render the body unfit for dissection. Ingenious bodysnatchers digging tunnels from a distance of six or seven yards down to the head of the coffin, removing the end and pulling the corpse out along the tunnel, leaving sentinel relatives or their paid proxies none the wiser. Bodies spirited through the city at the dead of night and delivered to respectable academies where they were met with surreptitious remuneration and carefully unasked questions. John might still find it distasteful but dissection of the unclaimed bodies of paupers and vagrants was generally regarded as by far the lesser of two evils.

If he had noticed the direction of my gaze, John did not mention it. In fact, he had been somewhat taciturn since we had left Glanteifi, rousing himself to answer any questions I asked but then lapsing back into silence. His reticence made my own near-euphoria at being away from Glanteifi seem inappropriate.

'Do you think I should have stayed at my father's side?' I asked. We were just passing what was obviously a substantial stable for the use of congregation members and, as we left its protective bulk behind, the wind buffeting across the fields hit us like a child running headlong.

His head jerked towards me as if I'd pulled a string. 'Why d'you ask that?'

'You're very quiet. I wondered whether it was the silence of disapproval – at me abandoning my father.'

'No! Not at all.' He stopped, then seemed to feel that a corroborative statement was required. 'In fact, if I was your father, I'd be glad you'd gone out. It must've felt as if you were sitting there waiting for him to die.'

I told him about the fear I had had that I might find myself sitting at my father's bedside, oblivious to the fact that he had breathed his last.

'D'you think that's an odd fear to have?' I asked.

'I don't know.' He sounded subdued. 'I've never been there when somebody died. By the time I knew about my parents and sister they'd all been dead for weeks.

'D'you know what I felt,' he went on, 'after the first shock? Stupid. Not sad, just stupid. There I'd been, imagining them going about as usual when all the time they'd been dead.'

'I'm sorry, John.'

I caught a shrug. 'I never would've got an education if my parents'd lived.'

And I wouldn't have ambitions to be a lawyer. The words might have been unsaid but I was acutely aware of their truth, nonetheless.

'How long have you been working for Mr Schofield, now?' I asked.

John took his time replying. Was he looking sidelong at me, trying to decide why I was asking?

'A bit more than five years. Mr Davies from Adpar school sent me to him when I was a few months off fifteen and I'm twenty next month.'

'Mr Schofield doesn't have any articled clerks, does he?'

'No.'

For somebody like Schofield it would be gratifying to pass on knowledge to an intelligent youth like John. 'How much law do you know?'

'A lot.' He spoke without boastfulness, simply offering it as a fact.

'Enough to pass the exams?' I knew, from frequent complaints at the bar, that the solicitors' examinations mandated by London's legal establishment were intended to guard against incompetence rather than to produce excellence and I wondered whether John was aware of this, too.

'I'd hope so.'

'Does Mr Schofield ever ask you questions on points of law? Test you?'

John hesitated. 'He does. Trying to catch me out.'

Had Schofield been intending to present John for examination without his being enrolled, formally, as an articled clerk? It would be irregular but not unheard of. If this had been his intention all along, he would consider himself very ill-used if I were to persuade John to work for me. Schofield had no sons and he might, conceivably, be preparing John to succeed him in his legal practice. Perhaps it would be as well to ask what his intentions were before I made any suggestions.

Why do you ask?' John wanted to know.

'I'm just thinking of your future.'

We rode on in an uneasy silence, both of us aware that I had not really answered his question.

The Reverend John Philipps Williams lived in an unpretentious manse on the hill in St Dogmaels and, this time, answered our knock himself. Doubtless there would be a servant or two about the place – a man of his standing would be expected to provide employment – but he did not flaunt them.

Two small boys having been located to find a patch of grass for the mares to graze, we followed Williams into his warm, street-facing study and I explained our errand.

'Little Lizzie Abel. Yes, we buried her last week.' His pleasantly deep voice was softened by what sounded like genuine sorrow.

'Please correct me if I'm wrong,' I said, 'but we've been led to believe that the little girl's death had neither been certified by a doctor nor registered by her parents before she was buried.'

I heard Williams's small sigh. 'Your information is quite correct. I know that, strictly speaking, we were in breach of the law, but I felt that it would be allowable to fall in with the mother's wishes, on this occasion, provided that I saw to it, myself, that the death was registered as soon as possible. Nobody was harmed by our actions – which is, after all, the point of the law – and a great deal of anguish was avoided.'

Though we were speaking Welsh it was not the easy, colloquial tongue I was used to but the high, Bible-cadenced language of a college-educated man. Williams seemed very sure of himself; not at all disconcerted at being found to have acted illegally, however technical the illegality. It irked me.

'Can I ask why there was such a degree of haste?'

'The child's mother – Margaret Abel – was in a state of near-collapse. I feared for her health if I did not bury little Lizzie in accordance with her wishes. She'd already seen to having the grave dug.'

'Do you know who did the digging, Reverend?' I turned at the sound of John's voice; from his tone I knew that he, too, was unimpressed by the minister's demeanour.

But, if Williams heard any disrespect, he chose to ignore it. 'Dan Bach,' he replied. 'He works as a labourer on a few of the farms near Blaenywaun. His family's come to depend on the extra he gets for digging graves and looking after things around the chapel.'

'You know for a fact that it was him who did the digging?' John persisted. It was clear – to me at least – that he was asking whether the child's father might have dug the grave himself in order to conceal her death from as many people as possible until she was safely in the ground.

'I didn't *see* him do it.' Now there was an edge of irritation to Williams's voice. 'But I know he'd have come running to me to complain if anybody else had. As I said, he depends on the money.'

John took his notebook out of his pocket and I wondered whether I should rein him in. I decided against.

'What's Dan Bach's proper name?' John asked.

Williams hesitated. In a congregation of several hundred, many of whom shared half a dozen surnames, he might know some only by their nicknames. 'Daniel Evans, I think.'

While John wrote in his notebook, I examined the minister's library. Bookcases filled one wall, floor to ceiling and, though the study was not large, such a collection implied a considerable outlay of funds. Either J.P. Williams was a man unusually showered with gifts or his congregation kept him in some style.

In my peripheral vision, John's face turned towards me; it was my turn to ask a question.

'You said, just now, that Mrs Abel was in a state of near-collapse,' I began. 'That's understandable, of course, but why did you *fear for her health* if her child wasn't quickly buried?'

There was a pause before Williams answered. 'You have to understand, Mr Probert-Lloyd, how very greatly a child's death can affect the mind of a mother.' The minister's tone had changed; he was speaking slowly, weighing his words as if they were unusually heavy. 'My wife and I lost our little daughter, last year, aged only three weeks. For some time afterwards, my wife would not be parted from a doll we had been given for the baby. She carried it everywhere, as if she, herself, had become a child again.'

Was it this willingness to reveal his own personal hurts that had made him so loved, so powerful a speaker, I wondered? And yet, it was not actually self-revelation at all, was it? It was his wife's private grief he was parading for us.

I waited for him to go on.

'Unlike my wife, Maggie Abel knew her child was dying. But all through Lizzie's illness, Maggie was convinced that a miracle would save her daughter. She felt certain that she needed only to have faith and Lizzie would be healed.'

'You didn't share her conviction?' I asked. His tone suggested as much: careful rather than fervent.

'I believe that God *does* perform miracles, Mr Probert-Lloyd. Indeed, I have seen more than one with my own eyes. But he does not do them *at our behest*. Simply to pray is not enough, else who would do anything else if it would grant them their wish?'

'We've been told that Lizzie Abel had a tumour on the brain,' John said, bringing us back to the point. 'Is that your understanding, too?'

Again, there was a brief silence but, this time, I had the impression that it was intended as a criticism of John's brusqueness. 'I know that's what the doctor who was treating her diagnosed and I have no reason to contradict him. After a few weeks he told the Abels that they must prepare for the worst. But Maggie would not accept that Lizzie was going to die.

'As I was saying,' he continued after a few moments, 'the death of a child can affect the mind quite profoundly. But, in this case, Maggie Abel's mind had already been thrown out of balance by Lizzie's illness *before* she died. She looked desperately for a meaning in her daughter's suffering. Eventually, she became convinced that Lizzie's illness was to be the means of drawing her husband back to God.'

An uncomfortable silence developed before I realised that Williams was looking for reassurance that I would wish to know this information. I had not announced my blindness and, now, I realised the folly of that omission. However sick I was of the need to advertise my limited sight, neglecting to do so made me look less competent, not more. My father's words of scarcely a week ago came uncomfortably to mind. *Why must you insist on behaving as if your faculties are unimpaired?*

'Go on,' I said. 'Why did Mr Abel need to be drawn back?'

'Previously, he had been a deacon at Blaenywaun—'

'He's not a young man then?' John interrupted. Evidently, he had been assuming – as I had – that, with a small child, the Abels were a young couple, but the diaconate was almost always filled with men in middle age and older.

'He's in his forties. Margaret is his second wife.'

'Why did he stop being a deacon?' John asked.

I could see the pale disc that was Williams's face; it did not turn towards John. 'David's first wife died in childbirth, along with their son – and he proved to be one of those people who, when misfortune befalls them, feel that God has abandoned them. A wrong-headed notion, of course, and one I could wish to see less often than I do. But, recently, David had decided to take his family to America and the prospect of a new start seemed to have rekindled his faith.'

'And his wife? Was she happy to leave home and family?'

'Initially, I think, yes. She is a very faithful, devout woman and I know it troubled her that David felt so far from God. If America was what it took to bring him back into the fold, then she was happy to go.'

'But not when Lizzie became too ill to travel,' I guessed. 'Was she their only child?'

'Yes, she was. But it wasn't simply a matter of the child being too ill to sail to America. As Lizzie's illness progressed, it became clear that the money the Abels had saved for an emigration bond would be needed to buy medicines to keep her from suffering constant pain.'

Money: the cause of half the murders in the world. Could it be that the rumours were true? Had David Abel seen his sick child standing between him and a new life?

'Also,' Williams went on, 'Maggie Abel had come to believe that going to America was no longer necessary to rekindle David's faith. She believed that the miracle of Lizzie's healing would draw him back to God.'

However, as a miracle failed to materialise and his child's condition deteriorated before his eyes, I imagined that David Abel had become more desperate to escape, rather than less.

Then I realised that I was making an assumption. 'Was Lizzie David Abel's child,' I asked, 'or has his wife also been married before?'

Easier, perhaps, to hasten the end of a child not one's own? But Williams firmly barred this line of thought.

'No, Maggie was not yet twenty when she married David. Lizzie was his child.'

I tried to frame the next question as delicately as I could. 'Benjamin Matthias indicated that there had been rumours about the child's death – that her father had, perhaps, ended her suffering himself?'

'What?' Williams sounded genuinely outraged. 'Who's saying that? Who would suggest such a thing?'

'No names were mentioned,' I said. 'Matthias just presented that as the reason for his coming to us. People were aware that Abel wanted to emigrate and there'd been speculation that he feared that the child's illness would keep the family here.'

'It's quite ridiculous,' Williams insisted. 'I cannot believe that anybody who knew David Abel would suggest such a thing. Quite apart from the monstrosity of the allegation, look at its timing if you want to see the fallacy of it. The emigrant ship isn't scheduled to sail until April. Why on earth would he–' He seemed unwilling even to repeat the allegation. 'Why would there be any need to do such a terrible thing *now*?'

'I'm afraid you put your finger on the problem yourself, Reverend,' I said. 'Because he wanted the money that would otherwise go on medicine for Lizzie in order to buy an emigration bond.'

With the mares happily grazing further up the road, John and I made our way down the hill to David Abel's workshop. We'd learned from the Reverend Williams that Abel was a cabinet maker and I wondered whether, just as his child's grave had been hastily dug, he had made the coffin himself for speed's sake.

We were met at the workshop's door by an aproned apprentice.

'I'm sorry, sirs,' he said, with a glance over his shoulder, 'the master can't see anybody at the moment – he's veneering. Got to work quickly, you see, before the glue sets.'

I longed to share a raised eyebrow with John at this outlandishly plausible excuse. 'How long will he be?' I asked instead, pitching my voice loud enough for the man inside to hear.

'If you come back in an hour,' the response came from within, 'I'll be able to speak to you.'

With an hour to wait, there seemed little to do but find some refreshment. John spotted an inn's sign further down the street and, soon, we were sitting in the White Hart before a huge fireplace where a small cauldron hung on a chain over the embers.

At my suggestion John went to sniff its contents and, given his enthusiastic verdict, I procured us a bowl each.

'I hope David Abel's not halfway to Pembroke by now,' I said, dipping the wooden spoon I'd been given into the broth.

'Not unless he and his apprentice are the best liars in the world,' John replied, taking me seriously. 'I think it's exactly what he said, there are some jobs you can't break off in the middle. Like killing a pig.'

We ate for a while but the silence between us was not entirely companionable and I felt compelled to break it with something more than a makeweight remark.

'I've decided that I'm still going to stand as coroner,' I told him. 'I've had all the time I need to think while I've been sitting at my father's bedside and I know that I can't go face sitting on the bench.'

'Why not? You'd be a damn sight better than most magistrates. At least you know how people live. The kind of people who find themselves in court, I mean.'

'Yes, but I'm afraid that'd make it worse. I can't change the law and, if the other magistrates saw me bending over backwards to be lenient, they'd be more severe in their own cases to make a point. I might be able to do some good for the people whose cases I heard but I'd just make it worse for everybody else.'

John made no audible response.

'Whereas, if I'm coroner,' I went on, 'I can make sure that what's happened to Teff Harris doesn't happen to other men. I can keep a watch on Billy Go-About and his officers, make sure that they're not just arresting the first person who comes to hand. Or that they're not writing off bodies that get fished out of the sea as victims of accidental drowning – like Bellis wanted to with Hughes.' I took another spoonful of stew. 'What do you think?' I asked.

Wooden spoon scraped wooden bowl with a solid sound as John finished the last of his meal. 'I think you'd be an excellent coroner. But the question is do the electors want somebody who'll be thorough, like that, or would they prefer somebody who's going to cost them less?'

I knew what he meant: the more painstaking an investigation, the greater the costs incurred. And the householders who paid county rates were the ones who elected the coroner. Justice for the dead was a noble aspiration, but could it compete with lower rates?

David Abel proved to be a small, wiry man. What remained of his hair was iron-grey but even I could see that most of his head was bare pate.

He seemed neither surprised nor unduly alarmed by our visit.

'You'll be here because Maggie didn't register Lizzie's death properly,' he said when I had introduced myself and John and expressed our condolences.

I nodded. 'If you wouldn't mind explaining the circumstances of your daughter's death and burial.'

Abel waved us to a settle at the side of the workshop while he sank on to a stool as if he had the joints of a man twenty years younger. The workshop smelled strongly of bone glue but, beneath that, there were the pleasanter smells of seasoned wood and linseed oil.

'You have to understand, sirs – all this has meant that my poor wife is not quite herself. Lizzie was ill for months and months.' His voice stopped abruptly as if his throat had closed up.

Months and months of watching your only child sink towards death. What could be worse? What could be more calculated to make a mother no longer herself? I imagined that having a steel bar rip its

way through her head would have been infinitely preferable to Maggie
Abel.

'At the beginning it didn't seem too bad. Lizzie complained of being
a bit dizzy and she had headaches where she'd never had them before.
Children don't, do they, as a rule? But then she started with the fits.
Maggie was worried she'd burn herself falling into the fire or she'd set
light to the house if she fell over with a candle in her hand. There are
any number of ways a child can hurt themselves when they fall into
the kind of fit Lizzie was having. That was when we first went to see
Dr Reckitt over in Cilgerran.'

I did not need to ask why he had chosen Reckitt. Being
unfashionable, Reckitt's fees would be modest.

'Did he know what was wrong with your daughter?' I asked.

'Not at the beginning, no. He said he needed to watch how things
went on for a while but he made up laudanum for us to give her if
the headaches got bad. We were glad of that. There's nothing worse
than seeing your child in pain.'

Nothing? Not even the notion that he might end his daughter's
suffering by his own hand? I shifted uncomfortably on the settle and
tried to breathe in through my mouth against the animal stink of the
wood glue.

'Over the weeks, as she got worse, she needed more and more
laudanum. We noticed that she had less of the fits when she took it,
so we didn't deny it to her. Then she started to go blind.' His voice
cracked. 'Couldn't walk far without falling over. It was then Dr
Reckitt said about a growth inside her head. Said it would grow and
kill her and there was nothing he could do about it.'

Abel's voice broke again. I drew breath to speak but it seemed that
the cabinet maker had only wished to master himself, for he went on.

'All we could do was give her laudanum for the pain. And for the fear. It's frightening for a child to feel her body fail her, sirs. Very frightening. And the laudanum took the fear away.'

This time, neither John nor I were eager to break the silence. We heard Abel's apprentice moving around in the room next door and I wondered whether he lived in. If so, it might be worth speaking to him, too.

'That must have become expensive,' I said, eventually, regretting immediately how crass and materialistic the words sounded when ranged against the suffering of his child.

'Dr Reckitt was very good to us,' Abel said. 'He made up the laudanum himself – it was cheaper than going to the chemist in town. But, by the time Lizzie went blind, Maggie was taking laudanum, as well, to help her sleep. Otherwise she was up all night, beside herself with grief about what was happening. And praying.' His tone was bitter. 'For all the good that did.'

'I gather,' I began, 'that you were planning to emigrate – with the Cardigan-Ohio Emigration Company?'

'Yes. Before Lizzie fell ill it was a chance to give her a different life. After…' He sighed. 'After she died, I knew I wouldn't be able to stay here. I tried that before and every day – *every day* – I saw my poor dead wife in my house, in the chapel, even here. I knew I couldn't do it a second time. I knew we had to get away else I'd be as bad as Maggie. Or worse.'

John Philipps Williams had been wrong. Abel hadn't been looking for a new life in America. He had simply been trying to escape the grief of his old one.

'Are you still planning to go to Ohio, Mr Abel? Do you have an emigration bond?'

'I do. But it was—' Again, he stopped abruptly but not, this time, I felt, because of his grief. He began again.

'I'd met Mr Jenkyn Hughes before Lizzie fell ill. He approached me about making some furniture for him to take back to America and we got talking. I'd been thinking of America for a long time and Maggie was agreeable. Before Lizzie was ill, anyway. We had some savings so I thought buying the bond would be no trouble. I didn't do it right at the beginning because I was hoping to come to an arrangement with Mr Hughes to accept the furniture as part-payment for the bond, so that we'd have more money to set ourselves up over in America. But it never came to that.'

I realised that Abel was no longer simply answering our questions, he was reliving the whole sorry history. People do that when a great tragedy has overtaken them; they feel compelled to speak of it, to dull the agonising edge of new grief.

'The weeks went by and we were spending more and more money on laudanum. And Maggie wasn't able to work as she had before. She's a seamstress,' he explained. 'She's always taken in fine work but with Lizzie being so unwell she couldn't do it. So the arguments started. She couldn't think about America with Lizzie so ill. All she could think about was getting enough laudanum to ease Lizzie's suffering while she waited for God to grant a miracle.

'Don't misunderstand me, Mr Probert-Lloyd. I didn't begrudge Lizzie the laudanum. Nor Maggie, come to that, poor soul. Not at all. I'd've spent every last penny we had on it, if I'd had to. But it was America, you see. Maggie started saying that she couldn't go. Not now and not ever. *If the worst happens and I lose her*, she'd say, *I can't leave her here on her own. I can't abandon my baby and go to America.*' He paused, to meet my eye, I supposed. 'She wasn't in her right mind, you see, sirs. '

I nodded, unable to think what to say to him.

'I thought she'd change her mind after – well, after a while.'

I said nothing, shifting slightly on the settle and plucking a curl of wood-shaving from my breeches, waiting for whatever he would say next. The doors to the workshop were closed, presumably to keep our conversation private but I wished he would open them and ventilate the place. I was beginning to feel sick from the thick smell of the glue. It was in my lungs, and I knew I would be tasting it on my tongue for hours.

'As the weeks wore on,' Abel continued, 'almost all our money was gone. Never mind a bond, soon I was afraid I'd have to insist on Mr Hughes giving me some money for the furniture before it was finished so that I could buy laudanum.' He took an unsteady breath. 'Dr Reckitt was here one day, seeing to Lizzie, and I told him how things stood. He said something terrible then – something that made me fear for Maggie's sanity if I had to tell her. He said that he didn't think Mr Hughes had the money to buy as much as a cabinet door or a chair leg, he was in so much debt.

'The thought of not being able to buy laudanum was terrible, sir, I can't tell you … The doctor could see what a state the thought of it had sent me into and he said we could strike a bargain that would give Lizzie all the laudanum she needed and see me and Maggie on the ship in April.'

'What sort of bargain?' John asked. From the sharpness of his tone I knew that his suspicions had gone in the direction which mine, too, had taken.

I saw Abel's hands move and had the impression that he had laid his palms flat on his thighs, as if he was about to push himself up and run away.

'He said he'd buy a bond for me and Maggie and see to it that we had laudanum for Lizzie. All he wanted, in return, was the chance to–' He faltered and when he continued, his voice wavered. 'To see what had made Lizzie so ill.'

Despite having anticipated as much, I still felt a chill go down my back, as if an icy feather had been drawn along the length of my spine. 'He wanted to perform an autopsy examination on your daughter?'

'Yes.'

I did my best to ignore the images which had sprung to mind, unbidden; images informed by my visits to Gray's dissection room before my sight had failed. The sawn edges of a skull, the tiny tears in the skin around the wound, the oddly-grey brain, the absolute wrongness of seeing a cranium bisected above the eyes so that what lay within could be seen and removed for examination.

'What did your wife say about this bargain?' I asked.

'She didn't know. Not until a few days before Lizzie died. The doctor had come to warn me that she wouldn't be with us much longer and to tell me what I had to do when—'

So hard did David Abel have to swallow down his grief that I heard the straining sound of it.

'Maggie heard what he said. She was beside herself. Absolutely beside herself. She made me give her the bond Dr Reckitt had bought and she went to see Mr Hughes herself. I couldn't believe that she'd leave Lizzie but she said she wouldn't take another teaspoon of laudanum from the doctor, we were going to buy our own from now on. She was going to make Mr Hughes buy the bond back and give her a down payment on the furniture. Said she wasn't going to take no for an answer and that she was going to pay Dr Reckitt back every penny for the bond and for the laudanum we'd had from him.'

I shifted on the settle. Its seat was narrow and my back was beginning to ache. 'Did your wife see Mr Hughes? Did she get your money?'

Abel sighed, ran his fingers over his bare head. 'No. She couldn't find him.'

'What about you, did you try?' John asked.

Abel did not reply so I repeated the question. After a moment or two, he raised his head. 'No. God help me, I didn't. And now it's too late, isn't it?'

There was nothing I could say to ease his guilt. 'Could we speak to your wife?' I asked.

The breath the cabinet maker drew in was long and ragged. 'I'd be happy for you to speak to her if she was here but she isn't. Once we'd buried Lizzie, she said she couldn't live under the same roof as me after what I'd done. She's demented – convinced Dr Reckitt'll be out at Blaenywaun digging poor Lizzie up unless she can pay him back.'

He shook his head. 'You'll find her at the chapel. Watching.'

John

As we left the village behind, I remembered Harry's father. 'I can go and look for her,' I told him, 'if you want to get on home.'

Harry chewed the inside of his lip, thinking. 'No. I'll go once we've found Margaret Abel. I want to talk to her about Reckitt.'

'You mean about this agreement he'd made with her husband?'

Harry chewed his lip some more. 'Not just that.'

What then? He didn't say anything more, so I started thinking out loud.

'If Reckitt was prepared to buy the chance to autopsy Elizabeth Abel,' I said, 'there's a chance he might've done more than that – is that what you're thinking?' Harry's head turned towards me and I started gabbling, wanting to get it out before he stopped me. 'I mean Reckitt's got some kind of mania about this, hasn't he – looking inside dead people? He's not a well-off man, you can see that from his house – he hasn't got the kind of money you need to go about buying emigration bonds just to give them away. And who ever heard of a doctor giving away medicine?'

'I know.' The way he said it, I knew Harry suspected what I did but wished he didn't. Enough laudanum dulls pain and suffering. But too much will kill you.

We hadn't seen Maggie Abel when we'd been out to the chapel earlier on, but then we hadn't been looking for her. We'd been looking for J.P. Williams.

But I thought I knew where she'd be.

'We should look in the stables,' I told Harry. 'You have to go past them to get to the graveyard, don't you? She could hide there and keep watch on who comes and goes.'

From the outside, the chapel's stables were big and impressive-looking. Inside, they were cold and bare. No tack hanging from the beams, no sacks and barrels of food standing about, only a basic manger in each stall for those who'd brought something to feed their horse while they were being preached to.

Margaret Abel was just sitting there, in one of the mangers. And that was enough to make her look mad, even if there was nowhere else to sit.

Harry gave me Sara's reins and walked up to her. 'Mrs Abel – you must come with us, now. We'll take you home.'

She cringed away from him, the way a cat flattens itself in front of an attacker. 'No! I can't. Go away.'

Harry put a hand on her arm. 'Mrs Abel,' he said, gently, 'your husband is worried about you.'

She pulled away. 'No! If I'm not here he'll come and take Lizzie. I know he will! He's owed. *He will*!'

Her eyes were bloodshot. From crying or lack of sleep? Both, looking at the state of her. Before her child died, she'd probably been pretty. But now her fair hair was in tangles and her face was drawn back onto the bones.

'No.' Harry might've been speaking to an over-tired child. 'Dr Reckitt is not going to come and take your daughter. I promise you.'

'But he's owed!' Her voice was shrill, desperate. 'He'll have her, I know he will!'

'No,' Harry was kind but firm. 'He won't. I promise you.'

'He will, he will, he will.' She fell to sobbing, and tearing at her hair. 'If we don't pay him back, he'll come for her,' she sobbed. 'He'll cut her flesh and look into every crack and crevice of her! It's unnatural. It's wicked! I won't let him have her! I won't, I won't!'

Harry grabbed her hands in his. 'Mrs Abel, listen to me. My name is Henry Probert-Lloyd of Glanteifi. I am the coroner. I am responsible for the dead and I promise you that Dr Benton Reckitt will not interfere *in any way* with your daughter's grave or her body. I give you my word.'

She pulled her hands away from him, but she didn't start tearing her hair again. 'I can't leave her,' she sobbed. 'I mustn't. Don't take me away,' she wailed. 'Don't take me away.'

I moved closer, pulling the horses behind me. Abel hadn't been exaggerating. His wife was deranged with grief and fear. And she looked starved.

'I can't see any food or water here,' I murmured into Harry's ear. 'We have to get her back to her husband before she dies, too.'

Harry nodded and took one of the woman's hands to help her out of the manger. 'Come with me, now, Mrs Abel.'

It was a tone of voice that would've worked ninety-nine times out of a hundred. But ninety-nine times out of a hundred you're not dealing with somebody who's lost their wits. Margaret Abel pulled her hand away and shrank down into herself again. 'No. No!'

Harry tried to pull her up but when somebody's decided to resist, their weight seems to double and he couldn't do it. I left the mares standing and leant a hand. Between us, we got Margaret upright. But I could see that she'd collapse in a sobbing heap if we let her go.

'I'll carry her,' I said.

Thin as she was, it was like lifting a child. 'If I can get up on the mounting block with her, I can put her in front of me on Seren.'

Harry didn't need telling twice. By the time I walked out of the stable doors, he was getting the mare into position. I staggered a bit up the steps under the weight of Margaret Abel and, when I stepped off the mounting block I couldn't see properly and almost overbalanced. There was a terrifying moment when I thought we'd both land on our heads on the mare's other side, then I managed to pull us back onto Seren. Shaking, I shifted Margaret Abel into a position where she was more or less secure. The fight seemed to have gone out of her and, when I looked down to reassure her that I'd hold her safe, I saw why. She'd fainted clean away.

Back at Abel's workshop, he was resigned.

'She won't stay, gentlemen. She'll be back off there like a rabbit. She won't live under the same roof as me.'

'Mr Abel.' Harry's tone to him was a sight less gentle than it had been to Maggie. 'Your wife is weak and ill. She needs food and water and care. I suggest that you close your workshop and ensure that she's provided with those things.'

Abel looked as if he wanted to tell Harry to mind his own business. Didn't dare say it, of course.

'She's in no fit state to run away, Mr Abel,' I said as I put his senseless wife into his arms. 'She's as weak as a hatchling.'

Abel looked up from Maggie's face to mine. 'Was she awake when you found her?'

'Yes. And spitting pins. But when it came to it, she didn't have the strength left to fight us.'

He looked me in the eye. 'You think you've done her a kindness, bringing her home,' he said, keeping his voice low. 'But you haven't. Once she wakes up, she'll be in such distress that it'll kill her if she doesn't go back and watch over Lizzie.'

'Abel, she's your wife. You must look after her.'

He turned to Harry. 'No, Mr Probert-Lloyd. This isn't my wife. This is a stranger. A mad stranger who hates me for what I did so that my child could die without pain and we could leave this place.'

'Whether you leave is up to you,' Harry said. 'But I'll see to it that you're paid for the furniture you've made. There will be no need to sell your bond, I'll make sure that Hughes's estate covers its cost and the cost of the laudanum Dr Reckitt gave you.'

'Make sure you tell her that when she wakes up,' I chipped in, nodding at his wife. 'Tell her that Dr Reckitt will be paid in full. I think she believes that he's bought your daughter's body and has a right to it.'

Abel nodded wearily. 'What did you want to speak to her about?' he asked.

I waited while Harry decided how to phrase his question.

'In the days immediately before your daughter's death,' he said, 'did Dr Reckitt come to your house more often than he'd done before?'

Abel lowered himself on to the settle we had sat on earlier, his wife's head lolling off his shoulder as he sat. 'No, I don't think so.' He gently lifted Maggie's head to rest against him. 'He generally came every week, to give us more laudanum. I don't think he ever came more often than that.'

'And the dose of laudanum – was that the same?' Harry asked.

'If you mean, how often did we have to give it to her, it was just the same, Mr Probert-Lloyd. But if you're asking was the laudanum stronger, I've got no way of knowing. Except…'

'Except what?'

I looked at Harry. His blind eyes were narrowed and he looked sharp, suspicious.

'Well, Maggie was taking it as well – from the same bottle. So if it was stronger, she'd have been bound to notice, wouldn't she?'

'Yes.' Harry's frown disappeared. 'Thank you, Mr Abel.'

The cabinet maker hung his head for a moment, as if the effort of holding it up had suddenly got too much.

'Dr Reckitt's a good man,' he said when he looked up at us again. 'He explained to me how what he wanted to do would help other children. How other children might be saved by what he learned…' Abel swallowed. 'You know, from Lizzie.' He looked up at us, lips pressed together, holding tears in. 'How could I think of another father suffering like I did,' he croaked, 'if I could do something to prevent it?

'The doctor could've just given us the laudanum,' he went on, his voice strengthening. 'He didn't have to give us the bond as well. I didn't ask him for so much. He's a good man.'

'What now?' I asked when Abel's apprentice had handed us the mares' reins and shut the door to the workshop behind him.

Harry swung himself into the saddle. 'Now, I need to go back to Glanteifi. On the way, we'll go to the Lloyd and Philips offices and find Shoni Jones's address in Moylegrove. They're bound to have it if he's claiming Jenkyn Hughes's share of the business. We'll go and see him tomorrow.'

I kicked Seren into a trot after him. 'I can go out to Moylgrove. You're needed at Glanteifi.'

Harry looked torn. I could see he wanted to be there, to hear how Shoni Jones justified taking possession of his cousin's papers before anybody knew he was dead.

'Let's leave it like this,' he said. 'If I'm not at the Black Lion by ten o'clock tomorrow morning, go without me. I'll come with you now, and we can check for messages and make sure they've got a room and supper for you.'

Supper at the Black Lion. No sarcastic remarks from my landlady. No thin gravy and tough meat. What was left of the day was suddenly looking a lot brighter.

Harry

My spirits drooped as I trotted Sara up the drive to Glanteifi, and I scolded myself, shamed at how little thought I had spared my father while I had been out with John.

And yet, in my own defence, had his finger not stabbed at the door of his room? *Work!* He had made it quite clear that I was to get out and be useful, not hover about him. The thought evoked an unaccustomed sense of fellow-feeling with my father; on the rare occasions when I was ill, I, too, wanted nothing more than to be left alone.

Mrs Griffiths greeted me at the back door. 'Harry, don't take your boots off yet. Mr Schofield sent one of his clerks over, earlier, with a note requesting a meeting with you at your earliest convenience. I think that was the phrase.' She withdrew what must be Schofield's note from a pocket in her apron and checked. 'Yes: *at your earliest convenience.*'

'I see. And is it convenient? Can I be spared for another hour or so?'

'Your father was asleep when I went up half an hour ago. Mr Arthur Philips has been with him most of the time you've been gone so he's been well entertained. And his speech is better again today. More sentences.'

'And the paralysis?'

'A little bit more movement, I think. He can get on and off the bed by himself now. He's out of bed and sitting in a chair by the fire.'

Progress indeed.

'Very well, I'll go and see Schofield then,' I said. 'I'll be home before dark if I go straight away. What's for dinner?'

I heard the boyishness of the question as soon as it was out of my mouth. I couldn't help it; standing here with the smell of cooking coming from the kitchen, the years just seemed to fall away.

'Cod. Nice and easy for your father to eat.'

'I'm sure Dr Reckitt would approve. Speaking of whom, has he been here today?'

'He has. And gone again. Expressed himself very satisfied with his patient.'

Since hearing the Abels' story I had been wondering what to think about Benton Reckitt. Previously, I had felt I understood his autopsy obsession. But, in the case of Elizabeth Abel, had he not overstepped some moral mark, taken advantage of a father's desperation? Had he not, as Mrs Abel obviously feared, effectively *bought* Lizzie Abel's body to do with as he wished?

Sara was already being rubbed down, so I took my father's usual mount, an elderly gelding. His official name was Major but, because of his docile nature, my father generally referred to him as Dobbin, and the grooms followed suit.

I managed to persuade the old horse into a decent trot down the drive and on to the road. It was a mild day and the oblique rays of the sinking sun set ivy leaves and holly bushes a-glitter in my peripheral vision.

Charles Schofield wanted to speak to me about John; there could be no other explanation for this requested meeting. I had estimated that I would need an assistant for a week, therefore, in the absence of any further communication from me, Schofield would have been expecting John back today. My failure to request his further assistance was discourteous, if excusable. Had my father not succumbed to his stroke, I would have ridden over on Saturday afternoon to speak to the solicitor and crave his indulgence for a further week. But apoplexy had struck and all consideration for Charles Schofield had gone by the board.

For John's sake if not for my own, I needed to make amends.

Astonishingly, the news that my father was unwell had not reached Schofield's office. Naturally, when I explained why I had not been to see him before this, he articulated all the conventional platitudes, but the question which followed rang with self-importance and told me how little genuine regard he felt for my father.

'I trust that in all this unforeseen busy-ness my clerk has given satisfaction?'

Stifling the antipathy his question provoked, I gushed like a geyser on the subject of John's excellence but to no avail. Schofield remained unmollified.

'I am quite well aware of John Davies's excellent qualities, thank you, Mr Probert-Lloyd. I have taken pains to train him and that is why I am sorely missing his presence in my office.'

'Yes, of course. And, please, do not think me unappreciative. As I mentioned, I would have come before this had my father not been taken so very ill.' I paused, delicately. 'However, I wonder if you might indulge me for a few more days? I have relied on John very much since I have had to be at Glanteifi but, as I'm sure you'll understand, there are things I cannot ask him to do alone and those have had to wait.'

In truth, John had done everything I would have done, entirely on his own initiative, but I could not afford to let his employer know that.

'Exactly how much indulgence do you feel you will need, Mr Probert-Lloyd?'

Unable to see people's faces, I was constantly having to guess at their expression in order to arrange my features into some complementary configuration; it was a wearying and probably futile process. Still, I gave Charles Schofield what I hoped was a look of realistic optimism. 'I'm confident that my investigations will be concluded at a public meeting in Cardigan on Friday,' I told him. 'That will furnish me with various material witnesses to whom I do not otherwise have ready access.'

'Friday?' Given that I had just doubled the length of time for which I had requested John's assistance, his tone was admirably non-committal.

'Is that entirely unreasonable of me?' I asked.

'I must admit, Mr Probert-Lloyd, its reasonableness or otherwise is not my primary concern here.'

'No?'

'If you succeed in being elected to the post of coroner for the Teifi Valley, have you asked yourself how you will provide yourself with an assistant who can always be available to you at a moment's notice?'

The question was both uncivil and indiscreet but, rather than bridle at it, I attempted to disarm him. 'Yes, that is a question I have asked myself. And I have decided to employ a private secretary. Even if unsuccessful in the election,' I added, 'I will clearly need a secretary as I assume my duties at Glanteifi. I would anticipate that, as long as I am careful in my choice, that person would have an interest in assisting me as coroner.'

'I see. And would that careful choice lead you to John Davies?'

'I understand,' I said, picking my words with care, 'that John's ambitions lie elsewhere.'

'Indeed?' The word was as sharp as a ruler over the knuckles. 'John Davies is an excellent clerk but, as I'm sure you are aware, Mr Probert-Lloyd, he has neither family nor means. He is not an *articled* clerk. Therefore, I fail to see in which direction his ambitions might extend.'

So, I had been entirely wrong about Mr Schofield's intentions; he was not preparing John to take his place.

'Of course,' I responded, 'as you say, he is not *presently* articled. But if articles were to be contracted for on his behalf... Would you welcome such a thing?'

'Is that John Davies's own impression? That I would welcome him here as an articled clerk – a would-be lawyer in his own right?'

'Not at all. He has given me no indication–'

'Because, if that is the case, I must disabuse him – and you, Mr Probert-Lloyd – of any such notion. I have a nephew who will sit, this very year, the examinations which will qualify him to practise as a solicitor. When the time is right, it is *he* who will take over my practice. He and nobody else, Mr Probert-Lloyd. And I hope, when he does, that – given this office's unstinting aid in endeavours that few others would have countenanced – he may count on your wholehearted support in the town?'

The intimidating effect of a verbal attack is far greater when you cannot see the person who is delivering it, and my body was tense with the atavistic fear of physical violence. 'Of course,' I replied, standing my ground though every nerve in my body was screaming at me to back away from danger. 'I've been very grateful for your help, Mr Schofield.'

'John Davies is undeniably an intelligent young man.' Schofield articulated each word as if he wanted to be absolutely sure I heard it clearly. 'But, if he wishes to take up articles, then he must do so elsewhere. This practice has room for only one solicitor and, as I have indicated, when I retire, that solicitor will be my nephew.'

I rode back to Glanteifi with the flaming oranges and purples of sunset ablaze in the western sky before me.

Neither Charles Schofield nor I had got what we wished from our interview. Schofield would have to do without John for another week and might, given our conversation, find him returned in a very different frame of mind from the one in which he had left. I, on the other hand, had seen my neat little plan dashed on the rocks of my own presumption. If John wanted to be articled, he would have to go elsewhere, which would inevitably take him out of my reach when I needed him. I could still do the right thing and find the necessary fees but, if I did so, it would be an entirely altruistic act.

Would John consider giving up the law and becoming my secretary? There was only one reliable way of finding out. But I would have to postpone that until after the inquest into Jenkyn Hughes's death.

John

I waited till ten o'clock on the dot then I went out to the Black Lion's stables. As I crossed the coachyard the clock down at St Mary's struck the hour, so I didn't have to worry that my watch was fast and I was leaving before time.

When she heard me, Seren's ears went up and she gave me her throaty greeting. I stroked her neck. I was going to be sad to take the little mare back to the stables at Glanteifi when this was all over.

'We're going out to Moylegrove, old girl,' I told her. 'Not that I know how to get there.'

It was all right when I was with Harry – he knew his way around because of hobnobbing around the county with the rest of the *crachach* when he was a boy – but I hadn't even been over Cardigan bridge before that week. I knew Moylegrove was in the direction of the sea, roughly west from St Dogmaels, but other than that I was just going to have to ask.

And that's what I did. Went up the hill out of St Dogmaels and asked where next. *Keep going* I was told.

So, I kept going past bent little trees and worn-out pastures, farms crouching with their backs to the wind, and gorse bushes half the size of the ones in the valley. I kept going and got enough rough-handling by the wind to make me glad of my overcoat till I saw the next person.

Left the next time you get to a bigger road, then the first right you come to.

The sky looked as if somebody was working it with a handle, and I hoped we were going to get to the Jones's farm, Penlanmeurig, before it started to rain.

We came to a little cluster of houses, and even though we hadn't got to the right hand turn yet, I decided to ask about the way again. Just to be sure.

There was a woman standing outside her house, beating the living daylights out of a mat with the handle of her broom. Something told me she had something – or someone – other than the mat on her mind. I called a good morning and got a curtsy when she saw me there on my horse. Hah! What would my mother've said if she could've seen that? Me getting a curtsy!

'Good morning, sir.'

I told her where I was looking for.

'When you get to a bend in the road like this'– she made an L-shape with her thumb and first finger– 'don't go this way.' She traced the long arm of the L. 'Just keep going over the hill. Penlanmeurig's on the other side, looking towards the sea.'

I told Seren to walk on and left her to her proxy beating.

Now I was nearly there, I didn't know whether to be glad Harry wasn't with me or worried about it. So far, nobody'd refused to speak to me. *I'm working for the acting coroner* had done the trick every time. And talking to somebody like David Daniels, James Philips's clerk, had been easier without Harry in tow. Daniels would never've told Harry everything he'd told me.

But the 'just one clerk to another' game wasn't going to work with Shoni Jones. At Penlanmeurig, what the family'd see was a man in a gentleman's overcoat, riding a gentleman's horse. I'd have to work a lot harder to convince them that, behind what they saw, I was just like them.

How big a farm was Penlanmeurig, I wondered? Within half a mile of where I'd grown up there'd been farms that were no more than a few scrappy fields held together with sweat and stone, and others that were a hundred acres and more of lush, green, fertile land. Farmers who held the most acres were always bidding for more, looking to take over tenancies where a lease was up.

Money makes money, as my father was fond of saying.

Mind, looking at the hard, stony ground on either side of me, it wasn't making much here. Even the hedge banks between fields seemed beaten low.

I shouldn't've started thinking about money. It just got me worrying. Because I shouldn't be here, should I? Not if I wanted to stay employed. I should be at the office on Adpar hill, doing everything I could to make myself necessary to Mr Schofield.

It all came from letting myself think I could be a lawyer. Which was as bad as thinking you could find the end of a rainbow and dig the gold up. Nothing more than a silly dream. I should just be grateful that I wasn't a labourer or a tenant farmer struggling to make a living like the poor bastards here.

Like my father.

My father. He'd been dead eight years and, sometimes, I couldn't remember what his face looked like. But I remembered his dream. And the hope of it had clung to me like my own shadow ever since Gwyn Puw and Dai'r Bardd brought us those coins.

America. A new life.

An old, cracked pot used to sit on the mantelpiece when I was a little boy. It was where my father used to put the 'America-money'. Every week the coppers'd go in and, when the pot was full, my mother'd go round the shops and exchange farthings, ha'pence and pennies for shillings and half crowns.

After my parents died, one of our neighbours held on to that pot for me. Presented it to me when I went back, and told me to count it, I'd find it all there. Didn't have the heart to tell him I had no idea how much we'd saved.

That money had all gone to Mr Davies, the Adpar schoolmaster who'd taken me in and educated me. I wished I had it still, it could pay for my ticket. Or for articles.

Did they make you pay for articles in America? Perhaps there was such a need for lawyers over there that they trained you for nothing. Especially in a completely new town like the one Jenkyn Hughes's emigrants were going to in Ohio.

Ohio. The name had a strange ring to it. Not even English. Foreign. What was it like, there?

We reached the top of the hill and the wind almost knocked the breath out of me. It was coming straight off the sea. From where I sat, on Seren's back, I could see wave furrows going all the way to the horizon. Grey and cold-looking, with white flecks where the wind was whipping them on.

I leaned forward in the saddle. Down the slope, a house had just come into view. Low and sunk into the ground, it was – as if it'd spent years cowering beneath the wind.

Not the house of a well-off man. No second storey. No range of barns and outbuildings. Just a longhouse that'd been added to and added to again at one end, each new room with its own window. At the other end was the holding's only byre with an open-sided cart shed going off at right angles.

The place was decently whitewashed, and I could see glass in at least one of the windows but, still, the buildings matched the land. Bare, starved, needing money spent if they were going to look anything much at all.

There seemed to be nobody about, so I dismounted and picked my way over the half-frozen mud to the house.

When I knocked, a head came round the door. A young woman.

'Shut the door!' I heard from inside. 'The chimney's smoking enough as it is!'

The girl blushed as she shut the door behind her and looked at me. She was pretty – hair the colour of a blackbird's wing, and big brown eyes.

'Good morning. Is this Penlanmeurig?'

'It is.' Then she added 'sir' just in case I was somebody important despite speaking her own language to her.

'I'm looking for Shoni Jones,' I said. 'Is he here?'

'Shoni? No, sir, he's not.'

'Do you know where I can find him?'

She went as if to look over her shoulder at whoever was listening, then realised that the door was shut. 'He's gone about all over the place,' she said. 'There's a meeting and he needs to tell people.'

'Can I speak to your father?'

'He's down at the forge in the village.'

Damn. That meant going all the way to Moylegrove and having to separate Shoni Jones's father from all the other men who'd be gathered round the blacksmith's fire, swapping news and gossip while they waited for tools to be sharpened or mended.

I thanked her and turned away. At least the wind'd be at my back for a minute or two.

I hadn't gone more than twenty yards from the house when I heard the door slam shut behind me and boots thudding.

'Please, sir, wait!'

It was going to be difficult to go back to being plain John Davies after all this sir-ing and curtsying. I pulled Seren up and turned in the saddle to see who was coming after me.

A man stumbled up, buttoning his jacket as he came. He didn't look much older than me – probably the girl's brother. His hair was shaved off so severely at the back and sides that, even with his hat on, I shivered looking at him.

'You don't need to go and find Dad, sir. He'll only tell you Johnny's not here – none of us knows where he is. He went off yesterday.'

'To tell people about the emigration meeting on Friday?'

He looked surprised. 'Yes.'

I dismounted. Couldn't talk to him man to man while I was looking down on him. 'You don't have to call me sir,' I said, pulling Seren's reins over her head so I could hold her more easily. 'I'm only a solicitor's clerk and this is a borrowed horse. But, for the time being, I'm the coroner's officer and I need to find your brother to speak to him on the coroner's business.'

'In trouble, is he?'

He wouldn't be sorry, that much was clear.

'That depends.'

'On what?'

'What d'you know about his involvement with Jenkyn Hughes and the American emigration scheme?'

He grunted and looked away. 'More than I bloody want to know. It's all he ever talks about.' Then he looked back at me, a sly look on his face. 'Going to come crashing down on him now, though, isn't it?'

'What is?'

'The whole thing!' He put on an American accent. 'The Cardigan-Ohio Emigration Company.'

'Why's it coming crashing down?' I moved slightly so as to put Seren between me and the wind.

He shook his head. 'Don't play stupid with me. You're the coroner's boy.' That was that, then. 'Sir' to 'boy' in half a minute. Still, he'd dropped the guard he'd've had up if he thought I was a gent.

'You'll know better than I do what's going on down there.' He jerked his head in the direction of Cardigan. 'Jenkyn Hughes, our so-called cousin, was a gambler. And not a very good one by all accounts. Now he's turned up dead and half the money for the scheme's been gambled away. More, if you believe some people.'

He was fishing for information so, in a spirit of give before you get, I obliged. 'No, it's not that bad. He only had a third stake in the company and he hadn't gambled away all of his share.'

That got me another grunt but I wasn't sure what it meant. I shivered. The frame of my specs was icy cold in the wind and it was making my head ache.

'Can we just walk over the hill?' I asked. 'We'll be out of the wind, then.'

He nodded and we stumped up the stony path until the wind stopped trying to blow the hair off our heads.

I pulled Seren up and faced him. 'If Shoni's invested in the scheme, I think his money's safe.'

He pulled a face. 'Invested? Shoni-boy's done more than invest. He owns the scheme now. Part of it, anyway. Got himself made heir to Jenkyn Hughes, didn't he? Did you know that?'

I nodded. 'Yes. We knew that.' Just as well to remind him that I wasn't working alone.

'All right then, I'm betting you don't know *how* he managed it?

How he persuaded cousin Jenkyn to sign his share away if he should *unfortunately* die?'

I let that hint of an accusation hang there for a moment or two. 'Go on then. Tell me.'

He shivered. 'He bought it.'

'*Bought* it? How?'

'Buy me a pint and I'll tell you.'

It looked as if he was afraid of being seen with me in Moylegrove because he led the way to St Dogmaels. We clopped down the high street to the White Hart where Harry and I'd eaten pot-stew the day before.

Once we'd sat down with our beer, I looked at him. 'I don't know your name, friend. I'm John Davies.'

He nodded. 'William Jones. But everybody calls me Wil Camlaw. *Camlaw.* Wrong handed.

'You're left handed?'

'They tried to make me use this one.' He raised the fingers of his right hand. 'You know, in the Sunday school, to write with. But I couldn't get used to it. Felt like I was trying to write with my toes. They grumbled and called me dull but, in the end, they let me do it with this one.' He mimed writing with his left hand.

Left handed. What had Reckitt said? If he was hit from the front, the killer was right handed. From behind, left handed.

'Right then. Tell me how your brother managed to buy his way into being Jenkyn Hughes's heir.'

He looked at me over his pint pot. 'Hughes needed money, didn't he? So when Shoni went to him and said he could help him out, our cousin was like a dog with a bitch on heat.'

'Where did Shoni get the money?'

The look Wil Camlaw gave me as he swallowed his beer was pretty sour. 'You mean how did a small tenant without two shillings in his pocket find the sort of money that'd interest somebody like Jenkyn Hughes?'

That was exactly what I'd meant. 'No, I mean—'

'It's all right. We're not as poor as you'd think from looking at the place. Or, rather, we weren't.'

I waited. He took another long pull at his pint then wiped his mouth on his sleeve and told me what I wanted to know.

It was a common enough story. His grandfather'd been a shrewd man who'd never spent a penny he didn't have to, so that his children and grandchildren could have a better chance than he'd had. And, at the end of his long life, he'd managed to put enough by to afford some land that had come up for sale quite near Penlanmeurig.

'He bought it for Shoni, on the understanding that our father would pass Penlanmeurig's lease on to me.'

Sounded like a sensible course of action. As far as I could see, their grandfather'd done the brothers a huge favour.

'I was happy with that,' Wil Camlaw said. 'It meant I had the bigger farm and I wouldn't have to work with Johnny.'

'You don't get on?'

'Never have, right from boys.'

'But your brother sold the land on, is that it?'

Will nodded.

'Did he give Jenkyn Hughes all the money?' I asked.

Wil's bark of a laugh had a grudging kind of admiration to it. 'Not him! Always known exactly what he's got to spend to get what he wants, Shoni has. How much effort, how much sucking up, how much work, how much money. Never spends an ounce more effort or a penny more in price than he has to.'

Sounded to me as if Shoni'd inherited their grandfather's shrewdness but I kept that thought to myself.

'So,' I said, 'he parted with some of the money he'd got for the land, and Jenkyn Hughes re-wrote his will making him his heir. Is that the sum of it?'

'Not quite. Johnny wanted to be part of the scheme.'

'The emigration scheme? He wanted to emigrate?'

Wil shook his head, swallowed a mouthful of beer. 'Wanted to be an agent, like our cousin. Wanted to be the big man, going around the countryside persuading people to leave their homes and their families and run off to America.'

Wil, evidently, was not friends with the idea of emigration.

'Had he been to America?'

'No. But Hughes came to stay with us when he first came over – must be nearly ten years ago, now – and then again last year, when he was nosing about for business partners. Filled Shoni's head with big ideas about life in America, he did. When he came over this time, Shoni wouldn't leave him alone – stuck to him like a tick every time he went out to talk to people about the scheme. Clever about it, mind. Said to Jenkyn that he knew who'd be most likely to want to go. Said they should talk to people he knew first, then go to people *they* knew and so on. Ended up halfway to Aberystwyth. And all the time, Shoni-boy was taking in every word our cousin said.'

Wil took a swift swallow of his beer. I could tell he had more to say.

'Came home with a book of notes this thick, he did.' He held his fingers an inch apart. Even if he was doubling the book's thickness for effect, that was a lot of notes.

'Reckoned he could do the agent's job now. Said he knew everything Jenkyn Hughes knew. Everything. He'd listened to the questions people asked and the answers they got and he knew what to say. All he needed was to go there, once – see Ohio and this town they were planning – and he could do Jenkyn's job for him. Better than him. He's always thought he could do a better job than everybody else, Shoni has.'

'Was that part of the deal he made with Hughes?' I asked. 'As well as being his heir, was he going to go out and see the new town in Ohio?'

'That's it. Got a ticket and everything. Wasn't going to trust Jenkyn's word, was he? He wanted the ticket in his hand. To be sure he was going.'

So. Shoni Jones had made it his business to find out how Jenkyn Hughes conducted the scheme. He'd planned to learn more by going to Ohio. And he'd made sure that, in the event of Hughes's death, he'd be able to take over, nice and neatly, where the American had left off. Had he decided that instead of setting himself up as an agent later, he'd just get rid of Hughes and take over his role in the American scheme, now? Then again, it wasn't quite that simple, was it? There were Hughes's gambling debts to consider. Shoni Jones would inherit them too.

A suspicion suddenly tapped me on the shoulder.

'Did your brother take out life insurance on Jenkyn Hughes?'

Wil put his mug down. 'No idea. Wouldn't surprise me. Careful, Shoni is. Very careful.'

I thought for a bit. What Wil had told me meant that there were suddenly a lot more questions I wanted to ask Shoni Jones. But I mustn't forget what I'd actually come here to find out.

'I've been told your brother owns a telescope – is that right?'

Wil looked surprised at the sudden change of subject but didn't ask why I wanted to know. 'Yes. Bought it off Jenkyn Hughes for ready cash.'

'Do you know when Shoni'll be back?'

Wil shook his head. 'Before Friday,' he said. 'That's all I can tell you. All the fires of hell wouldn't keep him away from that meeting.'

'All right then – when he comes back to Penlanmeurig, can you tell him that the coroner would like to see him before the meeting? He can find me or Mr Probert-Lloyd at the Black Lion in Cardigan.'

Harry

In spite of my best efforts, I was unable to leave the house in time to go to Moylegrove with John. My father did not wake till nine, and required help with dressing and getting to the close-stool. To have reached Cardigan in time, a door-to-door railway would have been necessary.

My father having managed to convey that he would like to leave his bedroom – *Down. Study.* – I accompanied him. Laboriously, two feet to each stair, he hecked his way down, his panted breaths alarming me slightly. I made a mental note to ask Reckitt whether that was to be expected after a stroke.

Assuming that my father's request to sit in the study arose simply from habit, I had ignored it and asked for the fire to be lit in the morning room. Quite apart from the fact that the study held no particularly fond memories for me, the morning room was a far pleasanter place in which to sit at this time of day; it looked out over the river and the meadows beyond and was filled with light from the rising sun.

I explained my decision to him on the way down the stairs but he resisted me when we reached the hall.

'Father, this way,' I pulled gently on the arm I was holding.

'No,' he panted. 'Study.'

'The fire's been lit in the morning room.'

'Study! Papers.' I heard a flash of his old spirit and knew exactly the kind of glare he would be giving me.

'Very well,' I said, allowing him to continue towards the study. 'If it's to do with papers, I'll ask Mrs Griffiths to come.'

I called out for Wil-Sam and sent him scurrying in search of Isabel Griffiths. Then, conjoined, my father and I shuffled to the study, where he disengaged himself from my supporting arm to make his ungainly way around the desk. He half-sat, half-collapsed into his chair and, after shuffling backwards and almost tipping the chair on its side, managed to pull out a drawer from one of the desk's pedestals.

I could hear his breathing and, anticipating questions from Reckitt, I tried to analyse its quality. Was it more of a wheeze or simply rapid, panting breath? Was it laboured or merely quick? I wondered when Reckitt would come. I would have to ask Mrs Griffiths if he had given any indication of when we might expect him.

My father started withdrawing documents from the drawer. His movements were stiff, clumsy, and I was afraid that, unused as he was to balancing his newly-altered body, he might topple from his chair. However, conscious of a need to restore some of the dignity stolen from him by the stroke, I did not go to his aid, simply watching as best I could while he bent, stiffly, to the drawer, reached in with his one good hand and straightened to put another sheaf of paper on his desk. The drawers were ordered for the convenience of a right-handed person and, as my father now only had use of his left, the whole procedure was awkward at best.

Isabel Griffiths appeared. 'Is everything all right, Harry?'

'Yes. My father wants to show me some papers, I think, but obviously…' I gestured at my eyes.

'Has he asked for me?' Her demeanour told me that she wasn't happy about invading the master's territory uninvited; her hands were clasped at her waist as if she was seeking reassurance from herself.

'No, it's me doing the asking.'

She hesitated but could not deny me for long. 'Very well.'

My father had finished emptying the drawer of documents and now sat, apparently looking down at the pile in front of him.

I turned back to Mrs Griffiths. 'Would you mind having a look at these documents, please? Just to see what they are?' As always, in my father's presence, I spoke to her in English.

She hesitated but, when I moved towards the desk, she followed. 'May I?' she asked my father. Clearly, he gave some visible permission because she drew the pile of papers to her and turned them around.

'This first one is Mr Probert-Lloyd's will,' she said, after a second or two.

I watched as she put it aside, unread. She had been asked only to say what the documents were: she would do that and no more.

'This one is a deed relating to a property on the estate.' She placed it on top of my father's will. 'As is this. And this. And this.' Each deed was placed on top of the last until the second pile was taller than the first.

'And this...' She moved her head closer to the desk, as if she was having trouble making out the writing. '... is ...' She stopped and turned to me. 'It's a mortgage document.'

'A mortgage? On what property?'

She turned back to the document. I heard a page turn before she spoke again. 'On Glanteifi. The whole estate.'

Involuntarily, my eyes fastened on my father and I had to shift my gaze until the whirlpool moved to one side and I could see him again. I could tell only that his face was turned towards me.

'Father? When did you take out a mortgage on the estate?' *More to the point – why?*

It was a futile question. How could he answer me?

'Kerr,' he said.

Llewelyn Kerr was Glanteifi's solicitor; he handled all the legal business of the estate and would, undoubtedly, have drawn up most, if not all, the documents on the table.

'Yes,' I said. 'I think I'd better pay him a visit.'

Kerr's Newcastle Emlyn office was at the top of town, on Water Street, near the recently-rebuilt Baptist chapel. That it was a more prosperous office than Mr Schofield's was evident from that fact that, whereas Schofield's had one bow window looking on to the street, the building occupied by Mr Kerr's practice was double-fronted and set back from the street a little. The brass plate on the wall had not just Kerr's name and title engraved upon it, but two others as well – that of his brother-in-law Edward Jervis and his late father-in-law's original partner, the venerable Joseph Evans. Three lawyers and at least six clerks, some of them articled. No wonder Charles Schofield had been adamant that there was room in his practice for only one solicitor; with Kerr, Jervis and Evans sitting at the opposite end of town, it was quite surprising that Mr Schofield managed to find enough business for one.

Having announced myself and relinquished my coat and hat to an attentive clerk, I was asked to wait and shown to a rather grand sofa in the spacious hall. No walking straight in off the street into a front office here.

Llewelyn Kerr had been my father's solicitor for most of the last decade but I would have been hard put to it to recognise him, even had my sight not been compromised. Fortunately for me, I was not required to do so.

'Mr Probert-Lloyd! Good morning to you. Come through to my office, will you? It's this way. Can you see sufficiently to follow me?'

I was glad to be spared the tedious business of explaining my anomalous sight and grateful that Kerr had handled it so adroitly, acknowledging my condition without assuming that it disabled me in any significant way.

'Thank you. As long as you don't require me to read or recognise faces, my sight is adequate to my needs.'

Kerr closed the door of a largeish office decorated in a rather unusual style. As far as I could see, no paintings of any kind hung on the walls; instead the solicitor had opted for wallpaper in a florid design of red and yellow on a royal-blue base, something geometric, or regularly repeating. It pulsed in my peripheral vision and made me feel slightly dizzy.

'Please, do sit down. I assume you're here, in your capacity as acting coroner, about Jenkyn Hughes's will?'

Providentially, we were both still in the process of sitting down, which allowed me a second or two to master my expression.

'Actually, I wasn't going to begin with that but, now you've brought it up...' I smiled.

'Yes. I probably should have come to you.' I heard a note of doubt in Kerr's voice. 'But you'll understand that it's a slightly delicate matter. I have to confess, I've been in a quandary.'

He seemed to be waiting for a response. 'How so?'

'I understand that the police have taken a man into custody. I have no idea how compelling the case against him is...' He petered out, inviting me to formulate the other half of his quandary for him.

'But the will offers a motive that might be compelling in its own right?' I speculated.

'Quite so.' Mr Kerr sat back in his chair, as if he felt that he had been altogether too forthcoming. But he had set himself upon the course of disclosure and he could not very well backtrack now. 'It's my understanding,' he said, 'that Mr Hughes's body was not found until some while after his death. Is that correct?'

I was finding it difficult to swap mental paths from my father's business affairs to Jenkyn Hughes's murder. I took a long breath, both to compose myself and to snatch a few seconds to order my thoughts.

'Yes,' I said. 'It's possible that he'd been dead as long as a fortnight before his body came to light.'

'And the discovery took place a week ago?'

'Approximately.'

Kerr took an audible breath. 'And therein lies the motive,' he said. 'On that estimation of timings, Mr Hughes made his new will less than a week before his death.'

A *week*? Was this the will in favour of the cousin, or a new one writing him out of it?

'Mr Kerr,' I began. 'I am not a policeman. I am not even the elected coroner, merely a temporary stand-in. However, I have already expended considerable energy and resources in investigating this case and I do not believe that the man currently in police custody is Jenkyn Hughes's murderer. I would consider it a great favour if you would tell me who stood to benefit most from Mr Hughes's death. I am quite sure, from your earlier remarks, that it is not Theophilus Harris.'

'No. It is not.' Even in confirming this much, Kerr sounded reluctant and I realised that I would have to help him tell me what he wished me to know.

'If I hazard a guess, will you tell me whether I am correct?'

There was a short hesitation. 'Yes, very well.'

If taken to task by his partners, Kerr would now be able to claim that he had simply confirmed what, apparently, I already knew.

'Is it his cousin, or near-relation, Mr Shoni Jones of Moylegrove?'

There was an exhalation. 'No, it is not.'

No? 'But I was given to understand, by persons who might reasonably be expected to know, that Shoni Jones was Hughes's heir.'

Kerr leaned his elbows on the desk and clasped his hands. 'Indeed. In the strictest possible confidence, I can tell you that he was the major beneficiary of Mr Hughes's *previous* will.'

'Go on.'

'Mr Hughes made that will on November the third. It left all his personal effects to his mother, to be returned to her at the executors' convenience. But all residual property and moneys were bequeathed to John – commonly known as Shoni – Jones of Penlanmeurig, Moylegrove.'

'And the executors of that will were?'

'Myself and the said Shoni Jones.'

'So Jones was aware of this will's existence? The one leaving everything to him?'

There was a small silence during which I wondered whether I had made some kind of *faux-pas*. Then I heard Kerr draw a breath. 'Not only did he know it existed, Mr Probert-Lloyd, but he sat where you are sitting now when it was being drawn up. Obviously, as a beneficiary, he could not be a witness to it but he watched as it was signed and notarised.'

'And the beneficiary of the more recent will? Is that person to inherit Hughes's share of the Cardigan and Ohio Emigration Company?'

'Yes.'

'And are they aware of the fact?' Surely it was not possible that a second would-be legatee had sat in Kerr's office watching as their prospects were substantially increased?

'I have not yet sought to inform the beneficiary,' Kerr said 'because, until the inquest has formally pronounced Jenkyn Hughes dead, probate cannot legally be initiated. As to whether the beneficiary is already aware that they have been named as Hughes's heir, I couldn't say.'

'Mr Kerr...' I controlled my voice, though I felt far from calm. 'My assistant is, even now, riding out to speak to Shoni Jones, convinced that he had a motive to wish Mr Hughes dead. If somebody else has a more compelling motive, I must know of it before the inquest.'

I paused but he said nothing. My mouth was dry as I asked my next question. 'Is the beneficiary Mr Hughes's partner, James Philips?' Who knew what convoluted legal arrangements the two of them might have put in place in each other's favour in settlement of gambling debts?

Again, an indrawn breath. 'No. Not *that* partner.'

John

I left Wil Camlaw and rode back to Cardigan. My head felt stuffed with everything he'd told me and I couldn't sort it properly. Did it make any difference that Shoni Jones had *bought* his way into Hughes's will? Did it give him more of a motive than if Hughes'd made him his heir voluntarily? Had he decided that he'd make sure Hughes couldn't change his mind?

With Hughes out of the way, Shoni would've been in the perfect position to step into his shoes and take over as agent to the Ohio scheme. He'd definitely moved up to the position of suspect number one in my mind.

But what had he seen on Tresaith beach?

I didn't want to, but I was going to have to speak to the big sailor again.

By the time I crossed the bridge in Cardigan, I had a plan. Problem was, I wasn't sure it'd work and there were about a hundred bees buzzing around in my guts as I paid a boy to look after Seren and walked onto the crowded quay.

I picked my way around, ducking under the seagulls that swooped on bits of God-knows-what on the ground and dodging between hand barrows and piles of crates until I saw what I was looking for. A sailor sitting by himself minding his own business. The tide was in and he was perched on one of those tying-up bollards, puffing on his pipe and looking up the river towards the stretch of river they called the Netpool where the ship-building docks were.

I walked up to him, hoping I was right and he was a sailor. If he wasn't, he probably wouldn't be able to help me. But he looked the part. He was wearing a knitted cap and those canvas trousers sailors wear. Must dry out better than wool. Nobody'd wear canvas for warmth.

Feeling like a pheasant on a duck pond in my office clothes, I said good day to him and asked if I could have a minute of his time. He was nothing like the big sailor, thank God. Just a little whip of a man with curly black hair sticking out from under his cap.

He shook his head. 'Sorry, matey. No speako the lingo.'

'Oh, well then,' I said, in English. 'Good morning to you.'

He nodded. 'Tha's be'er. What can I do for ya?'

'Do you know a big sailor with a bald head who carries his pipe behind his ear?' My finger went up to the side of my head and I snatched it down. He knew what an ear was.

'Yeh, I know 'im.'

'What's his name?'

'Dunno. They just calls him the Whaler. About somewhere, 'e is.' He began peering about.

'No, don't look for him! It's more than my job's worth to be caught speaking to him,' I lied. I dropped my voice, as if I didn't want anybody else to hear. 'It's a private matter, see. Can you tell him it'll be worth his while to come up to the Blue Bell in Pwllhai in half an hour?'

'An' who wants him?'

'John Davies.' I hoped the big man would remember my name. But, most likely, if he was 'about somewhere' he'd've noticed me by now.

'An' why should I bother?'

'Come with him and I'll make it worth bothering.' I wasn't going to pay him now – if I did, he'd have no incentive to pass the message on.

'Summink up front'd be a gentlemanly gesture – token o' good faith kinda thing.'

Harry'd given me what he called contingency money and I pulled some out now. Enough – I hoped – to interest the sailor but not enough to satisfy him. 'You'll get the same again if I see you with him at the Blue Bell. Come in half an hour. And don't tell anybody but him.'

I walked quickly back up from the docks to the area between the high street and St Mary's known as Pwllhai. Hopefully, the Blue Bell'd be far enough from the docks for the Whaler not to worry about being seen with me.

Trouble was, I'd been so busy thinking about him that I hadn't stopped to think about what it'd be like having to walk into a room full of strangers. I turned from closing the door against the cold outside and found every eye in the Blue Bell's taproom looking at me.

I didn't really want a drink but I couldn't sit there without one. I nodded to the man nearest the beer barrel in the corner, and he put a pint pot under the tap without asking.

The fear of offending somebody stopped me looking around, so I just smiled weakly as the landlord stared at me. Like everyone who drew beer for a living he did it by ear as much as by eye and he stared at me as the beer ran out of the barrel into the wooden mug. Then, without looking down, he shut the tap and handed me the pot.

'Tuppence.'

It was more than the beer was worth at Newcastle Emlyn prices but I wasn't going to argue. I paid up and found somewhere to sit in the corner, my back to the wall.

Half an hour I'd said to the English sailor. Best if people didn't see him and the Whaler leaving the docks hard on my heels. But half an hour was going to feel like a week with every eye in the place glaring at me like a magistrates' informer.

I would've liked to do something to pass the time – make some notes or read the ones I'd already written – but I was afraid to take my notebook out of my pocket in case somebody thought I was writing things down about them. So I just sat there and tried to drink slowly. A pint was plenty when I needed to keep my wits about me.

The men in the corner were speaking again but they kept their voices too low for me to hear. God knows what they thought I'd want to listen to them for. But then, if you've got something to hide, you probably think every soul you see is earwigging.

What are you doing here, John Davies, I asked myself. *Why are you still wandering around Cardigan asking questions when, more likely than not, it's going to cost you your job?*

But I'd come too far to go scuttling back to my clerk's desk now. I just couldn't face it.

I shuffled my arse on the bench and leaned away from the wall. It was striking cold right through to my skin. Cold and damp. I glanced across at the fireplace in the corner. The fire was what you might call grudging – if you'd sat right next to it your front would've been warm but your back would've been as chilly as the opposite corner.

I rubbed one boot up and down the other calf – there was a wicked draft down towards the floor. A strip needed nailing along the bottom of the door to keep the cold air from coming in.

The door opened and I felt something that was half fear, half excitement go through me. But the man who came in wasn't large or bald. Not the Whaler. He went over to three men near the back who'd called greetings to him, and I tried to get my thumping heart to slow down again.

Excitement. That's what was keeping me there, in the teeth of hostile looks and the prospect of unemployment. Excitement. I hadn't realised how bored I was with being a clerk until Harry'd walked in to Schofield's office that day back in November looking for an assistant. I suppose, apart from being a *gwas bach*, I'd had nothing to compare it with. But now I did.

I liked investigating. Finding things out. Getting the answers to questions. Perhaps I should give up clerking and become a policeman. If a miracle happened and Harry became coroner, I could be his officer then.

But working for Billy Go-About wouldn't be like working for Harry, would it? There was no way in the world Bellis would treat you like his equal. It'd all be Yes, sir, No, sir, Three bags full, sir. Not like now. Now I had people calling *me* sir.

What would my poor mother have said if she could see me now? Dressed in a good woollen overcoat with a gold watch in my pocket and an urchin holding my horse for me on the bit of grass under the castle wall?

But, when I thought about it, I didn't think my mother would've been all that surprised. I could see her nodding and smiling. *You always were a quick one, 'machgen i.*

She'd seen it even if my father hadn't. My nimble-wittedness.

I finished the last of my beer but the dregs. *To you, Mam.*

What would she tell me to do, now? Go back to Mr Schofield and grovel? Buy a ticket for America? Go up to the police station and see if they needed any more constables? *You could be Inspector one day, 'machgen i.*

John Davies, Inspector.

What would they call me? When I was a *gwas bach* nobody'd called me by my name, there'd been a John and a Johnny working there already. No, they'd called me Jac and then Jac Wap – quick Jack. It hadn't been a bad name even if it had come from what they shouted at me all day – *Come now, quick!*

Clerking, emigration or trying for the police. I had a choice to make.

The door opened again and, this time, it was the Whaler. Standing there in the low doorway, he looked even more huge and muscle-bound than before. He saw me but, instead of coming in, he moved his head sideways. *Come out.*

I'd forgotten the English sailor until I got outside. There he was, standing next to the Whaler as if he was showing off his prize bull.

'Here he is, matey. As requested.'

I put what I thought was reasonable into his black-stained palm and waited for him to complain. But he just marched straight in to the Blue Bell to spend it. I wished him a better welcome than I'd had.

The big man moved off, forcing me to follow.

'Why d'you want me?' he asked, without looking round.

I scooted up to his side. 'I wanted to ask you about Shoni Jones,' I said, keeping my voice as low as I could.

'What about him?'

I dodged around an open sack of sawdust that was standing outside a workshop door. 'That last time you saw Mr Hughes – when he was on the beach to meet you – when you came back to Cardigan after dumping the lime and moving the coal round the headland to Penbryn…' Moving, that was a good choice of word, I thought, when, to be strictly accurate, the phrase was 'feloniously taking away'. 'Did Shoni Jones come back to Cardigan with you?'

He stopped in his tracks. 'Why?'

'Because I think he saw something through that telescope of his that made him want to go back to Tresaith on his own.'

I was watching his face, side on, but he didn't so much as glance at me. It was as if he couldn't look at you and speak at the same time. 'Why should I tell you?'

A wagon came along the narrow lane then and we had to move. Now, I was standing behind him. 'You told me you owed a debt to Jenkyn Hughes,' I said, hoping he'd be happier with me speaking to the back of his head. 'If I know what Shoni Jones saw, it might help to catch Hughes's killer.'

He turned around. 'Jones, is it? Jones killed him?'

I swallowed. Something had sparked in those marble-blue eyes and I suddenly feared for Shoni Jones if I said yes. 'I don't know. But I need to speak to him about what he saw.'

The big man turned away from me and began walking again. 'Shoni Jones got off with the coal at Penbryn. Stayed there.'

I trotted after him. 'Why? To meet whoever was coming for it?'

'Said he'd walk back round to meet Mr Hughes.'

I drew alongside him again. 'So why didn't he just stay with him on Tresaith beach? Didn't he trust the rest of you to deliver the coal?'

He didn't answer straight away and I was so busy staring at him that I almost walked into an aproned man with his hand on the rim of a cart wheel.

'Mind yourself!'

I dodged round him and darted after the Whaler who hadn't slowed down at all.

'Why didn't Shoni Jones stay with Jenkyn Hughes in the first place?' I asked again. 'Why did he walk back from Penbryn?'

Abruptly, he stopped. Afraid of a fist, I hung back, but he half-turned. 'Mr Hughes was meeting somebody.'

I took a step forward. 'Who?'

'Don't know.'

There was more, I could tell. I waited.

'Said he was meeting a woman,' he said, finally. 'He said a word and they laughed. Albion and Shoni Jones. They laughed.'

'Do you know what the word was? D'you remember?'

'No.'

I tried all the English words I knew for prostitutes and he shook his head at all of them. Then it dawned on me that the word might've been to do with the meeting, not the person.

'Was it tryst?' I asked. 'Not *trist* in Welsh, there's an English word – tryst – means a lovers' meeting.'

'No.'

'What about *tête-à-tête*?'

'Sounds French.'

'It is.'

He shook his head.

'Assignation?' I suggested. A word he probably wouldn't know but a reasonably educated man like Hughes would. The kind of word men of the world like Jones and Albion might well have laughed at.

'Say it again.'

I did.

'Might've been. I wouldn't swear to it, mind. Not if a man's life depended on it.'

So, Shoni Jones had been ten minutes' walk from Tresaith beach where Jenkyn Hughes had had a pre-arranged meeting with a woman.

I wasn't sure whether things were getting clearer or more confused.

Harry

The news that Jenkyn Hughes had altered his will in Mrs Parry's favour mere days before he was murdered was, to say the least, surprising; though Reckitt might not have agreed, of course. Had the growth in Hughes's brain been responsible for this sudden alteration? Or had the intimate relationship Bets Parry had suggested between her mother and the American been at the root of his change of heart? In either case, assuming Mrs Parry knew that she was now the main beneficiary, it might represent a motive to wish Hughes dead. Especially as his gambling had made him a liability to the Cardigan-Ohio Emigration Company.

Carried home through increasingly insistent rain at Sara's brisk stableward trot, these – to my shame – were the questions that preoccupied me.

Had I been a dutiful son and a willing heir to Glanteifi, however, my thoughts should have been entirely occupied with what I had learned in the latter part of my interview with Llewelyn Kerr.

I had, I confess, been so disconcerted by news of the change to Hughes's will that I might have forgotten the real reason for my visit to Mr Kerr altogether had the lawyer not been practised in dealing with clients who had received surprising news.

'Your original intention was, I think, to speak to me about another matter, Mr Probert-Lloyd?'

I hope I did not look quite as witless as I felt in that moment. It required an actual effort of will to recollect what, in fact, I had come into town to speak to Kerr about.

'Indeed.' Briefly, I summarised my father's state of health and his keenness that I see the documents he had produced for me that morning.

'If you'd rather wait for confirmation, from Dr Prendergast or Dr Reckitt, that my father is as incapacitated as I say,' I suggested. 'I would take no offence.'

'My dear Mr Probert-Lloyd, that would be a very poor beginning to our association. I am perfectly willing to accept that matters are as you say.'

'Thank you. I'm afraid that practice at the London bar inclines one to forget that dependence on a gentleman's word still exists.'

I had expected Kerr to summon a clerk to procure a copy of my father's will but, instead, he said, 'I can give you the bones of your father's will without even consulting it. He revises it periodically as one might expect of a man whose minor beneficiaries predecease him. It's entirely uncontroversial. A few kind bequests to old or current servants and a trinket or two here and there to acquaintances for whom they may be supposed to have a particular significance. But the entire estate and all your father's assets are left to you as his only surviving offspring.'

I was relieved; a niggle of doubt had begun to worm its way through my mind after my father's performance in the library.

'And the other document?' I asked. 'The mortgage?'

A sigh from Kerr told me that the information he had on this subject would be less welcome.

'It cannot have escaped your attention,' the lawyer began, 'that recent years have not been kind to those who rely on land holdings for their income. When your father first came to Glanteifi at the turn of the century, he would have found an estate very different from the one he'd left in Worcestershire. Quite backward in all likelihood. Then the war came and, suddenly, ensuring that our agriculture was productive was not just about profit but about patriotism.'

For both Kerr and myself this was history, but the war against Napoleon had been the backdrop to my father's young manhood. His brother-in-law, Francis, had died fighting the French in Spain.

'Landholders got used to high prices during the war, but when it ended and we could import things again, their income slumped. Your father inherited the estate in eighteen hundred and eleven while the French blockade was still in place, and, from what my father-in-law told me when he handed over the Glanteifi account, Justice Probert-Lloyd was a very enthusiastic embracer of agricultural reform as a way of increasing production.'

That much I already knew. My father had spent much of his life trying to encourage his tenants to adopt agricultural innovations.

'I don't know how much you've had to do with the estate in recent times, Mr Probert-Lloyd, but that enthusiasm for new methods has recently begun to bear fruit. A new generation is acceding to tenancies and these younger men see what their fathers did not – that changes must be made if the land is to pay at all.'

'Farmers are not, by inclination, great revolutionaries,' I contributed.

'Indeed. And when change takes years to accomplish through generations of careful breeding or the nurturing of soils through successive plantings and harvests it's no wonder.' Kerr obviously felt that I was speaking whereof I did not know, that I was a naturalised Londoner who should be listening and not presuming to have an opinion. I bridled, but held my tongue.

'To come to the point,' he continued. 'In recent times, your father has been extending himself more and more, financially, in order both to acquire additional land as it became available and to modernise the estate's holdings. Instead of building up reserves of capital to see the estate through lean times, he has – quite literally – ploughed all his profits back into the land. And, when returns proved insufficient to meet the tenants' demands for new buildings and improved houses, he took out a mortgage on the estate so that he could get the work done sooner rather than later.'

'I hope you're going to tell me that this mortgage is for a reasonable sum and that it's not going to endanger the estate?' The question was intended to lighten the atmosphere. Kerr's tone had implied that he was preparing me for bad news.

'I am able to tell you no more than this. The mortgage is for a sum which makes repayments reasonable in years when nobody falls behind with their rent and when the home farm makes a healthy profit. Obviously, with the increased demand for produce of all kinds in Merthyr and the coalfields, farmers here have a ready market. But getting produce down to the ironworks isn't cheap, or easy.'

'Is the estate in danger?' I asked.

Llewelyn Kerr sighed. 'I'm not entirely privy to your father's accounts but my understanding is that a single bad harvest would put it on a very weak footing – even assuming that only a quarter of the tenants fell into arrears. Two bad years in a row would bankrupt the place unless matters were managed extremely efficiently.'

Something about the way he said 'extremely efficiently' made me suspicious. 'Are you suggesting that the estate isn't managed as well as it might be?'

There was a small silence. Kerr sat back in his chair and folded his arms. 'I don't know if you're aware of the fact that Mr Ormiston – your father's steward – suffered a tragedy two or three years ago?'

'When his daughter and her children died?' Their house had burned down with the whole family in it. I had been summoned home to attend the funeral.

'Yes.' The lawyer paused, and I remembered crowds at the graves' side, openly weeping at the loss of five souls in one terrible night.

'Since then,' he went on, 'I think it's fair to say that Mr Ormiston's heart has gone out of the job. He's a shadow of the man he was. And his wife ... poor woman.' It had broken Mrs Ormiston's health, I knew. From one of my father's weekly letters – read, when I was still able to do so, with the aid of the most powerful magnifying glass money could buy in London – I had learned that the steward's wife was now an invalid who rarely left the house.

'Tenants are not being given notice as they should for non-payment of rent,' Kerr said. 'Income is slipping, but outgoings – relating to your father's programme of improvements – remain high.'

'Why have they not been put on hold?' I asked. As little experience of estate management as I had, that seemed an obvious expedient to me.

I saw Kerr shake his head in incomprehension. 'Your father seems determined to push through his improvements as quickly as possible.'

Now, my body moving mechanically in response to Sara's brisk trot up the drive to Glanteifi, thoughts of Jenkyn Hughes were displaced by the agonising realisation that the indebtedness of the estate was my fault. My refusal to show any interest in its management had made my father fearful of the state into which Glanteifi would fall on his death and he had spent his declining years doing what he should have been able to leave in my hands.

Given his age and my resolute lack of interest in my inheritance, nobody could have expected my father to do more than preside over the estate's gradual decline; but he had behaved as if he had a son ready and eager to take up the reins, an heir with an eye to the prosperity of future generations. Had he assumed – *or hoped* – that I would prove to be such a man when the time came?

I recalled the letters that had arrived during my years of self-imposed exile; letters detailing rents my father had remitted, rebuilding he had undertaken, reductions in payment that he had sanctioned. Lazily, I had dismissed it all as the news of a man who had nothing more interesting to write about. Now, I saw that he had been providing me, year after year, with an education in how to be a good squire.

The guilt and anguish of that realisation made me resolve to be a better man. But it also raised an urgent question in my mind. Where was I going to find the money to stand as coroner?

John

The light was going as I rode down over the little Gwenffrwd stream and on towards Treforgan. It wasn't late but the day was cloudy and keen to be over. I turned Seren up the drive to the Glanteifi mansion and pulled my collar up against the fat drips coming down off trees that made the drive into an avenue. Down the slope, away from the house, the Teifi was running fast and brown and the swans who lived on this stretch had pulled themselves up onto the little island directly below the house. There they were, the pair of them, necks swung round to bury their heads between their wings. They'd decided night was coming on, too.

I left the mare with one of the grooms and went around to the front door. Still felt odd, not going in the servants' entrance, but the housekeeper'd been very clear about it, the first time I'd come here on my own – I was here on official business so I'd better present myself at the front door and be announced, not sneak in at the back.

The blonde maid, Clara, smiled when she opened the door. Then she remembered her place and asked me to wait in the hall for 'Mr Harry'.

So. Old George was still alive then. Harry'd be *Mr Probert-Lloyd* the second his father died.

I watched Clara hitch at her skirts to run up the stairs. She caught me looking and we both blushed. To distract myself from what was happening in my trousers I looked about the hallway. The black-and-white tiles were so clean you could've lain down and licked them. Clara, or one of Glanteifi's other maids, must mop and polish them every single day for them to look like that. Same with the bannister rail – gleaming, it was.

'John!' Harry came down the stairs two at a time as if he could see every inch, though I noticed that his hand was on the rail all the way, just in case. Perhaps it was him that was making it shiny not beeswax and turpentine.

We clasped hands like old friends, and he took me into the library. I hoped he was going to ring for something to eat. I'd had nothing since breakfast and my stomach was wrapped round my backbone.

As it turned out, no ringing needed to be done. Whether it was me he'd been expecting or somebody else, I don't know, but there was food laid out on trays already.

Not that that was the most surprising thing that happened in the next five minutes. Not by a long way. I could hardly believe the news Harry'd got from Llewelyn Kerr.

'*Mrs Parry's* Hughes's heir? Why didn't she tell us?'

'She might not know. Besides, the will probably won't stand. Jones could contest it, say that Jenkyn Hughes wasn't of sound mind when he wrote it. Reckitt'd back him up, I'm sure.'

'Be a hell of a blow to him if it did stand. To go to the bother of killing Hughes so he could inherit, only to find he wasn't going to.'

Harry picked up a pickled onion. 'Of course, we don't actually *know* that Jones is the murderer.'

'True,' I said. But Harry must've heard my reluctance to let Jones off.

'Very well, let's make the case against him.' He fished into the pickle jar again. 'You start.'

'Well, he had a motive: the inheritance,' I said. 'Then, he was on the spot where Hughes was last seen. He got off the boat at Penbryn while Hughes was meeting this woman at Tresaith.'

'And what he saw through his telescope? Do we think that's relevant?'

I felt myself blush. 'I suppose he might've been just watching. You know, watching Hughes. With the woman he was meeting.' Harry made a face. 'But, more likely,' I hurried on, 'Jones saw a chance for himself. To kill Hughes after the woman'd gone and he was there by himself. Or, if he saw someone else kill him, to turn it to his advantage.'

I watched Harry weigh that up. 'Another thing did cross my mind,' I said. 'Blackmail. What if Shoni Jones saw the murder, then tried to blackmail whoever'd killed Hughes? He might've ended up dead himself.'

Harry cocked his head. 'You think perhaps he *isn't* out there letting emigrants on the list know about the meeting?'

'He obviously *intended* doing that. But what if he stopped off to have a quiet word with the killer – feather his nest – and got bashed over the head like Hughes?'

I could see that the idea made sense to Harry. 'Judging by what you've found out,' he said, 'Jones is a man who doesn't mind chancing his arm. So it's possible.' Clumsily, he picked up a slice of beef with his knife and bit a chunk off it. Not very gentlemanly. I watched him think. 'What about the body being put in the kiln?' he asked. 'If Jones is involved, either he watched the murderer hide the body in the waste and was content to leave it there, or he put it there himself. Why?'

'Because he needed the body to stay hidden while he got his hands on Jenkyn Hughes's papers. Mrs Coleman wouldn't've just handed them over if news of Hughes's murder'd been common knowledge. She's too careful for that.'

Harry nodded. 'And Shoni Jones had Hughes's signet ring to vouch for him. He'd taken that from the corpse, I suppose? Do we know whether Jones was on that last lime boat – the day before Teff Harris found the body?' he asked. 'Because, if he was, he could have got them to leave him on the beach, moved the body out of the kiln, and been well away before Teff came to check that the limestone was there.'

Damn and blast it. I hadn't asked the Whaler whether the same people'd been on the boat for both the last lime shipments. I'd been so sure that it was the previous load's delivery that we needed to concentrate on, the one Jenkyn Hughes had been on the beach to meet. 'I don't know,' I admitted.

'Let's assume he was. How easy would it have been for him to move the body once the lime had been offloaded?'

We went to and fro with theories and decided that the one that fitted the facts best was that whoever'd dumped Hughes's body on the limestone had done it as soon he could, after the lime boat had rounded the Aberporth headland on the way back to Cardigan. And he'd probably used the rowing boat propped up at the gable end of Gwyn Puw's cottage. Teff'd said nothing about drag marks down to the sea on the wet sand so, most likely, the body'd been moved while the tide was still fairly high.

We both ate. For a man who said he was only eating to keep me company, Harry was putting away a good amount of cold meat and pickles.

'Mr Schofield asked to see me yesterday,' he said.

A hot rush of alarm went through me. 'I expect he was cross I wasn't back yet, was he?'

'Yes, he was. Blamed me rather than you, though. Which I encouraged, obviously.'

'Thank you.'

'Don't thank me yet. I made him even less happy, I'm afraid.'

I turned to look at him. 'How? What did you say?'

Harry's eyes were still on his plate, and not in a way that meant he was trying to see me. 'I asked him whether he'd welcome you as an articled clerk. With me buying you into the articles, obviously.'

I couldn't help smiling. Harry hadn't let me down after all. But the smile died as the truth dawned. 'He said no, then?'

'I'm sorry, John. Apparently, he's got a nephew who's going to take over when he retires.'

Damn. Because both of Old Schofield's daughters had married men with family businesses to inherit, I'd assumed that there'd be a vacancy at the solicitor's office when the old man retired. Wrong.

I felt my throat close up, and swallowed hard to clear whatever stupidity was lodged there. 'I've been thinking, actually. I might emigrate. Or go for a policeman.'

He looked as if I'd suddenly spoken French. 'Emigrate? To America?'

Didn't he think I had the nerve? 'Yes, why not? Or I could just go as far as London and join the detectives in the Metropolitan police.'

'If it's detecting you want, stay here and work with me!'

'Two problems with that.' In for a penny, in for a pound. 'One, you're not elected yet. Two, that would mean staying on at Schofield's and he probably wouldn't *let* me keep helping you. And, anyway, I've had enough of clerking. I told you, I want something better.'

'There is an alternative,' Harry said, slowly, as if he was convincing himself that what he was about to say was a good idea.

I waited.

'You're good with figures, aren't you?'

Where'd he got that from? I didn't ever recall telling him that. Not that it wasn't true, mind.

'Yes. Calculating's always come easily to me.'

'Ormiston – my father's steward – will be looking to retire shortly. In fact, I'm slightly concerned that, if my father dies now, he'll give notice immediately.' He stopped and I could tell he was trying to see my reaction. I didn't reply for fear I was getting hold of the wrong end of the stick.

'You must have picked up a lot of land law?' he asked.

'Quite a bit. That's a big slice of Mr Schofield's business.'

'If you were to become Ormiston's assistant or apprentice, you'd already know quite a lot of the job. And, if you can make sense of figures, you're most of the way there. It'd just be a case of getting to know the estate and how it runs.'

So, I had the shit-free end of the stick after all. I stared at him. Was he offering me this because he was guilty about making Mr Schofield angry? Because he felt he'd let me down over the business of him setting up as a solicitor?

'You're offering me a job as your steward's assistant? To be steward of Glanteifi when he retires?'

'Yes. What do you think?'

Harry'd offered the same job to somebody else once. His boyhood friend, David Thomas. Was this how he bound people to him – people who were important to him – by offering this job that would make you almost-but-not-quite a gentleman?

'The last person you offered the job to didn't turn out so well.'

He snorted a mirthless little laugh. 'True. I'd like to think I could expect better from you.'

'I guarantee it. But that's not setting the bar very high, is it?'

'Then you agree?'

I took a deep breath. 'I'm going to have to think about it, Harry. I'd talked myself halfway across the Atlantic on the way here from St Dogmaels.'

'Of course.' He nodded. Trying to pretend he wasn't disappointed that I hadn't said yes, straight off. 'Just so you know,' he said, as if it'd just come into his head, 'the estate would provide you with somewhere to live so you wouldn't have to go on living in your digs in town.'

'Right.'

He smiled. 'And, of course, if I do become coroner, the estate would have to take a back seat whenever we had an inquest to run.'

We. I couldn't help it, my spirits lifted at that. 'How would Mr Ormiston feel about that?'

'At the moment, he has no assistant at all. Even one that abandoned him from time to time would be an improvement.'

Harry opened the door, then, and called for Wil-Sam, the hall boy, to come and take our plates away. 'Ask for some tea for us, will you?' he said to the boy. 'And cake if there is any.'

'There is.' Wil-Sam looked up from balancing plates and cutlery. 'Mrs Griffiths said we'd need cake for all the visitors.'

Harry closed the door behind the boy and turned to me. I saw his hand go into a pocket and he took out what looked like a letter. Not much use to him, I thought. Unless it was one he'd written.

'This came this morning.' He stood it up in his lap with both hands. 'Usually, Mrs Griffiths reads my correspondence to me, but she was busy with my father when this came.' He chewed his lip. 'Would you read it for me?'

He was uncomfortable. I wondered what this letter was.

'If you like.' I must've sounded doubtful because he carried on chewing his lip.

'I'd generally wait. But–' He cut himself short. Sighed. 'It's from Miss Howell in Ipswich. We've been corresponding for some weeks now, and I'm afraid Mrs Griffiths is a bit shocked by some of Miss Howell's views. On the place of women. Particularly in church.'

Oh ho! So he and Lydia Howell were writing to each other. What was that all about? There'd been sparks between them when we met her in Ipswich, but I'd assumed that was because Harry resented the way she'd deceived him when she lived here.

As if he'd made his mind up, he held the letter out to me. I took it and opened it up. Lydia Howell wrote in a strong, legible hand. Scanning down quickly I didn't see a single crossing out. Either she had a clear mind or she'd made a clean copy to send.

'Dear Harry,' I read.

Dear Harry? I could see why Mrs Griffiths'd taken exception. Lydia Howell was an unmarried governess – she didn't have much business writing to him in the first place, never mind calling him by his Christian name.

'I'm writing this in more haste than usual as I've been thinking about your case.'

It was odd to be reading Welsh. I barely saw my own language written. Only in hymn books and the occasional public notice.

'I must confess, I envy you your investigation. It sounds unfeeling, I know, and I hope you know that I would never wish anybody dead.

But, given that the death has taken place, I envy you your part in seeing justice done.

I begin to feel, more and more, the confines of life here. The combined effects of your visit to this house and our subsequent correspondence have stirred up a dissatisfaction in me with my current circumstances. I find I long, increasingly, to be amongst my own people, to speak to those who share memories with me, to laugh easily in my own language at peculiarities that the English do not understand, to sing our Welsh hymns.

I feel like a boat adrift, torn from the anchorage of language and land; or like a plant, withering after being torn up by its roots and cast over the hedge. I have no stability, no nourishment here.

Hiraeth – that is what is plaguing me, I know it. But how could I come back? What would I come back to? And what as?'

What indeed?

Lydia Howell was an orphan, like me. And, like me, she was dependent on employment for her living. When the Reverend Mudge's children outgrew the need for a governess, she would be without a home. Her *hiraeth* – that longing we Welsh feel for home, for our past to be present to us again – must be tinged with fear for the future.

'I find myself dwelling on thoughts of the settlement in Ohio that your poor dead American proposed. If many people from Cardiganshire are going there to make their home, perhaps I should do likewise? I would then be amongst my own people and I might find those who remembered Nathaniel… It would be good to be able to speak of those days without fear of the consequences.'

Her words were guarded, as well they might be. Mrs Griffiths would know little, if anything, of Lydia and Nathaniel Howell.

'I must hurry to catch the post,' Lydia wrote, breaking off almost in the middle of a sentence as if somebody had come to stand over her, hand out for the letter. *'I remain, yours affectionately, Lydia Howell.'*

Yours? *Affectionately?*

Harry could school his expression when he wanted to but he couldn't keep from blushing. His reaction to her parting words told me more than he would want me to know, so I said nothing.

'She's an intelligent woman,' he said, his tone a lot blander than his complexion.

'I can see that. So what's she been saying that's made Mrs Griffiths so uncomfortable?'

'She's been engaging in spirited, intellectual conversation with a married man in the presence of his wife. Mrs Griffiths regards this as the moral equivalent of dancing naked in front of him.'

We laughed but I reckoned Mrs Griffiths was wiser than Harry on this subject.

Lydia Howell would do well to think about changing her circumstances.

Harry

Despite the fact that it would be dark before he got there, John insisted on returning to Cardigan and the Black Lion rather than staying at Glanteifi. He was adamant that he simply wanted to be there *in loco coronator*, as it were, but I could not help being convinced that he wanted to escape, that I had, somehow, misjudged things in suggesting that he become the estate's under-steward.

Fortunately, Reckitt's arrival forced me to put such thoughts aside and, after he had spoken to my father and pronounced himself pleased with the patient's progress, I prevailed upon him to eat dinner with me and accept a bed for the night.

I have no doubt that there was some surprise in the kitchen about my off-the-cuff invitation. In recent years there had been so few overnight guests at Glanteifi that Mrs Griffiths must have been obliged to have the spare linen removed from the presses occasionally and aired, lest it develop mould where it lay.

Things, I resolved, must change. If I was to make a credible fist of standing for coroner, I would have to gain the support of at least some of the local magistrates and I would not achieve that by keeping my distance from everybody.

I discussed this with Reckitt.

'Yes, going about in society is something of a necessary evil,' he agreed. 'If you're not seen from one month's end to the next, people are apt to forget that you exist. It's not the way to gain employment.'

I recalled Pomfrey's account of Reckitt's insistence on diagnosing a footman's ailment before a table of dinner guests, and wondered whether that was his idea of how to gain patronage. If so, it seemed an ill-advised kind of advertisement.

'Speaking of employment,' I began, 'I need to speak to you further about the case of little Lizzie Abel and her parents,'.

'I've told you – her father did not hasten her death. Unless it was by allowing her mother inadvertently to give her an excess of laudanum. It's possible that Mrs Abel's own dependence on the drug led to misjudgement.'

I had been intending to admonish Reckitt – one gentleman to another – for exerting undue influence over David Abel in the matter of the projected autopsy examination of his daughter but his answer distracted me. 'Was it always Mrs Abel who administered laudanum to Elizabeth?' I asked.

'Yes. She was obsessive in her care of the child. She barely allowed Abel to go near her. And, if you're going to ask if I believe that *Mrs* Abel deliberately administered an excessive dose of laudanum to end her daughter's suffering, the answer is no. Mrs Abel had a fanatical attachment to the belief that a miracle would cure her child. She had closed her eyes to every other possibility.'

So much so that she had been heedless of the bargain her husband had struck with Reckitt, believing that they would never be called upon to honour their part? Or had she, as Abel believed, been unaware of it until she overheard the doctor issuing instructions as her daughter lay on her deathbed?

'Reckitt, I know what you said to John, the other day about the necessity of conducting autopsies to further our understanding of disease.'

'And I stand by that opinion!'

'But, surely, offering Abel an emigration bond in return for the opportunity to dissect his child's body oversteps the bounds of decency?'

'*Decency?*' Reckitt sounded outraged. 'If you had seen the child in the last days of her life you would know that there was no decency in what that tumour inflicted on her. Its growth stripped her faculties from her, one by one. Walking, balance, sight, hearing, bowel and bladder control. By the end she hadn't the faculties of a newborn. There is no decency in that!'

'But does the indecency of disease justify your actions? Could you not simply have *given* Abel the laudanum and allowed him to make shift for himself as far as the emigration was concerned?'

'I tried! Do you think I'm some kind of monster? But Abel wouldn't take the laudanum from me. He has the stupid pride of those who are not quite poor. He was in agonies about it. He had saved so hard to take his family to America and now he was going to spend not only his savings but everything else he had on a medicine that would not save his child! And he was in fear for his wife. He truly believed that she would do something desperate to get the money she needed for laudanum.'

'You genuinely thought that making a bargain with Abel was the only way to ensure that Lizzie got the laudanum she needed? Couldn't you have commissioned furniture?'

'He would have seen that for what it was. Charity by any other name. I gave him what he needed in exchange for what he knew, with absolute certainty, that I wanted. We were equal in the bargain as we would have been in no other way.'

There was an inescapable, if heartless, logic to it. 'Would you do the same again, knowing the distress it has caused Mrs Abel?'

'Mrs Abel's distress arises from superstition and the debilitating effects of laudanum on her own system. It cannot be allowed to weigh against the future distress of other parents like her and other children like Lizzie.'

It was the first time I'd heard him say the little girl's name. And, for the first time, I felt that I might agree with him.

John

I ate the kind of breakfast I was beginning to get used to, working for Harry, then made my way to the 'Coroner's Room' to wait and see if Shoni Jones turned up. Seeing as Harry and I hadn't had much use out of the room for our money so far, I'd got the servants to make up a fire in there for me. Mrs Weston hadn't made any objection. Probably totting up the bill in her mind. Coal for a whole day – three scuttles at so many pence a scuttle, plus a bit more because the magistrates were paying.

Even in the warmth, I felt my spirits fall when I sat down and looked about at the cheerless little room. I didn't want to have to wait for Shoni Jones. I wanted to be out there, investigating.

But I parked my arse on the chair nearest the fire and got my notes out. Accounting for expenses'd keep me occupied for a bit. Starting with Harry's visit to Schofield's office, I went through the ten days or so that we'd spent investigating Jenkyn Hughes's death.

Jurors for the adjourned inquest – twelve, at one shilling a head.

Autopsies ordered – one at two guineas plus expenses.

Premises for the adjourned inquest – expenses to be paid to the proprietor of The Ship, Aberporth.

Witnesses for the adjourned inquest – two: Theophilus Harris, first finder; Jaci Rees, sub-registrar.

And so on and so forth. Stabling for our horses, dinners eaten at the public expense, rooms slept in ditto, sailors paid to produce informants and urchins paid to keep horses secure.

Once I'd finished the accounts, I went out to check that Shoni

Jones wasn't loitering somewhere in the Black Lion waiting for me. The servants'd jump to it if Harry was there, and send them to the Coroner's Room but they wouldn't be half as bothered seeing as it was just me.

I prayed I'd find him chatting up a maid or sharing a pipe with one of the bootboys. But no. No Shoni Jones. Nor anybody else wanting the coroner.

Back I went to the bare little room. Threw more culm on the fire. Went out again to get a pot of tea from the kitchen. Came back to my notes and started cataloguing evidence.

By the time I'd finished, things looked pretty bad for Shoni Jones. It didn't even matter much whether he knew about the will made in favour of Mrs Parry. By then, he'd got everything he needed to do Hughes's job.

The only unanswered question, as far as I could see, was what he'd seen through his telescope. According to the Whaler, Shoni had watched and watched. He wouldn't've done that if there'd been nothing to see, would he?

I was hungry again already and the chair I was sitting on had no cushion. My arse was used to riding about now, and I'd got out of the way of sitting on a chair for hours at a time.

I closed my notebook, gathered my notes into a pile and put them in Harry's writing box with the pen and ink. I could waste a bit more time taking it back up to my room, so that's what I did.

Back in the main hall, I took my watch out. Half past nine o'clock! I couldn't believe I'd only managed to fritter away an hour and a half.

It was no good. I couldn't stay here all day with nothing to do. Not when I wasn't even sure Shoni Jones'd come. It'd be a far better use of my time to go out to Penlanmeurig again and find him for myself.

Seren was getting more exercise than she'd probably had in years but she trotted out sprightly enough as we crossed the bridge and headed along the St Dogmaels road.

It was a sharp, bright morning. The sky was a high, clear blue that looked as if it'd ring like a china bowl if you could only reach up and flick it with your fingernail. My cheekbones ached with the cold but at least there was no wind to speak of. If I could just get a pair of gloves from somewhere, riding on a day like this would be a real pleasure. Maybe I could ask Harry for some old ones of his.

I sucked my teeth. Harry. What was I going to do about his proposition? If I said yes, that'd be it. I'd be Harry Probert Lloyd's man for the rest of my life. Was that what I wanted? Was that what *he* wanted? He'd taken great pains, when we first worked together, to treat me as his equal. If I was his steward, if he paid me, would he still do that? *Could* he?

It was becoming a lot clearer to me why he didn't want to be squire.

When I trotted over the hump of the headland to Penlanmeurig, I was ready for that wind off the sea. But, compared to the day before where it'd almost frozen my specs to my face, it was gentle, hardly more than a breeze. I pulled Seren up and looked across the fields to the sea. Cold, it looked. Blue under the sky, but cold. And it stretched all the way to the ruler-straight horizon. To America.

Did ships coming this way across the Atlantic get here more quickly than emigrant ships going out? The wind seemed always to be blowing *from* America, not to it. Perhaps there was a lesson there for me.

I imagined Jenkyn Hughes standing on the deck of a ship, looking out towards the horizon that'd turn into the coast and then the estuary and then Cardigan docks. Standing there in his white trousers and chequered waistcoat. Had Shoni Jones met him on the dock? I knew from Wil Camlaw that they'd got to know each other when Hughes had been over before, so more than likely he had.

Jones'd gone about for weeks – months, perhaps – with Jenkyn Hughes. Would he tell the same story as other people – that Hughes'd altered, got unreliable, changed his mind with the wind? Or would he say that his cousin'd always been like that – rash, apt to *let his mood take him* as my mother might've said.

A couple of gulls started their dead-soul screech overhead. How did sailors put up with that sound day in, day out? It'd drive you mad. I pulled my coat closer to me, held the reins in one hand so I could put the other on the warmth of Seren and trotted her down towards the farm.

Even if Hughes's behaviour had altered, it didn't have to be because of Benton Reckitt's famous lump in the head, did it? It could've been because he'd settled in, here. That happens, doesn't it? People're on their best behaviour at first so they make a good impression. Sit up straight, mind their pleases and thank yous. Then they relax, like a cat by the fire. Start showing their underbelly.

I arrived at Penlanmeurig in the middle of an argument. A big one. The kind families have before people decide they're never speaking to each other again. From what I could hear – and I didn't have to strain my ears – Shoni Jones had chosen today to tell his parents that he'd sold the farm.

I stood outside the door for a bit, listening. Not the best time to visit, was it, with everybody furious?

Then again, it might be the ideal time. Shoni'd be glad of the excuse to escape and relief might make him tell me things he wouldn't do otherwise.

I thumped on the door. No point being timid – might as well sound as if I had a right to be there.

The voices inside stopped. Just like that.

The knock of clogs came towards the door and the girl who'd opened it last time stood there. I watched her remembering who I was.

'Oh. It's you.'

'Here now, is he?'

She turned. 'Shoni.'

'What's this, now?' An older man's voice. He came into view, then – a small, grey haired man who moved as if every joint in his body hurt.

'Good morning.' I took my cap off to him – didn't hurt to be polite. 'I'm John Davies, coroner's officer. I need to speak to your son, please.'

He looked behind him. 'Take him and welcome. He doesn't belong here any more.'

I led Seren and walked alongside Shoni, same as I had with Wil Camlaw.

'Not impressed, then,' I said, jerking my head back towards his house. 'The will and so on?'

Looked quite a lot like his brother, Shoni did. Same small, wiry frame. Same dark brown hair, except his wasn't shaved as short as Wil's. But his eyes had a sharper, harder look.

'Can't stand the thought of me getting away, can they? Well good riddance to the lot of them, I've had enough.'

'Don't blame you.'

He looked at me sideways.

'I grew up poorer than you' I told him. 'Got farmed out for a *gwas bach*. But I wasn't going to spend my life half-starving and working in all weathers. Went for a clerk instead.' I didn't mention my parents' death. Let Jones think I'd stood up to my father, too. 'Anyway, I'm not here to talk about that.'

'What *do* you want?' He sounded curious. Was he covering up nerves? If he'd murdered his cousin, I'd've expected him to be nervous. But he just looked at me, waiting.

'Just so you know,' I said, before I got to the point, 'I'm not interested in whatever fiddle Jenkyn Hughes was playing with Mrs Parry's coal. I'm with the coroner, not the police, so whatever you say about that'll go no further.

'Fair enough.'

'You were on the boat that brought the limestone into Tresaith the night Jenkyn Hughes disappeared, is that right?'

'Disappeared? He never *disappeared-*'

I held up a hand. 'All right.' Seemed like a good idea to stop him before he could start telling me that Hughes'd gone up the coast to Aberaeron. It'd be harder for him to come out and tell me the truth if he was going to start off behind a wall of lies. 'To be clearer – you were on the last but one shipment of limestone to Tresaith. With Albion Thomas, Scrim Richards and the big sailor they call the Whaler?'

Jones looked at me. I thought he was going to ask why I wanted to know but, in the end, he just nodded. 'Yes.'

'And Hughes was on the beach? I mean, he stayed there while you all went up to Penbryn with the coal?' I held my hand up to stop him denying that he had any involvement in swindling Mrs Parry. 'I told you, I don't care. I'm just trying to get my facts straight, that's all.'

His eyes didn't leave me. 'Yes, Hughes stayed at Tresaith.'

'Was there anybody else on the beach?'

His expression changed then. He could see I knew something. He'd be wary, now. 'When we arrived? No.'

I filed away that *when we arrived* to come back to later. We turned off the farm track and on to the road. Apart from the ditch on each side, there wasn't a lot of difference – the parish wasn't working too hard to fill in ruts and potholes.

'So you unloaded the stone and you left Hughes on the beach while you went on around to Penbryn?'

Jones shot a glance at me. 'That's it.'

'And then you saw something, didn't you? You took your telescope out – the one you'd bought off Hughes – and you watched the beach.' I waited but he said nothing, just carried on walking, eyes forward. 'Isn't that right?'

'If you say so.'

'I do.' All right, he wasn't admitting it but then he wasn't arguing either. It looked as if the big sailor had told me the truth. 'So what did you see?'

He sighed as if he was giving up a struggle. 'Hughes.'

'Doing what?'

When he didn't answer, I stared at the side of his face, trying to make him look round at me. Didn't work. All I got was a really long look at his thin face with its two-day beard.

I tried again. 'What was Jenkyn Hughes doing? You may as well tell me. I'm not going to stop asking till you do.'

'Think you've got a right to know, do you?'

'I'm representing the coroner. Mr Probert-Lloyd. *He's* got a right to know.'

Jones shook his head, and I only just caught his next words. 'Some things're better not known.'

What did that mean? 'Did you see who killed Jenkyn Hughes?' I asked.

He was back to taking no notice of me. Eyes fixed on the road ahead as if his only concern was not tripping over something in front of him. But I'd've laid good money that he wasn't seeing the road at all. That, in his mind, he was seeing Tresaith beach with The Ship and Pantmawr cottage and the kilns at the back of it. That he was seeing whatever it was that'd taken place there after they'd left Hughes.

'If you know, you'd do better to tell me because, as it stands, all the evidence points to you. The will gave you the best motive to kill him. You went to Captain Coleman's and fetched all his belongings before anybody knew he was dead. You had his ring. And,' I finished, lit up by a sudden idea, 'you wanted to stop him losing even more money, gambling, because you thought he was putting the emigration scheme in danger of failing. And that would've left you with nowhere to go. You'd burned your bridges at home, hadn't you? If you couldn't go to America, you'd've had nothing.'

He stopped and faced me. 'You think I'd *kill him*?'

'It's what the evidence says. It's what everybody'll think after the inquest unless you tell me something different.'

He sucked his tongue, spat on the ground, started walking again.

I clucked Seren after him. 'Billy Go-About's got somebody locked up who looks a lot less guilty than you. When all this comes out at the inquest, he'll have you in gaol so quick you'll wish you were back at the farm listening to your father shout at you.'

'Not if I don't come to the inquest he won't. Not if he can't find me.'

'If you don't turn up, that'll make you look ten times more guilty! Why would you stay away if you've got nothing to hide?' I got no answer, but he was stiff with wanting to lash out, fists ready at his sides. 'And if you run off and hide,' I pushed it, 'that's the end of taking over as agent on the American scheme, isn't it?' I gave him a couple of seconds, but he still wouldn't budge. 'Come on! Either you give us the evidence to prove you didn't murder him or you lose everything!'

He stopped, then, and turned to me. The sun, still rising towards noon, shone into his eyes. 'Look,' he said, 'I didn't murder Jenkyn Hughes. Nobody did. He wasn't murdered.'

'*What*? Don't talk daft, man! I've seen the body. Seen that bash on his head. He didn't get that by accident.'

'I'm not saying it was an accident.'

'What then?'

He looked about then, as if he'd only just realised how far we'd come. 'Where are we going?'

I shrugged. 'I don't know. You just came out.'

The truth was, neither of us'd wanted to stand about in the yard at Penlanmeurig in case his father came out to start more shouting. We'd just started walking.

Shoni shook his head, lips all clamped up. 'I can't go back.'

'Have you got any money?'

'Not on me.'

'Then you'll have to.'

He looked back the way we'd come. Seemed to be weighing things up, coming to a decision. 'If you come with me, help me carry my things, I'll tell you what I saw.'

I didn't much fancy going back into that house. Nor being a glorified packman. But I didn't really have a choice, did I?

Harry

I sat in the study, my writing frame in front of me. After a weary few hours spent helping my father dress, eat and perform other basic functions, we had run out of things to say to each other. Or, perhaps more accurately, I had run out of things to say and his diminished communicative resources had been altogether exhausted. He was sitting quietly in a chair by the window now, though whether he was awake or asleep I could not tell.

I turned back to the letter I was writing to Lydia Howell and dipped my pen.

'I am sitting at my father's desk watching him out of the corner of my eye and wondering what now takes place in his mind. I would dearly love to put Reckitt's request to him – part of me feels it is only fair to do so – but how can you tell a man who has recently escaped death that, in the event of his imminent demise, a person with whom he is barely acquainted wishes to cut his head open? Perhaps others could. I am sure Reckitt himself would suffer no such reservations. But I cannot.

If the unfortunate event comes to pass, I will have to decide for myself.'

I stopped and considered. It is hard to write a letter when one cannot see what one has already written. One's flow necessarily becomes disjointed. But perhaps my blindly-written letters were actually a more accurate representation of my true thoughts than those I had composed when perfectly sighted. Letters are generally written in a form which implies that thoughts have flowed seamlessly and inevitably, one from another, whereas, if we were to write down our thoughts as they occurred to us, rather than as we would prefer them to have occurred, our correspondents would know us for what we are – beings who barely deserve to be described as rational.

'Perhaps it is the disordered nature of my life at present,' I continued, *'but I find it difficult to remember the order in which I have written things to you or, indeed, you to me. I find I am simply responding to the matters that press in upon me most at present.*

I mentioned to you, I believe, that I was considering the wisdom of offering John the post of private secretary. Quite how it has come to pass I am not sure but, instead, I have proposed that he become assistant to our steward. He has asked for time to give it due consideration and has disconcerted me by confiding that, like you, he has been mulling over the merits of emigration.

Is it simply envy that makes my heart sink at the thought? Such a course of action would be impossible for me for reasons which, I am sure, will be readily apparent, and I find it is hard to bear the thought of either of you abandoning me for life on a different continent.'

I stopped. What kind of declaration was I making to Lydia Howell? I was overwrought, half undone by lack of sleep and by concerns that had, suddenly, begun to overwhelm me. I was not thinking of the consequences of my words, only of their truth.

I steered away from the rocks of potential misunderstanding.

'I have never been the sort of man who has packs of friends as other men have hounds. One or two good friends have always sufficed at any given time. But, now, I see the folly of this failure to be generally sociable. I am

alone and without society and this has made me resolve to exert myself more. Indeed, I believe I am already making a friend of Reckitt. I suspect few will applaud this choice but he is an interesting man who is not afraid to speak his mind and I find that both refreshing and appealing.'

Then, despite my misgivings, I began a fresh sheet of paper and tacked recklessly back towards the rocks.

'Lydia, I find I cannot remember what this letter was supposed to be about.

Did you feel utterly alone in the world when your brother died? If you did, you will understand how I feel, now. Though my father has not succumbed, I know now precisely how alone I will feel when he breathes his last and that realisation has disturbed me.'

My pen scratched to a dry halt and I closed my eyes. Both edge-sight and whirlpool vanished. I saw what every person sees when they lower their eyelids. Nothing.

'Harry?'

I opened my eyes. 'Father?'

'Are you unwell?' The words flowed from him as none had since his stroke and I found myself smiling.

'I'm tired, that's all. But you sound better?'

'No. Sometimes.'

'Sometimes the speech just comes?'

'Yes.' The word was like a bullet. and it reminded me of something from my boyhood.

'There was a boy at school who had a terrible stutter,' I said. 'His speech would do that sometimes. It was as if something had unfrozen and words shot out.' I smiled. 'It was mostly when he'd been taking claret, as I recall.'

I detected something like a smile in my father's voice. 'I. Try.'

'Try the drinking cure? Why not indeed? We'll ask Moyle to bring some port in later, shall we?'

It might be wise, I felt, to finish my letter before the port arrived. God alone knew what I would find myself saying to Lydia Howell under the disinhibiting influence of alcohol.

John

Shoni Jones hadn't unpacked after his trip around the county, thank God, so he didn't take long getting his belongings together. Mind you, it felt long enough to me, standing there in the kitchen with his family. Not one of them spoke a word to me. His parents sat on either side of the hearth, Mr Jones just staring at the fire, ignoring me, and Mrs Jones busy with her spinning. She didn't have a wheel, just a drop-spindle. I thought the thread she was producing looked a bit uneven. Then I noticed how her hands were shaking and realised why.

The sister had a bundle of sewing on her lap – putting sides to middle on a sheet, it looked like – and she glanced up at me over her work as she picked the cloth up and moved it along.

It felt as if somebody'd died, with everybody sitting there in the middle of the day. Shoni's news had knocked them out of the normal run of things.

I found myself staring at a blue jug on the dresser. Its colour drew your eye and it looked bright and new. Had Shoni bought it for his mother out of the money he'd got from Jenkyn Hughes? If he had, I could see it having an accident before long.

About five seconds before the awkwardness in the room forced me to start talking about the weather, Shoni came down the ladder from the loft with a flour sack over his shoulder.

He crossed to his mother and looked as if he was going to bend and kiss her when his father reared up out of his chair.

'Out! Don't you lay a finger on your mother! She's worked herself to the bone for you and you've repaid her by throwing it all back in her face.'

His son squared up to him. 'You *wanted* us to have a better life – me and Wil. And that's what I'm going to have. A better life than this.' He waved a hand at the kitchen. At the scraped together, getting by-ness of it.

His father clenched his teeth on whatever words were trying to burst out and just glared. 'Go. Get out.'

Shoni Jones dropped a hand on his mother's shoulder. 'Bye, Mam. I'll see you in chapel.'

Mrs Jones didn't look up but her trembling hands had fallen into her lap. I looked down and saw that the strand of wool she'd been spinning had clutched itself together into a tightly-wound whirl on her apron.

I fastened the flour sack to the saddle by tying the stirrup-leathers up on top of it and trotted Seren down the lane after Shoni.

'I'll see if I can have Jenkyn's room at Captain Coleman's,' he said as I caught up with him. Good. I'd know where to find him. As long as he was telling the truth, of course.

He said nothing else, just marched along in front of me.

'Come on then. I've kept my half of the bargain. Tell me what you saw.'

He flicked a glance across at me but his mouth stayed shut. I knew what that look meant. He'd got what he wanted, hadn't he? All his stuff was out of Penlanmeurig, why should he tell me anything?

That got my dander up. I'd had about enough of being yanked around like a puppy new to the lead. 'I know Hughes was supposed to be meeting a woman,' I said. 'So that's what you saw, is it?'

'If you know, why are you asking?'

'Who was she?'

Jones didn't answer, just marched along, as if I wasn't there. Well it was my horse who was carrying his stuff and I wasn't standing for this. 'I heard you had that telescope at your eye until you were out of sight of the beach. Saw everything, did you?'

Before I knew what was happening, he had me by jacket. 'What are you saying? That I'm a pervert who likes watching–' he stopped himself. 'That's disgusting. You should be ashamed, boy of your age.'

Boy of your age indeed. I pulled away, straightened my coat, put a hand on Seren's neck to calm her. 'Well, if it wasn't that,' I said, 'tell me what you *were* looking at.'

Jones looked at me as if he had a nasty taste in his mouth. 'Wanted to know who he was meeting.'

'Why?'

His jaw clenched. 'Because I couldn't trust him. Slippery bastard, he was.'

I wasn't going to get sidetracked on to that. I needed to know what he'd seen. 'And it *was* a woman you saw?'

He gave me the barest of nods, as if it hurt him to answer me.

'Did you know her?'

He set off walking again. 'No.'

I practised my next question in my head. Wanted to sound matter-of-fact. 'Was she a whore?'

He glanced over at me. To see if I was blushing, most likely. He'd've laughed if I had been. 'What makes you think that?'

'Hughes had a reputation. Sorry, I know he was family, but it's the truth.'

Jones coughed, spat the phlegm onto the ground. 'I know his

reputation and it wasn't that. He had women but not ones he had to pay.'

'So not a whore, then?'

'Keep saying it, boy. In the end, it'll seem like any other word.'

I ground my teeth and kept my temper. 'So, what did you see? What happened between them?'

Jones kicked a stone out of his way into the dead grass at the side of the road. 'She went up to him and started talking – that's what it looked like – her talking, him listening.'

'Just talking?'

'Yes. But she wasn't persuading him, whatever she was saying.'

'How d'you know?'

Jones stopped and turned to me, folded his arms. 'Stood there like this, he did.' He glanced up as a flock of lapwings took fright at us and flapped their way into the bright air. I drew breath to bring him back to the subject but he carried on of his own accord.

'She showed him something.'

'What?'

'A piece of paper, it looked like.'

'A letter?'

'How should I know?'

A piece of paper. It had to be a letter, didn't it? Or a bank note.

'Anyway,' Jones seemed to be warming up to the task of telling me what he'd seen, 'then he started shaking his head. And she tried to lay hands on him.'

'Lay hands on him how, exactly?'

'Like this.' Jones turned to me and, before I could stop him, put one hand on my chest, made a fist with the other and started beating it against me. I backed off and Seren threw up her head so she almost hit me. I felt the graze of her cheek through my hair and my specs were suddenly crooked on my nose.

'Enough!'

He gave me a half-sneer then turned and started walking again. With one hand I pushed my specs back on and, with the other, I rubbed at my chest, shivering as the movement let cold air in under my shirt.

I dragged Seren on to catch him up. 'What then?'

No reply. His eyes stayed on the road.

'Come on, I need to know everything that happened.'

He walked on. But the way he was staring at the road ahead had changed. As if he was collecting his thoughts from a long way away. 'He grabbed her hands – to stop her hitting him – and held them.' He held his fists in front of him, miming the grip. 'Then *he* started talking and *she* started shaking her head.'

'Was he threatening her?'

He gave me a look. 'Thought you said you knew his reputation? He wasn't *threatening* her...'

I nodded, tried to look as if the possibility of Hughes propositioning this woman had been my next question. 'So she resisted him?'

'Yes. Pulled her hands away and turned to walk off. He grabbed her by the shoulder and pulled her back. Tried to kiss her. She pushed him off. Turned and ran. He ran after her. Grabbed her. Pulled her shawl off and was going to open her *betgwn*. She got away from him and started to run again. But then–' He stopped and looked at me. His face was pinched – was he making this up or was it the truth? 'She fell and he went down on his knees over her – one knee on each side to pin her down. I saw him go for the front of his trousers – you know, to open his...' he motioned at his own fly-buttons. 'Then I saw her arm move. She was holding something in her hand. Something she'd picked up off the ground.' He looked me full in the face. 'She hit him with it. Hard. Just once. On the side of the head. He went down sideways.'

'What then?'

'She pushed him off her, got up and ran away. But she couldn't run fast – that's why he'd caught her so easily. She had a bad limp.'

'Did she limp before, when she came up to Hughes? Or was she injured when she fell?'

'I think she was limping before. But she walked quite quickly, limp or not, as if she was used to it.'

That was useful information. 'Did you see her put him in the kiln?' I asked.

Jones looked away. 'I didn't see her do anything else. We rounded the headland to Penbryn.'

I frowned. 'If you could see well enough to see her hit him with something, you couldn't've lost sight of them that quickly.'

'You calling me a liar, John Davies?'

'I think you're trying to protect this woman.' Did I think that? Truth to tell, the words'd just come out of their own accord. Either way, it made him sound like a better man than he was, so it might encourage him to tell me more.

He thought for a moment. 'The truth is, when I lost sight of them, she was still lying there, with him on top of her. I think she was crying.'

Something made me look back at his sackful of belongings and I saw that it was slipping gently over to Seren's other side. I grabbed at it and re-tied it.

'One more thing.' I could see Shoni Jones out of the corner of my eye. He was tense enough to bolt. 'Was that why you went ashore with the coal at Penbryn? Did you walk back to Tresaith to see if your cousin was lying there injured? Did you go back to try and help him?'

I was pretty sure he *had* gone back – otherwise why had he got the lime boat to leave him at Penbryn beach?

'I've told you what I saw, John Davies. I saw a woman I didn't know hit a man who was going to rape her. That's it. That's all.'

I got nothing more out of him, all the way to Captain Coleman's.

Harry

John came to Glanteifi hot-foot from his conversation with Shoni Jones. Finally, it seemed, we knew how and why Jenkyn Hughes had come by his fatal head wound.

'Do you think he *did* go back to Tresaith?' I asked.

'Yes. Otherwise, when did he take Hughes's signet ring?'

'You don't think he's making up this story of a woman to get himself off the hook?'

There was a moment's silence but, when John answered, his tone told me that he had not been hesitating so much as giving my question proper consideration. 'If the Whaler hadn't told me about him watching whatever was happening on the beach with his telescope, I might. But, as it is, no. I mean, if you wanted to offload the blame for something like this, would you come up with a woman as the culprit?'

Possibly not, but somebody who was foresighted enough to plan a whole new career for himself might; and the story Jones had told did more than simply divert suspicion away from himself. He could present himself as a man who had allowed reticence at the thought of ruining a wronged woman's reputation to prevent him from coming forward to say what he knew. After all, in his version of events, she was innocent of anything but self-defence.

Furthermore, though this was hardly conclusive, his story fitted what we knew of Hughes's character.

'What's your opinion of Jones?' I asked. 'Is he clever enough to make all this up?'

Again, John gave the question consideration. 'He is. But I don't think he did.'

I raised my eyebrows, inviting him to tell me why. Projecting facial expressions into the unresponsive whirlpool felt contrived, but if I did not do it, I feared I would look like one of those blind, expressionless beggars you see on the streets in London.

'I think I know who the woman was,' John said.

'Really?'

'Yes. If you take a minute to think about it, you'll know too.'

I did not want to play guessing games. 'Tell me.'

John shifted position in the chair and I wondered if he was as confident as he sounded. 'I think the paper she was waving at Hughes was an emigration bond and she wanted him to redeem it.'

'*Maggie Abel?*' The bent and broken woman we'd found crouching in the manger at Blaenywaun chapel stables? 'She hasn't the wit, surely?'

'Not *now*, possibly. But this was before her child died. She was intent on redeeming the bond money to pay Reckitt off and get more laudanum without being beholden to him.'

'Does Maggie Abel have a limp?'

'I don't know. But her husband told us she took in sewing. That's the kind of work a crippled woman'd do, isn't it?'

I quickly shuffled through all that we knew and checked it against John's assumptions. I could not fault his reasoning, yet Maggie Abel seemed such an unlikely killer.

'Would she have the strength to drag his body to the limekiln and hide it?' I asked. Even before the decline precipitated by her child's death, she could not have been a robust woman and Jenkyn Hughes had been well built.

I could almost hear John thinking. 'No. I think Shoni Jones did that. I think he told her she should go home and he'd deal with it all. It would've suited him to have her out of the way so he could hide the body. He had things to do before people realised Hughes was dead.'

Leaning back in my chair I shut my eyes. 'How do you suggest we proceed?' It was his efforts that had brought us to this point, justice dictated that he should be allowed to decide what to do next.

'I think we should go and see David Abel again,' he said. 'Ask him if his wife has a longstanding limp. If the answer is yes, then I think we've got the truth. At least about how Jenkyn Hughes came to be hit on the head.'

It was a sensible suggestion. David Abel had told us that his wife had tried to speak to Jenkyn Hughes but had been unable to find him; perhaps he believed this to be the truth, perhaps not. In either case, hearing his response to Shoni Jones's testimony could only be instructive.

'You're not thinking of going back today?' I asked. Though it had been sunny all day, by now the light was nearly gone.

'No. I'll go back into Newcastle Emlyn this evening.'

'Why don't you stay here? Have dinner with me and we'll find a bed for you for tonight.'

Previously, John had refused such offers; that he did not immediately do so, now, made me hopeful that he was minded to accept my offer of employment. It had, after all, included the prospect of living at Glanteifi.

'Thank you, Harry,' he said. 'If you're sure that wouldn't be too much trouble, I will.'

In truth, it was not only this evidence that John was softening towards the thought of becoming under-steward that made me glad he had agreed to stay. With Arthur Philips and Reckitt both occupied elsewhere, I had spent a long and ennervating afternoon with my father trying to decide how to broach the subject of Glanteifi's mortgage with him.

Given that his current state made it almost impossible for him to explain, I could hardly ask him why he had not discussed the estate's precarious finances with me. Besides, no long deliberation was necessary to supply the answer: my father had been afraid that I would see it as some kind of lever to shift me and bring me home.

Look what a state things have got into here. Glanteifi needs new blood, new energy. Was that not what I would have heard, if he had told me he had mortgaged the estate? I would have felt pressed, forced, my good nature presumed upon.

In the end, during one particularly inexhaustible silence, I blurted, 'I'm so sorry you felt you could not tell me before – about the estate, the mortgage.'

He raised his good hand as if to say 'what's done is done.'

'Look at us,' I said. 'The blind and the mute. We're a pair well matched, aren't we?'

It was a phrase from my childhood: horses, matched for size and colour, or oxen, matched for strength and their pull at the plough.

'Not – blind,' my father said.

I knew what he meant. 'You're right. I'm not quite blind. And you're not quite mute. The imperfectly sighted and the communicatively inconvenienced, then.'

'Again?'

Realising that I'd spoken too quickly, I repeated my weak quip. I was discovering, to my chagrin, that it is difficult to slow one's speech without sounding condescending or pedantic.

My father let out a grunt of amusement, and I smiled. For the first time in my life, I felt myself to be on an equal footing with him. I suppose I might have felt more – that, now, I had the upper hand. But I did not. Not when I felt wholly unable to choose my own fate.

Had my father died of his apoplexy, would I have felt entitled to change my destiny, to sell the mortgaged estate before bankruptcy ruined me and seek my fortune, Dick Whittington-like, in the capital?

The question was redundant. My father was still in the land of the living, still, nominally, squire of Glanteifi. Time would tell whether he retained the mental acuity to make decisions but, as things stood, he was in no fit state to run the place. For the foreseeable future, I would have to take up his mantle, all the while knowing that I was being watched and judged.

I would need an ally.

'I have suggested to John Davies that he become Ormiston's assistant,' I said. Then, when my father did not respond, I repeated the information in short phrases. There was always the possibility that I had shocked him so greatly by my presumption that he was speechless but I preferred to imagine that I had spoken too quickly. When I had finished my reiteration, my father produced a single word.

'Local.'

This was hardly the response I had been anticipating. 'Yes. A local boy. Somebody who can speak to the tenants on their own terms. In their own language.'

In response, my father produced some incoherent noises in an attempt, I assumed, to add further thoughts. I tried to elucidate these to ease his struggle.

'You feel that a local man will do better than Ormiston, a foreigner?'

'Yes. No.'

'Yes and no?' I hazarded.

'Thassright.'

'With the mortgage and so forth,' I began, trying to keep my sentences short and simple, 'we're going to have to work more closely with tenants.' I waited for a response but there was none. Hoping that he understood what I was saying, I forged on. 'The estate can't go on paying for all improvements. We must ask the tenants to take some responsibility for their own farms.' I paused again. 'John understands their lives. He can help me win their trust.'

I hoped devoutly that that was true and that the tenants would not simply see him as a jumped-up solicitor's clerk. Apprenticeship to Ormiston, if handled wisely, should see to that.

Some strangled vowel sounds came from my father, as if he was trying to prime the pump of speech.

'What is it?' I asked.

'Coroner,' he spat after a few seconds.

It was time to establish myself.

'Yes. I have decided that I will stand as coroner. I don't know whether I will be successful but I think I am suited to the position.'

We had both left it at that.

Now, once I had helped my father upstairs to his bed and left him in the care of the footman who had volunteered for the more than usually onerous post of valet, I joined John in the library.

'I've been giving some thought to what you said earlier,' John began when we had settled ourselves.

'About taking the position of assistant steward?'

'Oh – yes – that as well. But I meant what you said about what we should do next. I've been thinking about Teff Harris.'

Stifling disappointment, I nodded. 'I see.'

'I think we should go and see Billy Go-About – tell him what we know and get him to let Teff go.'

'You've changed your tune. You were all for hanging him at one stage.'

'That was before we'd investigated properly.'

John sounded mulish. What had changed his mind? The attractive Mrs Harris? The little boy, Clarkson?

'Very well. I'll write a letter in the morning.'

'Thank you.'

'And the other subject?'

I watched his face as best I could. I thought he might have been moistening his lips but could not say with any certainty.

'I've given it a lot of thought.'

My heart sank. 'But?'

'Don't misunderstand me – I would like the job. But…' he gave a sudden, nervous laugh. 'Thing is, Harry, when I first knew you, you were all for selling the estate to the tenants, not being a squire, just making your living like anybody else. What'd happen to me if you decided to do that?'

'I'd make sure you were all right.'

'But how, Harry, *how*? If you were a private citizen with no estate, what job could you give me which would make up for losing the stewardship?'

It was a fair question and not one I had an answer to.

'So,' he said, his gaze so earnest I could feel it on my skin. 'I'd want to do the solicitors' exams while I learned stewarding. Then, if anything stopped me taking over from Mr Ormiston, I'd have another string to my bow.'

I was glad to agree. Quite apart from his own reservations, with the estate mortgaged as it was, it would have been negligent of me not to offer him some kind of insurance policy.

John

Early next morning, I rode out of the stableyard with more in my mind than just the conversations I was going to have with Billy Go-About and David Abel. Staying at Glanteifi'd given me a lot to think about.

I could see that living in the mansion would be very pleasant – a single night'd been enough to show me that. A feather mattress instead of a lumpy horsehair one. Warm water brought up to shave with instead of a jug of cold on the washstand. A dinner that was plentiful and delicious instead of stodgy grey stinginess.

The one thing I hadn't been taken with was the necessary closet next to my bedroom. I couldn't shake off the feeling that it was dirty to do your business indoors, right next to where you slept. If I moved in to Glanteifi, it was going to take me a while to feel comfortable about not going outside when I needed to.

But, still, the thought that I might be able to come and go at the big house *as of right* made my head swim.

Steward to the Glanteifi estate. The nearest I'd ever come to the position before was standing behind my father on the quarter days, watching him count out his rent and answer questions about our house and byre. What condition were they in? (*Good enough for us, thank you, sir.* Except we hadn't even had a privy, the field behind the house had always had to do for us.) Had my father made improvements? (*Not this quarter, sir, no.* And not any other quarter either, money being barely enough to keep us alive let alone think about making improvements.) Had we been able to pay our tithes on

419

time and in full? (*Yes, sir.* God knows why the vicar deserved our money. We never darkened the door of his church.) Takings from the market been adequate, had they? (*Yes, thank you, sir.* No. They'd been barely half what they'd been in my grandfather's time.)

I imagined myself asking those questions and Harry's tenants looking at me, caps in their hands, worrying about giving the wrong answer. One thing I'd realised since working for Mr Schofield was that tenant farmers often didn't understand the strong position they were in under the law. I'd be able to tell them that they were entitled to ask Harry to make improvements for them, that being a tenant gave them rights as well as duties.

But what was Mr Ormiston going think about having a solicitor's clerk foisted on to him for an apprentice? It was all very well Harry saying he'd not had an assistant till now and any help would be better than none but I wasn't sure Mr Ormiston'd see it in that light.

'He's not opened up today. Can't be home.'

I'd been standing in front of David Abel's workshop for the last five minutes, wondering whether I should go around the back. There'd been no reply to my knocking. 'Where is he then?' I asked the woman who'd spoken from her doorway.

She hitched her folded arms further up under her bosom, as if she needed the weight taking off it. 'I don't suppose that's your business any more than it is mine.'

'It is my business, as it happens. I'm the coroner's officer. I need to speak to Mr Abel.'

'Well, if he was going to come to the door he'd've come by now.'

She banged back into her own house with a look that was supposed to cut me down to size. I made a face at her door then looked about in case anybody'd seen me. Wouldn't do for the future steward of Glanteifi to be seen pulling faces on St Dogmaels high street.

I got back into the saddle and sat, thinking. Should I go looking for David Abel? As likely as not he'd gone to fetch his wife from the Blaenywaun stables to make her fit to be seen at the meeting tomorrow. He wouldn't appreciate me chasing about after him. And, to be honest, I wasn't over keen on another tangle with the madwoman.

Did Abel know what his wife had done? Always assuming it *was* Maggie that Shoni Jones'd seen on Tresaith beach. And, if he did know, would he take her away if he thought we'd come for her?

No. Maggie'd be desperate to get that bond redeemed and Dr Reckitt paid off. And a man who'd let his wife sit in a manger rambling wasn't going to subdue her by force. The Abels'd be at that meeting the next day. I was sure of it. There'd be time enough, then, to see whether Maggie Abel had a limp.

I turned Seren's head towards Cardigan and Billy Go-About.

Harry and I'd agreed that if we were going to get Teff Harris released we'd have to tell Inspector Bellis everything we knew. It wasn't as if he was going to press charges against Maggie Abel – if Hughes hadn't come after her, she'd've just left and limped her way back to Cardigan.

Had the lump in his head made Jenkyn Hughes think that any woman was his for the taking or had he always been like that? Short of going to America and asking, we'd never know.

Seren trotted down the hill, her shoes striking hard and cold. It was misty today and the dampness seemed to catch sound and hold it, so that it felt as if the sound of the little mare's hoofs hung in the air, wrapping itself around us as we went. Perhaps that's how it was for Maggie Abel – the fog in her head hanging there, keeping the fears for her daughter's body wrapped close. Reckitt with a spade. A small body on the dissecting table.

Without meaning to, I recalled the autopsy examination on Tresaith beach. The colours and smells of rotting flesh and bone and guts. The inside of Hughes's head.

What mother wouldn't want to keep her child from that?

Not Maggie Abel, that was for sure.

Poor mad Maggie.

Was it Jenkyn Hughes's death, as much as Lizzie's, that had driven her mad? She might not've intended to kill him but hitting him on the head with a stone had been the end of the American. And, if Shoni Jones's story was true, Hughes had lain on top of her while he died.

What had Reckitt said about how quickly Hughes might've died? *Possibly in a small number of minutes.*

I forced myself to imagine it. A person bleeding and breathing his last while lying on top of you. It was enough to make anybody mad.

Would Maggie Abel recover if she got the bond money and paid it back to Benton Reckitt? Would she comb her hair and wash her face and go back to being David Abel's devoted wife? Or had fear and grief – and guilt – affected her so badly that she'd never get her wits back?

Dr Reckitt believed that cutting a lump out of a person's brain might make them well again, turn them back into what they'd been before. And, if everything he'd said was true, one day doctors would be able to cut out growths in the head as easily as cutting out an eye in a potato.

But nobody'd ever be able to cut out pain and grief, would they? They say time heals but perhaps, sometimes, it doesn't. Perhaps, in a case like Maggie Abel's, the mind is altered for ever – damaged, like a spring stretched so far that it can't pull itself back into shape.

It wasn't my day for finding people in.

'Inspector's not here,' Morgan told me, as if it was the best news he'd heard all week. Perhaps it was.

'When will he be back?'

Morgan picked his nose and looked at the wad of snot he pulled out. At least he didn't eat it. Just wiped his finger under the table. 'Dunno. Tomorrow, for definite – for this meeting the emigration scheme're having. Dunno about today. Might just go home when his meeting's finished.'

'Who's he meeting, then?'

Morgan had a go at the other nostril. 'Not your business.'

Why were people so keen to tell me what was and wasn't my business today? 'You don't know, then,' I said.

He pulled his finger out. 'Not my business either, is it?'

I'd never've made a policeman. *Not my business* indeed. I sniffed. The police station smelled of pie. While the cat was away the mice'd been having a little feast. Was that gravy on Morgan's chin?

'I'd like to see Teff Harris, please.'

'You can't. He's gone.'

'Gone? Where?'

'Home. Mrs Harris went to a magistrate, didn't she? Got him to come and say that Mr Bellis couldn't keep her husband here without charging him with something. So he did. Charged him with failing to report a death and the magistrate bound him over to appear at the next sessions. Then off he went.'

So. Even Billy Go-About wasn't allowed to keep people locked up just because he felt like it. Perhaps he wasn't as popular with the magistrates as Harry thought. 'Right. When did he let him go?'

'Yesterday.'

I nodded. 'All right. Good.' I had a pretty shrewd idea that Harry'd be pleased if Billy Go-About had to find out who was responsible for Jenkyn Hughes's death at the inquest, like everybody else.

Harry

After a late breakfast, when I had left my father resting on his bed, Moyle intercepted me on the way from the stairs to the library.

'Excuse me, Mr Henry, I have a communication for you.'

I stifled an automatic irritation. 'What kind of *communication?*'

'A note, Mr Henry. From Dr Reckitt. At least, that's what the person who brought it claims.'

A *person* was Moyle's designation for anybody he regarded as inferior, a class which included included every Welsh person drawing breath.

'Where is it?' I asked.

'I have it here.' As he spoke, he produced it, holding it out to me.

I drew in a long, calming breath. Moyle was making a point; I had not seen fit to inform him, personally, of my diminished sight so he would behave as if he did not know. 'If you'd be so good as to read it to me, Moyle, I would be grateful.'

'Very well, Mr Henry.'

Moyle removed his pince-nez from his waistcoat pocket and took his time unfolding them. I wondered if they were the same antiquated, uncomfortable-looking pair he had worn when I had last been able to see them clearly. Then he unfolded the note. Evidently Reckitt had had no sealing wafer to hand and had simply folded the ends in on themselves.

'There is no salutation,' Moyle began. 'The doctor was obviously in some considerable hurry.'

Being somewhat acquainted by now with Reckitt's habits, it seemed more likely that he simply saw no point in addressing me when he had sent the note specifically to be read to me.

'*I have been summoned to the Abel household,*' Moyle read. '*Mrs Abel has attempted to end her own life. I am going to do what I can but you may wish to attend. Her husband tells me you want to speak to her. Reckitt.*'

End her own life? Given the religiosity her minister had described, I could not imagine the state of desperation the poor woman must have fallen into even to contemplate such a thing. I wondered how near she had come to succeeding and what Reckitt meant by 'do what I can'.

I decided to take the Cardigan route to St Dogmaels. If John had gone to the police station only after visiting the Abels – as I would have – there was a good chance that I would meet him on the way back.

And, half way to Cardigan, on the long hill up from Ponthirwaun, I saw a rider approaching. Sara knew Seren before John could hail me, and there was much whickering and tossing of heads as the stablemates greeted each other.

When I told John what had happened, he swore softly. 'Back we go then,' he said, turning Seren around. 'If she was lying at death's door inside, that explains why her husband's workshop was closed up.'

Abel's apprentice was waiting for us. 'The master and Dr Reckitt are inside.'

We gave him the mares' reins and went through the workshop into the Ables' lodgings at the back.

Reckitt's voice greeted me before my eyes could accustom themselves to the ill-lit kitchen. 'Ah, the coroner's here.'

My heart sank. 'Am I here to view a death?'

'No. Thanks be to God.' The voice was Abel's. Faith restored? Or simply falling back on old forms? 'Sit down, sirs.' He moved aside, leaving us to occupy the settle opposite Reckitt.

'What happened?' I asked.

I had directed the question at Abel, but it was Reckitt who answered me.

'As I understand it, in the early hours, Mrs Abel swallowed an immoderate amount of laudanum. With a presence of mind few would have shown, Mr Abel induced her to vomit and sent his boy to fetch me. On my arrival, finding Mrs Abel still living, I put the boy on my horse and sent him to you, Probert-Lloyd.'

I nodded. 'How did you know that I wanted to speak to her?'

There was a brief silence during which I formed the distinct impression of some wordless communication between the doctor and David Abel.

'Dr Reckitt came to see me yesterday,' the cabinet maker said. 'He'd heard from you what a desperate way Maggie was in, and he wanted to do whatever he could for her.'

He paused as if he was inviting Reckitt to speak for himself, but the doctor said nothing.

'I thought it'd be good for her to hear from the doctor's own mouth that he had no intentions of—' Abel pulled himself up, then went on. 'Well ... you know. So, I went to fetch her from the stable. I brought her back here last night. Dr Reckitt was going to come this afternoon and talk to her.'

Now Reckitt did intervene. 'From what Mr Abel has told me, it seems that Mrs Abel had descended into a state of delirium while she was at the stables. Some food and a bath may have calmed her nerves and restored her sufficiently to herself to attend to what he was saying but not enough to hear the news rationally. Early this morning, while her husband was procuring a drink for her after she had woken in distress, she consumed all the laudanum that I had brought here.

'As I intimated,' he continued, 'if it had not been for Mr Abel's prompt and decisive action in forcing her to bring up the contents of her stomach, she would, very swiftly, have fallen into a comatose state. And she would not have awoken.'

I saw John turn away from Reckitt towards Abel. 'Where is your wife now?'

'Through that door. In our bed.'

'Alive and well?'

'Alive, at least. Go and see, if you wish, Mr Davies.'

John did not move, though whether from a wish to take Abel's word for his wife's wellbeing or from fear of what he might find in the bedroom, I could not say.

'It might be as well, John,' I said. 'For Mr Abel's sake as much as for our own.'

For a second or two, John hesitated, then he rose and crossed the room.

'After I had made her bring up the medicine,' the cabinet maker said, 'I walked her up and down to keep her awake.'

'Again, showing an enormous presence of mind,' Reckitt contributed. 'I doubt that one man in a thousand would have thought to do such a thing. Including some who are medically qualified.'

'I thought, if I made her walk, made her stay awake, then she couldn't just slip away,' Abel said. 'So I dragged her up and down, in and out, even when she begged me to let her be.'

John closed the bedroom door behind him and rejoined us.

'Asleep,' he confirmed. I imagined him standing over Maggie Abel, watching for the rise and fall of breath, desperate not to wake her and cause her to throw herself, once more, into a delirious fit of self-harm.

'Why did she do it?' he asked. 'When you'd told her that the doctor didn't mean Lizzie any harm?'

I saw Abel shaking his head. 'I don't know. She isn't in her right mind. And, after all she's had to bear, I don't wonder at it.'

He knew. I was sure of it. 'You know what happened between your wife and Jenkyn Hughes, don't you, Mr Abel?'

Abel sank his face in his hands and I heard the scrape of calloused palm on stubbled skin.

'Shoni Jones saw what happened,' I said. 'He'll give evidence that your wife struck the fatal blow in self-defence.'

The cabinet maker sighed and sat up straight once more. 'Will you grant me one favour?'

I heard the immense weariness in his voice. 'I will if I can.'

'Don't call Maggie to bear witness. Call me. She's told me everything.'

I thought I knew what he meant. It transpired that I was mistaken.

PART FOUR

PART FOUR

John

I hadn't expected to see David and Maggie Abel at the bondholders' meeting. But there they were, standing quietly at one side of the Corn Exchange floor. I can't say Maggie Abel looked well but she didn't look mad either. Just gaunt and tired.

I bent to speak into Harry's ear. 'Abel's here with his wife. Do you want to speak to him?'

He shook his head. 'No. Best not to agitate Maggie. It may just be that Abel's persuaded her to go to Ohio after all.'

That seemed about as likely as her deciding to swim all the way to America. Far as I could see, Maggie Abel was here to get her bond redeemed and for no other reason. She wouldn't be able to rest until Reckitt was paid off.

I looked about for Shoni Jones. I'd been all for going to see him the day before, after we'd left the Abels, but Harry wanted to hear more from Benton Reckitt. Over a pint in the White Hart he'd made the doctor go over his autopsy findings again. Was he certain that it was the blow to the head that'd killed Hughes? How long would it've taken him to die? Was it possible the blow on the head hadn't killed him – that he'd been smothered afterwards?

You might've expected Reckitt to be irritated at his conclusions being questioned but he wasn't. Matter of fact, he seemed pretty taken with Harry's questions – even started asking his own. Did Harry have evidence of suffocation? Did he think Hughes might've fallen face down and suffocated on the sand, for instance? And, if not that, then what? Obviously, with his face in the condition it was, there'd be no signs of pinching or small cuts around the nose and mouth to show that they'd been held closed. He'd noticed no sand in the airways and, yes, he had looked for that.

'You have to understand, Probert-Lloyd, that though I've undertaken many autopsies I've always been looking for disease processes, not for evidence of murder. Our victim certainly wasn't strangled – there was no damage to the trachea, no bruising to his neck. And he didn't drown, as we've already established, so he wasn't left face down in the surf after he'd been hit. But, beyond that, I can't tell you more than I have already.'

So, no evidence to say that Shoni Jones'd found Hughes alive and finished him off.

A big crowd had gathered for the meeting. As well as bondholders, a lot of people would've come just out of curiosity or hoping to hear more about the murder. But I still couldn't see Shoni Jones.

Harry'd asked for a few minutes with the emigration scheme's partners before they addressed the meeting. Perhaps Shoni was waiting with them in the Shire Hall upstairs.

I forced a way for us through the chattering and gossiping with a combination of politeness and a sharp elbow. All around us, voices were raised so they could be heard above the hubbub and I caught snatches of what they were saying as we pushed through.

'... gambled their money away.'

'Soldier Harris out of ...'

'... farms as big as Cardiganshire.'

'... surprised Billy Go-About's not ...'

I excused my way between two women in Sunday best who were arguing about chapel ministers. One thought a pastor would be chosen to go out with the emigrants but her friend didn't agree.

'There'll be a chapel there already, for the people building the houses and everything. They won't need *another* minister.'

How many of these people were bondholders? Emigrants needed to be sure what was happening but nobody'd want to lose even half a day's pay. More than likely, families that knew each other would've sent one person on behalf of them all.

Once we were through the crowds, Harry and I made our way up the stairs to the Shire Hall. I'd never had any reason to go up there before, and I looked about as we reached the top of the stairs. The meeting hall turned out to be a high, panelled room that ran the whole length of the building. After the gloom of the Corn Exchange downstairs, it was very light, with one row of tall windows looking up the high street and another, less grand row facing down towards the docks. A raised platform at the front must be where the judge sat when the assize court was in session.

Off to one side there was an oddly shaped room, open to the main court, where Mrs Parry, Mr Philips, and Shoni Jones were standing. Apart from a table and chairs, the room was bare but still impressive with its own many-paned windows and high ceiling.

Harry walked over. 'Good day to you.'

Shoni Jones sprang up and James Philips raised his arse a few inches off his chair before Harry made a 'sit down' gesture and we took our seats. Mrs Parry returned his greeting but, all the while, kept her eyes fixed on me. It made me uncomfortable – people weren't usually so barefaced about Harry's blindness. And that half smile of hers was unsettling. Brought to mind what Bets had told me about her mother and Hughes.

'Thank you for agreeing to organise the bondholders' meeting,' Harry said. He was speaking English, out of deference to his cousin,

I supposed. James Philips probably thought it was beneath him to speak Welsh.

'We're happy to help.' Mrs Parry'd elected herself spokesman again.

'I trust you'll all be at the re-convened inquest on Monday?' Harry asked.

James Philips's face looked as if Harry'd asked him to come and watch a dog pissing up a tree but the other two nodded.

'You may all be called as witnesses,' Harry went on. 'You most certainly will, Mr Jones.'

'Of course.' Shoni Jones's eyes flicked from me to Harry and back again. Wondering if I'd passed on everything he'd told me to Harry, more than likely. 'I suppose the will won't be read until after the inquest?'

Harry nodded. 'The solicitors will be happier if probate's not applied for until then.'

'But what if people ask? Everybody downstairs is expecting to hear who's taking over from my cousin. Here and in America. What are we going to tell them?'

Mrs Parry opened her mouth to say something but Harry got in before her. 'As you've pointed out, Mr Jones, many of the bondholders already know you. They'll accept you as agent in Mr Hughes's stead without question as long as Mrs Parry and Mr Philips are agreeable.'

He turned his face towards Mrs Parry, then his cousin. He was asking for that agreement, now.

James Philips didn't look too pleased to be put on the spot. 'Haven't much choice, have we?'

Mrs Parry fixed her eyes on Shoni. Then, just as I thought she was going to refuse, she said, 'That would seem sensible. For the time being at least.'

In other words, *till the will's been read and we all know where we stand.*

'Very well' Harry said. 'That's all that matters today, I think. The will is a private legal matter and can be dealt with, as such, after the inquest.'

'Right then.' Mrs Parry rose from her seat and headed for the stairs. We went to follow her but James Philips hung back. 'Mr Probert-Lloyd, a moment of your time, if you please?'

I saw Mrs Parry look over her shoulder, but she didn't break stride. Shoni Jones followed her.

Harry turned to face his cousin with a smile. They hadn't met before today and Harry looked as if he assumed James just wanted to acknowledge him.

Philips glared at me. I obviously didn't rank anywhere near the organ grinder's monkey at that moment, more like the shit on the monkey's arse. 'It's of a personal nature.'

Harry stood his ground. 'Not related in any way to Jenkyn Hughes's death?'

'It's about the inquest—' James began.

'Then I should like John to remain, if you don't mind,' Harry cut in. He wasn't smiling any more. 'Anything relating to the inquest is official business and John is coroner's officer.

'*Official business?* Listen to yourself, man! I'm asking to speak to you as a kinsman—'

'We may be cousins but, in this, I am the coroner.'

James Philips stared at him, hard. 'Forget I asked. Let's go downstairs.'

But Harry grasped his arm as he tried to walk past. 'If there's something I need to know, it had better come out now rather than in public, under oath. Especially if it's something to do with Jenkyn Hughes's will.'

Philips flinched at Harry's directness. I looked away before he could catch me eyeballing him.

'Very well.' The words couldn't've been colder or sharper if he'd chiseled them out of ice. 'The point is, I really don't feel that there will be any need for me to give evidence at the inquest. I can't tell you anything that Mrs Parry wouldn't be able to. And it's not as if I had anything to gain from Hughes's death. In point of fact, his death is nothing to me but a huge inconvenience.' He seemed to be expecting a response, but Harry just waited.

I kept my eyes away from him but I could feel James Philips glaring at me. . 'I believe that my father made free with my private business.' His voice was as tight as a snare. 'Told you that I had incurred certain … expenses, where Jenkyn Hughes was concerned.'

Incurred certain expenses? I'd never heard gambling debts referred to like that before.

Harry inclined his head. Yes, he knew that.

'Hughes came to see me about a month ago,' Philips went on. 'Just me. Said he wanted my help.'

'What sort of help?'

'My support. For a new will he'd written.'

I expected Harry to say, *The will in favour of Mrs Parry?* But he didn't. Discretion. 'Go on.'

'Previously, he'd been persuaded to leave his share of the business to Jones. But now he'd thought better of it. He felt the company would be in better hands if he left it to Louise – Mrs Parry.'

'And why exactly did he need your support in that?'

At the other end of the room, I saw Shoni Jones's head rise up from the stairs. 'The meeting's waiting,' he said.

'Just one moment,' Harry said, without turning around.

Jones's head sank down again. Now I'd been made aware of it, I could hear the restiveness of the crowd below. They weren't happy at being kept waiting. Especially now that Mrs Parry and Shoni Jones were in front of them, doing nothing. They'd be wondering what quiet deals were being done up here.

'Hughes needed my support because he knew his cousin would be livid. And he wanted me to speak up if there was a court case brought against the new will.'

'And he ensured your support by remitting your ... *expenses* as long as you agreed to speak in favour of the new will.' Harry was nobody's fool.

Philips sucked in his cheeks and raised his chin. 'Yes. He made me sign a statement saying that I both witnessed and supported the will, without any inducement or benefit to myself.'

I hid a smile. Jenkyn Hughes had been a sly one.

'I think it would be better,' James Philips said, 'if Jones could be prevented from making any statements, today, about his being the heir to his cousin's portion of the business, don't you?'

Harry nodded. 'Very well. If he looks likely to make any such statement, I'll ensure that he's prevented from doing so. It would be humiliating to him to have the truth made public after such a declaration so I'm sure he'll be grateful to you.'

James Philips's expression told me exactly how much he cared about Shoni Jones's humiliation. All he wanted was to make sure that there was as little gossip as possible about him or the emigration scheme.

'Very well,' he said. 'Shall we go down, now, before we're called to heel again?'

Not far from the foot of the stairs there was a dais which I hadn't noticed when we went up. Something to do with the grain-trading that went on there, I supposed. Now, the three representatives of the emigration scheme got up on to it and Mrs Parry opened proceedings.

She'd barely begun to speak when I saw Maggie Abel move away from the wall and start pushing her way through the crowd. She'd taken her husband by surprise, setting off like that, and she was a few paces ahead of him before he caught up with her and stopped her. I couldn't hear what he was saying but he was speaking very intently. I watched Maggie. If she was listening to him, she gave no sign of it. She was just staring at the three people on the platform. And, the way she was looking at them, I was glad it wasn't me up there.

I told Harry what was happening. He nodded but said nothing, just carried on listening to Mrs Parry.

'As far as we know at the moment,' she said, 'there'll be nothing to stop us sailing as planned on the fourteenth of April. All bonds will be honoured and, I believe, there are still some places left.' She looked around at Shoni Jones.

'Yes, there were a few unsold bonds at my cousin's lodgings so we can still offer them.'

'That's all I've got to say,' Mrs Parry concluded. 'Any questions?'

'We heard the scheme'd gone bankrupt,' a voice called from the middle of the crowd. 'That's not true, then, is it?'

'No. It's not.'

'What about Jenkyn Hughes's gambling debts?'

That question started the crowd grumbling and chattering and heckling. As if she'd been waiting for the noise to hide her, Maggie Abel was on the move again. Her husband moved with her but, this time, he didn't try and hold her back.

When she got to the front of the crowd, she stopped. Just stood there, looking up at the dais like everybody else.

I waited, heart thumping, stomach like a fist.

She said nothing. Didn't move. Just stood there, looking at Shoni Jones. Then she started nodding. Like you see very old people doing, sometimes, as if now they've started, they've forgotten how to stop.

She was agreeing mightily with herself over something.

Mrs Parry was answering the question about Hughes's debts. 'Any debts will be the responsibility of Mr Hughes's legal heir. But if anybody thinks it'd be a good idea to start turning up saying they're owed money, they can think again.' Her eyes scanned the crowd as if she was trying to spot likely turners-up. 'The solicitors acting for Mr Hughes's heir will want to see IOUs. If you've got no IOU in Mr Hughes's handwriting, you'll get no payment.'

That got the hecklers going, though God knows it shouldn't have. Who pays up without a valid IOU? Anybody who'd been thinking they'd get away with that must never've had dealings with Mrs Parry, that's all I can say.

There were a couple of other questions about what'd been promised in Ohio and whether it would still be on offer now that Hughes wasn't there to take them. I listened with half an ear but my eyes were on the Abels. Maggie was staring up at Shoni Jones as if she was trying to suck the life out of him with her eyes.

You could tell he was rattled – he didn't so much as look at her. He was trying to pretend he hadn't noticed her standing there like a basilisk. But, fair play to him, when Mrs Parry asked him to answer a question, you wouldn't've known there was anything wrong.

'I've never been to Ohio, but I've spent months with my cousin and I've got his notes and his articles of agreement with various businessmen in the new settlement. I can promise you – if you had an agreement with him, there'll be a record of it and I'll make sure it happens just like he said it would. I'm the agent now.'

There were some sarcastic cheers then, and Jones went red, out of anger or embarrassment.

Then, suddenly, Maggie was shouting. She was up on the dais, shouting in Shoni's face. 'Nobody should believe your promises! You're a liar. *A liar!*'

And she hit him with a small fist to emphasise her point. Abel tried to pull her away but Mrs Parry put a hand on his arm. 'Leave her.'

Maggie took no notice of her husband anyway. 'You said you'd tell the police,' she raged. 'You said you'd tell them what you saw. Make it all right. *But you never did!*'

The whole room was listening now. The people who'd come for scandal and gossip were agog, they hadn't expected anything as good as this.

'I waited and waited and *they never came!*'

This was what David Abel hadn't wanted to tell us, what he'd wanted to say only once, at the inquest. That Maggie had been sitting at her child's bedside, watching her die, praying for a miracle and, all the while, waiting for the police to knock on the door. To question her about the humiliation she'd suffered on Tresaith beach. To demand to know how Jenkyn Hughes had died.

Maggie hit Shoni Jones again and he staggered back. James Philips grabbed his arm, though whether it was to keep him from falling or to stop him from running away was anybody's guess.

'Nobody said *anything* about him!' Maggie shouted. 'Nobody knew he was dead! *Nobody!* You *lied!* And I was a miserable sinner and I did nothing. I did nothing *and Lizzie died*. She *died!* Because the iniquity of the fathers shall be visited on the children!'

What was she saying? That no miracle had saved her daughter because she'd believed Shoni Jones and not gone to the police herself? That was madness if ever I'd heard it.

Whatever it was, it was enough for David Abel. He took his wife by both shoulders and turned her around. I suppose he was going to try and get her out and home but he never had the chance. With more strength than I'd ever've credited her with, Maggie Abel pushed her husband backwards into Jones and his partners. Then, while they all fell in an air-grabbing tangle, she turned and limped quickly away.

The crowd parted for her like the Red Sea. As if they were afraid her madness was contagious.

Of course, somebody should've gone after her, straight away. Easy to say that, later. But there was something so shocking about what she'd just done, about seeing four people tangled up with each other on the floor, that it froze you. And, then, the crowd surged into the space where she'd been and started helping the partners to their feet, each wanting to be the first to see if one of them was really hurt.

In the end, we came to our senses and fought our way out of the Corn Exchange, David Abel scrabbling to follow. But by the time we reached the high street, she'd gone.

'This way,' Abel said. We followed him down a narrow lane towards the docks, clattering down the cobbled hill, squeezing past foot- and cart-traffic. I looked past Abel but I couldn't see his wife ahead of us.

'Are you sure she won't be over the bridge and on the road home?' I panted. This looked like a wild goose chase to me.

'She's not going home.'

Harry was quicker than me. 'You think she's going to do away with herself? Throw herself in the river?'

'She did once before.' Abel stumbled on. I looked round at Harry but all his attention was on following Abel and not bumping in to anything.

David Abel darted down the first alleyway that would take us to the river. I could see his reasoning. If his wife wanted to jump in, this would be the quickest way.

But we got to the quay and there was no sign of her. No crowd looking into the water or shaping up to get her out. She hadn't come this way.

I looked for Abel. He was staring upstream, looking to see if she'd carried on to a spot further along the quay. I left him to it and turned the other way.

It was down to the two of us. Harry couldn't be expected to look for her.

I wish David Abel had looked downstream instead of up. Then I'd've been spared the sight of his wife falling from the middle of the bridge.

Arms held out to the sides as if they could steady her against the rushing air, legs bent, the wind filled the skirt of her *betgwn*, freed her apron to flap like a flag and cover her face. I didn't want to see her hit the water so I turned away and my last sight of her was her hair trailing up into the air as she fell.

Harry

Maggie Abel could not swim and, even had she been a proficient swimmer, she could not have survived; her clothes filled with water and the rushing tide dragged her under. Of course, that was what she had wanted; she had jumped from the bridge for no other reason than to secure her own death. Whether that action had been a rationally taken one would have to be decided later. The inquest into her death would, inevitably, hear of the circumstances attending the death of her child and that of Jenkyn Hughes, and the jury might well come to the conclusion that the balance of her mind had been disturbed.

Once a boat had been dispatched to recover her body and Reckitt summoned to certify death, John and I sat with Abel on the quay to wait. A respectful crowd made space for us in the lee of one of the huge dockside warehouses, and tea chests were produced for us to sit on. Those who work on the ships and wharves of a busy port are rarely famed for their compassion but death inevitably brings a certain reverence to the fore in even the most worldly soul.

Feeling that it would be crass to speak about anything else, I asked Abel what he had meant when he said that Maggie had tried to end her life by throwing herself into the river once before.

He sighed and looked down at his hands, fingers splayed on his thighs.

'It's how we came to be married. I saved her from the river.'

I said nothing, waiting for him to continue.

'I had recently lost my first wife and newborn son and I was almost lost to myself. I could not sleep and I'd been wandering most of the

445

night along by the ferry over on the other side. When I saw Maggie wading into the water as the tide was rushing out, I didn't stop to think what I was doing. I just could not bear the thought of another death.'

Her spirit broken as much by his kindness as her own despair, Maggie had poured out her sorry tale to him.

'It was Jenkyn Hughes,' Abel told us. 'Did your investigations tell you that he had been over from America before?'

'Shoni Jones said that he'd met his cousin on one previous occasion.'

'I believe he made two or three trips before this last one.'

As Abel told his story, it became clear that Hughes's eye for the ladies had been well developed prior to the growth in his head, as had his tendency to pursue his quarry relentlessly. If what Maggie had told her future husband was to be believed, his seduction of her better deserved the name of rape and he had left her with a child growing in her belly when he returned to America.

A man of deep faith, and understandably tender where misfortune was concerned, Abel had seen Maggie's situation as an opportunity to be an agent of God's grace. He had offered her marriage and respectability.

'Of course, when it became clear to folk that she was already with child when we married, there was a lot of talk. It seemed best to allow everybody to think that I'd tried to forget my grief in the embraces of a young girl and I claimed Lizzie as my own. Nobody but the two of us knew the truth.'

Nobody, that is, until Maggie told Hughes on Tresaith beach. She had not gone to him simply as a representative of the Cardigan-Ohio Emigration company but as her daughter's natural father.

'She hadn't wanted him to know about Lizzie,' Abel said. 'But when she was in such a state about Reckitt's offer, she got it into her head that he was the one person who could save her. She decided that it was a means of forgiveness and reconciliation sent by God. That Hughes could provide us with the money we needed to repay the doctor as a way of expiating his sins.'

Abel gave a small grunt which might have been a sob. 'Hughes took a different view,' he said. 'He laughed at her.'

I heard anger in Abel's voice and I wondered whether he, too, had petitioned Hughes to no avail.

'How can a man refuse to help when his own flesh and blood is suffering?' he asked. 'How could he laugh at what Maggie told him and do nothing?'

It was the question only a good man could ask, a man who could not begin to fathom the lack of concern another might feel for his own child.

'And he didn't just refuse to help, he insulted her as well,' Abel went on. 'He told her that any man might be the father of the child. I suppose, because he was immoral, he believed all men were like him. And he told her it was her fault, that she'd tempted him. So she took the blame on herself and started to believe it was her fault Lizzie was ill.'

Abel shook his head. 'Worst of all, he offered my poor wife the same violence that had left her with child all those years before. She hit him with that stone to save herself. He left her no choice.'

He stopped then, and I nodded. 'Of course.'

I heard Abel swallow. 'When Lizzie died, Maggie ran mad. Not just distraught like any mother might be but truly mad. She was tormented by the fear that no miracle had saved Lizzie because *she* was a sinner. That her sins had been visited on our child.'

'The sins of the fathers shall be visited upon the children,' I said. They were the words Maggie had shouted at Shoni Jones.

'Yes. The *fathers*!' Abel's tone was suddenly belligerent. 'If anybody's sins were to blame it was Hughes's. And it was his sins that brought about his own death. My wife was defending herself as any honest woman would!'

'Nobody can deny that, Mr Abel,' I reassured him. 'It was self-defence of the purest kind. Mr Jones will testify to that at the inquest, I can assure you.'

'Shoni Jones is not guiltless in this either! Maggie blamed herself for trusting him – for not going to the police straight away. And when she heard what had happened to Hughes's face – that somebody'd tried to make sure he couldn't be identified...'

I shook my head. 'No, Mr Abel. We think that was an accident – an unintended effect of hiding the body in one of the lime kilns on Tresaith beach.'

While Abel digested this piece of news, I looked about to see if I could spy Reckitt. His clothing, I was confident, would be sufficiently different from the surrounding sailors and docksmen for me to identify him.

'It's as we thought, then.' John ventured after a silent minute or so had passed. 'Shoni Jones saw what had happened through his telescope, then went ashore at Penbryn and made his way round to Tresaith?'

'Yes.' Abel's voice was bitter. 'He told Maggie to go home before she was missed. Said he'd see to it all. Summon the coroner. Go to the police and tell them what he'd seen.'

But, instead, Jones had dragged Hughes's corpse to the limekiln and buried it, leaving both coroner and police in ignorance for another fortnight.

When Reckitt arrived on the quayside, I asked him to wait with Abel and John for Margaret's body to be brought out of the river while I returned home. I felt a pressing need to return to Glanteifi. Perhaps it was the effect of Mrs Abel's sudden and unforeseen death but I was very conscious of the fact that, though my father might have cheated mortality thus far, it was by no means certain that he would continue to do so. I had never been a believer in premonitions nor did I feel myself to have experienced one now; nevertheless, I felt an unease which would be assuaged only by my going home.

As I quit the docks and made my way back up to the Black Lion's stables, I considered those two weeks during which Shoni Jones had concealed the death of his cousin and of all that had befallen me because of them. Had he reported what he knew immediately, had he not concealed the body, it was quite possible – probable, even – that I would not have been asked to stand in as coroner. With Jenkyn Hughes' identity never in doubt and Jones's eyewitness testimony as to cause of death, only a brief inquest would have been necessary and one of the magistrates could have deputised. But, with an anonymous corpse discovered in an apparently mutilated state, an investigation had been necessary.

Shoni Jones's actions might have had purely selfish motives, and they might – when an inquest was held into Margaret Abel's death – be found to have contributed to the balance of the poor woman's mind becoming disturbed, but they had also benefitted me enormously.

It was a sobering thought.

John

Rumours that Maggie Abel had murdered Jenkyn Hughes brought flocks to the inquest. We'd known it would happen and Harry'd asked me to arrange for the hearing to be held in the Black Lion's assembly room – the biggest space we could reasonably expect to get in Cardigan.

Mrs Weston had taken a minute to consider whether she wanted the town's gawpers under her roof but, in the end, the prospect of the magistrates' money and the free advertising the Black Lion'd get from being mentioned in the papers as far away as Carmarthen and Haverfordwest brought her round.

It was strange, sitting there, watching Harry preside while I took notes of the proceedings. Barely three months before, I'd sat in the ballroom at the Salutation Hotel in Newcastle Emlyn, watching Leighton Bowen conduct the inquest into the bones that turned out to belong to Margaret Jones. Then, Harry'd been a curiosity and I hadn't known him at all. Now, I hardly knew anyone better.

We hadn't expected to learn anything new in the inquest, and we weren't surprised. It was more or less a case of laying out what we'd uncovered. We got confirmation of a few things and clarification of some others – Teff Harris, for instance, admitted that he'd stripped the body because he was afraid of being accused of the murder.

'Why was that, Mr Harris?' Harry asked.

'Because I knew people'd heard me threatening Mr Hughes.'

'Again, why?'

'He was double-selling coal. I found out and didn't like it. I told him if he didn't stop, I'd come for him.'

'Come for him?'

'He knew what I meant.'

And Harry, who also knew what he meant, left it at that.

Then there was Obadaiah Vaughan. He'd been taken off the jury so he could give evidence and I don't suppose it was just me who saw him as a bit of a pathetic figure standing there, trying to look like something he wasn't. Like one of Iolo Morgannwg's great bardic circle when, in reality, he was just a small farmer who wrote verses to seduce women.

He was there to give evidence about finding the American coins in the lime waste but Harry got him to admit that it was him who'd written the anonymous note to Billy Go-About.

'I did, yes, and I'd do it again.'

'Why didn't you just come forward?'

Vaughan'd seen that question coming. 'Teff Harris and I aren't friends. I knew my motives would be suspected if I said what I'd seen. But I wanted to report it so that seemed the best way.' The words slipped off his tongue like honey off a warm spoon

Harry stared at where Vaughan was standing for a long while. How many people in the room knew that, with his eyes pointing there, Vaughan was the one person he was guaranteed not to see? But Dai'r Bardd didn't know where to look. Or what to do with his hands. He tried putting them in his pockets but then you could see he'd felt how that looked and pulled them out again.

Witness after witness, I watched Harry summoning facts and questions without the use of notes and knew how impressive that would look. The people who were gathered in the assembly room didn't know that we'd gone over and over the facts the previous night at Glanteifi, that we'd drawn up the witness list, in order, and gone through it again and again until Harry knew exactly who to ask for at any given moment.

Who comes after Teff Harris?

Matthias the registrar.

Who's after Mrs Parry?

The Whaler.

The inquest was the beginning of Harry's campaign to be elected coroner for the Teifi Valley. And when he accepted the jury's verdict on Jenkyn Hughes's death – manslaughter in an act of self-defence – and called for an hour's break before he began hearing the facts surrounding the death of Margaret Abel, he sounded like the coroner. Every inch.

To spare witnesses the need to give their testimony twice, Harry'd taken the unusual step of asking the Hughes inquest jury to sit for the hearing into Margaret Abel's death as well.

He began the second inquest with the words, 'Gentlemen of the jury, you viewed the body of Mrs Margaret Abel and have stated that you are content that this was, in fact, the deceased's identity. You have heard details of Mrs Abel's state of mind before, during and after the events on Tresaith beach and you will now hear details of the events immediately before her death.'

And then he called me to bear witness.

I'd seen Maggie Abel's actions at the public meeting and heard every word she'd said. I'd chased her down to the docks, along with her husband and Harry and I was the only one of us to see her jump from the bridge. My opinion – that she'd jumped and not fallen off the bridge – was confirmed by witnesses who'd been crossing the river at the time and had seen her climb onto the parapet. One had even tried to prevent her from harming herself but was left with nothing but guilt at what'd happened.

'Perhaps, if I hadn't run towards her,' he said, 'she might've taken a moment to consider what she was doing and stepped back from it.'

But Harry disagreed. He reassured the witness that he was quite certain Margaret Abel had climbed on to the parapet with the sole intention of ending a life which – *in her grief and madness* – had become intolerable.

The jury took notice of the emphasis he'd put on that phrase and brought in a verdict of suicide while the balance of her mind was disturbed. So David Abel had permission to bury her in the churchyard at Blaenywaun alongside her Lizzie.

Meanwhile, after the second inquest, Billy Go-About arrested Shoni Jones on charges of failure to report a death. Although Harry hadn't questioned him too hard during Jenkyn Hughes's inquest on why he'd left the body in the limekiln for two weeks, during Maggie Abel's hearing Jones'd had to admit that he had promised to tell the truth of what he'd seen and had failed to do so in order to serve his own ends. The hecklers had hissed him then and I can't say anybody at the inquest blamed them. Unless Harry could persuade the magistrates to fine Jones instead of putting him in gaol, it seemed unlikely that he'd be going to America with the emigrant ship in April.

Perhaps it was true, what my mother always said – it was possible to be too clever for your own good.

Harry

On the Saturday after the inquest, I sat in the morning room with my father, looking out over the gardens and the drive to the river beyond. It was a glorious, spring-like day and I was trying to remember the exact state of trees and flowers at the beginning of February. What would be in bud or early leaf – snowdrops, daffodils?

My father's condition remained largely unchanged and I knew that, soon, I must take up the reins of the estate and exert myself to understand its workings.

For now, however, my limited capacity for monologue having been exhausted, I was considering going down to see if the post had yet been collected from town when I heard the sound of a vehicle approaching. Only a single horse by the sound of it, but coming at a fair speed. Neither carriage nor cart, then. As it came on to the sweep of drive before the house, I could see that it was a little trap, and watched as the driver jumped down and helped a lady out.

My pulse quickened at the prospect of a visitor and, with a hasty warning to my father that he might be required to receive company, I hurried downstairs.

Moyle had not yet answered Wil-Sam's scurrying summons, so I loitered on the bottom stair; the butler would be displeased if I answered the door myself and, besides, it would be embarrassing not to be able to recognise the caller.

Moyle, as ever, opened the door as if his master was the Duke of Devonshire and not an obscure Welsh squire. 'Good day,' I heard him say to whoever stood before him.

Footsteps came closer to the door. Then I heard a voice that almost winded me. 'Good day. Is Mr Henry Probert-Lloyd at home?'

My legs less steady than I would have liked, I descended the remaining step and called, 'I'm here, Moyle. Do show Miss Howell in.'

A brief historical note on Welsh emigration to the Americas

The Irish diaspora and the influence that Irish people have had on the development of the United States is well known but few people are aware that the Welsh influence is also significant. There were several distinct waves of emigration from Wales to the Americas and each had a different impetus – religious, cultural or economic.

Pennsylvania

The first wave of emigration to America came about as a result of religious intolerance following the restoration of Charles II to the throne in 1660. When the Court of Great Sessions in Bala threatened to burn Quakers, a group responded by acquiring land in what is now Pennsylvania and emigrated there in 1682. The following year, having bought land on the banks of the Delaware, Baptists from mid and west Wales went to settle in Philadelphia. These settlements were in what was known as the Welsh Tract or Welsh Barony.

The original settlers negotiated with William Penn – Quaker founder of the Pennsylvania colony – to make the tract into a separate jurisdiction which would be administered in Welsh. This did not come about, but the Welsh language was used by the families that lived there and they gave Welsh names to their settlements, some of which still survive today, including Bryn Mawr, home to one of America's most famous liberal arts colleges for women.

By 1700, a third of families living in the Pennsylvania colony were Welsh.

Almost two centuries later, in the mid-1800s, a new wave of emigration brought coal miners from south Wales to the mines of

Pennsylvania. Many became managers and executives rather than coal-cutters and they were also influential in union politics.

To this day, Pennsylvania boasts the largest number of Americans of Welsh descent – approximately 200, 000, most of whom live in the coal producing regions of the state

Ohio

The nineteenth century saw the mass emigration to Ohio that forms the backdrop to the fictitious Cardigan-Ohio Emigration Scheme in *In Two Minds*. Early in the century, most emigrants were farmers but, as other industries developed, miners and quarrymen began to be needed in the new towns of the state. Many of these emigrants made for the Appalachian part of southeastern Ohio, including the two counties mentioned in the novel, Jackson and Gallia. So many emigrants made their way to the area that it became known as 'little Cardiganshire' and Welsh was still spoken in those communities well into the twentieth century.

As of 2010, over 126, 000 Ohians are of Welsh descent.

Interestingly, Cardiganshire emigrants ended up in Jackson and Gallia counties by accident. In 1818 a group arrived in the French settlement of Gallipolis, having made their way from Baltimore by wagon then boat on the Ohio, en route to the Welsh settlement of Paddy's Run near Cincinnati. Somehow, during the night, their boats became unmoored (there is speculation that it was the work of some enterprising member of the Gallipolis commercial fraternity who saw his chance to vastly increase the population and create a 'boom town') and, as aconsequence, the emigrants gave up their journey to Paddy's Run and settled in nearby Gallia county.

There were other, more minor, Welsh settlements in Tennessee,

Indiana, Minnesota, Kansas, Maryland, Virginia, California and New York State. Utah, meanwhile, was the destination of choice for many Welsh Mormon missionaries, while others went to Idaho where they founded the city of Malad which still boasts the largest population of people with Welsh origins outside Wales (around 20%).

The Influence of Welsh Emigrants in the Development of America

Though, in comparison with emigration from other countries, the population leaving Wales and making their home in America was relatively small, their influence was disproportionate to their numbers. For instance, sixteen of the original fifty-six signatories to the American Declaration of Independence were of Welsh descent and one, Francis Lewis, was a first-generation immigrant.

The family of Thomas Jefferson, third president of the United States, came from a village on the foothills of Snowdon and other presidents also had family roots in Wales, including James Monroe, Abraham Lincoln, Calvin Coolidge and Richard Nixon.

Yale and Brown universities were both founded by Welshmen. Elihu Yale's parents were first-generation immigrants to Boston and, when he died, he was buried in the parish church near his family's home in Plas-yn-Iâl, Denbigh.

Morgan Edwards, co-founder of Brown University, came from Pontypool in Gwent.

Patagonia

Some early Welsh emigrants to America had attempted to set up Welsh colonies in order to retain their linguistic and cultural identity. One of the earlier Pennsylvanian settlements – Scranton – had been established with that intention but the Welsh residents soon found themselves being assimilated into a wider Anglophone society. However, in the 1860s, at a time when migration from the countryside to the industrial heartlands of the south Wales valleys was causing concern to those who feared that Welsh culture and identity was being lost, a new wave of emigration began. This time it was to somewhere few people had ever heard of: Patagonia.

Staunch nationalist, Michael Jones, principal of Bala college, had negotiated with the Argentinian government to allow a group of Welsh emigrants to settle in an area called Bahia Blanca. There, they would be self-sufficient and able to maintain their language and culture in a 'little Wales over the seas'. (This was not a purely altruistic act on the part of the Argentinian government, however. The authorities hoped that the Welsh settlement it would resolve a dispute as to who controlled the land, sovreignty over which was claimed by both Argentina and Chile.)

The first group of settlers – mostly from north and mid-Wales – arrived in 1865 and their descendants are there still. Until a generation or two ago, Welsh was still spoken as a first language, along with Spanish, and links between Wales and Patagonia remain strong, with young people coming to Wales from what Welsh speakers know as Y Wladfa (the Colony) to re-establish familial ties and to improve their Welsh. In return, Welsh-speaking young people go to Patagonia to encourage the use of Welsh and to strengthen cultural links.

Acknowledgements

As ever, first and greatest thanks go to my other half and first reader, Edwina, for all her endless support and constant positivity. Not to mention her ability to rein me in when my enthusiasm for planning publicity events threatens to leave me with no time to actually write the books I'm supposed to be publicising.

Huge thanks to Rebecca Lloyd and Emily Glenister at The Dome Press who are an absolute joy to work with. No author could possibly enjoy working with an editor or publicist as much as I enjoy working with you guys. You are awesome!

I love designer Jem Butcher's cover so much. It's so great to have Harry and John going out into the world so beautifully dressed. Thank you, Jem.

Authors, being solitary workers without colleagues to keep us positive when the going gets a bit sticky, depend on others to remind us that we can actually do this writing lark. In this respect I am so grateful to have had a decade's support from the Macmillan New Writing crew: Eliza Graham, Len Tyler, Aliya Whiteley, Frances Garrood, Tim Stretton, Deborah Swift and Roger Morris. More latterly but no less importantly, I have enjoyed much support and encouragement – not to mention joint festival appearances – from the Crime Cymru authors. Particular thanks in this context must go to Rosie Claverton, Bev Jones, Thorne Moore and Katherine Stansfield.

And while I'm mentioning support, thanks to my book group friends – Viv, Jo, Rachael, Alison, Maria, Sarah – thank you for the fun, the chat and the prosecco!

Jacky Collins, aka Doctor Noir, is a new but enthusiastic supporter of Harry and John and I'm very grateful for her commitment to putting us, and Crime Cymru, on the map.

And finally to my family – Sam and Nancy, Rob and Flo, Mum, Dad and Jim. Thank you, my loves, for always being there and for not being surprised that it all worked out in the end. Your faith has always meant everything to me.